# THE LAST TRUE HEIRS

## THE HEAD, THE HEART, AND THE HEIR
### BOOK FOUR

ALICE HANOV

Gryphon
Press

# Gryphon Press

Published by Gryphon Press
Waterloo, Ontario



First Edition

Paperback: 978-1-998835-07-2
Hardcover: 978-1-998835-08-9
Special Hardcover: 978-1-998835-09-6
Ebook: 978-1-998835-06-5

Edited by Sam Pollock, SE Fleenor and Supriya Saxon
Cover design by The Book Designers

*For my husband Steve,*
*who always believes in my crazy ideas and supports my dreams.*

Dear Reader,

This extended edition of The Head, the Heart, and the Heir was created because my readers wanted these extra scenes, and I was happy to oblige.

I now understand the importance of being prepared when you read a book. While this book deals with coming of age, and feeling different from everyone around you, there are themes or memories that could be hard for people to read.

If you'd like a list of what exactly this book will touch on, (both warnings and tropes) please see my website, AliceHanov.com, or scan the code below with your phone.

Happy reading, and take care of yourself.

Alice

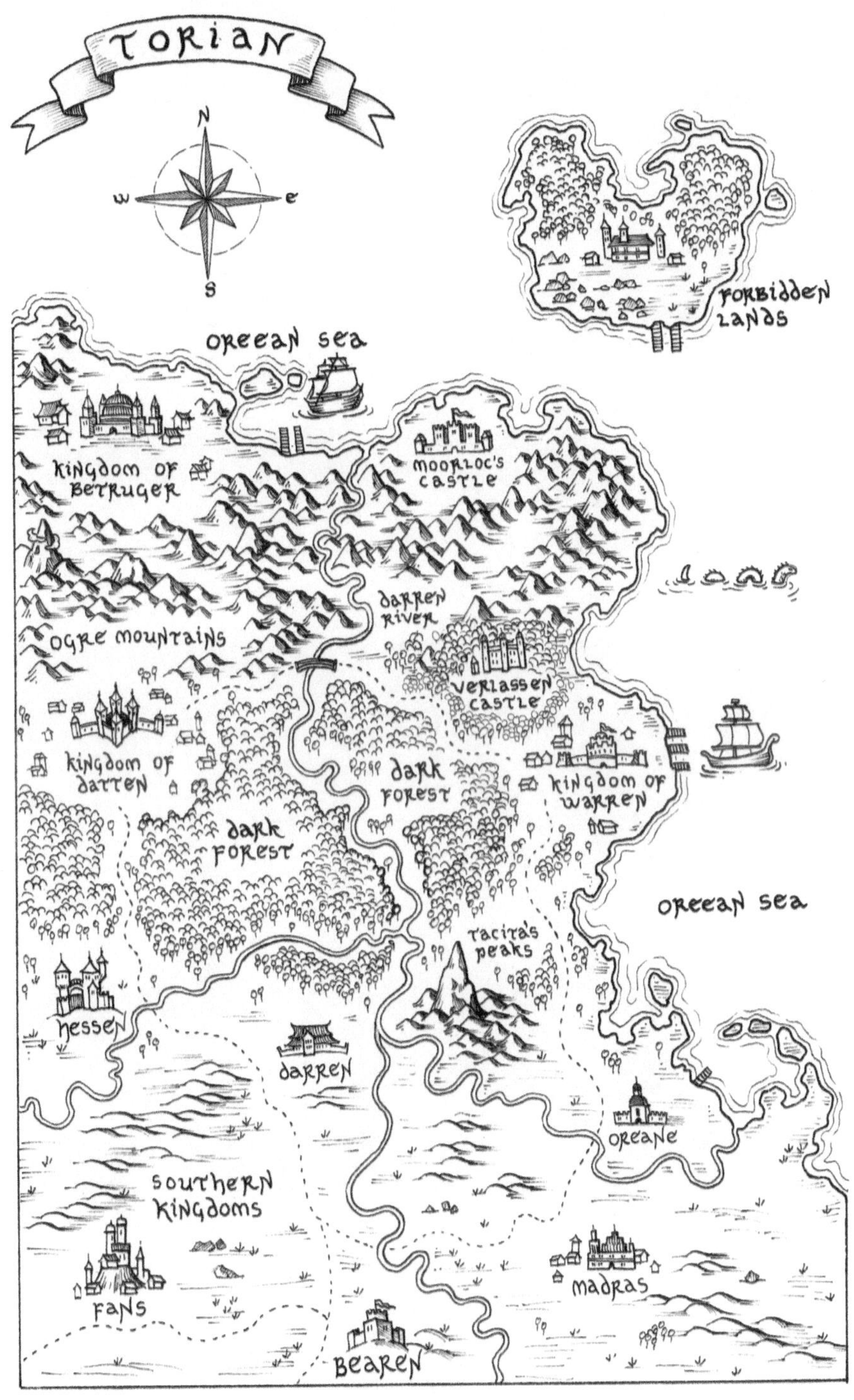

TORIAN
N
W E
S
FORBIDDEN LANDS
OREEAN SEA
KINGDOM OF BETRUGER
MOORLOC'S CASTLE
OGRE MOUNTAINS
DARREN RIVER
VERLASSEN CASTLE
KINGDOM OF DARREN
DARK FOREST
DARK FOREST
KINGDOM OF WARREN
HESSEN
TACITA'S PEAKS
OREEAN SEA
DARREN
SOUTHERN KINGDOMS
OREANE
FANS
MADRAS
BEAREN

Forbidden Lands
Salem
Cassandra
Tiere
Merlin
Ares
Celtics
Mire
Hades
Mystics
Poseidon
N

# CHAPTER I
# GRYPHON

The sorcerers stood in silence, watching Aaron's body jerk on the stone floor of Datten's throne room. No one moved until he stopped and felt cold to the touch.

Megesti looked up from the chilly stones beside Aaron, his eyes filled with dread. "Gryphon ... did we kill him?"

Gryphon scoffed. *I'd never be that lucky.* If Aaron died from a curse after attacking Alex, that would be Gryphon's best shot at getting rid of him.

"No," Kharon replied.

Birch moved behind Megesti and rubbed his shoulder. "I gave him a potent sleeping draught. It knocked him out and will settle whatever magic is controlling him."

Gryphon rapped Aaron's shoulder with his boot to make sure he wasn't faking. "I suppose I can see what attracted Alex to him. When he's not ranting about me, he's not terrible-looking ... for a mortal. Even if he makes stupid faces in his sleep."

"Gryphon," Birch said, smacking Gryphon upside the back of his head. "He can't defend himself."

"That's the point, Auntie Birch," Gryphon said.

1

"Just do your job," Megesti snapped. "We need to see what we're dealing with."

"Ares ..." Gryphon muttered.

He squatted beside Aaron and cracked his fingers. All sounds vanished as he threw open his well, releasing his Mystic powers and setting himself alight in a blue glow. He placed his fingers on Aaron's temples and rushed into the man's memories. He hopped from one to another—Alex smiling, laughing, kissing Aaron. It made Gryphon's heart ache, even if he'd never admit it aloud. Soon he found a memory filled with hatred. It was of himself, seen from Aaron's point of view. This memory felt different—disconnected from the rest. Gryphon dug deeper into this dark area and found dozens of moments with Alex. Gone were the love and warmth. These memories were fixated on Alex and Gryphon. Anytime Gryphon was there, Aaron's jealousy took over, and his temper turned on Alex. It was clear any mention of him triggered the curse. Somehow it bypassed Aaron's conscience and turned him into a different person.

Gryphon's own temper stirred. He went further back until he saw a flash of orange and found exactly what he was dreading. A broken coach and an old woman he recognized. *I've never been able to reverse one of her spells.*

"It's Eris," Gryphon said, releasing Aaron. He swayed from standing too quickly after expending so much energy. "My hexa cursed him. She did it when he was coming back from Verlassen Castle with Harold."

"That long ago?" Kharon asked. "How did no one notice?"

"Alex would have, if she weren't so busy healing and helping mortals all day."

"Gryphon," Birch scolded.

Gryphon rubbed his forehead. "There's more. Aaron has no memory of these events. When we cure him, he won't remember what he did to her."

"That'll destroy him," Megesti said.

"Considering how he forced Alex to go through the same thing, it's what he deserves."

"Gryphon!"

"I'm entitled to my opinion, Birch, even if you don't like it."

"Can we get him out of the throne room and into his suite?" Megesti asked. "I'm worried someone will find us in here."

"We can, but I don't promise not to drop him." Gryphon and Megesti grabbed Aaron under his arms, and Kharon took his feet. They cracked to the Datten King's suite and dropped Aaron onto his bed. Birch arrived with a potted plant and slid it under the bed. Using her Celtics powers, she grew the plant and bound him to the bedposts with vines.

"Megesti, you stay here," Birch said. "Kharon, keep an eye on his mother so she doesn't find him. Gryphon and I will review the books in the lab."

"What if he wakes up actually himself?" Megesti asked.

"Then you'll explain what happened and why he's tied up," Gryphon said. "You're his friend, so he should believe you."

Megesti glanced from Aaron to Gryphon. Finally, he nodded and took a seat on the chair beside the bed.

Gryphon stared at the wall. Unbidden, Aaron's memory of attacking Alex burned through his mind. The terror on her face when he grabbed her arms and held her down while trying to find some imaginary mark would haunt him for the rest of his days. *Unlike him, the only mark I'll ever leave on her will be my bond mark.* Gryphon exhaled and turned to Megesti.

"If he isn't himself, you may have to hurt him to contain him, Megesti."

"Don't say things like that," Birch said, pinching Gryphon's arm.

"I'm not being vindictive. He went after *Alex.* If he wakes up angry enough ... who knows what he'll be capable of?"

# CHAPTER 2

# ALEX

Alex sat on the foot of her oversized bed in her mother's old bedroom in Verlassen Castle watching the fire crackle. They'd fled from Datten so fast she hadn't even told her father where they were going. The thought of him worrying added to the guilt eating away at her. Stefan took a gulp of his ale and focused on her.

"What happened tonight—it isn't your fault, Alex," Stefan said.

"How is it not my fault? If he'd married some mortal girl, this never would have happened. *I'm* the reason he's cursed."

She tucked the blanket around her lap.

*I know that look. You had it the day I fell through the ice and the day Aaron and my grandfather came to Kirsh. You're afraid.*

Her shoulder had stopped bleeding, but she was too emotionally exhausted to safely heal it. Stefan knew how her powers became chaotic when she was upset. He'd dutifully washed and wrapped it in silence, and now they sat in her room, staring at the fire and drinking.

Neither had bothered to change. In the firelight, she could see the blood on Stefan's Datten tunic and the drops that marred his pale skin. It was her blood—from when he'd ripped her from Aaron's grasp. The pure rage on his face at that moment would forever be burned on her soul. Remembering made her tremble. She knew what Stefan was capable of, but she preferred not to be reminded. He took another swig of his ale and caught her studying him.

"I'm not leaving you. Don't even suggest it. This chair is my bed tonight."

Alex sighed. "I could sleep in your quarters, like old times."

"After tonight, you deserve to be in your own bed." Stefan groaned. "Who'd have thought our old lives at the camp would be the simple part?"

"There, we only had to worry about starving or freezing to death in the winter." Alex took a sip of her ale but spit it back into the mug. It reminded her of Aaron. The same ale had been on his breath. "Just say it, Stefan."

He looked at her quizzically.

"You were right. I shouldn't have fallen in love with Aaron. Say it didn't have to be this way, and it's exactly what you knew would happen." She sniffed, tears welling in her eyes.

"That isn't what I was thinking."

Alex moaned. "Then what were you thinking?"

"How sorry I am that you and Aaron can't simply be happy. That something or someone is always trying to rip you apart. And how shameful it is ... that I was one of those things."

Stefan's words cut deep. Alex put her ale between her knees. Terrified tears ran down her cheeks, and a sob escaped. "What if they can't cure him and he's stuck like this forever?"

Stefan took her ale and placed it on the table with his. He sat beside her, and she fell toward him when the mattress bowed.

"You'll get through this—if by stubbornness alone," he said.

Alex laughed in the middle of a sniffle and snorted.

"That's my Alex," Stefan said, rubbing her shoulder.

"I hate you."

"You wish you could."

Alex shoved him hard, and he slipped off the bed, making her truly laugh.

"I think we both need rest." Stefan stole her blanket and got comfortable in the chair.

All her fears of losing her future with Aaron slammed into her at once. "Thank you, Stefan."

"Always."

# CHAPTER 3

# AARON

Aaron pounded on the cold stone wall and screamed until his lungs burned. No one heard him. He'd awakened on the floor of this strange room, imprisoned by stone walls on all sides. The air was crisp and the floor damp. There were no doors or windows, yet it was bright enough to be midday.

*How long have I been here? It feels like days, but I'm not tired or hungry. I need to get back to Datten and to Alex. She'll be so worried about me.*

Aaron paced the small distance between the walls, feeling like a caged animal. All he could do with his time were think, worry, and walk, as his mind wandered to his friends, his wife, and his regrets over what had happened between him and Alex.

# CHAPTER 4

# GRYPHON

G ryphon picked up another book at random and flipped through it. "How are things with Megesti?"

Birch hesitated, gathering her thoughts like so much scattered seed. "Slow. I'm trying not to push him. This last year has taken a toll on him."

For several hours, Gryphon and Birch dug through the books in the lab, searching for protection spells and remedies against curses. They reviewed and eliminated every book in the room. After that, Birch headed to bed, and Gryphon relieved Megesti. Alone with the mortal, he took the spot next to Aaron's bed, placed his hand on Aaron's face, and stretched his fingers over his temples.

*Maybe if I can figure out the spell Eris used, we can better counteract it. Otherwise, we might do more damage.*

Gryphon relived his hexa cursing Aaron over a dozen times. A kiss on the cheek administered the spell and only affected Aaron, sparing Harold. When he couldn't watch anymore, Gryphon strolled around the room. With each lap, he replayed Aaron's memory of attacking Alex in this room before he'd left for the southern lords.

On his third trip, he spotted a tiny fleck of blood on the wall. "You're going to feel so horrible after you wake up."

"Clearly, since I have to look at *your* hideous hide."

Gryphon whipped around to face Aaron. The sneer on the mortal's face made Gryphon grind his teeth, but his visage often did. It didn't mean the princeling wasn't himself.

"Are you actually *you* right now?" Gryphon asked.

"What a stupid question. Untie me," Aaron ordered, struggling against the restraints.

"Not until I know."

"Know what? That I intend to ram my sword through your gut for putting your hands on my wife? Untie me now."

"That's an answer. Not the one I wanted, but an answer, still." Gryphon walked over to Aaron. "If you're in there, Princeling, fight this. You're not going to like what this side of you did to your wife, but the sooner it's over, the sooner you can grovel for her forgiveness."

Aaron laughed. "I'll never grovel after what she did with you."

"As disappointed as I am, we haven't done anything. You're cursed and delusional." Gryphon turned to leave.

"So she didn't rip off your clothes after she killed those men in the castle?"

Gryphon's blood ran cold. He slowly turned around. "What did you say?"

The hatred on Aaron's face was startling, making his eyes look darker. "She told me everything. Murdering those men, killing her innocent maid, wanting you to take her when you showed up glowing orange like some fire pumpkin ..."

"It wasn't like that. We kissed, that's it. You're twisting her words to get a confession for something she *didn't* do. Alexandria isn't perfect, but you always forget she's a sorceress. We aren't prudish like mortals, but she'd never intentionally betray you. What happened in the basement resulted from the onslaught of her Ares powers and her inability to control that level of magic. I'm *her* Head, and she is *my* Heart, so her powers want me. Nothing more."

"You say that as if you wouldn't have bedded her if I wasn't in her life."

Gryphon scoffed. "If you didn't exist, I'd have claimed her on the beach the day I met her. But you do exist, and despite what I want, I'll do what she asks. I'm getting Birch so we can give you something to help you sleep while I figure out what to do with you."

# CHAPTER 5
# ALEX

Alex couldn't sleep. Every time she closed her eyes, Aaron's enraged face appeared, and it sent her into a panic. Stefan had no such problem. He was sprawled out across the chair, snoring.

*You and Michael can sleep almost anywhere. It's not fair.*

Alex put on her green sparring clothes and braided her wavy chestnut hair before heading out of her room to get some food from the kitchen. She made her way down the hallways of Verlassen Castle, unable to stop thinking of Aaron.

*It's too soon for them to have figured anything out. I have to remember what Emmerich taught me about keeping control of my emotions when I can't control anything else.*

Alex stopped and took a few deep breaths to calm the raging typhoon in her heart and gut. Finally calm again, she hurried to the kitchen. As she slipped into the room, her hair stood on end, and she scanned the darkness.

"Who's here?" Alex threw her hands forward, bringing the fireplaces to life. The flames illuminated the worktables and the pots and pans hanging on the far wall.

"Hello." Lynx was standing in the center of the room, holding a loaf of bread. She took a bite and slowly chewed it, watching Alex. "Didn't anyone teach you it's dangerous to stare at wild animals?"

"Sorry. I didn't expect to find anyone down here."

"I couldn't sleep and wanted a snack." Lynx wiped crumbs from her lip with the back of her hand and looked at Alex carefully. "There are more." She nodded her head toward the pantry.

Alex strode to the small door and snatched another loaf. She also grabbed a bottle of Warren wine and a small bag before hopping onto the worktable. Lynx looked at the wine curiously.

"The mugs are up there." Alex pointed behind Lynx and winced at the pain in her shoulder. By the time Lynx retrieved the mugs, Alex had opened the bag and removed the corkscrew. Lynx opened the bottle, and Alex poured them each a full mug as Lynx hopped onto the table beside her.

"So why can't you sleep?" Lynx asked after a few minutes of awkward silence.

"Nightmares."

"About what?"

"Everything. My mother's death. My time at the castle. The memories Gryphon took, which I got back. I spent eight months trying to live with what happened there, and I was finally feeling as if I could. But now with Aaron … I have too many scars on my soul."

"What happened at the castle?" Lynx asked, softly, as if Alex were glass and might break at too sharp a sound.

Alex shook her head.

"Maybe telling someone who understands your experiences would help. I'm a titan and a powerful sorceress, like you."

Alex chewed another bite of bread. She didn't want to be judged. *But then, so what if you judge me? It's not as if I have to worry about you telling Gryphon.*

"I'm Gryphon's confidant, so clearly, I can keep a secret."

"Is there a history with you and Gryphon?"

"Are you asking if I've ever been to his bed?"

Lynx asked it so frankly that Alex spit out her wine in shock. Lynx laughed so hard she nearly fell off the table. "Gryphon's practically my little brother. I helped Birch bathe him when he was an infant. That's how I know about that butterfly birthmark. So, never. Not even if he was the last sorcerer in Torian."

"I understand," Alex said, trying not to laugh.

"Why did you ask? Do you have feelings—?"

"Nothing like that. I love Aaron. I know Gryphon and I are supposed to be something ... someday, but that's a lifetime away for me. All I care about now is my life with Aaron."

"All right," Lynx said, sipping her wine. "Then tell me about the castle, and why you look as if you have the weight of the entire mortal race on your shoulders."

Alex hesitated, and then it all poured out of her: Moorloc's teaching, the kiss with Gryphon, the death of Reinhilde, the moment she decided she couldn't take any more, and finally, her battle with the evil ghost of her grandfather. Lynx listened silently until Alex was done.

"That's a lot to hold inside. You know those men deserved it, and what happened with Gryphon wasn't your fault either. He's an Ares male. Of all our lines, they are by far the most aggressive in claiming a partner. That it took you losing control of *your* Ares powers to wake up his instincts is impressive."

"His restraint was, too."

"So that leaves the accident and its consequences. How many people have you told?"

"Very few. Harold knows some things but not everything. And Emmerich and the generals were helping me sort things out, but after Emmerich's death ... we stopped."

"No wonder you're struggling with your powers. You should talk about this more."

"I can't. I'm responsible for enough death."

"What does that mean?" Lynx asked.

"It means she blames herself for the deaths of the people who protected her when she was taken away from her grandfather," Stefan said.

Alex's eyes widened as she turned around to face Stefan. He marched over and hugged her.

"How much did you hear?"

"Everything. Seems you left out some things when you told me what happened. Kruft and his men are lucky they're already dead, because if they weren't, I'd rip them apart with my bare hands."

"I hate when you spy on me." Alex couldn't face Stefan's glare, so she looked down and picked at her bread. *Please don't hate me.*

"It was unintentional. You were gone when I woke, and I know to check the kitchen before I start to worry." Stefan grabbed the last of Alex's bread and ate it.

A quiet moment passed between the three of them until Stefan caught Alex's eye and winked. The secret sign between them that everything was okay. Alex felt the weight leave her heart.

"What was her name?" Lynx asked. "The woman you killed. What was her name?"

"Reinhilde."

"You said she was from Warren. Do you know her last name?" Stefan asked.

"Vinur."

"Felix's family name. When we're back in Warren, we could visit the Barron."

Alex opened her mouth and Stefan patted her knee. "And yes, I'm coming with you, whether or not you want me to," he said.

Alex smiled. "Thank you." She reached up to hug him and winced as she tugged her stitches. "Of all the places to stab me, why the shoulder?"

"It's not even a proper wound," Stefan said. "You bled, but

there won't be any permanent damage. I'd have expected better from him after all those years training with my father." Alex jumped down and tried to push him with her good arm.

"Actually," Lynx said before gulping the last of her wine, "for a sorceress, it makes perfect sense. You can't raise your arm right now, and you need to be able to raise it to do magic."

"So, he took my magic away? Or my control, at least."

"Yes."

"Okay, now I give him some credit," Stefan said. "But that's enough night adventures. It's back to bed, you two. You can take your bread, but I'm keeping the wine."

"Is he always this bossy?" Lynx asked.

"You get used to it," Alex said.

❧❧❧ ❧❧❧

AFTER THE WINE, Alex slept until lunch and was surprised to find the room empty. *Why'd they let me sleep in?* Still in her sparring clothes, she made her bed perfectly and fixed her braid until not a hair was out of place.

Sir Colten was guarding the hallway door. When she peeked out, he offered to summon Stefan and bring them lunch. Alex thanked him and was about to go back in when he spoke again. "Did you figure out the premonition, Your Highness?"

Alex looked back at Sir Colten. "Premonition?"

Sir Colten reminded her that she'd woken half the inhabitants of Verlassen Castle with a premonition dream, which was why she'd been in Datten—to inform Aaron.

"What exactly did I say?"

"I'm sorry, I didn't get the whole thing down. Gryphon got the rest."

"You wrote it down? Please bring me the note with whatever you can remember."

"Of course, Princess." He nodded and strode down the hallway.

Alex watched until he rounded the corner, then darted inside her room. *What premonition? What did I say? Did I know Aaron's attack was coming? Did I cause it?*

Waiting for Sir Colten felt like an eternity. When Stefan arrived, Alex was already spiraling. He grabbed her into a hug to settle her, but she wiggled free and kept pacing.

Lynx bounced into the room. "I thought I'd find you here." She stalled when she saw Alex's face. "What happened?"

"Alex had a premonition before all this started," Stefan said. "Sir Colten is getting his notes. I've instructed her guards to write down anything strange she says, assuming it's a premonition."

"That's clever," Lynx said.

"I like my men prepared," Stefan said.

"Hmm. So do I," Lynx purred.

Stefan stepped back, almost tripping over the couch. Alex was considering whether to rescue him from Lynx when Sir Colten arrived. He set down a tray of bread and cheese, then handed Alex a sheet of paper with hastily scrawled words. "I hope it makes sense to you. Gryphon and I were very confused."

"Gryphon?" Stefan asked.

"Yes." Sir Colten reiterated to Stefan what had happened and then returned to his duties.

Alex's magic pumped through her, growing wilder with every breath. Lynx stole a piece of cheese and watched Alex almost as carefully as Stefan did as she read the premonition.

*"If he fails to protect her, Warren shall fall. If she fails to save him, the sorcerer will fall. If they fail to unite, then everything will fall. Chaos will spread across the lands and fill the rivers with blood."*

"That's disturbing," Lynx said, sitting down.

"They always are. But how do we get the missing bit from Gryphon? I ... I can't go to Datten. Not until I know he's okay." Alex's breath hitched, and she fought back short, ragged breaths.

"I'll go," Lynx said, reaching over and squeezing Alex's hand.

"Thank you," Alex said. "Could you grab the gray bundle at the back of my wardrobe too?"

"I'll be back soon." Lynx winked and cracked away.

As soon as Lynx vanished, Alex pushed her plate away and stood to pace the room.

"Eat," Stefan said.

"If I eat now, it's just going to come back up."

"Exactly. It's easier on your stomach if something is in it." He held out a small loaf of bread. It was only after he shook it that Alex exhaled and took it from him. She paced the room, nibbling on the loaf.

"What if they can't fix him? What if he's a monster forever because of me?"

Stefan sighed and grabbed Alex's hands. "We are only having *this* conversation once. Gryphon loves you as much as Aaron does. He will not let something bad happen to Aaron, because he knows that would devastate you. I don't like him, but I know he'll get Aaron back."

Alex leaned against Stefan and sighed. "I need a distraction."

"Riding or sparring?"

"Will you let me win?"

"Never."

"Then sparring."

# CHAPTER 6

# GRYPHON

"He's stronger than he looks," Kharon groaned, wiping their hands on their robe. They left with Birch to find more herbs for sleeping potions, leaving Gryphon, Megesti, and Michael to watch Aaron.

Gryphon growled. It had taken four of them to force Aaron to drink the sleeping draught Birch made, and he'd gotten kicked when Aaron got his leg out of the restraints.

"What do we do now?" Michael asked. "Edward and Jerome are handling his duties, and Jessica has been keeping his mother occupied. Did you find anything useful in the books?"

"No, I did not," Gryphon snapped. He leaned against the wall in Aaron's room, idly opening his palm and summoning his fire power only to close his hand into a fist and extinguish it.

"Doesn't that burn you?" Michael asked.

Sometimes Gryphon forgot how little mortals knew about sorcery. It used to enrage him, but the curiosity and concern in Michael's eyes amused him. More importantly, the knowledge would help him better support Alex. "No, it helps me think."

Lynx appeared at the door. "He's been doing it since he was a little sorcerer. Any luck?"

Gryphon and Megesti shook their heads.

Lynx sighed. "I was hoping to have something for Alex."

"How's she doing?" Michael asked before Gryphon could. "I mean truthfully, not how she says she is."

"I left her with Stefan."

"That's good. I'm glad he's with her," Gryphon said.

Lynx and Michael looked at each other and then at Gryphon.

"Since when do you like Stefan?" Megesti asked.

"I don't, but I can't stand the idea of Alex sitting alone worrying about Aaron. This curse has twisted him. We knocked him out, but the things he said before were horrible. I don't know how they're going to get through this."

"The same way they get through all the other issues. With faith in each other and with love," Michael said.

"Sometimes that's not enough," Gryphon said.

"Listen to the sentimental mortal." Lynx winked at Gryphon.

"I meant, they've been through a lot, and I think they'll get through this too," Michael said.

"On that lovely note," Lynx said, "I'm here to get the first half of the premonition Alex had when you two were at the castle. Her knight could only remember the last half."

Gryphon groaned. "I already forgot about her premonition." He paused a moment in recollection before he recited the start of it. "*There is a debt to be paid, and the price shall be steep. Their plans have been set, it shall be with blood. A son for the son, the father for the father.*"

"Have you figured it out?" Lynx asked.

"No. The princeling preoccupied me." Gryphon gestured toward Aaron.

Lynx stepped closer to the bed. She looked Aaron over carefully and sniffed. "He still smells wrong. I don't like it."

Gryphon and Megesti updated Lynx on what they had discovered so far.

"Well, you can give me a list of spell books you found in Verlassen Castle, or Megesti could come back with me and he can deliver them to you," Lynx said.

"Where are you with the protection spells?" Megesti asked.

"Alex and I found five books at the castle that showed promise, but after her premonition nightmare, I forgot them. I can't focus on fixing the princeling *and* protecting this castle," Gryphon said.

"You still want to go through with the protection spells?" Lynx asked. "Don't we have our hands full at the moment?"

"He's the reason we have to try them. I want to see if protecting the castle casts out whatever was done to him."

Lynx sighed. "True. If he's possessed, it'll remove all the unwelcome sorcerers."

"Exactly."

"He is rather handsome," Lynx said. "I can see why Alex picked him."

Gryphon elbowed her. "On that disturbing note ..." Gryphon wanted to change the subject but did not know what to say. Megesti came to his aid.

"I'll go with you," Megesti said. "Alex will need me to get into the lab so we can check the Cassandra journals. They're our best bet for healing this."

"Lynx, keep Alex busy," Michael said. "She does better when she's focused on something."

"If she needs a distraction, we'll test out some of those spells. Can't hurt to see if they work better for her," Lynx said.

"Tell her we're doing our best and we won't give up," Gryphon said.

Lynx crossed the room to a pair of wardrobes. She opened one, saw it was Aaron's, and then shut it and opened the other. She rooted around until she found a gray bundle and tucked it under her arm.

"What's that?" Michael asked.

Lynx shrugged. "Alex was desperate to have it, so I'm bringing it with us. Ready, Megesti?"

Megesti nodded, and they cracked away.

Gryphon turned to Michael. "I'm fine here. You can go see how things are going with the knights."

Michael nodded and headed out of the room. Aaron was snoring loudly enough that Gryphon knew he'd hear him anywhere in the suite. He headed downstairs and snooped through Alex and Aaron's things. Everything was dull and very Datten. *Armor, swords, shields—don't they have anything better to show off? Maybe these are his father's things. Once Alex redecorates it, it'll probably look like a library.*

Gryphon helped himself to some parchment and a pencil and sat at the giant tables to make some notes about different spells he remembered reading in his father's library.

# CHAPTER 7
# ALEX

Stefan kept his word and didn't let Alex win a single round. By the time they finished, both were sweaty, bruised, and exhausted—exactly what Alex needed. They returned through the main hall and past the stairs that led down to the lab. There used to be a portrait hiding them, but after taking away all the paintings with Moorloc and Lygari, Alex had decided not to cover the entrance. Looking down the dark stairs, Alex noticed a face out of the corner of her eye. Turning, she saw her wedding portrait with Aaron, and a chill ran through her. Her father had it finished fast enough for it to already be displayed up here.

*How was that only three weeks ago?*

A warm hand squeezed her shoulder, and she looked up. Stefan gave her his best big brother face, clearly trying to comfort her. She sighed and let him lead her toward her room.

When they stepped into the library, Lynx was sitting on the couch, watching the door. "There you are," she purred. "I wondered how long you'd be."

Alex rushed to her. "Did you see him? Is he healed? What did Gryphon say?"

Lynx pursed her lips and glanced briefly at Stefan.

That was all Alex needed.

"I came for the books," Megesti said from above. He was on a ladder, holding a pair of books. "Specifically the Cassandra ones, to see if they have any healing spells that can help."

Alex swallowed hard against the emotion rising in her throat. "Did you get the bundle?" she asked.

"I did." Lynx stood and pulled out the gray cloth from under the couch.

"Thank you." Alex took it from Lynx and unwrapped it, revealing three smaller bundles. She peeked inside the first but set it aside. The second was the one she was looking for. She set it on the table and slid it over to Stefan, then carefully wrapped the other two back up.

"What's this?" Stefan asked, pointing to the bundle in front of him.

Alex smiled. "Part of Harold's coronation gift for Aaron. Open it."

"Why would I open Aaron's gift?" Stefan looked confused.

"You'll understand when you open it." Alex pushed the bundle closer to him.

Stefan obeyed. Inside was a gold-hilted sword with a red blade. The handle had a large obsidian stone at the end.

"Red steel," Lynx said. Her eyes widened in fear.

"Where did you get red steel?" Stefan asked.

"From Harold," Alex said. "Red steel is deadly to a sorcerer."

Stefan's eyes grew larger. "How many?"

"Three. Besides Harold's and Macht's blades. One each for Aaron, you, and Michael, plus a few arrows for me since I already have my mother's red steel dagger." Alex placed her dagger on the table.

Lynx gasped. "You carry red steel around? Are you mad? Do you want a slow and excruciating death?"

"That dagger already saved my life once. I'm at more of a risk from other sorcerers than hurting myself with my blade."

Lynx's mouth dropped open, and she turned to Stefan.

"She's only cut herself on her own blade three times in her life, and two of them were Michael's fault," Stefan said. He removed his old blade from his scabbard and replaced it with the new one.

"You're going to *wear* that?" Lynx asked.

"My job is to protect Alex. Lately, every attack has come from a sorcerer. If I have a weapon that can help, it's never going to leave my side," Stefan said. "Besides, I have a sturdy scabbard, so I won't accidentally cut any sorcerers."

Lynx glared at him, and with a snap of her fingers, she cracked away.

*Ferflucs. Now Lynx is mad at me.* Alex adjusted her braid and tried to not think about that.

"Megesti, let's go get you those books," Alex said.

"We also need the books you and Gryphon picked out. He wants to try those spells first," Megesti said.

"Stefan, could you take Lynx to my father's room? Sir Colten put Gryphon in there."

"Of course."

After Stefan left, Megesti followed Alex toward the lab. Alex made sure they were alone as they walked into the hall.

"Be honest. How is he really?" she asked.

"He spouts deranged nonsense, and the hatred on his face is— well, it's not Aaron. I've never seen him like this."

"What if they can't fix him?"

Megesti stopped on the stairs and faced her. "Alex, it's only been a day. Give us a proper chance before you jump to worst-case scenarios. We know who cursed him, and Birch thinks that's a start."

"So who was it?" Alex asked. At the bottom of the stairs, she pulled the dagger from the wall to slice her palm, knowing it would be healed in minutes.

"Are you sure you want to know?" Megesti took the dagger and sliced his palm, curling a fist to drip the blood necessary to open the door. When it swung inward, the fireplace burst into flames, illuminating the lab for them.

"I *need* to know, Megesti."

"Gryphon's hexa," he said softly.

Alex groaned. "His grandmother? Why is his family out to get us?"

"Take your pick. His father was obsessed with your mother, which probably annoyed his mother and hexa. Birch is Gryphon's mother's adoptive sister, and she married my father, so there's that. It could also be because you're the Heart and you're already more powerful than many living sorcerers ten times your age, which makes them jealous. Lastly, you're here, and that's keeping Gryphon here. I'm pretty sure the next Head fleeing the Forbidden Lands to save mortals wasn't in anyone's plan."

Alex cringed. She couldn't believe she was in the middle of a second family dispute, all because her parents fell in love and she was born. "I know you're right, but that doesn't make it easier for me."

"And that's because nothing about this is easy." Megesti patted Alex's shoulder as they got to work.

Soon they had pulled every Cassandra book from the shelf and set them on the table. They sat and, without speaking, went through each one to pull out anything with notes on curses or possessions.

After an hour, Lynx and Stefan came to check on them. Lynx asked to help, and Megesti tried to explain that the books were protected, but Alex grabbed one and whispered to it, asking it to show itself to Lynx. Megesti's jaw dropped when Lynx was able to read it.

"How did you do that?" he asked.

"Gryphon taught me," Alex said without looking up from her book. "Our line merely needs to ask the books to show themselves." Megesti whispered to his book and passed it to Stefan.

Together, the four of them worked tirelessly to find all the healing spells in the Cassandra books. By the time they were done, it was well into the night, and the stack to send to Datten was large enough that Stefan volunteered to help Megesti. But Alex refused to let them go until she and Megesti had copied out the handful of spells she wanted to try out.

"I'll keep an eye on the Heart while you're gone," Lynx said and winked at Stefan.

Alex bit her lip to stop herself from laughing at Stefan's flustered look.

"Have Gryphon send you back when you're done. Ready?" Lynx asked, and before they could reply, she ran her hand down Stefan's biceps and cracked him and Megesti away. Turning back to Alex, a mischievous grin spread across her entire face. "He's so much fun to play with."

Alex crossed her arms at the gorgeous sorceress before her. "Lynx, what exactly are your intentions with my Stefan?"

Lynx shrugged, still smiling.

"I'll warn you now, he's very honorable and won't be open to being a sorceress's plaything, no matter how beautiful you are," Alex said.

"I enjoy a challenge."

"If you want a real challenge, you should let me teach you to spar," Alex said.

"Not with red steel!"

"Of course not! We train with wood, and honestly, Stefan has never once cut anyone he didn't mean to. I trust him with my life, and I trust him with red steel. You can too."

Lynx's nose scrunched the way a cat's would, but after a loud huff, she nodded.

Alex started laughing and picking up the papers. *Stefan doesn't know what's coming for him. I think he's in for a battle he'll lose.* As she looked down at the books, the words seemed to swim together. "Should we try these tonight or tomorrow?"

"In the morning. It'll be easier for you after some rest," Lynx said.

"That's fair."

"Aaron'll be okay." Lynx came up to Alex and held out her arms. "I know we aren't friends yet, and that you take time warming up to people, but now that Bossy is gone, how about we go find that wine? Then, after a few mugs, you can have a good cry and maybe even hug someone."

Lynx's brown eyes were soft like her father's. *I don't know why, but something tells me I can trust you.* Alex stepped to Lynx and hugged her.

Lynx stumbled but hugged Alex back.

*Aaron will be okay. Birch and Gryphon won't give up. As long as no one else notices he's not himself—*

Alex sucked in her breath. "I was too worried about *if* Aaron would be himself again, but if the Rassgats find out he's lost control, he could lose his throne."

"Your father and the general will not allow that to happen. Neither will Harold. Gryphon and I were there for the signing. The peace with Betruger is between Edward, Harold, Aaron, and you."

Alex's heart pounded, and her palms grew slick. Lynx grabbed her hands and tugged them until Alex looked at her.

"Aaron's throne is not in danger," Lynx said. "You are the Queen of Datten. If the king is ill, the general and the queen will handle things. And if anyone tries to take your throne, well, Gryphon might have to use those Mystic powers of his to convince them otherwise."

Alex exhaled. "I forgot he can implant thoughts into people's minds too, not only remove them."

"Of course you did. He avoids doing it. Now let's get that drink." Lynx slid her arm over Alex's shoulders, the same way Stefan would, and with a mischievous gleam in her eye, she pulled her into the hallway toward the kitchen.

⁓⟐⟐⟐⟐ ⟐⟐⟐⟐⟐

ALEX SLEPT RESTLESSLY. She awoke soaking wet and gasping for breath. In her mind's eye, she could see Aaron's face, contorted with rage as he attacked her in the throne room. Then he was Ridge, using his face like a mask when he attacked her at Betruger Castle. Shaking her head to push away the last terrible memories, she tossed her wet nightgown over her chair and put on clean sparring clothes. With a wave of her hand, the fireplace sprang to life, sending sparks dancing across the ceiling. Alex looked at her crown and necklace on the table beside her bed. Aaron had given her the necklace on their wedding day. Three stones hung from it: a ruby from Daniel's sword, a sapphire from her grandmother's brooch, and the strange black stone from her mother. She cleared her throat to banish her tears and fastened the necklace around her neck, tucking it into her shirt.

She picked up the spells that she and Megesti had copied down in the library. The hallway was empty, so she crept into the courtyard and sat on the wet grass to read. It was still dark, so she created a floating sphere of fire to illuminate the page. She whispered the words of Merlin and waited. When nothing happened, she placed both her hands on the ground and read the words louder. A small golden light left her hands and spread across the grass in front of her like ripples on a pond. Spurred by her success, she shifted to her knees and pressed her hands on the ground as hard as she could. She took a deep breath and screamed the words

28

at the ground. The light flew from her hands and hit the edge of the courtyard.

"What are you doing?"

Alex gasped and turned. Lynx and Stefan were watching her, standing with their arms crossed.

"I couldn't sleep."

Lynx walked over and kneeled beside Alex. "You're not supposed to try these spells alone. I know you want to prove yourself, but they can drain you. You need someone here to stop you if it goes too far."

Alex bit her cheek and looked up at Stefan.

"I'm not mad," Stefan said. "I know you. When I couldn't find you in your room, I went to your usual places."

"Powerful magic needs to be handled properly," Lynx said. "I can help you with this spell, but from what I witnessed, you *need* more training, and only one person is qualified to train the Heart."

"Can we talk about Gryphon after we've put the spell on my home?" Alex asked.

"So long as we actually talk about him," Stefan said.

Lynx gestured back at the entrance to the courtyard. "Stefan, we'll need food. Alex is going to need to eat after this spell."

Stefan nodded and headed inside while Alex waited for Lynx to speak.

"Straighten your back and lock your elbows. I'll say the words with you, but your power will carry this spell, since it's from your line and your mother's home."

Alex inhaled deeply.

"And it's not the volume but the focus that matters," Lynx added.

Alex pressed her hands into the ground and pushed the lid off her well. Lynx kneeled beside her, matching her position. Together, they read the spell repeatedly until Alex knew the words by heart.

Once again, the golden light rippled across the grass and climbed the walls of the castle.

"Focus. Take deep breaths," Lynx whispered encouragingly. "Try to cover everything. I'll check outside and come back when you've finished."

Lynx cracked away, and Alex pushed herself harder. Sweat trickled down her back, and her hands burned as the light sped out of them. She was nearing the bottom of her well when Lynx reappeared.

"You're done," Lynx said. "The light made it into the surrounding woods."

Alex lifted her hands off the ground and sat back on her legs. The golden light simply faded slowly until it vanished.

Stefan watched from the entrance. "You covered everything from the stones to the tables to the food."

Alex smiled at him. "I'll still eat it."

"Good, because you need it." Lynx held out her hand to Alex.

Alex took a moment to catch her breath before accepting. She limped toward Stefan and let him help her into the library to eat.

As they ate their food, Alex caught Stefan staring at her. She stared back as she took an extra helping of bread and cheese.

"Someone has an appetite," he said.

"I'm starving."

"You completed a challenging spell without emptying your well," Lynx said. "Young sorcerers eat a lot of food when they are learning to master their powers, and the more powerful the sorcerer, the bigger the appetite."

Alex took a huge bite of her bread and waited for Stefan to look away. As soon as he did, she threw a piece of cheese at him and laughed when it hit him on the chin.

Never one to waste food, Stefan ate the cheese without taking his eyes off her. Alex knew that look. He was worried but didn't want to upset her.

"I can't sit here and worry, Stefan. Keep me distracted." An awkward silence fell over them as they ate their food. Once her plate was empty, Alex asked Lynx, "So, when can I do the next spell?"

Lynx choked on her cheese. "Not until tomorrow." She turned to Stefan. "Is she always this ... determined?"

"If you mean impulsive and stubborn—yes," Stefan said.

Alex stuck out her tongue at both of them. "Well, if we can't go cast the spell over the Stronghold today, can we at least go to Warren?" she asked.

"Why Warren?" Lynx asked.

"It's where King Edward and my sister are telling everyone we are," said Stefan. "Yes, I think it's time for Alex to make an appearance."

# CHAPTER 8
# GRYPHON

Gryphon knew how disappointed Alex would be when he sent Lynx back without an update, so he left Jessica and Michael to watch Aaron while he, Birch, and Megesti gathered in the lab. They laid the books out on the table.

*I know how long sorting out and curing a curse can take, but Alex doesn't. If I don't fix you soon, Princeling, I'll lose her before I even have her.*

Megesti looked bewildered by the pile of books in his lab. "What do we try first?"

"We should go try the protection spells," Birch said.

"Already?" Megesti asked.

"Yes. If he's possessed, the protection spell should force out all unwelcome sorcerers."

Gryphon scoffed and crossed his arms.

"What?" Megesti asked.

"He's worried he'll be thrown out when the protection spell goes up," Birch said. "Clearly Aaron doesn't want him here, so there is a risk he won't be able to stay."

Megesti spoke to Gryphon in earnest. "Gryphon, regardless of what my current king has to say, the queen and I would be honored for you to remain."

"Thank you," Gryphon said. He spun around a spell book toward Megesti. "Your home, your protection spell."

Megesti gulped and pulled the book closer. "You'll help, right?"

"Your line originally cast the spell, so only you or Alexandria can properly strengthen it, and she's indisposed."

Sweat gathered on Megesti's forehead. He picked up the book and whispered the words.

"Louder, so we can correct pronunciation, Sapling." Birch smiled sweetly.

Megesti raised his eyebrows. "Sapling?"

Gryphon snorted. "Birch gives everyone plant nicknames. It's a penchant of the Celtics line. I'm Sprout, Alex is Petal though she doesn't know it yet, and now you're Sapling. Lynx was Seedling, but she doesn't like nicknames, and after a few incidents where animals dug up Birch's garden, she stopped calling her that."

"I'm not sure how I feel about Sapling."

"You'll get used to it," Gryphon said. "Now read."

It took Megesti a few tries, but once he got the spell right, a violet light left him and spread down the table and across the floor. As the sweat continued to roll down his face, the light grew darker. When Birch came back from outside the castle walls and shook her head, Megesti slammed his hands on the table in frustration.

"It's okay, Sapling," Birch said. "You're still getting used to using your stronger powers."

The door knocked and opened, revealing Michael. "A violet light just swept through Aaron's room."

"Did it cover him?" Gryphon asked, and Michael nodded.

"Did he wake up?" Birch asked.

"No," Michael said.

"So it didn't help. Michael, let us know if anything changes," Gryphon said.

Michael nodded and left.

"What do we do now?" Megesti asked.

"I don't know." Gryphon groaned.

"Well, at least we know for certain it's a curse and not a possession. A possession would have been removed as the spell hit him," Birch said.

"How does that help?" Megesti asked.

"It won't help *us*, but I can assure you it will help settle Alexandria's mind when she hears about that possibility."

Both Gryphon and Megesti hesitated.

"Why?" Gryphon asked. "We aren't any closer to finding out how to fix him."

"Maybe not. But he was cursed weeks ago. That's a long time to live with a possessed person, and this means it was only ever her husband in there."

"I still don't get it," Megesti grunted.

Gryphon slapped his forehead, finally realizing what Birch was alluding to. "Ferflucs, I hadn't even thought of that. We have to make sure she knows."

"Knows what?" Megesti demanded.

Gryphon turned to him. "That in their most intimate, private moments, it was only ever Aaron in there, and not another sorcerer acting through him."

Megesti's eyes grew enormous when he realized what Gryphon meant. "That happens?" he asked, horrified.

"It's disgusting, and only a monster would do it," Birch said.

An awkward silence filled the room. They were getting nowhere, but they all knew the stakes. It wasn't only Alex's nerves they were trying to settle. With so many Torian royals arriving in Datten for Emmerich's funeral, they couldn't delay things any further without raising a lot of questions. Gryphon groaned.

Megesti closed the book he was holding. "It's getting late. I understand if you two need some rest, but I'm going to keep working. Aaron's my best friend, and Alex is family. As long as he's like this, I'll work as hard as I can to fix him."

Birch reached across the table and took Megesti's hand. "We'll stay here with you, Sapling. You've spent more than enough time alone."

Megesti pulled another book closer. He took a deep breath and read the next spell.

They worked through the night, trying spells and potions that might be relevant. Shortly after sunrise, Michael burst into the lab.

"He's worse. I don't know how it happened, but Jerome, Kharon, and Edward are struggling to contain him. I got Jessica out, but we need your help!"

Gryphon grabbed Michael and cracked them into Aaron's room, where pandemonium had broken loose. Kharon had revealed the ghosts of Emmerich and Daniel. The apparitions were trying to talk to Aaron, but it was clear he wouldn't listen. Aaron had broken Birch's restraints and was out of the bed, threatening Edward and Jerome.

They were yelling so loudly that despite the large space, Gryphon had no trouble hearing what they were saying.

"I don't care what you think," Aaron growled. "Bring me my wife!"

Edward pushed Aaron back. "You're not going near my daughter like this. Get yourself under control, and I'll consider it."

"Don't bother trying to reason with him. He won't listen to anyone," Gryphon advised.

"Catch your tongue, you worthless fire pumpkin."

"Sticking with that name, are we, *Princeling*? Why don't you leave everyone alone and come deal with me man-to-man?"

"Gryphon! Are you insane?" Michael asked, rushing to his side.

Gryphon noticed Jerome sneaking closer and nodded to him. Edward leaped back as Aaron lunged for Gryphon, but Jerome grabbed him from behind. Michael clambered across the bed and grabbed Aaron's other arm. Aaron fought them as hard as he could, but Michael and Jerome tightened their grip and locked him in place.

Gryphon examined Aaron's face. The blue eyes he'd seen gaze lovingly at Alex so many times now glared at him coldly. He was almost unrecognizable, his face twisted by hatred.

"If you ever touch my wife again, I'll gut you," Aaron spat.

Straightening his back, Gryphon freed his well, and his body glowed orange. He stepped up to Aaron and stared down at him. "If you ever raise your hand to my Heart again, I'll burn you alive."

"That's enough, children." Birch pushed Gryphon back to separate them. She placed her hand on Aaron's shoulder. A green light left her hands and flooded into Aaron, relaxing his body.

"Drink this," Birch said, holding out a mug to him. Gryphon recognized the stench of Birch's sleeping potion from several feet away.

Aaron looked at the mug she held out to him and then turned to Edward. Alex's father nodded, and as Aaron reached for the mug, Jerome and Michael released his arm enough to let him drink.

# CHAPTER 9
# ALEX

Alex cracked them into Warren's spare hall. Despite her improved skills, she was tired, and the sound reverberated through the space. Lynx wrinkled her nose in distaste. The throne room doors flew open, revealing Generals Bishop and Nial.

"Your Royal Highness," Matthew said, bowing to her.

Alex strode over to her father's men. "In Warren, I'm only a crown princess, Matthew, so please dispense with the titles." She gestured toward Lynx. "This is Lynx—the sorceress who helped Birch and Gryphon make the Stronghold suitable for everyone. She's my honored guest."

"Welcome, Lady Lynx," Randal said as he and Matthew bowed. "Your father sent word you'd be coming. Is it true? Did Aaron attack you?"

"Between only us, yes," Alex said. "But please don't hold this against him like my father does."

"I'm so sorry, Alexandria," Matthew said.

"Megesti, Birch," Stefan began. "Gryphon and the other sorcerer, Kharon—"

"Sorcerous," Lynx said.

"Pardon?" Stefan asked.

"Kharon is a sorcerous. Sorcerers are male, sorceresses are female, and sorcerouses have forgone the shackles of gender," Lynx said.

"Oh. I think I'll owe him an apology then," Stefan said.

"Them, not him," Lynx corrected.

"Really, Stefan? I thought you were the observant one," Alex teased.

Stefan set his shoulders. "Let me begin again. All the remaining magical beings are working hard to help Aaron. We have high hopes they'll be successful."

"I'm glad to hear that," Randal said.

"Under the circumstances," Matthew said, "we'll continue to act on your father's behalf. If you're here to recover, people will expect you not to perform any royal duties."

Alex rolled her eyes. "If that's what's *expected*, I'll behave, but it's unnecessary. Everyone forgets I'm a healing sorceress."

"Still," Stefan said. "If your people expect you to stand back, take advantage."

"Is Edith around?" Alex asked hesitantly.

"Yes, but if you want to be on your own, she'll understand." Randal motioned to the hallway door.

Alex nodded gently at Matthew, silently dismissing him in the way Aaron had taught her. "I don't want her to leave Harold's side because of me. Things are going well for them."

Randal chuckled and led them down the hallway. "She didn't come with me because of you. As for King Harold, I must agree. I worried we'd never find a man worthy of my daughter, but then she went and found herself a king."

"Worthy?" Lynx asked, and Alex explained loudly, teasing Randal in the process.

"I *don't* have a favorite!" Randal said, making Alex laugh so loud it echoed down the hall.

Lynx asked about the art on the wall and in the rooms they passed. Stefan answered every question, giving Alex a pleasant distraction. When they arrived inside her room, Lynx twirled and stopped to examine all the books and art pieces. A moment later, Edith came in from her suite. Without a word, she hurried across the room and threw her arms around Alex's neck. After she got her breath back, Alex hugged Edith back.

"I'll be all right. But I don't want to talk about it," Alex said.

"Fair enough." Edith spun to face Lynx. "Hello, I'm Edith Nial, daughter of—"

"Me," Randal replied from the doorway. "If you need anything, Alexandria, have Stefan or Edith summon myself or Matthew."

"I will. Thank you," Alex said.

Randal nodded and closed the door behind him.

"Why do you wear pants so much? I've never seen another lady in pants," Lynx asked Alex, motioning to Edith's dress.

As expected, Edith was dressed in the proper Warren style, although this dress was more elaborate than her usual ones. The skirt was puffy with a fancy silver lace trim and long sleeves that went slightly past her wrists. But it was the neckline that caught Alex's attention. It was much lower than the style Edith normally wore. *Trying to impress a certain king? It seems your mother's willing to risk you ruining a more formal dress.*

Edith crossed her arms. "My mother has insisted I wear more formal gowns. She has high hopes I'll find a suitable match in the next year."

"Dressed like that, you certainly will," Lynx said. "I'm Lynx, Titan of the Tiere sorcerers."

Edith looked at Alex.

"She's an animal-sorceress."

"Ah. Well, if you're a friend of Alex's and Stefan's, you're a friend of mine."

"'Friend' is a little strong," Stefan said.

Alex playfully pushed his shoulder. "Hush, you. I pick my own friends." Alex turned back to Lynx, who was still in her titan robe. "And as your friend, it would be rude of me not to offer you something else to wear, if you'd like. I have dresses and sparring clothes."

"I like pants," Lynx said. "Animals don't like the sound my coat makes, and dress skirts would be even worse."

"I'd be happy to take you into town to get some Warren attire," Edith said. "Care to join us, Alex?"

"I'd rather set my hair on fire."

Edith shook her head. "Her Highness has a strong dislike of shopping for dresses or anything besides books. Luckily, the royal seamstresses only need her for fittings with formal gowns. Everything else they can make from her measurements."

"Take Stefan with you," Alex said. "Our men are well-behaved, but I suspect you'll need an escort to keep the nosy nobles away if you intend to actually accomplish anything."

"If you think I'm going to leave you alone—" Stefan said.

"I give you my word that I won't leave the castle."

"No, give *me* your word," Lynx said.

"Why?" Edith asked.

"I can smell when someone lies," Lynx said, smiling.

"What?" Alex asked, stepping away from the sorceress.

"Not the lie itself, but the way your body reacts when you lie. Your breathing and scent change." Lynx's eyes flashed dark green as she sniffed the air between her and Alex.

"That's unnerving," Alex said.

Stefan grinned at Lynx. "Alex, give Lynx your word, and I'll escort the ladies to the pier."

Alex wrinkled her nose and then exhaled. She wiped her hands on her pants and held one out to Lynx, who took it. "I promise not to leave the castle unless escorted by a general."

Lynx's eyes flashed dark green. She turned to Stefan, and when he nodded, Lynx shook Alex's hand. Her eyes went back to brown.

"Now we can go. When we return, you can ask her if she left the castle, and if she lies, I'll know."

"Happy?" Alex glared at Stefan.

"Very. Maybe having more sorceresses around has some advantages."

Edith giggled. Alex rolled her eyes and told her and Lynx to go have fun. She walked up the stairs to the second floor of her room and waited for them to leave. As soon as they were gone, she hurried to the top floor and the door that led to her father's room. Since Edward was still in Datten, his room was dark and the curtains closed. Alex lit a fireball and let it float high enough to illuminate the room. She slipped around the bed and opened the bedside table drawer.

Inside was a pile of letters. The top one had her father's name, written in her mother's handwriting. Alex pulled out the bundle, unwrapped the ribbon, and opened the first letter. *My dearest Edward, I cannot wait until you return to Datten to see Emmerich, and I can feel your lips on my—*

Alex gasped and closed the letter. *Ew. I knew you spent years courting before me, but ew.* Alex cringed as she tied the letters together. She rummaged around the drawer until she spotted what she needed. She grabbed it and cracked away.

The door to the treasure room closed behind her, and she rushed past the stacks of jewels, trinkets, and treasures, heading for the last row, where the secret door lay behind the old paintings. This time, Alex got a whiff of stale, damp air. Carefully she moved the paintings aside. She knew Stefan would never find out, since she wasn't leaving the castle, but he wouldn't be gone very long, so she'd need to hurry.

She spun the strange key all the way around in its tiny keyhole and stepped back as the door swung away, giving her access to the narrow and dank tunnel. She produced a fireball and walked into the dark, toward the whispers of the spell books. She stepped across the threshold, and her grandfather's study was illuminated.

The whispers came from the bookshelf across the room. Alex avoided looking at the wolf pelt she stepped over. Scanning the books, she saw nothing unusual, and she struggled to pinpoint the origin of the unsettling sound. She pulled the first book off the shelf, finding it to be a copy of a journal she'd already read in the library. She flipped through the next few and found the same. The entire shelf held copies of the same journals that were held in the library. Flabbergasted, Alex put her ear against the shelf and listened for the whispers, but they'd gone silent.

The ceiling flames crackled, and Alex shivered. Her breath fogged before her. Reaching deep for her courage, she locked her face in a grimace and turned to face her grandfather.

"Get out," he snarled at her.

"No. Not until I figure out what you hid down here."

Alex crossed her arms while her grandfather screamed at her. He tried to slam his hands on the desk, but they went through. When he turned around, he stared at her for a long while before a smirk spread along his lips.

"Is the gossip true? Aaron turned on you?"

Alex's blood drained from her face, and she shivered.

Arthur stalked toward her, his cold eyes locked on her face. "That's a yes. Apparently the boy isn't as foolish as I always thought."

"It wasn't his fault. He was cursed."

Arthur laughed at her, but there was no lightheartedness to it. "Seems sorcerers aren't all useless after all."

"We do a lot of good. My mother helped hundreds of people."

"Your mother killed people, too. People who trusted her."

Alex didn't back down. "Every physician loses patients, even magical ones."

"Maybe you should go heal your husband and see how true that sentiment is."

"Get out, or I'll go to your tomb and make sure no one remembers what you looked like."

Her grandfather growled but faded away. Alex could still feel his presence in the icy chill that hung in the air. She fought to keep her teeth from chattering and heard a whisper coming from his desk. Alex pulled out the chair and examined the desk. Arthur had covered the top in bits of paper with scribbled writing, along with bills and receipts. When Alex read Kruft's name on one, she didn't want to read any more and flipped the paper over. The whispers grew louder, so she opened the main drawer and pushed all the papers into it, clearing the desk.

The whispers were coming from the back of the desk, but there were no books on it. Alex put her ear to the desk's surface and heard them there, so she knocked on it until she heard a hollow sound. She could feel lines on the wood in that area. She pushed on them, and one side popped open. She reached inside and pulled out two books. Both were Cassandra books—one was her mother's missing book, and the other was from the original Cassandra.

Alex stared at the books and thought back to what her grandfather had said. She looked over her shoulder at the portrait of her grandmother, Elizabeth.

"You're the ghost I never see. Why? Are you upset with me? Or ashamed of what he did?"

Alex looked at the painting, and a book fell off the shelf. She leaped to her feet and spun as the room went warm. The book on the floor was small, and when she opened it, she saw her grandfather's handwriting. It was a journal addressed to her grandmother. Having unintentionally read her mother's love letters, Alex cautiously flipped through the pages.

. . .

My Dearest Elizabeth,

I have finally found the truth, and I want you to know I forgive you.

You wanted nothing more than to be a perfect wife and give me a son, but what you failed to see was that I only needed you. I would have lived our lives out together childless as long as I had you by my side. I tried to tell you, but when you put your mind to something, there was no stopping you. Your courage and drive were unmatched.

None of this was your fault. The blame lies with that witch, and now she has ensnared our son.

ALEX'S HAND flew to her mouth as she finished reading.

# CHAPTER 10

# AARON

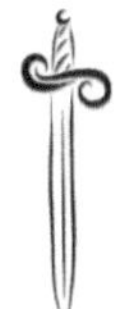

Aaron opened his eyes and felt the stone walls closing in on him.

*Still here ... in this cell.*

His fists were bloody and his knuckles were raw from punching the stone. His hands were aching, but he did not feel hungry or tired or even the need to urinate.

He shuffled back and leaned against the wall. When he closed his eyes and her emerald eyes floated into his mind, the overwhelming terror subsided, and his breathing slowed. The memories that came were ones he hadn't thought of in a long time.

She stood in Warren's garden, dressed in one of her many blue dresses. She despised those ones. Her giggle made him smile. When her eyes shifted down, he followed them to the flowers he'd picked for her.

*I remember this day.* It was cold, but Victoria's magic kept the flowers blooming all year.

He offered her a bouquet with a rose, tulips, dahlias, lilacs, snapdragons, and a single white lily. Alex glided toward him. Even shy of five, she moved gracefully. She took the flowers, and when her hand brushed his, a heat rushed up his arm, and he trembled. He closed his eyes and shook it off. When he opened them, her emerald eyes stared into his, and she kissed him.

Lightning erupted through Aaron, and his shoulder stung. Without taking his eyes off Alex, he slapped away whatever had stung him and followed Alex as she skipped back to their mothers. Another woman was with them, but he couldn't remember who she was. Her smile was soft, and her brown hair was braided into a bun, the same as his mother's. Her blue eyes stood out from her warm tan skin.

A boy came from around the hedges with Daniel. He was about Aaron's age.

"I found Percival. He was in the stables." Daniel playfully pushed the boy toward the women.

The boy's mother crossed her arms. "What do you have to say for yourself?"

Percival gulped and stepped back. He noticed Aaron and narrowed his eyes at him, then thrust a doll he was holding toward his mother. It was Alex's doll, the one with the green dress. "The princess dropped her favorite doll in the stables, and His Highness pretended not to hear me when I asked if I could retrieve it. So I snuck away and got it. Father would have been disappointed if I hadn't. He always says a Veremund protects their Warren."

Alex squealed, grabbed the doll from him, and clutched it. The boy bowed so low his black hair fell into his face, making Alex laugh when he righted himself and shook his head to get it out of the way.

*Percival Veremund, I remember you. Before Alex vanished, the Veremunds were around Edward and Victoria as much as the Nials were. What did Alex call you? She hated the name Percival, but I forget what she called you.*

Aaron rubbed his eyes and covered them with his hands. In the dark of his mind, he could see Alex's face on their wedding day.

"Today, I make you mine for the rest of your days. As long as you have breath, I will be yours, and you will be mine, and nothing will come between us."

Aaron felt his throat go dry. He opened his eyes and stared at the stone wall. "I shall find a way back to you. I swear."

# CHAPTER II
# GRYPHON

Gryphon dropped onto the bench at the library table. The pages of the books in front of him fluttered, and he let out a loud sigh. "Birch, there are too many spells here. How are we ever supposed to figure out which ones will help rather than make things worse?"

"We're not giving up, Gryphon," Megesti scolded. Annoyingly, he refused to sit and nervously paced the room, patting his hands. It was making Gryphon anxious.

"Easy for you to say. Aaron doesn't tell you how he intends to gut you every time he wakes. All of his aggression is aimed at me."

"Why not try them all?" Michael asked from the other side of the table.

"Could these spells hurt him?" Harold asked.

"It's more complicated than that," Birch said patiently.

Megesti groaned and resumed his circuit. The pounding of his feet was sending Gryphon into madness. He took a deep breath. Aaron was asleep, giving them some time. Birch's potion had enough nutrients to keep him going for a week.

"What about this one?" Michael held up a violet journal. The spell at the top of the page was titled *Removing a Line Curse*.

"That one sounds promising," Birch said. "But I suspect he'll need to be awake for us to test it."

"How do we try it without the entire castle hearing?" Harold asked.

There was a soft knock on the door. Megesti lunged to answer it, and Jessica walked in.

"King Edward is taking Guinevere to visit the widow Countess Veremund. She's one of the few nobles who was alive when Emmerich was crowned and is still sharp enough to remember the details."

"You left Aaron? Jerome and Kharon are still there, right?" Michael asked.

"Don't worry. He's sleeping quite soundly," Jessica said. "My father and I were speaking, and we realized that you'll need to take Aaron somewhere away from prying eyes when you try to fix him."

"Yes, we will," Harold said.

"We have a solution. The dungeons are where they keep Dattenites who are waiting for their court dates, along with those who are guilty and serving out their punishments. However, below the escape tunnels is another level of dungeons. That's where former kings of Datten kept prisoners of war and anyone charged with treason."

Harold looked at Jessica, surprised. "Your dungeons have dungeons?"

"Yes. Only the most trusted families know how to get into them."

Megesti shrugged. "If my father knew, he never told me."

"Will you take us there?" Gryphon asked.

"Naturally."

"And how is it that you know how to get into the bowels of the castle?" Michael asked.

"Children play in places they aren't supposed to. Aaron, Caleb, and I liked to hunt for monsters and ghosts." She smiled at the men and leaned against the door frame. "Sadly, we found none."

"None you could see," Gryphon said.

"Well, we're grateful for your childhood monster hunting," Birch said.

Gryphon stood. "Birch and Megesti, grab the books. Jessica, please lead us to these dungeons."

Jessica nodded and held out her hand to Michael, who hurried over and took it, and they followed her to the dungeons. The first basement of the castle was cold even though it was early September and the sun was high in the sky. Jessica gracefully weaved them through the maze of halls until they arrived at an old wooden door. It was decaying and had no handle or hinges. Jessica let go of Michael and stepped up to it. She pushed on the left edge of the door with all her might, and it pivoted in the middle, revealing the entrance to a dark tunnel.

Gryphon lit several balls of fire, letting them float into the darkness.

"Thank you," said Jessica, and she stepped into the tunnel. The space was narrower than Gryphon had expected. They arrived at a crumbling set of stone stairs that spiraled down into a dark pit. Gryphon released more fireballs for light, and they descended hundreds of stone steps to the bottom. Soon they were at an impenetrable stone door. Jessica produced a large brass key and unlocked it. Gryphon pulled the antique brass handle for her.

The hall they entered was twice the size of the previous one. As they filed into the room, Gryphon waved his hand, igniting all the torches. Despite the fires, the air grew colder.

"Is it always freezing down here?" Michael asked.

"As long as I can remember," Jessica replied.

"The souls who died down here never left," Gryphon said, trying to silence his Hades magic. The dungeons had six cells, all larger than he expected. Each could easily hold a dozen men—or one violent, cursed king. The cells themselves looked as if someone had carved them into the bedrock that the castle was built on. Rough iron bars stretched from deep in the floor up into the ceiling.

Harold walked past Gryphon and tried to rattle the bars, but nothing moved. "That should hold him."

Gryphon nodded. "Sorcerers could escape, but not a mortal."

"I'll come with you to collect Aaron," Michael said.

Gryphon looked at him in surprise. "That's a terrible idea."

"I don't care. I gave Alex my word that I'd look out for Aaron, and I won't let her down."

"Fine," Gryphon relented, and he cracked away with Michael.

A short while later, Gryphon, Jerome, and Michael laid Aaron onto the makeshift straw bed Birch had set up on the floor of the cell. Jessica set down the jug of water and the plate of bread and smoked venison they'd brought for him. Megesti paced the small path outside the cells, his face growing paler by the minute.

Michael was the last to leave the cell and slammed the door behind him, but Aaron didn't even flinch.

"He needs to sleep off my potion," Birch said. "I'll take the first shift watching him."

"I'll stay with you," Megesti said.

Gryphon nodded and cracked everyone away.

# CHAPTER 12
# ALEX

Rain poured across the entire kingdom of Warren. Alex sat in the garden under her favorite willow tree, letting the rain beat down on her.

Stefan ran up to her and put his hands on her shoulders. "Alex, what in the Forbidden Lands are you doing out here?" When she didn't respond, he shook her. "Alex! Look at me."

She turned her face to him. "He killed her because he found out."

Stefan's face softened, and he kneeled down beside her. "What did who find out?"

Sloshing footsteps arrived behind Stefan, but Alex didn't move her eyes from his. "My mother helped my grandmother. It makes perfect sense, but it's twisted, and wrong ... I'm wrong."

"What are you saying?" Edith came to her other side.

"Elizabeth Veremund, my grandmother. My mother's ledger had *her* name in it, on the same page as Cameron's mother. My grandmother ... was barren. She used her lady's maid to seek help from my mother."

"How do you know?" Stefan asked.

"I found a note in my grandfather's sick room. It was in my mother's handwriting and addressed to R. Vinur. Reinhilde Vinur ... the woman I killed. She told me she worked in the castle. She was my grandmother's lady's maid. The note included the directions and the price. 20 gold coins. Success was guaranteed."

Edith touched her arm. "Alex, that doesn't mean—"

"It does," Alex shouted. "I found his study and the journal he wrote to my grandmother, explaining his plans. He fired Reinhilde after my grandmother died and he learned the truth. His beloved wife died because of my mother. He hunted her, but she was hiding in the forest or in Datten ... untouchable. So when my father brought her home pregnant with me, Arthur made plans."

"If that's true, why did he wait for over five years?" Stefan asked.

"He wanted his proper heir first. A ... a boy. But my mother wouldn't give him one. When he realized that she'd only ever have me, he planned to get rid of us so my father would have to marry again."

"That doesn't mean you don't belong here—that you weren't meant to be," Edith said.

"Of course it does. Moorloc told me my mother married my father for a reason, not out of love. To make me *what* I am. I didn't want to believe him, but she ensured Warren had an heir ... so he'd be my father."

*But the letters. The letters show she loved him. No, they just show she desired him. I wish my father was here.*

"Alexandria, your mother helped so many people with her potions. Without her, Cameron never would have been born, and my grandfather would have died of illness very young," Edith said.

"She helped the Wafners too. And so many other families in Datten in her time there," Stefan said.

Alex let out a sob. The rain came down harder, and thunder drummed nearby.

Stefan sat on the wet ground beside her and pulled Alex against his chest, wrapping his arms around her. "I know this is hard. But it's been ages since you lost control of your powers like this. Remember the law you made: the sins of a parent do not carry to the child. We won't hold you responsible for the choices your mother made. If you're guilty, then Edith and I are guilty for our fathers' failings. Mine for failing to protect you, and the Nials for failing to protect you and your mother."

"Stefan's right," Edith said. "You're not your parents or grandparents. You're determined to do things better and are one of the kindest people I've ever met, and I know many people."

"Even if you have a nasty temper," Stefan added.

Alex chuckled and wiped her nose.

"At least you know now. Hopefully, you can put that pain to rest, now that you know why he did it," Edith said. "I know not knowing has tortured you."

Alex glared at Edith. *Easy for you to say. Your family is nothing but honorable, while mine is filled with liars and monsters.*

Stefan was looking at her with narrowed eyes. "And tomorrow you're going to show me this study you found."

"You can't be angry," Alex said. "I never left the castle."

Stefan still eyed her suspiciously. "Let's go inside. I don't want you to catch a cold."

"I don't get colds," Alex reminded him.

"Well, I'd prefer Edith and I not catch one."

Back in her room, Alex put on dry clothes and climbed into bed. Without Aaron, it felt enormous and empty. She moved all around until she finally ended up on Aaron's side. She clutched his pillow to her face, inhaled the scent of pine, and sniffled back tears. Stefan was in his chair on the far side of her room. Alex knew he wouldn't say anything if she cried, but she didn't want to burden him more than she already had. Biting her lip, she clung to the pillow and willed herself to sleep.

ALEX WOKE BEFORE DAWN. It took a moment for everything to hit her, and she covered her eyes, commanding herself to be brave. When she sat up, she found an empty room. Only a blanket remained on Stefan's chair. Alex stretched.

"Where's Stefan, Sparta?" She scratched her bear skin rug's head with her foot and crossed her room to the stairs. When she descended the stairs to the main floor, the only sound she heard was her nightgown swishing against her legs.

Stefan had fallen asleep on her couch as usual. He was sitting up on the side furthest from the stairs—but he wasn't alone. Lynx had fallen asleep beside him. Her head rested on his shoulder, and he'd draped his arm around her.

Alex couldn't help but grin. *That was faster than expected. You always proclaimed you'd never marry, that you planned to stay at my side and protect me as so many Wafner men have done for royals for generations, but I knew the truth. I saw Lynx's face years ago as the woman who'd win your heart and change your mind. Apparently, I was wrong about the mortal part.*

Alex cleared her throat loudly and crossed her arms. "Who'd have thought it would take a sorceress to convince my brave knight to abandon his post in favor of other activities?"

The pair stirred, and then Stefan leaped from the couch, almost making Lynx fall. She recovered and settled into his spot.

"There were no activities. Just talking and sleeping."

Alex giggled at Stefan's flushed face. "I can't tell if you're blushing because you're embarrassed or because you're angry at being caught."

Lynx snorted, stood, and adjusted her new tunic. "Perhaps it's both."

"I don't need you two ganging up on me."

"Would you prefer three? You two make a handsome couple," Edith added, coming out of her room.

Stefan muttered to himself and stormed toward his room before spinning back to Alex. "Don't think I forgot about that secret room you were snooping in yesterday. As soon as everyone's dressed, you're taking me there."

"You left your sword on the floor." Edith pointed under the couch.

"How are you still so bossy?" Alex grabbed his sword and presented it to him. "I assumed sleeping with a beautiful sorceress would loosen you up."

Stefan's face became nearly as red as his hair. He slammed the door behind him, and the three ladies erupted into giggles.

Dressed in sparring clothes and with a baguette in hand, Alex led Stefan, Lynx, Edith, and Randal to the treasure room entrance. When she arrived at the door, Randal gave her a look that reminded her of her own father.

"My father showed me this room, Randal. I didn't snoop."

"He took you here to retrieve jewels for your wedding. When I caught you here, that wasn't the case." Randal rubbed his forehead with his fingers. "You found the room then, didn't you?"

"Yes."

"And kept it secret all this time?" Stefan asked.

Alex nodded.

Randal growled, but Edith put her hand on her father's arm. "That was less than a month ago, and a lot's happened since then. It isn't an excuse, but I think Alexandria would have told us eventually."

Alex nodded instead of speaking. A nod felt like less of a lie. When she looked around for something to prick her finger with, Randal stepped forward. "Allow me. No need for you to cut yourself when a Nial can do it."

Once inside, Alex headed straight for the paintings without

sparing a glance for anyone. As she pushed them out of the way, Randal joined her. In only a minute, they had cleared the wall.

When Alex spun the key around and the door moved, everyone else jumped back. She stepped into the pitch-black tunnel and rubbed her palms together. When she pulled them apart, an orb of fire floated ahead of her and lit up the tunnel.

Stefan leaped in after her and pulled her arm back. "What is this place?"

"A tunnel. But it's what's at the end of the tunnel that matters." Alex shook Stefan's grip off her and walked into the slightly lit tunnel.

When they arrived at Arthur's office, Edith gasped. "Father, this looks like your office at home."

Randal looked around and nodded to Edith. "It also matches Matthias's office. The founding families all made their offices the same so if something ever happened to one line, we'd know where the secrets were."

"What secrets?" Lynx asked.

Edith half smiled and crossed her arms. "They wouldn't be secrets if he told you."

Stefan was already at the table, flipping through the journal Alex had found the day before. He sucked in his breath and looked at her.

"I told you it was my fault," Alex said.

Randal stepped beside Stefan and read with him. Alex flinched when his hand clenched into a fist. Stefan turned the page. *I should have warned you, Randal. Reading Arthur's words on how he manipulated you so he could murder my mother can't be easy. You swore to protect her.* Edith stood before the painting of Queen Elizabeth, while Lynx kneeled at the wolf rug.

"He writes as if he's proud of it," Stefan growled.

"He was," Alex said. "Killing my mother was his way of getting revenge for my grandmother. A life for a life."

"How did you find this place?" Edith asked.

Alex stepped toward the books. "When Gryphon and I were going through my ancestral journals looking for protection spells, he realized a few were missing. They're here. They whispered, and I heard it in the treasure room."

"And then you returned alone to investigate," Stefan said. He and Randal both turned toward her, scowling.

"I'm allowed to explore inside my home unaccompanied. Even my father would allow that."

Stefan and Randal exchanged a look. "You're right," Randal said. "Inside these walls you've mostly been safe."

Stefan went back to the pages on the desk while Alex returned to the journals. Edith joined her to keep track of which ones she'd checked. They worked, and Alex hummed her favorite tune.

"I haven't heard that song in years," Randal said.

Alex spun to face him and found Stefan looking at the general, as surprised as she felt.

"What is it?" Stefan asked. "Alex and Michael have been humming it since they were little."

"It's an old Veremund family lullaby. Only the Veremunds know the whole tune. I only ever heard a few lines, but it's lovely."

"So my father sang it to me?" Alex asked.

Randal nodded.

"But if my grandmother died, how did my father hear it?"

"His uncle. Elizabeth had a brother, Bruno—Matthias's father. Edward spent a lot of time with Bruno's family when he was young. He was closer with them than with his own father."

"Then how does Michael know it?" Edith asked.

"Easy," Stefan said. "Michael was the only boy, other than Ian and myself, who was allowed to be alone with Alex."

Alex shivered, and an icy hand gripped hers. She gasped as her grandmother, Elizabeth, stood beside her. The late queen smiled at Alex and pointed at the desk. Alex followed her finger.

"Is Daniel here?" Stefan asked, shivering.

"It's not Daniel," Alex whispered and squeezed between Stefan and Randal. She laid her ear on the desk and tapped until she found a second hollow area on the opposite side. She fiddled with it, then pulled open the door. Alex pulled out a second journal and turned around. Her grandmother winked and slowly disappeared.

"What is it?" Lynx asked.

Alex opened it and scanned the first page. "Arthur's rambling notes and plans. He has notes on red steel and ideas of where to get it. A list of how much he paid Kruft to spy on Datten, and how successful he was in influencing Emmerich and—" Alex's hand covered her mouth.

"What?" Stefan asked.

Alex's breath quickened, and she looked at Stefan and Randal. "And how successful he was at turning Emmerich and Aaron against each other. He was working with Kruft to get a Rassgat on the Datten throne, because Emmerich's grandfather had allowed my uncle and mother to settle there."

"He really was a monster," Edith said.

Alex flipped through a few more pages and stopped to read a particular passage. She read it three times. "Is there a painting of Bruno Veremund?" she asked Randal.

"Yes. I think it's in the spare hall or down here. Why?"

Alex's entire body trembled as she clutched the book. Lynx stepped beside her and squeezed her shoulder. Alex swallowed and turned to Stefan. *"Once Matthias and Catherine are out of the way, Kruft will deal with the boy."*

"Who?"

"Matthias and Catherine Veremund. My father's cousin. Now shush and let me read it aloud. *It pains me to get rid of the boy who so reminds me of my dear friend Bruno, but his parents are getting too close to figuring out that I orchestrated Victoria's demise. So it was they, not I, who sealed their boy's fate. I've ordered Kruft to follow the carriage all the way into Datten territory and get rid of the boy in Kirsh. The town where the honor rites take place will bear the guilt for the death of the last Veremund heir."*

"Why do *I* know that town?" Edith asked.

"Because it's where Alex, Michael, and I grew up," Stefan said. "Do you think they figured out what your grandfather was planning?"

Alex looked up at Stefan and half sobbed, half laughed. "Stefan, it's dated ten days before I found Michael."

"What does that mean?" Lynx asked.

"I think Alex believes Michael is Percival Veremund," Randal said.

Alex snorted. "Who names a kid Percival?"

"It would explain why you brought a boy covered in blood home with you," Stefan said. "Some part of you deep inside must have recognized him from when you were in Warren."

"And why Michael and I connected in a way I only ever connected with one other—" Alex hesitated. "I always trusted him. Never doubted his loyalty to me."

"A Nial and a Veremund always protect their Warren," Edith whispered.

"Could it be possible? Could Michael be my Veremund, like Matthias was my father's?" Alex asked Randal.

"Only one way to find out," Randal said.

# CHAPTER 13
# ALEX

They dug through all the paintings in the treasure room until they found one of Bruno Veremund. Alex stared at the painting. His clothes were in an older style. His hair was neater, and the man was clean-shaven, but the face that looked at her could have been an older, paler version of Michael.

"It's similar," Lynx said.

"As a boy, he always resembled his mother. I never would have expected him to end up looking like his paternal grandfather," Randal said.

"Bruno's old in the painting. Are there any of him as a young man?" Stefan asked.

"There are, but we'd have to go to the Veremund estate. I'm sure we could go this afternoon."

Alex's heart pounded in her chest. "Do you know what this means?" she whispered.

"The Veremunds aren't gone," Randal said. "There was a prophecy passed down through the founding families that when one of us died out, Warren would fall. For centuries, we have protected our lines and ensured we carried them on, and I thought my failure had ended one."

He turned toward Alex and held out his hand to her. Alex took it, and Randal kissed the back of her hand. "I never should have doubted the Warrens' ability to protect *us*. We've protected you for so long I forgot that there was a time where the Warrens protected us."

Alex smiled at him as Stefan came over and hugged her. He squeezed her so hard Alex couldn't breathe.

"If he *is* Percival Veremund, then you're stuck with both of us forever," Stefan said.

Alex tried to laugh but couldn't until he released her. "Percival and Patrick ... I'm going to keep calling you both Michael and Stefan. They suit you better." She pulled on the hem of her shirt and exhaled.

"What is it?" Stefan asked.

"I'd like to go to the crypt."

"Of course—"

"Alone," Alex said. "My grandmother was the cold we felt. She helped, and I'd like to thank her."

Stefan tensed. "I'm happy to wait outside if you want, but—"

"Randal said I'm safe inside the castle," Alex said.

"I think Alex deserves a little privacy while she speaks to the dead," Edith said.

"Why don't I crack us all to the dining hall? After we figure out lunch, we'll come back down to retrieve Alex," Lynx said and winked at Alex.

"Will that give you enough time?" Randal asked.

"Yes." Alex nodded to them and hurried out of the treasure room.

Soon, she was in the enormous cavern that held the five doors. She opened the door that led to the newest crypts and made her way down the dirt path. The torches came to life, and Alex watched them dance in the breeze that swirled around her. *I'm so tired. I won't admit it to Stefan, but a nap would be nice. The protection spell took more out of me than I realized, and the emotional strain is even worse.*

The path crunched beneath her shoes. Before her were two rows of statues, and behind each was a stone tomb containing one of her ancestors. Looking at the faces of the long-dead kings and queens of Warren made her sad. *Datten tradition dictates Aaron has to be laid to rest in Datten, but where will I go? Will I end up in Datten, Warren, or the Forbidden Lands?*

Alex stopped for a moment to catch her breath. The idea of being buried away from Aaron overwhelmed her, considering their current situation. *I should probably get him back before I worry about this.* She turned to the right to see how far she'd come. The statue beside her was her mother's. Alex kissed the ends of her fingers and touched them to her mother's cheek, bringing tears to her eyes.

"Today I'm not here to see you."

She turned around and walked past Arthur's statue to her grandmother's. Elizabeth Veremund had the same beautiful smile on her statue that was on the painting in the room. The shape of her eyes and the way her hair fell were identical to Edward.

"Thank you for helping me in the office. I hate knowing he worked with Kruft for years, and that the brute betrayed Aaron and Emmerich, but I can put one part to rest now. We know why he came after me and killed my mother, and I can give Michael back the past he lost. Now I hope I'll be as good to him as he's always been to me." Alex chuckled. "With Stefan as his brother-in-law now, and me as a distant cousin, he really is stuck with us."

Alex wiped her clammy hands on her tunic, and when she looked up, Elizabeth's ghost was standing beside Arthur's statue. Her face stoic, she beckoned Alex closer with a curl of her finger. Alex's feet moved on their own as if her grandmother had somehow bewitched them. The ghost kissed Alex's forehead and took her hand. She led her to Arthur's statue and pointed to the stone sword in his hand.

Alex wrinkled her nose. "Why are you showing me his sword?"

Her grandmother tapped her hand, and Alex lifted it to her face. An icy chill crept up her arm. The large ruby on Aaron's grandmother's wedding ring sparkled in the candlelight. Alex gasped, remembering the day Arthur killed her mother.

"His sword's red steel!" Alex dropped her hand and looked around the tomb to find the sword. When she couldn't, she hesitated and then turned to her grandmother. "They bury kings with their swords, don't they?"

The queen nodded and faded away.

Alex remembered the iron candelabras that stood at the entry of the crypt. She ran back to grab one and went after Arthur's tomb. The wooden door leading into the stone room was easy enough to break open, but inside, Alex faced the obsidian stone coffin. She circled it, but there were no obvious handles or openings. Breathing deeply, Alex wedged the candelabra into the lid and threw her entire body weight against it. The lid unsealed, and a terrible stench escaped. Alex retched from the smell, but she slammed the candelabra into the side of the lid until she could get her fingers under it, and then shoved it with all her might until she could push it aside. Alex held her breath and climbed up the side of the box.

Her grandfather's corpse had liquefied and stank. Alex's eyes burned as she peered into the casket. Thankfully, it wasn't long before she spotted the sword. The red steel blade he'd used to kill her mother was clamped in his skeletal hands. Alex reached in and tried to take the sword, but the corpse's grip was strong. She retrieved the steel rod again and pried the sword from Arthur's grasp. The sound of his bones snapping made her grimace, but she grabbed the hilt and wrenched it free from his grave.

Alex stepped out of the tomb to examine the sword in the light. She spun it in her hands and watched the steel shimmer as the blade sliced through the air.

"Grave robbing now, little witch?"

Alex froze. The voice dripped with the same hatred as her grandfather's, but now it was full of life. *No, it couldn't be.* Her throat went bone-dry. She opened her fist and sent a strong wind down the path, extinguishing the torches and sending the entire crypt into darkness. She slipped toward the door.

"You can hide, Titaness, but you can't run." A ball of fire appeared on the path only a small distance away from her.

*Ember.*

Alex dropped soundlessly to the ground and slipped between her grandparents' statues. She set the sword on the ground and considered her potential escape options. The main door was too far away. The dungeons were closer, but she didn't want to get trapped down here with Ember. Months earlier, the psychotic Titan of Salem had tried to kill her when she was with Stefan on her way to Warren.

"Don't bother trying to crack, little witch. I've cast a spell to stop you from doing that."

The last option was to run to the end of the crypt tunnels. Alex wasn't sure what was at the end of the tunnels, but she remembered reading that they sloped downward and led to the sea in case of flooding. *If I can just get to the water, I'll have a chance against Ember. But here, sealed in the crypt, I won't stand a chance against her fire.* Fighting to calm her raspy breaths, Alex slid her hands along the dirt. She pulled the sweat from her brow and the water from the moist ground around her. Silently, she crawled away from the statue and peeked down the path. Ember's back was turned, and she was walking toward the main door. *Thank you, Stefan, for pushing me so hard and never letting me give up.* Alex felt her adrenaline surge as she leaped up from the ground and sprinted down the path.

Every torch in the room roared to life.

"Found you," Ember shouted, and a second later, a ball of fire ignited in front of Alex. Panic fueled her, and she threw the water she'd gathered ahead of her. She leaped over the smoldering rubble and ran harder.

The sorceress screamed in frustration. There was a thump, and Ember arrived so close to Alex she could hear Ember's panting behind her.

Alex knew the tunnels were too narrow to crack through without knowing what came around the corner. She tore through them, and Ember struggled to keep up well enough to throw fire. Alex did her best to throw water at Ember, but she couldn't stop to look back because if she did, Ember would catch her.

After what felt like hours but could only have been a few minutes, a dim light appeared ahead. Alex rounded a corner, and the path forked. Daniel's voice rang out. "Left. Go left." She tore down the left tunnel.

Ember's frustrated scream echoed down the tunnel before Alex felt the heat. She glanced over her shoulder for a split second and tripped. As her body slammed against the hard tunnel floor, Alex felt the fire rolling over her back and screamed. The pain was excruciating. Flames burned her shirt and flesh, but Alex forced herself to her feet and kept running. Around the final bend, the darkness of the tunnel gave way to the light of day and the Oreean Sea.

The fire spread, and she could feel the skin on her shoulder burning. The light at the tunnel's end was blinding. She looked out over the sparkling waters of the Oreean Sea, far below. She'd have to jump. Behind her, Ember's laugh grew louder. Alex took a deep breath and dove headfirst from the tunnel ledge.

As the icy water surrounded her, Alex fought the panic that

threatened to drag her into oblivion. *This isn't the river. You aren't a little girl anymore. You can swim. You can do this. You will do this.* Alex sank down further and further into the water. When she couldn't hold her breath for another moment, her legs finally obeyed, and she fought against the current and pushed herself to the surface of the sea. She burst out of the water and gasped for breath.

Ember's screams reached Alex from across the beach. She turned back and glimpsed Ember throwing flames everywhere in frustration. Alex struggled to keep herself afloat in the rough waves. She knew if she settled them, Ember would see her and she'd be finished. As soon as she could breathe, Alex screamed for her mother, Merlock, Daniel. She begged them to get Kharon.

# CHAPTER 14

# GRYPHON

Gryphon paced the path in front of the cell, never taking his eyes off the young king. Aaron had been asleep for an entire day while the group gathered more spells. He didn't stir when they returned and remained placid while they attempted to break the curse with incantation after incantation. For extra measure, Harold and Michael stayed with Aaron in the cell.

Megesti dropped another failed spell book on the ground. "Which one do we try next?"

"The one I suggested three books ago," Gryphon snapped. "The one for line curses."

Birch hesitated and then acquiesced. "Gryphon, you'll need to read it. These sorts of spells work best if read by someone related to the one who inflicted the curse." She took the book from Megesti and offered it to him.

Gryphon turned to Aaron and spoke the words from the book, but nothing happened. He tried again, louder and more clearly.

"Could it be he'll stay asleep even if it works? Maybe he needs to be awake," Megesti said.

"You said these memories shift when he becomes jealous or angry. What if we need to provoke him?" Harold asked.

A mischievous grin spread across Gryphon's face. "That, I can handle."

Birch glared at him. "You should not be enjoying this."

"I'm not!" he replied innocently. "I simply excel at making him mad."

"How do we wake him up?" Michael asked Birch.

"It's usually better for them if they wake up naturally, when the potion wears off."

"We don't have time for that," Harold said. "If it won't injure him, I think we should wake him up."

Birch sighed loudly and cracked away. When she returned, she had a bucket of icy river water with her. She handed it to Harold through the bars of the cell. He hesitated.

"Are you worried?" Michael asked.

"A little," Harold admitted. "If this hurts him, I don't think Alex will be happy with me."

"She'll know you meant well," Gryphon said. "Let's get it over with."

Harold walked over to Aaron with the bucket, and Gryphon entered the cell. Megesti stayed in the doorway in case he needed to distract Aaron so Harold could get to safety. Gryphon could see the sweat on Megesti's face and hear his nervous breaths. None of them were sure what would happen when Gryphon read the spell, but they were ready for anything. He moved toward the back wall so Harold would be closer to the door. "If anything happens, Harold, get out and lock the door. I'll crack away."

Harold swallowed hard and lifted the bucket.

Birch spoke up. "Is everyone ready?"

They all nodded, and before anyone could change their mind, Harold dumped the cold water on Aaron's face, waking him instantly.

"Harold, what are you doing?" Aaron snapped, looking around. "Where are we?"

"The dungeon," Gryphon replied.

Aaron's head whipped toward Gryphon, and his lips curled into a scowl. "What is *he* doing here?"

The disgust on his face was clear. Aaron stormed over to Gryphon. "Get out of my castle and kingdom before you make me do something I'll regret."

"Worse than beating your wife?" Gryphon pushed Aaron's shoulders, and he stumbled backward.

Aaron reached for his sword, but it wasn't there.

"Tsk, Princeling. You don't think I'd actually leave you with a sword? After you stabbed Alex, who knows what you are capable of?"

"I'll handle my wife how I see fit. She's *my* queen, not yours."

Birch and Gryphon exchanged a look.

"Well, I'd ask Birch to get her for you, but she's gone. She left for Warren after your fight," Michael said. "We worried for her safety."

Harold took a step back toward the door as Gryphon approached Aaron. "If you don't want me here, I'll head over to Warren. Comfort *your* wife in her time of need, since it's obvious she's not coming back to you soon."

Aaron's eyes twitched, and he breathed so hard he was almost panting like a dog.

Gryphon stepped even closer to Aaron and whispered, "How long do you think it would take for me to replace you in her bed?"

Aaron went feral. His eyes bulged, and his face contorted into a snarl. Then he let out an animalistic growl and lunged for Gryphon.

"*NOW!*" Birch shouted, and Gryphon cracked away from Aaron, causing him to stumble.

Harold rushed out of the cell, and Michael slammed the door

shut before Aaron could reach it. Megesti and Gryphon both chanted the words. Aaron banged his fists against the bars, screaming curses and threats at Gryphon.

Almost as quickly, Aaron fell silent. He released his grip on the bars and crumpled to the ground like a stone. Everyone outside the cell stared. He convulsed and then lay still. Harold and Michael threw open the cell door and rushed to his side. Gryphon moved his hands into a spell position, holding them in front of him at shoulder height with his fingers at the ready, and they all waited.

"Aaron?" Michael kneeled beside him and gently shook his shoulder. "It's Michael. Are you all right?"

Aaron's eyes popped open, and everyone jumped back.

# CHAPTER 15
# AARON

*Not again!* Aaron groaned as he focused on the gray stones above him. *Not another stone box with nothing but my thoughts or my pain. Wait, I'm not in pain!* Aaron examined his hands. The cuts and bruises from days of punching the stone wall were gone.

"That makes no sense."

Whispers came from all around him. Aaron rubbed his eyes hard enough to make himself wince as the voices grew louder.

"Aaron, are you all right?"

"Michael?" Aaron turned and found Michael kneeling beside him with Harold standing not far behind.

*I'm free. I got out of that horrible room … but how? I don't remember how I got here, or where* here *is. I don't even know what day it is.*

Aaron rolled over and rose to his knees. Suddenly his stomach felt as if snakes were trying to slither out. He barely caught himself as he fell forward and vomited. It was thick and black like tar. Harold and Michael stepped back. Aaron heaved three more times until a large puddle of thick, black sludge was beneath him. He gasped for breath, and the last bit of it dripped from his lips. The taste lingered. It was worse than the time he fell into the horse manure while helping at his uncle's stables. He wiped his mouth with the back of his hand and looked around at the solid stone walls. There were thick bars holding him in.

"Is *that* the stone cage?"

"The what?" Harold asked.

Aaron shook his head and scooted away from the puddle to take in his surroundings. "Why am I in the dungeons?"

"For safety," Megesti replied.

"You were cursed," Michael offered.

Aaron blinked, trying to focus on what Michael had said. *Cursed? Is that what put me in that room?* He scanned the faces of his friends. "Wait … where's Alex?"

"Do you remember what happened?" asked Harold.

"No." Aaron shook his head. "Why isn't she here?"

Harold, Michael, and Megesti glanced toward Gryphon, but they all stayed silent.

"I think we should let you get cleaned up before we have this conversation." Birch approached the bars and held out her hand.

⁕ ⁕ ⁕

Aaron scrubbed himself raw trying to remove the black sludge that stuck to his face and hands. Finally free of it, he grabbed his closest shirt and pants. Since he'd become king, even his simplest clothes were more formal than his old clothes had ever been. *Why is everyone acting weird? I just need to know where Alex is. I didn't fight to get out of that stone box to end up away from her.* He pulled his royal tunic over his head and paused abruptly at the sight of their bed.

*What day is it? When did I last see Alex? I'm so confused and disoriented. It's infuriating. I know we had a fight, but about what?* An image of Gryphon in sleeping pants holding Alex flashed in his head, and Aaron felt sick.

Desperate for answers, he hurried to the library, where the others had promised to meet him. When he arrived, only Edward, Michael, and Megesti were there, seated at the table.

"Where is everyone?" Aaron asked.

"We thought it would be best for us to speak with you first," Megesti said.

Aaron crept to the table and stood peering at his friend. "Why?"

"Because you're more likely to believe us," Edward said. He was drumming his fingers on the table.

"Gryphon warned us you wouldn't remember the ... incidents," Megesti said.

"What *incidents*? Someone tell me what is going on. Now!"

Michael opened his mouth to speak, hesitated, and then started again. "You don't remember hitting Stefan? Jerome tackling you? Trying to stab me? Actually ... stabbing Alex?"

Aaron's throat went dry, and sweat gathered on the back of his neck. "That's ridiculous. I could never hurt Alex—"

"*You* wouldn't, but that other version of you—the cursed version—did," Megesti cut in.

"No." Aaron ran both hands through his hair, trying to calm his breathing, before looking back at his most trusted friends. "There is no version of myself that would lay a finger on my wife."

Michael stood and moved around the table toward him. "Aaron—"

"Enough. I demand to see *her*. Where is she?"

Edward crossed his arms. "That will not happen, Aaron."

"I didn't ask for your opinion." Aaron's fists slammed on the table, making Michael jump away from him and Megesti flinch. "Tell me where my wife is!"

Edward didn't bat an eye. "Safe, in Warren."

"I need to see her," Aaron said. He searched his mind for when he had last seen her, or for any recent memory of her, but a wave of nausea knocked him to his knees. His stomach roiled, and he threw up more of the black sludge. Terror filled him when he failed to recall anything about his moments with Alex. *Ferflucs. Why can't I remember anything?*

"You need to get well before you see her. I won't have you retching black slime in front of her and scaring her half to death," Edward said, staring Aaron down. "She's been through enough."

"And what does *getting well* entail?" Aaron rubbed his sleeve against his lips to remove the sludge that clung to them.

Edward and Michael kept quiet, but Megesti spoke up. "Well ... we aren't sure."

Aaron crossed his arms and scowled. "You refuse to let me see my wife, days before we bury my father and I get crowned King of Datten. Do you know what the other kingdoms will think if my wife isn't at my side?"

Edward slammed his hands on the table, making Michael and Megesti jump. "Stop worrying about the useless southern kingdoms and pompous Datten nobility. Instead, worry about whether *I* will ever trust you with my daughter again."

*You wouldn't ... No, you can't.* Aaron gulped and stood, careful to avoid the sludge on the floor. "She's my wife. You have no right to keep me from—"

"I have every right," Edward shouted. "On your wedding day, you swore to honor and treasure her until your dying breath. Your actions of late have not lived up to that promise. Until we crown her Datten's queen before your people, she can walk away, and right now, I'd encourage it."

Aaron tried to swallow, but his throat went dry. Edward's hardened stare and snarled lips reminded Aaron of Arthur.

"Edward ... you can't mean that. I love her. You know that."

Edward let out an exasperated sigh. "I do, but that other side of you, the cursed side, was reminiscent of my father when he was angry. It will take time for me to forget."

Aaron shivered, remembering the terror Arthur brought to any room he entered. "*What* did I do?"

"Besides stabbing her?" Megesti said. "You shouted at her, threatened her—struck her ..."

"And I suppose Gryphon told you that?" Aaron asked. "Why do you all simply believe him?"

Michael exhaled and gripped the table. "Jessica saw the bruises, Aaron. Lynx bandaged Alex's bloody shoulder, and in the throne room, you attacked me for protecting her."

Aaron shook his head. "No. I don't believe you."

"The Wafners spoke with me as well," Edward said. "To make me aware of what occurred the day you left for the southern lords. You attacked Alex in your suite. She barely got away. Warren law allows any woman—even a queen—to leave a marriage if abuse is present."

"Alex is *not* leaving me!" Aaron shouted.

"That's not your decision to make!" Edward shouted back.

Aaron desperately tried to hold in his temper, but his head was pounding, and his stomach threatened to be sick again. "I need water before we discuss any more." He fled the library, but as he rounded the corner, he found Birch and Gryphon outside his suite.

"Why are you outside my room?" he asked.

"Your Royal Highness, we wanted to make sure that everything went okay with your talk. We know how difficult this is," Birch said.

"We didn't get very far," Michael said, coming up behind him.

"He didn't like what we had to say," Edward said when he and Megesti joined them.

"How did you expect me to react when, rather than answering my questions, you implied you want Alex to divorce me?" Aaron snapped.

"I have no intention of convincing my daughter to abandon her marriage. Rather, I wanted to make it clear to you that she has options should *you* decide to follow in the footsteps of older kings of Datten. I understand it wasn't you, but I will not allow my daughter to remain married to a man who puts his hands on her ... who hurts her."

Aaron shook his head. "Birch, would the spell Alex used to get back her memories allow me to see what I did while I was cursed? I need to know the truth. What they're saying ... it can't be real."

She shook her head. "That spell returned *Alex's* memories. From what Gryphon discovered, the memories of what you did while cursed aren't yours."

"So there's no way to get—"

"Megesti! Gryphon!" Kharon came running out of the stairwell. Their robe was on crooked, their eyes wide and their face as pale as death. "Thank Hades I found you."

"Kharon, what's wrong?" Gryphon's voice softened as he spoke.

"Go to Warren."

"Why?" Megesti asked.

"Because I have six ghosts screaming at me that Alexandria's hurt and needs your help."

"How?"

"I don't know. I just know that Victoria, Daniel, and—" Before Kharon could finish, Gryphon grabbed Megesti and Edward by the shoulders and cracked them away.

Kharon groaned and turned to Birch. "It was them and Merlock and a few other royals I didn't recognize who told me she's been seriously injured."

"I'll let Jessica and Jerome know what's going on." Michael hurried down the hall.

"I'll prepare some potions. Whatever has happened, she'll need rest to heal from it. I'll come find you both when I'm finished." Birch nodded to Kharon and Aaron and hurried to the stairwell.

"Thank you," Aaron called after Birch. Once she was out of

earshot, he spun to face Kharon. "I need to get to Warren and make sure she's all right."

"Of course, King Aaron." Kharon patted Aaron's shoulder and sent him to Warren.

The moment his feet hit the floor in Warren's throne room, Aaron ran. The others would have brought Alex to either her own suite or her father's. Aaron burst through the door to Edward's room without knocking, but it was empty.

Chest heaving, he heard shouting from the suite he shared with Alex. He crossed the room and wrenched open the adjoining door.

Edward's attention was on him before the door closed, and his frosty glare made it clear that Aaron should remain quiet. "I don't understand. How did she end up in the sea with her entire back burned?" Edward asked.

Lynx and Stefan shared a look.

"Alex wanted to go to the crypt alone to speak to your mother," Stefan said. "She requested privacy. We only intended to leave her for a quarter hour at most, but that was all that witch needed to find her." His hands clenched into fists, and his body shook.

"And the sea?" Edward asked.

Lynx spoke up. "To escape Ember, Alex leaped from one of your tunnels into the sea. Her back was so burned she could barely swim, but a family of colossal seahorses brought her on their backs to the pier where Stefan and I waited."

Aaron moved closer, unable to stay quiet. "How did you know she'd be at the pier?" he asked.

Lynx glanced back at Aaron. "The seagulls told me."

Aaron was about to ask about colossal seahorses when a loud scream echoed through the room. The force of it made the stone walls of the castle rattle. *Alex! What are they doing to you?* He leaped toward the stairs, but Stefan blocked him.

"Move," Aaron commanded.

"No."

He tried to shove past, but Stefan thrust out his arms, blocking him.

"Stefan." Aaron's voice deepened to warn the knight that he wasn't asking.

"I said *no*," Stefan said and pushed Aaron back with his free arm. The push wasn't hard, and it only sent Aaron back a step, but Aaron's Datten temper roared inside him.

"You won't keep me from my wife." Aaron lunged at Stefan and shoved him as hard as he could in the chest with both hands.

Stefan regained his balance quickly and leaped toward Aaron. With lightning speed, he struck and punched Aaron in the cheek, making him bite his tongue. As Aaron's mouth filled with blood, he wiped it with the back of his hand.

"Alex doesn't need you two fighting," Lynx said.

Aaron wouldn't shift his glare from Stefan. "I've had enough of people telling *me* what my wife needs!"

Edward pinched the bridge of his nose. "Aaron, that—"

"What she *needs*," Stefan growled down at Aaron, "is a husband worthy of her—one who won't abandon and abuse her when she needs help."

Aaron dove at Stefan and rammed his shoulder into Stefan's stomach, slamming him into Alex's reading couch, which went sliding across the floor. Lynx hissed as Stefan jumped up and started pummeling Aaron's back and side. A punch landed on the scar on Aaron's belly, and Aaron cried out in pain. He released his grip on Stefan and doubled over. Stefan staggered to his feet.

"Did you two get that out of your systems?" Edward snapped.

"No," Stefan grumbled, and Aaron leaped at him. Stefan tried to dodge Aaron's fist, but Aaron predicted the direction he'd go and sent his right hook into Stefan's face.

Blood poured from Stefan's lip, but he charged Aaron and grabbed him by the tunic. Lynx growled and scurried aside right before Stefan shoved Aaron backward into the stone wall. Aaron clawed at Stefan's arm, but his grip was unrelenting. Aaron tried to punch him, but Stefan's fists were faster. Blow after blow struck Aaron's face and stomach.

"Stefan, stop it!" Lynx pleaded.

"It's fine, Lynx," Aaron grunted, and the blows slowed. "He's just upset that Alex loves someone more than him."

Stefan laughed. The tone grated on Aaron's nerves. "I don't care who she gives her affection to as long as he's worthy of it, and you've never been."

Aaron snapped. He punched Stefan's elbow, and when Stefan snapped his arm back, Aaron pounced and threw a few quick punches. The two of them whaled on one another until the loud roar of an animal sent them scrambling apart.

A massive sand-colored lynx crouched before them and snarled.

"Where did that come from?" Aaron asked, putting his hands up and moving back.

Stefan stepped toward the giant cat. The cat's ears moved straight up and turned slightly forward as it cocked its head to the side. "I think it's Lynx."

The cat hissed at Aaron.

"Are you two ready to behave yourselves?" Edward demanded, crossing his arms. "I understand this fight between you has been a long time coming, but it's the last thing Alex needs."

Lynx rubbed up against Stefan's leg and purred so loudly Aaron and Edward shifted their focus to her.

"What is she doing?" Stefan asked.

Aaron groaned. "Showing her interest in you, Stefan. No wonder Alex couldn't tell when the suitors were showing her affection."

"Catch your tongue, Princeling!" Stefan said.

"Enough," Edward barked. "Lynx, send my son-in-law back to Datten."

Aaron stood his ground. "I'm not leaving."

Edward stepped toward Aaron. "You might be King of Datten, young man, but I'm King of Warren, and in my kingdom, you have no right to force my daughter to see you. The second she asks for you, I will have you brought back, but until then, go home."

"Edward ..." Aaron pleaded.

"Go *home*, Aaron."

Aaron wiped his hands on his pants and frowned at Edward. *I never thought you'd try to separate me and Alex. I always thought you were so excited to have us together.*

"Lynx, could you?" Edward asked the cat that was Lynx.

Her ears twitched, and she emitted a dark green light. With a soft *poof*, Lynx's human form stood before them, naked.

Edward coughed, and Aaron shifted away from Lynx. Stefan's face turned bright red, and he seemed frozen in place. Lynx strutted past him and squeezed Aaron's shoulder, sending him back to Datten.

# GRYPHON

The stench of burned cloth, flesh, and hair filled the room.

*It doesn't matter how often I smell it. I'll never get used to this.*

Chaos and rage burned through his soul.

*When I get my hands on Ember, I will burn her until she is suffering as much as she's made Alex suffer. I don't care how long it takes.*

Alex was sprawled out on her bed before him. The back of her shirt had completely burned away, and black, crispy bits of skin surrounded deep, bloody wounds on her back and shoulder. The stench was horrible, but Gryphon wouldn't let Alex see how uncomfortable he was. She needed him to be strong. Megesti sat on her bed, holding her hand. He was glowing gold like her, but even together, they were struggling to heal the burns on her back.

Megesti shifted on the bed, and Alex let out another wall-rattling scream. The pain in her cry brought Gryphon's Ares powers to the surface, and he erupted in an orange glow. Alex buried her face in her pillow and sobbed.

"Gryphon, this isn't working," Megesti said.

Gryphon squatted beside the bed and stroked the tears off

Alex's cheek. "How are your healing powers progressing? Do you still need to touch what you heal?"

"Yes," Alex whimpered.

"Then we'll make a circle."

Megesti pursed his lips. "Why?"

"You're a Usurper. That means you can take and transfer power. You can take Alex's healing power and pass it to me, and I can heal her wounds with it."

"We can do that?" Megesti asked.

"It's challenging, and it takes a lot of power, but I think the three of us are strong enough to manage it."

Alex whimpered, and Megesti nodded in resolve. "We have to. She can't stay like this."

Gryphon turned back to Alex. "I need you to open your well and release as much of your healing power as you can. Megesti will pull it from you and pass it to me. I'll use my Salem powers to pull out the heat and your Cassandra powers to heal the burns."

Alex nodded.

"It will hurt before the healing kicks in. As badly as when I cauterized the whippings."

"I can't even breathe without pain, Gryphon. Do what you need to."

Gryphon stood and held out his hand to Megesti. The Merlin sorcerer gulped and held out his shaking hand to Gryphon. Gryphon squeezed it and motioned to Alex's hand. Megesti gently picked up her hand and stroked it with his thumb.

"Are you both ready?" Gryphon asked. His calm tone belied the sweat running down his back. He would need to work quickly, or Megesti would be in danger of draining Alex's powers for good with his inexperience channeling power.

Megesti and Alex said, "Yes."

A dim golden glow slowly moved down Alex's arm into

Megesti. When it hit him, his eyes flashed violet, and he lit up a brighter gold all over.

"Gentle, Megesti. Don't take too much from her at once."

Gryphon tugged on Megesti's powers and felt a warm rush fill his chest. *Cassandra powers feel like a loving hug. All my powers feel like chaos and violence. It never occurred to me that there could be powerful magic that was still gentle. Her powers really are the opposite of mine.* The fingers on his free hand glowed now. He drifted them down to Alex's back, touching the charred flesh. Alex flinched and sucked in her breath. He gently danced his fingers along her back, the golden light leaving his fingertips to spread across her skin until it sank into her back all at once.

Gryphon was astounded when her wounds lit up. Alex squealed as the charred skin melted into her normal flesh and the red parts faded back to pink.

Megesti watched, wide-eyed. "It's as if the wounds are being sealed from the inside."

"They are," Gryphon said. "The healing powers are hers. We're sending them to the right place. They pull the rest of her magic to her wounds."

"I'm tired," Alex whimpered.

"It's from all the magic Megesti's taking. We're almost done, and I'll stay with you until you wake up."

"Thank you."

They sat in silence as the wounds on Alex's back closed. Finally, when the last one was gone and her back was perfect again, Gryphon asked Megesti to release Alex first, and then him.

"Have Birch make you a sleeping draught. You'll need rest too," Gryphon told him.

"I don't know if I should leave."

"Aaron needs you now. You never finished telling him what he did."

Megesti groaned.

"I won't stay alone with her if that's what you're worried ab—"

"No," Megesti said. "I trust you."

"Send Stefan up. He needs to be updated about Datten too, and I should be the one to explain to Alex what I found." Gryphon picked up the blanket at the end of the bed and covered Alex.

Megesti got up and stretched. "I'll talk to Edward and send Stefan."

"Good luck with the princeling. Get him to understand as much as you can. I'll talk to him when I get back."

Megesti sagged his shoulders as he walked down the stairs. Gryphon stood beside Alex's bed and watched her sleep until heavy footsteps came into the room.

"Is she all right?"

Gryphon turned to Stefan and nodded.

"Is she asleep from overusing her powers, or—?"

"The pain. Healing is usually draining, but there was so much damage ... it was excruciating."

Stefan moved to the bed and gently sat beside Alex where Megesti had been. He cleared his throat, then picked up Alex's hand and squeezed it. "Will she be okay?"

"The scars are gone." Gryphon told Stefan everything he and Megesti had done.

Stefan gingerly peeked under the blanket. He sounded astonished when he said, "How is that possible? There's nothing left except her birthmark. It looks different, though. Less 'pumpkin with an arrow' and more 'sword through a heart or crown.'"

Gryphon smirked.

Stefan dropped the blanket. "Thank you. She'd never admit it, but her scars bothered her," he said.

A comfortable silence came over them.

"She needs us both, Gryphon. Me to protect her from men, and you to protect her from the sorcerers."

"Is protecting her how you got that bloody lip?" Gryphon asked.

"That story can wait until she's awake. Would you care to tell me what you learned about Aaron's curse while you were in Datten?"

"That's complicated, and I only want to tell the story once."

"I'll grab us some chairs while we wait," Stefan said.

# AARON

Aaron returned to the library. Rage still coursed through his veins. He wiped the back of his hand against his bloody mouth and roared in frustration. *Drawing blood from a royal is treason. I don't care who he is. Stefan's going to the dungeon the moment he sets foot back in Datten. Punching his own king! What a boor.*

Aaron marched to the large meeting table in the middle of the room and kicked a bench under the table. He was about to kick another when he spotted the pile of books on the small walnut table in the back. It rested between Alex's soft red couch and chair. Whenever they visited, Alex would spend hours immersing herself in Datten's history and culture. Thrilled with her desire to learn about Datten, Emmerich had the royal carpenter craft couches for her eighteenth birthday. They matched the set in the queen's suite, though those were gold. Aaron had requested red for Alex, wanting to distinguish her from his mother.

Aaron remembered her curled up on the couch, reading about the history of his kingdom or debating with his father and Jerome about a decision the previous kings had made. *So I didn't lose all my memories. I still have older ones.* Without her, the corner looked empty and wrong, and Aaron choked back a sob. He could still hear their last conversation, where they'd debated with his father and Harold about why Betruger was kinder to its women than Datten, despite so many other similarities.

*Could everything be true? Did I actually hurt you? They said I lost days and did things I can't remember ... what if that side of me is the real me? So many Datten kings of old were horrible. What if I'm actually the monster they claim I was?*

There was a knock on the door.

Aaron took a moment and composed himself before he called, "Come in."

"There you are. Michael and Jessica told me about what happened. I assumed you went to Warren with Edward."

"I tried, but I was unwanted." Aaron turned to face Jerome, and the general winced slightly. Anyone else would have missed it, but Aaron knew him too well.

"What happened to your—?"

"Your son is what happened. You'll be throwing Stefan into the dungeon when he returns. Give him some time to think about how he treated his king."

Jerome tensed, but only for a second before his stoic mask was back in place. "There are a few lords asking for an audience with you. I've put them off for the last two days, but people are becoming suspicious about your absence so close to tomorrow's funeral and coronation."

Aaron groaned. "Give me a minute to clean myself up and then I'll see them in the throne room."

AARON'S FOCUS drifted from the squabbling lords before him to the empty throne beside him. *Is Alex all right? Did Megesti and Gryphon help her? Will she come home? I don't blame her for staying away. If even half of what Michael said is true ... I need to know what I did. I can't beg for forgiveness without knowing what I'm begging to be forgiven for.*

"Your Royal Highness?"

"Yes, Brendon," Aaron snapped.

"Have you made your decision?"

Jerome was standing behind the lords, and when Aaron hesitated, he shifted his weight. He must have known Aaron hadn't been paying attention. Aaron narrowed his eyes, and Jerome nodded his head to the right, then cracked his neck.

*Thank you.*

"I am siding with Lord Ainsley," Aaron said. "I'm sorry, Lord Oakes, but the land has been in the Ainsley family for generations. Just because your fathers had an understanding that you could hunt on the land does not mean this generation is required to uphold it. Try offering the Ainsley's something that *they* value, and I'm sure you two can find some sort of agreement. You are both honorable noblemen, after all."

Lord Ainsley bowed low to Aaron. "Thank you, Your Royal Highness."

Lord Oakes snorted and, catching Jerome's eye, reluctantly bowed.

Aaron waved for them to go, and once they had gone, he slumped back on his throne in a huff. "Lords acting like children. Is there any duty more tedious?"

Jerome glanced around the room. "Your father said the same thing when he dealt with squabbling nobles, although Her Royal Highness seems to enjoy it."

"That's because she didn't grow up here and doesn't know the old system or the old families." Aaron groaned and dropped his head into his hands. Thanks to the magic of Alex's late mother, his crown didn't even move.

"How are you holding up with all this?"

"I don't think I've actually processed most of it. All I know is what I'm feeling doesn't matter. I just ... I need things with Alex to be okay ... then I can deal with everything else." *It's only been days since my father died, and I can't even think about that.* Aaron exhaled and asked his general, "Do we know who's attending tomorrow?"

Jerome's lips pursed. "Edward and Randal have confirmed, but no word on Her Royal Highness."

"Is what Michael and Megesti told me true? Did I ... ?"

Jerome nodded. He repeated everything their friends had told him earlier, as well as the incident in the hallway where Jerome and Stefan had kept him from seeing Alex.

"She must think I'm a monster."

"Arthur was a monster. You are not."

"Edward certainly thinks I am."

"Why do you say that?"

"I saw it in his face when I arrived in Warren. What if that side of me is the real me? We know Datten kings for their rage and violence ... what if that jealous, crazed side of me is all there is?"

"Absolutely not," Jerome said.

"You can't be sure—"

"I can. I knew your grandfather, father, and brother. They had tempers but were capable of real violence without them. It's why your father and grandfather were so feared on the battlefield. I've known you your whole life, Aaron, and you are not capable of that sort of violence. Your conscience is too strong." Jerome squeezed Aaron's shoulder and smiled.

"I don't know if I believe that. How am I ever going to face her again?"

"She'll forgive you in time."

"You can't know that." Aaron stood and paced the room.

"She forgave you when you believed Cameron and Stefan over her and thought she was using you."

"She forgave me because I promised to do better—something I have repeatedly failed at."

"You forgave her for the arrow and for the battle at Moorloc's castle."

Aaron turned to Jerome. "That's completely different. The arrows were self-defense, and I only forgave her for Moorloc's because *she* needed to be forgiven. I don't think she did anything wrong there, including the kiss that Gryphon planned."

"You and I know that, but she felt differently. Your forgiveness mattered to her. At least you'll comprehend her struggle now."

Aaron paused at the doors. "How so?"

"Now that she has her missing memories back, she's struggling to process what happened at Moorloc's. You now understand that pain of not knowing what you did. Perhaps you'll push her less. Allow her to process things in her own way."

Aaron scoffed. "You mean Randal's and your way."

Jerome stiffened. "How long have you known?"

"Months. She never told me, but you're terrible at hiding things from me. I watch people, Jerome. I always have."

"Well, know that we're available to you too, if you need us."

"Do you think Matthew and Randal will actually help me after they find out what I did?"

"That will depend on your actions over the next few weeks and months. They are Warren generals, and she is their crown princess. Their forgiveness must be earned. You hurting her will impact Warren and Datten's relations in ways we don't know yet."

"Wonderful. More to stress over."

"Judging by your swollen lip, it's Alex's guards, my son included, who won't forgive you so easily."

"Your son forgets his place too often for me to let this slide."

"My son takes his role as Alex's guard very seriously. As do Michael and Julius. Even your friends Caleb, Hunter, and Lucas would defend Alex with their lives."

*How many of them know what I did?* Aaron shook his head. "When they hear the truth, my friends will understand. They'll forgive me."

Jerome crossed his arms and looked down at Aaron. "While they may express forgiveness to you out of obligation because you are their king, I promise you they will not forget. Nor will I. You may be the current King of Datten, but it is through Alexandria that we will have our next king."

Aaron ran his hand along his neck. "That was something my father always stressed to the royal guard. We value our queen equally to our king. If we were ever attacked, Avery was charged with getting Mother out at all costs."

"Correct, Your Royal Highness." Jerome uncrossed his arms and straightened.

"It's Aaron."

"Not when you hold my son's future in your hands, Your Royal Highness."

Before Aaron could reply, Michael and Jessica rounded the corner. "Aaron! I'm so glad to see you up and about." When Jessica caught the look on her father's face, her smile vanished. "Is everything all right?"

Jerome nodded. "It's fine, dear."

"We're on our way to dinner, if you'd like to join us. You must be starving."

"No, thank you, Michael," Aaron said. "I'll be eating in my room tonight. I have some last minute things to take care of for tomorrow."

"Of course. Jerome?"

"I'll be along in a moment."

Jessica narrowed her eyes at Aaron but allowed Michael to lead her to the dining hall.

"Is my mother aware—?"

"No," Jerome said. "I spared her those details. She's been through enough this week."

Aaron nodded and left for his room, alone.

# CHAPTER 18

# ALEX

Alex woke awash in orange, red, and purple light. The sun reflected off the Oreean Sea into her room, dancing across her floor over the feet of Stefan and Gryphon, who were both at her bedside. She felt relieved to find herself wearing one of Aaron's training shirts.

"Edith dressed you," Gryphon said.

"And why are you both watching me sleep?" Her memories slammed into focus all at once. She threw the blanket aside and crawled to the edge of her bed. "Do you have information on Aaron?"

Alex's heart broke when Gryphon's face fell and he turned to Stefan.

"No! You promised to fix him!" Alex cried.

Stefan climbed onto the bed beside her and held out his arms to her, but Alex gawked at his swollen eye and cut lip. She turned to Gryphon and growled, "What did you do to Stefan?"

"Me?" Gryphon threw his hands up in surrender. "Oh no, Princess. Your husband did that damage. According to Lynx and your father, Princeling and Stefan here finally went after each other."

Alex shoved Stefan off the bed. "You fought Aaron? What is wrong with you? He's cursed. What if he'd hurt you?"

"You've seen me fight. He's the one hurting right now," Stefan said.

"Does that mean he's here?" Alex trembled. It was only a moment, but that was all Stefan needed.

"*That* is why I went after him," Stefan said, thrusting his finger in her direction. "You're afraid of him."

She slapped his hand away. "I am not afraid of *my* Aaron."

"There is only one Aaron. Your Aaron and cursed Aaron are the same person," Stefan said. "No matter how badly you want to separate them in your mind."

"What about the Aaron who did that to you?" Gryphon pointed at Alex's bandaged shoulder. Alex bit the inside of her cheek. She didn't know how to respond to either of them.

Stefan stood up. "Stay out of this, Gryphon. None of this started until you came into her life!"

Gryphon erupted in a blinding orange light. "So I should have left her alone at Moorloc's castle? Let them beat and torture her until her magic made her lose her mind? Is that what you're saying? Or have you already forgotten everything she endured there?"

"Enough!" Alex shouted. She slammed her hands on the bed and sent a gale through the room, pushing Gryphon and Stefan further apart. "I have enough loved ones fighting with one another. I don't need any more."

Gryphon huffed and crossed his arms, and his orange glow faded. "I'm sorry. I stayed in Warren to give you the news about your princeling, not fight with your brother."

Alex swung her legs over the edge of the bed. She patted the spot beside her, and Stefan took a seat. Alex grabbed Stefan's hand, squeezed it tightly, and turned to Gryphon. "What about Aaron?"

Gryphon pursed his lips and kicked at the ground with his foot. "We cured him—"

A high-pitched squeal escaped from Alex as her hands flew to her mouth.

"There's a 'but'—a very large one."

"You tell her," Stefan said, moving his hand protectively to Alex's shoulder. His touch stilled the trembles that raked her body.

"He was *cursed*, not possessed," Gryphon continued. "So, it's like Stefan said. While he was violent and chaotic, it was only ever him—albeit the worst version of him. Now, with that other part of him locked away, he has no memories of anything that happened."

"Wait. He doesn't know anything?" Alex whispered.

"Correct. Michael, Megesti, and your father tried to tell him, but they didn't get far. We hoped he'd listen to them. Because Aaron has no recollection of what he did to you, he's going to have a hard time believing it."

Stefan groaned. "No wonder he was so adamant to see you when he got here."

Alex rubbed her shoulder. Gryphon and Megesti had been so focused on her burns that they'd missed it, and she'd been too drained to heal it herself. Luckily, Lynx had stitched it for her. She still felt too upset to heal it.

"How did the curse work?" Alex asked.

"Think of the cursed part of him as another Aaron—all the horrible parts of him in one place, buried deep inside his mind. It keeps those memories locked away. It only woke up when he became jealous ... of me. The spell worked because he saw me as a rival—a threat, regardless of how you feel. It's why it took me so long to realize something else was wrong."

"I should have done what he asked, maybe—"

"No!" Gryphon and Stefan shouted in unison. Alex startled.

"You aren't responsible for Aaron's actions, cursed or not," Stefan said. "I wish you had told me, Michael, your father, your ladies—*anyone*—what was going on when you were alone with him, but you are not to blame. Please know we would have helped you, never judged you."

Alex looked down and tugged on the hem of the shirt she wore.

Gryphon cleared his throat, and Alex thought she heard a hint of sadness in his voice as he spoke. "I completely agree with Stefan. If anyone is to blame, it's me. I'm the reason my hexa cursed him, and *I* should have noticed something was off. If I'd paid more attention, I would have noticed the magic he was giving off. No mortal should have a magical presence."

"Magical presence?" Stefan eyed Gryphon suspiciously.

"It's a tingle we feel around magic. Like when your foot falls asleep," Alex explained. "If Aaron doesn't remember any of what happened, what do we do?"

"That's up to you, Alexandria," her father said from the door that connected their suites. There were bags under his eyes, and his hair was a mess. Alex could almost feel the exhaustion radiating from him. She'd been so focused on Gryphon and Stefan that she hadn't heard him come in.

"Up to me how? He's my husband."

"Only if you still want him to be." Edward walked over to them. "Warren law allows for immediate divorce in the event of abuse."

Alex stared at her father, aghast. "Loving me is what got him cursed. I won't abandon him." She exhaled, steadying her voice, and made a point not to look at Gryphon. "I'll never love anyone else as fiercely as I love him."

"Love changes over time. You can't say that you won't love anyone else."

Gryphon shifted awkwardly beside Edward, but Alex wasn't done. "Then why did you never remarry after my mother?"

"Your mother is not Aaron," Edward snapped. "To imply so is

an insult to your mother."

"Aaron loves me. He forgave me for everything I did. What kind of wife would I have to be to leave him for what he's done?"

"Again, your behavior at Moorloc's was justified," Gryphon said.

Alex turned to him. "I'm not merely talking about that. I shot him with my bow when he came to our camp. I lost *my* temper arguing with Moorloc, and my wind ended up gutting Aaron and impaling a torch in Stefan's chest. And while I was justified for most things in the castle, I killed someone." Alex's voice broke as she took in the men around her. "How can you forgive me so easily but vilify Aaron?"

Edward crossed the room and kissed the top of Alex's head. "Wait until you have children, my dear."

Alex groaned and turned toward Gryphon. "How do we fix him?"

"He's cured, but he'll have to decide how much he wants to know and what to believe." He sounded genuinely concerned.

"I'd like a minute alone with Gryphon. Could you get me something to eat? I'm starving," Alex said.

"Of course. Stefan." Edward waved for him to join him. "You can deliver the food. Randal's desperate to have me make all the decisions he's put off."

Stefan stood and walked to the door. "Hurt her and I'll break you," he said as he walked past Gryphon.

"You can try." Gryphon smiled mischievously.

*Sunset, behave.*

His eyes immediately shifted back to Alex when the others left the room. Once the door closed, Alex slipped off the bed, and Gryphon snorted. A chill hit her legs—she wasn't wearing pants. Aaron's shirt was long enough that it went halfway down her thighs, so she tugged on it a little to make it longer. She closed her eyes to calm her nerves.

"Is he really cured?"

Gryphon nodded slightly. "But you know how disorienting it is to realize you have lost memories and time. While he's back to himself, he won't be *normal* for some time."

"What did you not say in front of them?" she asked.

Gryphon dropped his hands and began to light and extinguish flames in his palms. "What he did ... infuriates me. From your little speech, I suspect you've already forgiven him, but I can't. A primal part of me will always want to punish him for what he did to you. And honestly, I think Stefan and Michael feel the same."

"Whom I forgive is my business and no one else's. I forgave you for kissing me at Moorloc's castle, and I wanted to set you on fire that morning for it."

Gryphon closed his palms, extinguishing the flames, and took a step toward Alex. "But have you forgiven yourself? I kissed you so you could save yourself. You kissed me under very different circumstances."

Alex's cheeks heated. "But not so different from the circumstances that Aaron finds himself in. I was under the influence of my Ares powers, and they cursed him."

"True. But he doesn't know what he did."

Alex closed the space between them. She narrowed her eyes and barely breathed as his golden eyes pierced her. "But I know what he's going to feel now. If anyone understands magic taking you over and making you lose control of yourself, it's me. I spent years having my emotions cause havoc with my magic."

"It's not the same."

"Yes, it is. I burned down a mill, set part of the camp on fire, and nearly burned Stefan and Michael countless times. That's without even taking into account gutting Aaron or killing Reinhilde."

"Alex—"

"Look me in the face and tell me that Aaron cutting my shoulder, when he could have done much more damage to me, is worse than me killing someone."

Gryphon stared at her, his face full of confusion and doubt. Finally, he rubbed his forehead and shrugged.

"Now how are we going to explain to him everything that happened?"

"I have a plan, but it's between me and the princeling."

"If you intend to do anything to my husband, it's *my* business too."

"Not until he makes it yours." Gryphon turned, but Alex grabbed his biceps and gulped.

"Thank you," she whispered. "For telling me ... and everyone the truth."

Gryphon ran his hands along her biceps. His face held a compilation of pity, sorrow, and something Alex couldn't place.

"I can't lie to you. Not about something this important. I could tell you an ugly dress was pretty, or that you needed more guards to protect you, but I could not mislead you about matters of the heart. If I risked Aaron, you would never forgive me, and then anything that was supposed to happen between us one day would die before it could even begin."

Alex wrinkled her nose. "So, you were honest for selfish reasons?"

Gryphon grabbed her hands and squeezed them. "A little. But I want you to be happy. Happy and safe."

"*Gryphon.*" Alex exhaled and took her hands back. "Your plan ... you won't hurt him?"

"I promise not to intentionally harm him."

Alex stood on her tiptoes and kissed Gryphon's cheek. "Thank you. Are you staying for dinner?"

"No. Go eat with Stefan and your father. I have Ares magic to undo."

# CHAPTER 19

# AARON

Aaron paced his bedroom. Everywhere he looked, the space was tainted. All the rooms he shared with Alex were filled with love, but this one now brought shame, even if he couldn't remember what had happened. Confusion and anxiety hit him anytime he racked his brain trying to remember what he had done to her on the day he left for the southern lords.

*She fled from here ... from me. Jerome wouldn't lie. Michael and Jessica saw her bruises. What did I do? What ridiculous thing did I make up in my head to set off my temper and make me attack my wife? I hate not knowing. This is as horrible as when I lost Daniel ... like a part of me has been ripped away.*

Unable to stay in their bedroom anymore, Aaron took the stairs down to what had been his father's war room. The large table still held a dark stain from when Alex had bled on it the day she got her memories back—the day he'd almost lost her. More guilt wormed its way into his gut and settled there like a stone. Fighting back tears, he traced the outline of the stain and tried to think of the good times with her. Finally, he removed his crown and set it on the table, then grabbed some parchment and supplies. He sat and began to write. He needed to figure out what to say to her and explain everything he was feeling.

*There are no words to apologize for what I've done.*

"Too common."

*You know I would never—*

"That sounds like I'm blaming her!"

*I'm sick with the guilt of what I've done.*

"She shouldn't care that I feel guilt. I should feel guilt."

Aaron crumpled up page after page of failed explanations and apologies. A pile of illegible sheets soaked in tears amassed at his feet. He begged for her forgiveness, telling her how sorry he was and how much regret he felt. At some point, Jerome brought him dinner, but Aaron didn't touch it. Instead, he continued to write to Alex. When he finished, it was several pages long, and while nowhere near perfect, it mostly explained how he felt. He walked upstairs, placed it on Alex's pillow, and returned to his food.

Aaron finished the cold venison and some of the cheese, but he couldn't bring himself to eat the bread. He always waited to eat his bread until Alex was full, in case she wanted his. Emotionally drained from the letter, he couldn't take looking at the bread anymore. He walked to the shield and swords on the wall above the fireplace—his father's first set. Something in him snapped. *Generations of war-hardened kings gave me this temper. There shall be no more war in my home.* He grabbed the shield and wrenched it from the wall. He tossed it into the corner and moved on to the next war symbol on the wall.

Soon there was nothing left on the wall save for a small bookshelf. He'd thrown everything on the floor and stood there, panting, when he heard a faint rattle.

"Aaron?" His mother was standing at the open bookcase, staring at the pile on the floor. "I see you've redecorated. I was looking for Alexandria."

Guinevere could read Aaron like a book, so he looked down, avoiding her gaze.

"I see." She walked into the room, letting the bookcase close behind her. "King, friend, or husband?"

"Husband."

"Tell me what happened."

Aaron's head shot up. "No!" He shook his head as his eyes widened.

"I can't help if I don't know what happened, Aaron. Whatever you did won't change my love for you."

"I can't tell you what happened, but I can say it was my fault," Aaron whispered. "I haven't been the best husband lately, and since becoming king—I've only gotten worse." He wasn't lying, but it felt odd not to tell his mother the whole truth. At the same time, he couldn't bear to see the shame that would be in her eyes if she knew everything.

"I need more."

Her hand rubbed his shoulder, and it spilled out of him. "I hurt her, and I don't think I can make up for that."

"Physically or emotionally?"

Aaron slunk back from his mother, wiping the tears that ran down his cheek.

"I see." Guinevere spoke with the tone she'd only ever used to scold his father. "Marriage is a partnership, young man, and it takes work. Work that you cannot hide or run from. If you want Alexandria's forgiveness, you will have to earn it."

"I don't know if she'll ever forgive me."

"I know my goddaughter and she sees how you've been struggling since your father died, but I will not condone violence, least of all against your wife."

Aaron looked up at his mother and swallowed.

"But if you put in the work to prove you are sorry and you apologize like a king—not a prince—she could forgive you."

"Apologize like a king?"

"Princes say they are sorry without always meaning it because they are always forgiven for their misdeeds. But a king apologizes not only with words, but also with actions—to prove he means it."

"And you know that from experience?"

Guinevere pulled her shoulders back and straightened her skirt. "I'm not proud of this, but when we were just married, your father smacked my bottom on our way to dinner one night, and I reacted badly."

"Reacted how?"

"I punched your father in the face in front of his men."

Aaron's mouth dropped open.

"I reacted before I could stop myself. A past suitor had made me uncomfortable once, and my brother taught me how to put a stop to it. It took work on both sides for us to overcome that. For me, I had to deal with the guilt of hitting my husband and humiliating him in front of his men. For him, it was the guilt of making me uncomfortable. We both had to forgive each other."

"Is this why you never kissed him in front of the knights?"

"Yes."

"He always said it was because of the sound."

"Which was the excuse he used because he knew I was uncomfortable showing my affection to him in public."

*I wish I'd seen that.*

"Stop thinking of me hitting your father, young man."

"How do you always know?"

"I'm your mother." Her focus narrowed on his lip and eye, which were still swollen from his fight with Stefan. "There is something else you will need to keep in mind."

"What?"

"Her guards and her father."

"Edward will forgive me. He's my godfather."

"I'm not so sure. He loves you dearly, but she's his daughter, and the love of a parent for their child is stronger than anything you will ever find. You hurt her. He might be able to move on, in time, but he'll always remember, and your relationship with him will never be the same."

Aaron felt like he'd been punched again. *I didn't even consider what this would do to Edward and our relationship. It's not fair. The curse wasn't my fault, and now I could lose everything, including the closest thing I have to a father figure in my life.*

"Judging by your bruised and swollen face, the young Wafner has done his duty."

"And I have plans for him."

"Forget them."

Aaron's head snapped toward his mother. "Assaulting the king is treason."

"It is, but if you want Alexandria to feel safe around you again, you need to think about what exactly you expect of Stefan. If his job is to keep her safe, shouldn't that include keeping her safe from *you?*"

Aaron froze. Guinevere crossed her arms and stared at him. "It won't just be Stefan watching you closely. All of your guards, Michael, Jerome, Caleb even. If they forgive you, it's likely out of obligation because you are their king, but don't expect them to be as permissive around Alexandria as they were before."

Aaron's mind was racing. Guinevere walked to him. "I have faith you'll put in the hard work it will require to fix this. You are a Strobel, after all." She kissed his cheek and headed back to her room.

Aaron put his hands on the table and closed his eyes to let his thoughts catch up. He was only alone for a minute when he heard footsteps above him.

"Are you here, Princeling?"

"Go away, Gryphon."

A wicked laugh echoed down the stairs, followed by footsteps. Aaron pushed himself off the table and turned to face his rival.

"I thought you'd want an update on your wife after the little Wafner stopped you from seeing her by putting his fist in your face."

Aaron tensed. *Does Alex know about my fight with Stefan? If she didn't already think I was a monster, she does now.*

"How is she?"

"She's fine. Better than fine, actually. When Megesti and I healed her burns, all the scars from her time at Moorloc's disappeared too."

"How?"

"Didn't Megesti tell you?"

Aaron shook his head. Gryphon told him what had happened and that Alex knew about Aaron's situation.

Aaron gulped. "So, she knows I remember nothing?"

"Correct. She feels for you—why, I have no idea—though little Wafner doesn't. He's holding you accountable for your crimes, regardless of what Alex says. Someone should, after all."

Aaron rolled his eyes. "So why are you here?"

Gryphon held up the letter Aaron had written to Alex. "I found this on her pillow. Apologies don't come easily to you, do they?"

"That is private."

"Was ... be glad I read it," Gryphon said, holding out the letter to Aaron. "Now you can write a better one."

"What do you want?"

"To help you get your memories back."

Aaron scoffed and crossed his arms, leaning against the table behind him. "Why would you want to help me?"

For once, Gryphon's arrogance vanished. "The sorceress who cursed you is my hexa."

"Hexa?"

"Mother's mother?"

"Ah. Your grandmother."

Gryphon nodded. "I feel responsible for what she did."

Aaron eyed Gryphon suspiciously. "I thought Megesti said she was working with Lygari. I doubt she picked me because of you. Besides, Alex would insist you aren't responsible for the poor choices of your parents, and I tend to agree with her on that."

"I'm well aware of Alex's opinion on this matter. But I also know that you see yourself as a monster after this, and having lived much of my life believing the same about myself, I feel you deserve the truth before you make your decision about that."

"Can you give me the memories of what the cursed side of me did to her?"

Gryphon rubbed his forehead before he shifted his gaze to Aaron. His eyes flashed blue for a second. "Yes. Not only will they help you understand what happened and what you did to Alex, but they'll serve as a suitable punishment for you."

"Punishment?"

"They start out stupid, as simple, petty jealousy, but quickly turn violent. You threatened her in your bedroom, and the fear on her face will haunt *me* forever. And the stabbing—" Gryphon growled like an animal, and his clenched fist burst into flames. He stepped away from Aaron and closed his eyes, taking slow, steady breaths until the fire died. "You deserve to be haunted too."

"I understand," Aaron said. "I need to know for myself what happened. Not hear it secondhand. The only chance I have of making amends is if I know what I did."

"What if you can't live with what you did?"

Aaron glanced back at the blood on his father's table. He straightened his back and turned back to Gryphon. "Alex has to live with the memories from her time at Moorloc's castle. My having to live with hurting her seems fair."

"Agreed."

Aaron moved toward Gryphon. "What do I need to do?"

"You'll need to fully trust me. I have to dig inside your head, find those buried memories, and pull them out. I've never done this before, so I don't know what it will do to you. It could hurt. Or it could kill you."

"Kill me?"

"I can't go home, so I can't consult any of my Mystic texts. Magic of this level has real risks even when done by someone as powerful as me. But Alex is too weak to heal you, should something go wrong."

"I won't ask her to heal me under these conditions."

Gryphon smiled. "Then sit down. I need you to hold perfectly still."

Aaron sat on the bench beside the table, and Gryphon placed his fingers on Aaron's forehead and temple. Heat spread through his head like fire, and it quickly rose to a searing pain. Aaron sweated and clenched his fists. *You're doing this for Alex.*

A sharp pain hit him as if he'd been struck in the head, and a sudden rage flared up. An image appeared—the old woman Aaron had helped on the side of the road. Beside her was her grandson. They shimmered like the sun on the sea, and then she became an even older woman with a clear resemblance to Gryphon, while her grandson shifted into Lygari. In a flash, Aaron was bombarded with memories—angry words snarled at Alex about Gryphon, jealousy at their wedding, rage and hatred as she justified healing Gryphon in the stable. Aaron trembled as Gryphon worked to free the darkness in his mind.

*Lies. She lies.* His own voice echoed through his mind. *She's making a cuckold of you. She's a whor—*

Alex's cries broke through the voice. He saw her below him on their bed, begging him to stop. He felt the stitches of her shirt ripping in his hands as he struggled to find the mark that would prove her unfaithfulness—the mark that Gryphon must have left on her. *How would he leave a mark on her? That makes no sense. I was clearly mad.* Following that, Aaron saw Gryphon, in his night-clothes, holding Alex, in hers, with Sir Colten. A fury like he had never felt exploded through his mind, making him sick to his stomach, until he saw Alex follow him into the throne room. Her eyes sparkled, and her face was full of love.

When he spoke to her, it was his voice, but there was vile anger and hatred behind it. He wanted—no, he *needed* to put her in her place. He felt the weight of the sword in his hand but didn't even remember grabbing it. In a blink, blood soaked Alex's shoulder, and Michael leaped between them. The sound when he hit Michael made Aaron flinch, but Alex's cry sickened him. Jerome took him down, and he fought back until Gryphon trapped him with fire and Alex slammed him into the wall with her wind. The pain and heartbreak on Alex's face when she shouted at him would forever be burned into Aaron's mind and heart.

Gryphon released him, and the pain and heat vanished. Aaron trembled and dropped forward, but Gryphon caught him.

"Are you all right?" Gryphon asked.

Aaron struggled to breath. *How could I? I promised to cherish her ... protect her. I should have stopped myself. I'm weak ... pathetic ... everything Arthur and the Rassgats always said I was. How is anyone going to listen to me as king? How will I fix this? Do I even deserve to fix this? She should have married Cameron ... he would never—*

"Aaron?" Gryphon shook him. "Are you in pain?"

"Not physically."

"I'm sorry."

"I don't want your pity," Aaron said, pulling away from Gryphon and dropping to his knees on the ground. "You're probably loving this."

"As entertaining as it is to see you suffer, the pain it's causing Alex isn't worth it. She's hurting too."

Aaron looked up at him.

"She's afraid of you. You need to wait for her to come to you when she's ready. You can't force her to see you. And anyway, Stefan and I won't let you near her until she's ready, so don't even try."

Aaron nodded and hung his head. *Mother was right.* "Tell her I'm sorry, and that she can have as much time as she needs."

"I'll be right back." Gryphon cracked away, and Aaron let his head drop into his hands.

A moment later, a mug hit the table beside him. Aaron sniffed the green liquid and made a face.

Gryphon smirked. "It tastes even worse. But don't worry. Birch made it less potent, so you won't spend several days asleep."

Aaron sighed, gulped the potion, and dragged himself to his bed, knowing that nothing but nightmares awaited him.

# CHAPTER 20

# ALEX

Alex rushed to get changed into sparring clothes. When she arrived in her receiving room, Stefan and Edward were standing beside a small feast.

Alex grabbed a piece of bread. "I've changed my mind. We need to determine this while the sun is out." She ran between the two confused men to Edith's door and knocked loudly. "Edith, I need your father. We're going on an adventure. I think my father needs to see this for himself to believe it."

Edith opened the door and hurried through the room and into the hallway to summon her father. Alex began humming her music box tune as she chewed her bread and waited for Randal and Edith.

Edward listened to her humming intently. "You remember the Veremund lullaby?"

"Not only I."

"What do you mean?"

"When we were little, I'd hum this tune that no one knew."

"We assumed she made it up," Stefan told Edward.

"But then, the first time I hummed it in front of Michael after he came to the camp, he hummed the end with me."

"Could he have heard you earlier?"

"No. It was his first night at the camp."

Stefan nodded. "Alex found him in the woods. He was in shock and bleeding from a large cut on his head. Michael still has the scar under his hair."

Alex shrugged. "He was scared, and I wanted to help, so I hummed him the song and he joined me."

"So, you believe he's from Warren?"

"We know he is," Randal said from the doorway with Edith. "He changed a great deal—grew taller, lost his baby fat, and his hair darkened. But there's one way to be sure."

"What's that?" Edward asked.

"We'll visit the estate. As a young boy, Percival resembled his mother. But now, Michael resembles his grandfather, with his dark hair and sharp facial features. The paintings of Bruno as a young man are either in the Veremund estate or with his widow in Datten."

Alex clapped her hands. "We're going to the Veremund estate."

Edward put his hands on his hips and then shrugged, giving way easily before his headstrong daughter. "You heard your princess."

The group rode down the cobblestone road to the Warren noble estates. Alex kept steering the conversation away from Aaron, preferring to question Stefan endlessly about Lynx. She admitted she'd seen him with her in visions, and that only made Stefan grow more silent. Alex turned her attention back to the lavish estates they rode past. Each estate manor was ornate in its own way. Nothing compared with the castle, but when compared with the simple houses in town, these were elegant. Cobblestone paths led from the road right to the front doors, ensuring the noble ladies would never dirty their skirts, even in the worst weather.

Miniature versions of the royal garden ran from the front to the back of several properties. It was fall, so the flowers were gone, but as they rode past, Alex made them bloom again with her Celtics powers.

Randal stopped at a worn path, and everyone came to a halt. The house had clearly been beautiful once but was now desolate. Its stones, once black and glistening like the other noble estates, were now weathered and gray. Over the years, the sea storms had damaged most of the shutters, and they lay in pieces on the ground. The gardens were overgrown, and the cobblestones were lifting from the earth from lack of use. The other estates all had servants and families wandering around, brimming with life, but this one was as still as a graveyard.

"This is the Veremund estate?" Stefan asked.

"Every estate belongs to the highest level of nobility in Warren. All of them have a blood connection back to the original three founding families," Randal said.

"Although none have as strong a tie as ours, the Nials', or the Veremunds'," Edward said.

Alex couldn't figure out how she felt looking at it. Part of her was excited at the idea of finally learning Michael's truth, but she feared what she might find waiting inside. *If he is a Veremund, he's actually an orphan, and that would be my fault as well.*

Alex swallowed hard and trotted Snow beside Randal. "You don't have to go inside if you don't want to," she said. "I know you're the one who found them."

Edith gasped. "You found Matthias and Catherine? I thought Matthew did."

Randal turned to his daughter and shook his head.

Edith reached over from her horse to take his hand. "Oh, Daddy. I'm so sorry."

She'd never heard Edith call Randal anything other than "Father" before. Edward shrugged.

"Let's head inside," Randal said. "The Veremund estate has the same floor plan as our manor. It won't take long to find the painting."

They tied up the horses out front. The front door had been so weathered into the doorframe that it took Stefan and Randal's combined force to get it open. Once they freed it, the stale air hit them all like a slap in the face. The house hadn't been aired out in over a decade. Alex felt her heart race. *This is the same stale air in the crypts. Death and decay. Can we really expect Michael to live here?*

Inside, the foyer branched in multiple directions. Alex peered through the openings that lead to various rooms. All the paintings, tables, and furniture were covered in white fabric. When Alex took a step into what was clearly the receiving room, something inside of her stirred. Before her stood the ghosts of a beautiful young couple, and she gasped, stumbling backward.

"Alex?" Edith asked.

Alex turned to Randal. "You found them in here, didn't you?"

He nodded, and the heaviness made Alex feel as if the air was crushing her. Stefan grabbed her hand and pulled her from the room, and her father held her until she calmed. When she glanced back, the ghosts had vanished. The group followed Randal down the hall, listening to the echo of their footsteps and a few loud breaths from Alex. At the end was another door.

They stepped into the formal dining room, and Alex shivered. The air was ice-cold. Without thinking, she waved her hand and winced as she tugged the stitches in her shoulder. The fireplace and candles came to life. Unlike those in the other rooms, this table was left uncovered. The layer of dust on it showed how long it had been since anyone was in this room.

Edward and Randal strode toward a sheet hanging on a painting at the end of the table. Edward ripped the sheet off the painting, and Alex's breath caught in her throat. The man in the painting looked exactly like Michael—except for his eyes. But the nose, lips, and chin were identical. He had the same black hair that fell to one side and the same tanned skin.

"He has his mother's eyes," Edward said.

"This is Bruno Veremund as a young man. The older brother of Queen Elizabeth Veremund," Randal said.

"I spent most of my childhood in this house," Edward said. "When Arthur was fighting against Betruger with the Datten kings, I stayed with my uncle. It's why I always let Aaron hide in Warren when he needed to get away from Emmerich. Bruno did that for me."

"What do we do now?" Stefan asked.

"The last step is to visit the duchess," Randal said.

"The duchess?" Edith asked.

Edward pointed at the woman beside Bruno. "Duchess Veronica Veremund, Bruno's wife. She's the only living Veremund who can corroborate that Michael is, in fact, Percival Veremund."

"Though after seeing this, and Judith reminding me what you called him, I have no doubts," Randal said.

"What I called him?" Alex asked.

Randal smiled at Alex. "You could say 'Aaron', 'Daniel', 'Cameron', and the names of all the other noble children, but according to my wife, you refused to call Percival by his name because you hated it."

"You were that stubborn as a little girl, too?" Stefan asked.

Randal nodded. "You picked a different name and wouldn't be swayed. Not by his mother, not by yours, not by anyone."

Alex turned back to Stefan. "Michael. I called him Michael."

Randal nodded. "Always Michael."

❧❧❧ ❧❧❧

Alex stood at her balcony, basking in the warmth of the setting sun on the Orean Sea. The cool breeze sent her hair blowing behind her, but her thoughts kept going back to Aaron. *What am I going to do about you? I know everyone's worried about me going home, especially Stefan and my father, but I miss you, and I want to be there for you tomorrow to support you as you say goodbye to your father.*

There was a knock, and Alex spun to see Lynx standing beside her bed.

"I called up, but there was no answer," Lynx said.

"I was lost in thought."

"Thinking of Aaron?"

"How—?"

"I can smell certain emotions. It's a Tiere trait. I can always tell when Birch is scared or if Gryphon is lying."

Alex couldn't help but laugh.

"I wanted to see how you're feeling physically."

"Stronger. Do you think we'd be strong enough to go to the Stronghold and cast the protection spell on it? It's larger than my mother's castle but much smaller than Datten or Warren."

"I'm willing to try, but if you drain yourself again, Gryphon will have my head."

Alex smirked. "Don't worry about it. You can always have Stefan defend your honor."

"What does that mean?" Lynx held out her hand to Alex.

"Nothing. Is it true you turned into a lynx and then walked naked through the room to break up Aaron and Stefan?"

"The lynx got them to separate."

"And the nakedness?"

"A consequence of transformation. When we shift into animals larger than our bodies, we ruin our clothes."

*That makes sense.* "Ready to go?"

"I'll get us there. You conserve all the magic you can."

A moment later, Alex peered up at the exterior of the Stronghold. "When did it get another floor?" she asked.

"Gryphon, Birch, Kharon, and I added it after the Datten men were trying to find homes for all the displaced people of Betruger."

Alex tugged on her shirt. *I'd forgotten about that. After everything that's gone on with me, I forgot about the pain of an entire kingdom. I have to do better as a queen.*

"This place smells cursed," Lynx said as they stood outside.

"That's because of all the ghosts that remain." Alex motioned to the field behind them. "This is where Moorloc and I killed each other. It's where Lygari raised my grandfather from the dead, and where he would have succeeded in killing me if Gryphon hadn't given me Daniel for protection."

A warm comfort filled Alex's chest. Lynx's hand rubbed her back. "You're not alone any longer. And if those monsters who tortured you try anything while we're here, Kharon has the power to deal with them."

Alex's voice was almost a whisper when she said, "I didn't know that."

"After things settle down, I'll sneak them here. They can banish all the dead if they won't go willingly."

"Would they be able to bring the dead somewhere else?"

"I've never asked. Guess we'll find out." Lynx grinned, and her sand-colored skin sparkled in the dying light. "Shall we crack, or would you prefer to walk?"

Alex held out her hand to Lynx and let her crack them into the courtyard. They stood at the door leading to the middle tower. *You can do this. You aren't alone, and you are stronger than you think. If only Aaron or Gryphon were here.* Alex pushed open the door and gasped.

"What's wrong?" Lynx asked.

The space echoed. The floor, once bare earth, was now covered in beautiful, glistening stonework. She walked to the middle of the room and spun. Gone were the broken bed and wardrobe, and in their place was a lovely desk flanked by bookcases. Alex recognized several of Stefan's favorite training books, and next to them were ones from Warren and Betruger.

Lynx wrinkled her nose. "This room looks lovely, but it feels … terrible."

Lynx was right. Even though it looked different, the room still filled Alex with dread. "This is where Moorloc kept me as punishment for fighting back. Two days alone without food or water," Alex said.

"Merlin's beard! And I thought our schools were awful." She looked up at the ceiling.

"We should perform the spell from the top," Alex said. "It's the highest point, or at least it was, and we could see it spread over the castle."

They began the ascent to the top. As they climbed, Alex noticed that sections of the stone were new, giving her hope that Gryphon had thought to raise the tower too. When they arrived at the top, Alex moved to the railing, and icy sea air filled her lungs. The waves crashing below filled her with peace.

"This area is lovely." Lynx walked to the west side and looked from the mountains to the small forest near the castle. She grinned and turned to Alex. "Your work, I presume?"

Alex nodded.

"Celtics is my other power. We can always spot the work of another of our line. Your trees are magnificent."

"Thank you. I've been told I'm gifted with plants, like my mother was."

"Many Cassandra sorceresses have been. Celtics sorcerers are also some of the best with potions, which comes in handy for healing."

Lynx motioned to the stone railing beside her, and Alex placed her hands on it. They both recited the spell, softly at first, then louder and more aggressively, directing their magic to protect the castle and the people within. The Stronghold was larger than Verlassen Castle, but it was the extra people that caused Alex to groan. Lynx's eyes lit up a dark green, and Alex pushed harder. She felt the rush of her well opening and fought to let out just enough power to cast the protection spell without draining herself. When they finished, both of them sat and pressed their backs into the cold stone railing. The sun had gone down, and they were sitting alone in the dark. The glow of the spell faded into the surrounding stones.

"Are you all right?" Lynx asked.

"Tired, but that isn't unusual for me."

"Then allow me to take you home."

Alex grabbed Lynx's outstretched hand, and they arrived back in the receiving room of Alex's suite in Warren. Exhausted from her efforts, Alex didn't notice Stefan until he cleared his throat. She and Lynx spun around to find him staring at them with crossed arms and the Wafner scowl filling his entire face.

"Care to explain why you felt it was appropriate to leave your head guard behind?" he asked through swelling lips.

Alex groaned. "You *cannot* be upset with me for going unescorted to Moorloc's. We have men from Betruger, Datten, and Warren there."

"We had men here too, and yet you were still cornered and attacked in the crypts." Stefan winced as he spoke.

"That's why we went. The Stronghold is our closest location to the Forbidden Lands. We've now protected it, so only sorcerers who are welcomed can get in." She paused and then asked, "Will you let me heal you?"

"Is that your way of apologizing?"

Alex chuckled. "No. I took Lynx. You don't get to control every moment of my life, even if you think you do."

"You're supposed to be resting, not draining your powers," Lynx cautioned.

"It won't take much." Alex looked up at Stefan. "Healing—yes or no?"

"You're so difficult," Stefan said. Then he uncrossed his arms and leaned down.

"Thank you. I hate seeing you hurt." Alex placed one hand on Stefan's swollen cheek and the other on the opposite temple.

"I know," he whispered.

A faint golden light made its way across Stefan's face from one of her hands to the other, healing him completely.

"Perfect," Lynx purred from the side of the room.

Alex smiled at the praise. She still wasn't used to being able to control her powers so well. She waited for Stefan to respond, but he merely turned red. "You should say something, you big oaf. Don't be like Jessica and Michael," she whispered.

"Go get some rest," he scolded. "I can tell you're tired, and that means you're actually exhausted—and not just magically."

Alex stuck out her tongue at him. She waited a moment before she finally turned around, winked at Lynx, and headed up the stairs to her bed. When she was out of sight, she stopped and kneeled on the ground, peeking around the corner of the open stairs and straining to listen to the conversation she knew would come.

"How'd it go?" Stefan asked Lynx, almost too softly for Alex to hear.

"Well, but it took more magic out of both of us than I expected. Her to perform it and me to stabilize her. The real challenge will be Warren. She'll need both Megesti and Gryphon to do it. I hope Megesti managed to put the spell on Datten. She'll need proper rest before she can do another one."

"She doesn't follow instructions."

"Clearly not. But at least she brought me to the horrid place instead of going alone."

"You really care about her, don't you?" Stefan asked.

"She's my Heart too, not just Gryphon's. We haven't had a ruling sorceress in generations, let alone one so kind. I'll protect her with my life. She's our future—a chance for us to be better."

"I love her the same, but I feel I failed her after what happened with Aaron."

*You didn't fail me, Stefan. You had no way of knowing he was losing his mind.*

Lynx chuckled. "Curses are tricky. Gryphon is descended from the line that cursed Aaron, and even he didn't catch on. You have nothing to feel guilty for."

Alex strained to listen, but whatever was happening was too quiet for her to hear. She was about to climb another floor to go to bed when she heard Lynx's voice one last time.

"She was right about one thing. You need to stop being an oaf and admit you desire me."

"I already did!"

"I know, but I enjoy hearing it."

Alex swallowed a squeal of delight. She had remembered that face for seven years—the face of the woman Stefan would marry. Despite all his protests and assurances that he'd never marry, that he'd remain her guard and had no desire to have anything else, she had always known the truth. He only needed to find the right woman. *Or the right sorceress.* She smirked.

# CHAPTER 21

# AARON

Aaron woke to a loud crash. He threw off his blankets and ran to his table to grab his sword. His heart cantered in his chest like Thunder trotting at full speed as a second clang sounded from the suite's first floor.

Aaron blinked, but when he opened his eyes, the room was just as dark. "Ferflucs!" The sky was black through the balcony doors, and the fire at the end of the room was nothing more than glowing embers. As soon as his eyes adjusted to the light, Aaron crept down the stairs, in his sleeping pants, to see who dared come after the King of Datten.

Torches illuminated the first floor from either side of the door. Before he even hit the ground, Aaron realized the noise had come from the pile of armor and weapons he'd removed from the wall. A cloaked figure stood in the middle of it, trying to navigate out of the mess.

*Thought you could catch me unawares, huh? Well, I'll have to show you what the new king is truly capable of.*

Arriving behind the figure, Aaron leaped forward, grabbed the intruder's shoulder, and shoved them toward the wall beside the door.

"What in the Forbidden Lands?"

Aaron held an empty cloak in his left hand and his sword in the other. He heard a gasp behind him and swung on the balls of his feet to thrust his sword at the intruder behind him. A pair of sparkling emerald eyes came into sight, and he leaped back.

"Alex!" Horrified that he'd once again threatened his wife, Aaron released his sword, sending a clattering through the room. Alex flicked her wrist, bringing the fire to life—she was dressed in only her favorite green nightgown. Her flowing locks shone in the firelight, except for the side bits that caused her so much trouble. She'd braided those and pulled them behind her head. In her hand, her Datten crown sparkled from the light of the flames. Aaron took the tiniest step toward her to gauge her response. She trembled and slid her foot further behind her, but she stalled and set it back.

*My grandmother's crown—your crown. Tell me how to fix this. I'll beg, grovel, anything! Just please forgive me. Please let my mother be right. Please take me back. I'm so sorry, and I'll do anything you ask to make this right.*

Alex's terrified face flashed across Aaron's mind, distracting him. When he could focus again, he realized she had spoken to him and he hadn't heard a word she said.

"I'm sorry ... I didn't hear you."

Alex swallowed and moved back a step. "I asked how you're feeling. Gry—" She gasped. "Megesti and my father told me how hard the cure was ... on you."

*Say his name. Let me prove I won't lose my mind over it.* Aaron took a cautious step toward her, and her whole body tensed. He slid back before speaking. "The cure was excruciating, but it doesn't even come close to the pain of knowing what I did."

"Are you yourself again? No lasting effects?" Alex's lip trembled, and she kept tugging on the necklace around her neck.

*You're afraid of me ... I have to fix this. But you're wearing my gift, so that means there's hope ... right. I'm so sorry. I'll learn to live with what happened as long as I didn't break us.*

Aaron forced a smile. "I'm back to the jousting, Warren-loving, terrible Prince of Datten, except with a bigger crown."

"That's a relief." Alex's grip on her crown tightened as she alternated between looking at him and the changes he'd made to the room.

*Look at me! Please!*

"Alex?"

Her head turned, and her eyes locked onto his.

"Say his name."

"What?" Her eyes grew wide, and her skin paled as she sucked in a breath.

"So you can see it's really me. Say 'Gryphon', and I won't change."

"Aaron—"

"You kissed Gryphon at the castle," Aaron said.

Alex's hand flew to her mouth to stifle a gasp, and she dropped the crown she was holding.

Aaron bent to pick up the crown. When he stood, he waited until she'd summoned the courage to glance at him again. "Gryphon kissed you at the castle. He's seen you undressed and saved your life more than once, and you *need* him to gain control of your powers, and ... I'm okay with that."

"What?" Her hand dropped to her chest.

He stepped toward her, and she didn't flinch or back away. "I love you, and I need you safe. If that means I must put up with him ... I will."

Alex gulped, and Aaron closed the remaining space between them.

"You're all right?" Alex's hand moved toward his face but hung in the air. Aaron didn't move, convinced she'd flee if he did. Finally, she caressed his cheek, and her eyes shifted from his split lip to his black eye. "Mostly."

Aaron took her hands in his and kissed them. "Nothing justifies how horrible I was. I'm so sorry for what I said. For what I did, and what I allowed to happen to you. I should have been stronger."

"Aaron, that wasn't you—"

"It was. Maybe not all of it, but enough." Aaron nodded. "I promised to protect you, and I didn't. Even worse, *I* hurt you. You deserve better than a mortal who can't even control his temper and allows himself to be manipulated into believing lies over his own wife. I don't deserve you."

"Aaron." Alex's tone was stern. "I decide who's worthy of me. The men in my life have no say in the matter." She pulled her hand away from his. As she moved it back to his face, it glowed gold. Her thumb ran across his lip, and a tingle spread across his face wherever she touched him. When the tingle left, the pain from his fight with Stefan had vanished.

Alex lifted her face and moved her hands behind his neck. "I could never stop loving you. The man who attacked me was the darkness in you, and we know I have my own darkness. We both made unforgivable mistakes this year, but we'll get through this. I came back tonight because I want to make things right with you, not chastise you. I can't say how long it will take to properly heal us or what 'making things right' even means for us, but tomorrow, I'll stand at your side and show our kingdom a king and queen who support each other."

Aaron felt her tremble and pulled her closer. "But?"

"I was scared your healing could be a ruse."

"There is no ruse."

"I know. I checked when I healed you."

Aaron closed his eyes, trying to summon the right words. *I need to say the perfect thing to make you see what you mean to me, so you know how truly sorry I am. I'll do whatever you need me to.*

But before Aaron could open his eyes, Alex's lips pressed against his. Startled, he tried to step back, but Alex pulled him closer. Her arms tickled as they snaked around his waist and locked around him. Aaron shifted his weight and pressed himself into her. As her kiss deepened, he gripped her face, kissing her back hungrily.

When they came up for air, Alex smiled at him. A faint pink crept across her cheeks, and her grip on him tightened, a personal signal only Aaron recognized. *What exactly are you thinking, Your Royal Highness?*

"Gryphon wouldn't tell me how he planned to help you."

"I couldn't hold myself accountable for my actions if I didn't know what they were."

"He gave you the memories?" Alex released him and stepped back. Her eyes widened, and she looked him over as if she could find some physical change in him. "Why would he punish you?"

"Because I asked him to."

"Why? If you give me some ferflucsing nonsense about honor, Aaron, I'll slap you."

"It would be hypocritical of me to insist you remember the worst days of your life if I wasn't willing to do the same."

Alex's lip quivered. "What were you think—?"

Aaron kissed her again before she could finish.

"I still wish you didn't have to bear that burden," Alex whispered and placed her palm on his chest.

"What do you need from me?" Aaron asked. "You came here, so do you need to talk? Do you want me to hold you? Apologize? Beg?"

Alex pressed her fingers gently to his lips, silencing him, then smiled coquettishly and nuzzled his chest. *No. You don't want to ... do you?* Before he could respond, she ran her hand behind his head and smiled up at him. He wanted to be gentle with her, but she wasn't having that. A deep moan left Aaron's chest as she pressed her body against him. In a moment of strength, Aaron pulled away from her and gasped for breath.

"Alex … do you want what I think you want?" Aaron asked, stepping back from her.

Alex closed the distance between them. She ran her hands up his chest and narrowed her eyes at him. "Yes, and you don't get to tell me how to forgive you. You're supposed to let me heal however I want."

"I didn't mean it like that." Aaron breathed deeply. The smell of sea air and flowers coming off Alex made it hard for him to focus.

"I need to feel connected to you—treasured by you."

Aaron slid his hand around her hip and pulled her closer.

Alex looked deep into his eyes. "The last time I was in our bed with you, that other you … hurt me. But he's gone now, and I need to erase that memory. Sorcerers connect with touch, and I feel most connected to you when we're intimate. So if you want to apologize to me, get out of your head, hear what *I* need, and give me that."

*You don't have to tell me twice.* Aaron wrapped his arms around her waist and backed her up against the bare wall behind them. Alex gasped when she hit the icy wall, and as Aaron's hands gripped her hips, she cracked them upstairs and set their fireplace roaring to light the room for them.

"If you change your mind about this, I'll understand."

"Aaron, I want what *I* want. Don't shame me or make me ask again."

Her fingers snaked in his hair, and she kissed him. Aaron pressed her against the wall. The memory of shoving her, of wanting to hurt her, flashed into his mind. Aaron's heart pounded, but Alex didn't notice. When she finally came up for air, he tried to hide his concern, but Alex caressed his cheek.

"I know. We'll replace that one too."

Aaron smiled, swallowed his fears, and focused on her. When he kissed her neck, a soft moan left her, and he ran his hand up her thigh, slowly pushing up her nightgown. She shivered as the chilly night air hit her skin. Aaron gripped her thigh tightly and picked her up, pressing her into the stones behind her. Alex's arms wrapped around his neck, and he pushed himself against her harder, making her moan louder.

"Aaron—" Alex's voice was raspy as her nails dug into his back.

Aaron peppered kisses up the side of her neck until he reached her ear and whispered in a deep, husky voice. "Yes, my queen?"

"I want the Princess of Warren's husband, not the King of Datten."

Aaron felt the smile leave his lips. *We'll work on that fear, eventually.* Alex turned her face to his, and he pushed his forehead against hers.

"After the last few days, I can't imagine being anything but gentle with you. But I meant what I said ... if you want to stop, just say the word."

Alex nuzzled against his neck before she whispered, "Bed."

Aaron locked his arms around her and spun her around toward their bed. He laid her down and caught Alex observing him as he dropped his pants to the floor. The only light up here came from the fireplace Alex had brought to life. As he moved toward her, Alex held up her arms for him, allowing him to remove her nightgown and drop it beside his pants.

He couldn't help looking her over in the dim light. She'd been hurt so much, but the scars were almost nonexistent. Only the mark on her shoulder that he'd made was left. Aaron knew that even though the marks were gone, their pain would remain.

As Alex slipped into bed, Aaron playfully stalked after her. "We're going to have to talk about quite a few things, Your Royal Highness," he whispered.

"Not tonight."

Aaron caged her head with his arms. Alex smiled at him, then grabbed his face with her hands and kissed him. Aaron could feel the need behind her kiss and dropped onto his elbows to get closer to her. He moved his kisses to her neck and felt her chest tighten when she gasped. Settling between her legs, Aaron felt her cling to him when he moved into her. It didn't take long for their moans and breaths to quicken, and Aaron pushed his forehead to hers.

"I love you," she said. Her breaths were shaky, and she trembled beneath him.

Aaron kissed her softly as her fingers dug into his back. He put aside everything in his mind and focused on Alex so he could be in the moment with his wife. After they were satiated and spent, Alex curled against him and fell asleep with her head on his shoulder.

As the fire died, Aaron pulled the blankets over them. He gently ran his fingers along Alex's spine. Just as Gryphon had said, the scars were gone and her back was smooth. She twitched and snuggled closer to him as he tickled her.

When a knock broke the silence, Aaron reluctantly threw on his pants and hurried over to find a nervous Jerome.

"I don't want to alarm you, Aaron, but Stefan and Edward sent Lynx here. They can't find Alex. She's vanished, and no one knows where she is."

Aaron scoffed and shook his head. "Figures she wouldn't tell anyone."

"What do you mean?"

Aaron jerked his head toward his bed. "She's here. Arrived a few hours ago."

Jerome groaned.

"Have Lynx bring everyone from Warren if they're up anyway. Then ask the kitchen to prepare an early breakfast."

Jerome nodded and headed down the hallway. Aaron sat on the

edge of his bed. Alex had moved into the warm space he'd vacated and was sleeping on her front. Aaron tucked her braided lock of hair behind her ear and kissed her cheek.

"Thank you for giving me the chance to make things right. I'll do whatever you ask to help you feel safe with me again."

# CHAPTER 22
# ALEX

Sunshine streamed into the room. Alex reached for Aaron, but his side of the bed was empty. She sat up, clutching the blanket to her bare breasts, and saw him with Michael on the balcony. He was still in his sleeping pants, and the sun shone over his broad chest as they spoke. Alex couldn't help but smile.

*Despite everything, I still see the same strong and loving man who found me in the woods. Curse aside, that is. Thank you for not losing yourself with your new crown and title. Even with our friends, you're not a hard, commanding king. You're just you.*

Alex climbed out of bed. Her lady was at the wardrobe, examining some black dresses. Alex slipped into the robe Jessica had left at the end of the bed and crept onto the balcony toward the men. She wrapped her arms around Aaron, but he'd clearly been expecting it and snatched her arms, pulled her in, and kissed her passionately.

Michael groaned. "You're already back to this?"

"Good morning, my queen," Aaron whispered.

"Good morning, Your Royal Highness."

Michael made a gagging noise. Alex turned and shoved him.

"When did you arrive?" Michael asked, holding out his arms to her.

Alex hugged him tightly. "Early morning. I didn't want to wake anyone."

"No, you made everyone in Warren worry about you." Michael pointed to Jessica. "Better not keep my wife waiting."

Alex laughed and headed to Jessica. "Have you decided on a dress?"

"No. They're so different."

"They look exactly the same to me."

Jessica rolled her eyes. "They're completely different. One is Warren styling and the other, Datten. Look at the lace, the necklines."

"I missed you." Alex hugged Jessica. She released the sleeve she was holding and hugged Alex back.

"It's only been a few days," Stefan said, coming up the stairs from the main floor with Edith and Lynx behind him.

"I brought your fathers and a few nobles early this morning. Your father was irate that you left without telling him," Lynx said.

Alex swallowed the lump in her throat as Aaron and Stefan tensed and stared at each other. She pulled away from Jessica and scurried across the room to them. "Aaron ..."

Aaron glanced at her for only a moment and held up his hand. Bile crept from her stomach.

"I don't regret my actions. I accept whatever punishment you deem appropriate," Stefan said, standing taller. "Even if it means the dungeon."

Aaron ran his hand through his hair, sighed, and held out his hand. Stefan's eyes narrowed on Aaron's hand before he glanced over to Alex. She shrugged, feeling as confused as Stefan looked.

"I had intended to throw you in the dungeon, but then my mother set me straight."

Stefan accepted Aaron's hand and shook it.

"What did Her Majesty say?" Jessica asked.

"She reminded me that Stefan's only job is to protect Alex. That means with his life, if necessary, but also means protecting her from me. When I followed Edward to Warren, I didn't know what I'd done, and the last thing Alex needed was me barging in and demanding to see her. You did your duty and protected your queen. I won't punish you for that." Aaron released Stefan's hand and turned back to Alex.

"Understood. I was surprised how well you fought. I didn't think you had that in you." Stefan winked at Alex, making her groan.

"I was trained by your father," Aaron replied.

"This Datten dress is beautiful," Edith said, drawing everyone's attention. "I love the intricate Oreean lace."

"See?" Jessica said, pointing at Edith.

"Wear the Datten dress," Aaron said. "My mother will appreciate it. Michael and Stefan, downstairs."

ALEX RODE in the carriage with Stefan, Randal, and Edith, twisting and untwisting the skirt of her dress in her fingers. Aaron had gone ahead with Edward, Guinevere, and Jerome to make sure he was there to greet the other royals. Everyone agreed that with Alex having been away to "recover," she should arrive just before the ceremony began. Stefan grabbed her hand and squeezed it. Ever since she was little, he always knew when her insides were twisted and terrified.

"I won't leave your side unless you are beside Aaron," he said. "I know you still hate crowds."

"You can also leave her with us," Edith said. "The Nials always protect the Warrens."

"So do the Veremunds," Randal said. "Have you decided how you're going to tell Michael?"

Alex wrinkled her nose at Stefan.

"It's your call," Stefan said. "He asked you to help him."

"He knew asking me meant you would be there too," she said.

"True, but he still asked you."

"Considering what we discovered, it makes sense. Veremunds stick with their Warrens," Randal said.

"My father suggested we speak to the Countess first to make sure she believes it before we get his hopes up. I'd hate to disappoint him if I was wrong," Alex said.

Edith looked up at her father, and he nodded to her. "There *is* a way to know for certain. The treasure room."

Stefan raised his eyebrows at her, and Alex played with her braid. "The first time my father took me there, he showed me how the blood of a Warren, Nial, or Veremund is needed to unlock the room. If Michael's blood opens the door, he's Percival Veremund."

"After everything calms down, we'll take him," Stefan said.

The carriage jolted to a stop, and Alex peeked out the window. They weren't at the hall yet. Instead, they were behind the many other carriages of Datten nobles heading to mourn their king. Randal opened the door and turned around to speak to the driver, but Alex climbed out.

"Your Royal Highness, you should remain inside. I intended to ask the others to move out of your way."

Alex motioned for Stefan to get out of the carriage. "I understand, General Nial. However, I won't hide from my people. I'll walk the rest of the way and accept the Dattenites' condolences on behalf of Aaron."

Randal smiled down at her. "You truly are your father's daughter."

"Thank you." Alex held her chin high and held out her arm to Stefan.

He was scowling. "I don't like it."

Alex pursed her lips. "Then it's good that I'm in charge." She held out her arm to him again, but he didn't move. Alex huffed and turned to walk away when Stefan's words stopped her in her tracks.

"Lynx. Gryphon."

A moment later, the two sorcerers appeared before her. Both were dressed in their formal titan robes—Lynx wore emerald green, and Gryphon had chosen the less intimidating cobalt blue.

"You called?" Lynx purred. She spared a glance for Alex and then turned her attention completely to Stefan. Her eyes slowly moved across his formal uniform and lingered for long enough that Gryphon elbowed her.

"Stop devouring the oaf with your eyes. What do you want, Little Wafner?"

Alex snickered at the name, but Stefan's only reaction was to narrow his eyes at Gryphon. "My queen wishes to walk the rest of the way. I can protect her from men, but I need help where magic is involved."

"Of course we'll escort the Heart." Lynx smiled. She pushed Gryphon toward Alex and slipped her own arm through Stefan's.

With Randal and Edith in front of her, and Lynx and Stefan behind, Alex walked alongside the crowd of people. She talked to anyone who wanted to give condolences. Not everyone would fit inside the hall, and Alex wanted to allow them all to say their piece. By the time they arrived at the hall, all the other guests were inside. Alex worried how it would look for her to arrive late.

As they entered, a tingle went through Alex, and her stomach dropped. *Why didn't I give Aaron his sword this morning?* Emmerich's casket was sitting on a large stand at the front of the hall, surrounded by the highest-ranking knights. Jerome and the general of archers, Avery Reinhart, flanked the casket. Aaron stood near the stand, accepting condolences from royals and nobles.

Alex's breath sped up as her eyes landed on Daniel's and Emmerich's ghosts near the casket. They nodded at her, and Gryphon squeezed her elbow, startling her.

"Are you all right?"

"No. Where are Michael and my father? I need to know where everyone is." Alex scanned the hall for them.

"Alex—" Stefan began, but she cut him off.

"I have a bad feeling about today. You know how my feelings get."

"It's a funeral, Alex. I'd be concerned if you had good feelings," Megesti said as he came over to her.

"Megesti is right. Funerals are challenging for sorcerers," Lynx added.

"Even more so for those who can see the dead," Gryphon whispered to Alex. "Michael's over there." He pointed Michael out to Alex.

"Are you sure that's all it is?"

"Positive. Now let's get you to your husband. I'm confident your only job today is to stand beside him and look pretty." Alex punched Gryphon. "Ow. I didn't make the rules."

Stefan and Lynx took Gryphon with them to find a seat while Megesti took Alex up the main aisle. She greeted the other royals and her father, who was sitting with Guinevere, before taking her place beside Aaron. For the next hour, Aaron introduced her to the royal families of the southern kingdoms. Alex had met a few of their sons at her birthday celebrations when she'd first arrived home. Most had not impressed her. Soon enough, she spotted Aaron trying to hide his smirk when he greeted Prince Jesse and Prince Rudolph. Both princes had tried to win Alex's affection, but their aggressive tactics resulted in one being slapped and the other being pushed off the pier.

A familiar little old woman kissed Alex's cheek while Aaron spoke to one of Datten's southern lords.

"You look exactly like your mother, dear," said the woman.

"Thank you. I'm sorry, I don't know your name."

"Of course you don't, Your Royal Highness. I'm the Duchess Veronica Veremund. My late husband's sister was your grandmother."

Alex's royal composure abandoned her as she gawked at the woman, looking for some piece of Michael in her features. But her hair was completely white, and her skin wrinkled, and her eyes dark brown.

"Alex, do you need to sit down?" Aaron's voice sounded far away as he pulled her from the duchess. Alex didn't even remember having taken the woman's hand.

"No, I'm fine." She pushed Aaron off her and turned back to the old woman. "If you are available, Veronica, my father and I would love to have you for tea very soon."

"I would be honored, Your Royal Highness." She curtsied to Alex and slowly made her way to the other nobles.

"What was that?" Aaron whispered in her ear.

"I'll tell you tonight."

"Alex..." His eyes locked onto hers, and tension filled his face. She squeezed his bicep and smiled sweetly.

"I promise. It's wonderful news."

Aaron relaxed, and they turned to finish their talks with the guests. Once everyone else was seated, Aaron and Alex took their seats and the funeral began. Edward was Emmerich's oldest friend, so he had accepted the difficult job of giving the welcome address. He gave a lovely speech detailing Emmerich's many accomplishments, honors, and passions. He followed it with fond memories of his friend.

Tears ran down Alex's cheek, and Aaron squeezed her hand. "You see him, don't you?"

"Yes," Alex stammered as she squeezed his hand. "Your speech is next."

Aaron quickly kissed her cheek and walked to the front of the hall to address his people. She could tell from the way he cleared his throat that he was struggling. *You can do this.* She nodded at him, and he kissed his hand and placed it on his father's coffin before he turned to the crowd.

Alex turned to the row behind her. "Kharon." She whispered to the Hades titan, and they nodded to her and then to Aaron.

As Aaron spoke, his father appeared beside him, visible to him thanks to Kharon. "King Emmerich was many things." Aaron began swallowing hard as his father nodded to him. "He was a fearless warrior, a devoted husband, a charismatic leader, and a great friend. He dedicated his life to improving things for the people of Datten. Thrust into power at the tender age of thirteen, he never really had a proper childhood. My father was many great things, but a gentle man he wasn't. He was harsh, easy to provoke, and occasionally violent, but he lived through things I can't even imagine—war, losing both parents while he was young, and the loss of a child. As a new husband who hopes to be a father one day, I can only imagine the pain he and my mother have gone through, and it makes his behavior much clearer now.

"My father wasn't angry at me. He was angry at the world that took my brother. He wasn't being mean, he was being protective. I stand before you today a stronger man, a more decisive king, and a better husband because of what my father taught me. So, while we argued more often than we agreed, he was the father I needed, and for that, I will always be grateful. He made me the man I am today, and I will ensure he is proud of the legacy he left behind." Aaron finished and glanced at his father. Emmerich rested his hand on his heart and bowed to Aaron. As he rose, he gave him the same mischievous smile Aaron had given Alex a thousand times. Emmerich touched Aaron's cheek and patted it before Aaron exhaled and turned to take his seat.

It was Alex's turn. She went to the front of the hall and turned around. "I didn't know King Emmerich as long as most of you here, having only really met him a little over a year ago. We didn't start off on the best footing, considering that I yelled at him and, some might say, threatened him." Alex paused and locked eyes with Emmerich's ghost. "Later, I learned he admired princesses who spoke their mind, a quality he expected from the nobility of Warren. I also discovered he truly embodied the motto of Datten. Honor above all. So much in my life is thanks to him: my father's happiness while I was gone, my husband and, by extension, our future children, and even my life. He tried to protect me from my grandfather, helped me learn how to deal with the loss of men in battle, and saved my life. King Emmerich was all that Datten asks for in a king. He will be missed, but the legacy he left behind will be here for years to come."

Emmerich crossed his arms and winked at Alex as she made her way back down to her seat.

As the funeral ended, Aaron invited everyone back to the castle for a feast in honor of their fallen king. Edward escorted Guinevere in the procession from the hall to the castle. Alex squeezed Aaron's arm as they walked between their parents and Emmerich's casket.

"It's okay," Aaron said when Alex exhaled loudly for what felt like the hundredth time. "We need to get through the meal and then the ceremonial carrying of the king to the crypt."

Alex's eyes darted across the expansive tournament field where tables had been set up. She was scared to think of what might happen if sorcerers suddenly showed up. "Why did we have to have the meal here?"

"I know you're anxious after we were attacked at the Warren tournament, but this was my father's wish, and you inspired it. Edward had to convince my mother to break with tradition, but now, all the knights, nobility, and common people can attend together. My father wanted to ensure that anyone who wanted to attend could."

The sentiment was lovely, but Alex didn't feel any better. The midday sun illuminated the tournament field. It was decorated as if an actual tournament were taking place. Bonfires surrounded the area to help keep off some of the late fall chill. Aaron went to join his mother in greeting the guests, but Alex turned around and went to find someone else who understood sorcerer intuition.

Alex weaved through rows of wooden tables piled high with food. Each table had two barrels of ale, one at each end. Over a dozen boars were spinning on spits, and the tables were laden with even more roasted venison. Beside them were countless gold bowls overflowing with potatoes, beets, carrots, turnips, and a few vegetables that Alex couldn't identify. She snatched a roll from the closest of the three bread tables and headed away from the main crowd, trying to sense where the other sorcerers were hiding.

When she finally spotted them, she waved, and they came toward her. Suddenly, all the hair on her arms and neck rose at once. She froze in place as the wind felt heavier around her. Alex locked eyes with Gryphon, and the moment she blinked, he was beside her.

"What is that?" Alex asked. Her voice came out in a wheeze.

"What exactly do you feel?" Gryphon replied.

Alex turned back toward the field and found Michael and Stefan marching toward her. She swallowed hard and turned back to Gryphon. "The air shifted. Didn't you feel it?"

"No."

"The air feels heavy, like before a storm."

"It's magic." Gryphon's eyes grew wide. He closed his eyes, and when he opened them, they shone with blue light. "Someone powerful is here."

Panic rushed through Alex, sending her chest heaving.

"Stay calm. If you get worked up, you'll struggle to control your powers. The last thing we need is hail."

"How did you know about that? Stefan?"

"Lynx. But I assume your Little Wafner told her. I've noticed those two seem to be getting close." Gryphon nodded to Stefan and Michael.

"What's wrong?" Michael asked.

"We saw your panic from across the field," Stefan said.

"The air isn't right."

They looked at Gryphon. "I don't feel it, but that doesn't mean she's wrong. Cassandras are more perceptive."

Michael took her hand and squeezed it. Alex exhaled slowly and felt her heart slow down. Like Aaron, Michael excelled at calming her down. But during their brief conversation, she'd lost track of her father and Aaron.

The three men around her sensed her fear.

"Alex?" Stefan asked.

"I can't find Aaron or my father."

"We'll find them. Don't panic," Gryphon said.

Before she could reply, the ground rumbled beneath their feet. Alex spun toward the castle and protective walls. Her eyes shifted to the cobblestone roads that took people from the castle into town.

The stones were hopping in their spots.

Gryphon noticed it too. "This is bad. Get everyone inside."

"Michael, stay with Alex. I'll get the knights," Stefan ordered.

Gryphon nodded and dropped to his knees. His hands erupted in a bright orange glow as he slammed them on the ground. The rumbling stopped, and Alex picked up her skirts and ran across the field with Michael at her side.

When they reached the crowd, she turned to Michael. "Find Aaron and my father. Tell them what's happening." Michael bolted through the gathering. Despite everything, the guests were loudly talking over one another about what this could mean. She stopped and shouted at them. "People of Datten, hear your queen. Everyone, go inside the castle walls. Run and don't stop. Knights, guards! Help the women and children, *now!*"

No one seemed to hear Alex. They continued chatting. The few who noticed her nodded politely and went back to what they had been doing.

"I said, *run!*" Alex screamed as the ground rumbled again. Before anyone could move, a mound of dirt rose from the ground behind her. As she turned, she came face-to-face with the brown-skinned, brown-haired sorcerer who had impersonated Aaron during the attack on Betruger Castle.

# CHAPTER 23
# ALEX

"Hello, little witch. Sorry I'm late for the celebration." Ridge's brown eyes fixed on Alex as he smoothed out his brown titan's robe. A pair of mountains were stitched on the chest and matched the single line mark on his neck. He leaped from the mound and stalked toward her. "Where are your friends?"

She threw a gust of wind at him, but all it did was move his hair.

"Wind cannot move stone." He strode closer, smirking. Vines burst out of the ground and slithered up his muscular thighs. He looked to the side, where Lynx stood in her green Tiere robe.

"Leave before you make Gryphon angry, Ridge!" Lynx growled.

Ridge sneered at Lynx. "You reek of mortals."

"I'd rather live with them than spend another day with a brainless pet of Garrick's."

Ridge snorted and spun his wrist so fast Alex barely saw it. The earth beneath Lynx vanished, and she dropped into a hole that immediately filled in, leaving only her head exposed.

The people behind Alex finally dashed toward the castle. Ridge glanced at them, but his attention quickly returned to Alex, making her tense up.

"I wasn't sent here for them."

A sorceress wearing a golden robe appeared beside Ridge, clapping her hands and cackling. "Ah! I see you finally got Lynx under your control." The hatred in her eyes made Alex stiffen. "So, this child is supposed to be my replacement?" She moved her light brown hair off her shoulder and fixed her emerald green eyes on Alex. *The same green as Megesti and me. You're a Cassandra.* An explosion freed Lynx, and Gryphon planted himself in front of Alex.

His voice shouted into Alex's mind. *Don't argue with me, just stay behind me.* Alex took a step behind him.

Ridge glared at the green-eyed sorceress. "Penelope, this is *my* job."

"Garrick wanted me to keep you in line. He's worried your attraction to Lynx might sway you."

"She reeks of some mortal male. Imagine degrading yourself enough to fornicate with one of them. You might as well take an animal for a lover."

Lynx hissed at them as she came to Alex and Gryphon's side.

Penelope snickered. "She probably has, in her feline form."

"Get out of my kingdom!" Alex shouted, moving beside Gryphon.

"Well, at least the child can speak," Penelope said.

"You can leave now of your own choice, or I can make you," Gryphon growled at them.

"Who should we listen to, Penelope? Our current Head, or his pup?" Ridge asked. He snapped his fingers, summoning a staff. He slammed it into the ground, sending an earthquake rushing away from them like ripples on a pond.

Alex spun to see the towers of the castle wobble. She turned back to the field, and it seemed everyone had finally realized something unnatural was happening. Guests were fleeing in every direction. Alex desperately searched for Aaron, Michael, Stefan—any of her loved ones, but there was too much chaos. She cracked whatever groups of people she could focus on to the castle until the ground beneath her shifted, sending her sprawling.

Gryphon roared and lunged for Ridge, leaving Penelope to Alex and Lynx. Penelope stalked toward them with a small ball of fire in her hand. Lynx shrieked into the sky, and a flock of birds appeared out of nowhere and attacked. Penelope screamed and tried to fight them off as Lynx leaped to Alex's side and pulled her up.

Out of the corner of her eye, Alex saw Ridge moving toward her, but Gryphon punched him in the face. Ridge's staff flew from his hand, making the earthquake worse. They all lost their footing and slammed into the ground. Alex wiped the blood from her chin as she clambered to her feet and cracked another group of guests into the castle. With so many of the guests safe, Alex could finally recognize the people who were left. She saw several of her knights heading to safety. Generals Nial and Wafner were escorting Guinevere, Edward, her ladies, and several royals from the southern kingdoms. Aaron was on the far side of the field with Michael, Macht, and Harold. They were helping people into one of the escape tunnels. Stefan and Kharon were directing people near the castle gates.

*Where's Megesti?* Alex searched for him in vain, and an icy wind announced Daniel's arrival beside her.

"Where's Megesti?" she asked.

He pointed to the edge of the Dark Forest, where it met the training field.

Alex checked behind her. Lynx and Gryphon were keeping Ridge and Penelope at bay. *This was too easy.* Alex cracked to the edge of the woods where Daniel had pointed and ran into the forest. Her large skirt slowed her down, and branches scratched and ripped at her dress and skin, but she ran harder and harder until she heard voices.

Alex pushed herself one last time and broke through the foliage into a clearing. Megesti was unconscious and slung over the shoulder of a tall, dark-haired sorcerer, and beside him was Gryphon's mother, Imelda. She limped slightly, clearly favoring her right side. The sorceress sniffed the air. Her blue eyes flashed dark green, and she howled.

*How is she still alive?* Alex was moving toward them when snarls came from all around and two gargantuan wolves padded toward her.

Imelda narrowed her eyes at Alex as if she'd heard her thoughts. "Strong sorcerers can live two weeks after a red steel wound. I'm very much dying, you little witch, which is why I came to get my revenge. But it seems someone beat me to it."

"Beat you to what?" Alex asked as the first wolf snapped its jaws at her.

"You took my son from me, so I came to take yours. But as you're no longer with child, someone beat me to it." Imelda sniffed the air. "Very recently."

Alex bit back the pain and rage that flooded her heart. *Don't let your emotions take over. Focus.*

"So rather than leave empty-handed, I took the last link to your mother. How surprising to find out he's our current Usurper. It seems my sister's been keeping secrets."

"Usurper or not, he's useless," a male voice said.

*No.*

"Hello, cousin."

Lygari turned around to face Alex, and her heart leaped into her throat.

"Lygari? How? I banished you."

Imelda laughed. "Banishing a sorcerer doesn't get rid of them forever, little Heart. It merely removes them from *you*. Didn't

Gryphon tell you? Lygari found his way to us months ago. He's been most helpful in figuring out all your secrets." She stepped so close to Alex that she could touch her, but the wolves snarled, and Alex stood still. "We know all about that little castle you hide in, and where Datten and Warren are weakest … we know everything."

Alex gulped but wouldn't back down. Emmerich's advice filled her heart, and she stood taller. "I never took your son from you. You chased him away."

Imelda slapped Alex so hard she bit her cheek, drawing blood.

"You know nothing of my son, witch. For half a century, Gryphon stood at our side, the perfect Ares son, the next Head. He was ruthless and took whatever he wanted without concern for anyone else. But then *you* arrived. You summoned him and ruined everything. Sticking your nose where it doesn't belong. Just like your mother." Imelda's icy blue eyes bore into Alex's soul.

Alex threw her hands forward and sent a gale force wind at Imelda and her wolves. She tried to crack Megesti away, but her cracking powers weren't working.

"Gryphon!" she shouted. "Gryphon, I need you!"

Penelope and Ridge cracked beside Imelda as Gryphon arrived at Alex's side.

"They have Megesti!" Alex cried.

*We'll get him back. I promise.*

Gryphon flicked his hands, and fire erupted out of his palms. The flames snaked their way up his arms. Penelope hid behind a tree while Ridge and Imelda moved to shield Lygari as he ran.

"Don't hurt Megesti!" Alex shouted as Gryphon grew fireballs in each hand.

Alex chased after Lygari, but Ridge must have spotted her because the ground shook again. Alex jumped at the last moment, escaping most of the tremors, but Lygari faltered and almost dropped Megesti. Gryphon was preoccupied fighting his mother and Ridge. Fire and rocks flew back and forth between them. She was on her own.

Stefan's lessons from the forest came to her. *Use what you have around you. A rock, stick, even a snake can be a weapon in the right hands.* Alex sprinted toward Lygari. A fallen tree blocked their path. He ran around it, but Alex leaped over it, tearing her skirt on a branch as she pressed onward. Ahead, Lygari reached the riverbank. It was an offshoot of the Darren River that brought water to the castle moat and surrounding towns. It flowed quickly and was too wide to jump across, so Alex caught him.

"Let him go, Lygari," Alex barked. Her legs and lungs burned from chasing him through the woods in her stupid dress, and she felt her grasp on her powers slipping.

"No. Once he's dead, I'll be Titan of Merlin." Lygari backed toward the rushing river behind him.

"No, you wouldn't—I would," Alex said.

"Merlin is a male line. I'd be the last male."

"Except *I'm* the Heart. I have more powers than all the males in our line put together. It would pass to me."

Lygari cursed at her, but Alex brought her vines up to hold his legs in place. Lygari struggled against them, trying to burn them off and keep hold of Megesti.

A deep growl came from behind Alex, and she ripped the lid off her well. Power rushed through her as Gryphon joined her. He was glowing orange and glaring at Lygari.

"How are you enjoying second place, Gryphon?" Lygari struggled against the vines.

Gryphon smirked as he moved closer. "Let Megesti go, and I might not kill you." His voice was so calm Alex trembled in fear.

"That doesn't work for me." Lygari's legs burst into flames, burning away the vines. "I value my life too much." He shifted his stance, and Megesti slid off his shoulder and tumbled down the riverbank.

"No!" Alex dashed to the edge in time to watch Megesti land in the raging water and sink. Without hesitation, Alex leaped in after him. She couldn't risk her powers hurting him in her terrified state and knew she didn't have much time. Downstream were the rapids that joined a river. Half would carry on into the Dark Forest, and the smaller stream would feed the castle moat and provide water to Datten's well in town.

The water was freezing, and Alex fought her body's instinct to panic like it had when she fell into the icy river as a child. The river was deeper here than it had been by the camp, and the weight of her soaked dress quickly pulled her to the bottom. It took her a moment to get oriented in the murky water, but she managed to fight to the surface. She surfaced and saw that Megesti was being pulled downstream. She caught up with him before the rapids.

With one arm clamped beneath Megesti's armpit, Alex kicked off the riverbed and pushed them to the surface of the water. She gasped to fill her lungs and coughed as the water splashed in her face, filling her mouth and nose.

"Alex!"

Gryphon and Lynx were on the riverbank, shouting at her. Lygari was nowhere to be seen.

"I can't ... crack," Alex shouted.

Gryphon reached for her as her dress pulled them down. The next thing she knew, her legs gave out from under the weight of her soaked dress, and she hit the grass. Megesti lay on the ground beside her. Gryphon had cracked them both to safety, but Megesti was barely breathing. Alex put her hand on his chest and let her healing powers do their work. Gold light left her and filled Megesti. When the light returned to her, his breaths were loud enough for them to hear.

"Gryphon, take him to Birch and Aaron. I have to find Lygari."

"Lynx can do it. I'll stay with you."

"No," Alex said. "Birch is his family. You take him back to her. Lynx can stay with me."

"Alex—"

"Gryphon! You could have brought him and been back already," Lynx said. "I know it goes against your nature, but stop being difficult."

Gryphon stiffened and did what Alex asked of him.

# CHAPTER 24
# GRYPHON

Gryphon arrived in the Datten courtyard with Megesti's arm over his shoulders, practically dragging him along. The guests were gone, but the yard was full of knights in Datten armor being ordered around by General Wafner and another older man.

"Birch! Little Wafner! Princeling!" Gryphon shouted over the noise.

Birch rushed to him, followed by Stefan.

"What happened?" Birch asked. She cupped Megesti's face with her hands. He groaned and opened his eyes a slit before closing them again.

"Where's Alex?" Stefan asked as he moved to support Megesti's free arm.

"With Lynx, in the woods," Gryphon said.

"Why are you not with Alex?" Aaron bellowed. The rage in his voice reminded Gryphon of the Aaron the curse brought out.

"Because I don't answer to *you*. She begged me to bring her cousin here, and unlike you, I actually listen to her." Gryphon took

Megesti's arm and slung it around Aaron's shoulders. It jostled Megesti enough that he let out a low moan.

"What happened to him?" Aaron asked.

"Lygari and my mother happened." Gryphon tried to crack, but nothing happened. Surprised, he tried again. His eyes widened with panic as he turned to Birch. "Can you crack?"

She tried and shook her head.

"What do you mean, you can't crack?" Stefan asked.

"It means someone, most likely my mother, put a spell on the castle so we can't leave. I could leave the forest but can't leave here."

"It's a trap. I'll take the knights and we'll bring Alex back," Aaron said.

Birch pursed her lips. "I'm sorry, King Aaron, but if sorcerers can't leave, mortals certainly won't be able to."

"So we're supposed to leave her out there defenseless?" Aaron snapped.

"Alex is never defenseless," Stefan said, glaring at Aaron across Megesti's sagging head.

"Who is out there with them?" Birch asked, turning to Gryphon.

"Ridge, Penelope, my mother, and Lygari."

Birch sucked in her breath. "That's a lot of powerful magic."

"I know," Gryphon grumbled.

"You know what you have to do," Birch said, and Gryphon nodded.

"What does that mean?" Aaron asked.

"The only way to break out of here is to let my Ares and Tiere sides take control."

"*That* doesn't sound good," Stefan said.

"It'll be fine," Birch said, squeezing Gryphon's shoulder. "Lynx and I are here, and combined with Megesti and Alexandria, I'm sure we'll get you under control afterward."

*The Celtics titan, an unconscious Usurper, and a drained Heart. Why do I feel like this is a terrible idea?*

Gryphon shook his hands, beckoning his fire. The familiar orange glow washed over him. "You're going to want to get away from me."

"Why? Is your *temper* going to explode?" Aaron mocked.

"Something like that," Gryphon grumbled.

Aaron and Stefan stepped back, carrying Megesti with them.

"Be careful, Sprout," Birch said as she ushered the mortals further back.

Gryphon closed his eyes and thought of the one thing that infuriated him more than anything else: Alex at Moorloc's castle. He thought of the terror on her face when Kruft had come to the beach, and that day she'd finally broken and tried to end her life. He tapped into that rage, released his well, and all of his Ares power flooded into him. Chaos and rage engulfed him, and his fire grew into a swirling inferno.

"What is happening?" Stefan asked.

"Gryphon's going to break out of here. We need to move back," Birch answered. "You're about to learn why Tiere sorcerers don't name their children after mythical beasts."

Pain ripped through his limbs as a roar erupted from his lungs. The flames burned away his skin and replaced it with fur and feathers. Thick golden fur coated his rear and legs, and feathers burst out of him from the waist up. Talons ripped through his fingers, and claws broke through his toes. He dropped onto four legs and eyed the mortals before him with eyesight so perfect he could see the pores on their cowardly faces. The stench of fear was all around him. He snapped his beak at them to remind them what he was capable of. Stretching out his monstrous wings, he cracked his neck to the side and roared again as he took to the sky.

# CHAPTER 25
# ALEX

"Come out, little witch. We won't hurt you ... *much*," Ridge cackled.

Alex had lost Lynx when they ran, and now she hid behind a tree, trying to catch her breath. She still couldn't crack, and Gryphon hadn't returned. Her mouth tasted like blood, and her arm throbbed where Ridge had struck her with a rock. Closing her eyes, Alex bit her lip to hold back the whimper that was trying to escape. A branch snapped. Instinctively, Alex dropped to the ground, and the tree burst into flames.

"Found you," Lygari laughed as he and Ridge moved in on her.

Panting, Alex pushed herself off the ground to run, but vines burst up and dragged the sorcerers to the ground. Lynx appeared from the trees behind her.

"Are you all right, Alex?"

Alex nodded, letting out a gasp of relief and grabbing Lynx's hand.

"You're too drained to fight. We have to run," Lynx said.

"Can't you crack us?" Alex asked as they ran through the woods toward the castle.

"It isn't working," Lynx said.

"Is that why Gryphon didn't come back?"

"He'd never leave us. This reeks of his mother."

They made it out of the trees onto the training field before the earth shook again.

"Little witch, exactly like your mother, sacrificing yourself for your family." Imelda stepped toward them while Ridge and Lygari flanked her.

Lynx pushed Alex behind her and growled.

Imelda lifted her head and howled into the air, and in seconds the wolves returned, stalking toward them.

Lynx stood her ground. "You won't hurt Alex. We haven't had a sorceress Heart in millennia."

"Of course not. The wolves are for you, Lynx. I intend to bring our Heart home to the Forbidden Lands, where she belongs. Once she's there, my son will follow." Imelda's gaze was fixed on Alex. "Typical sorcerer, following his cock instead of his head."

A wolf snarled at them, and as it jumped, Lynx transformed and attacked it in her animal form. The other wolf leaped at her and sank its teeth into her back. Lynx howled. Terror flooded Alex, and winds erupted out from her. Alex took advantage of the distraction. Her temper gushed inside her as she flicked her wrist at the trees behind Lynx. The roots erupted from the ground, untwisting and striking at the wolves like enraged cobras.

When the largest root snapped one wolf's neck, Imelda shrieked in anger. She cracked directly in front of Alex and struck her, sending Alex to the ground. Alex lost her focus, and the roots released the second wolf. "Stupid witchling. You will not defeat me again!" Imelda shouted.

*Again?* Alex pushed away and caught sight of Lynx, still bleeding but doggedly fighting the wolf. When Imelda raised her arms to strike her again, the sleeves of her robe fell back, revealing a large scar on her left arm. Its shape was burned into her memory from long ago. *The wolf at the camp when my powers came in. If I beat you then ...* Alex did her best to look scared, but as soon as the sorceress was back in range, Alex kicked her in the knee. Imelda lunged forward, and Alex scrambled to her feet and used the surrounding wind to throw her back.

Ridge slammed his fist into the ground, and Alex stumbled.

*I hate Mire powers. Stefan and Jerome need to help me work on my balance.*

Lygari cracked in front of her, holding a blade that she hadn't noticed before.

"I'm going to enjoy making you suffer for what you did to my father."

"Why get revenge on behalf of someone you hated?"

"Because it's fun."

"You're as psychotic as he was."

"Runs in our family, *Princess*." Lygari thrust out his sword and sliced open her shoulder.

Alex screamed and retreated from him. She was struggling to summon her fire when a colossal explosion echoed from the castle and lightning shot up from the ground. The sorcerers all startled and looked at the sky. Penelope muttered something and vanished. Ridge cursed under his breath, and Lygari looked at Imelda. She went red with rage and rushed at Alex and Lynx.

Throwing her wind, Alex held Imelda at bay until a gust from above knocked Alex back. A giant, winged beast slammed into the ground between them, making the earth shake and sending rocks flying up all around them. It stood twice her height, and the roar that it released was so loud Alex had to cover her ears. The beast crouched and stalked Lygari, Ridge, and Imelda, keeping them away from her. Alex removed her hands from her ears. Under the claws, fur, and feathers, the beast was a solid mass of muscle that looked like it could crush or shred her with one swipe. The family books said that gryphons were large, but Alex hadn't realized *how* large. Despite everything she'd survived, she wet herself when the creature roared again, this time so loudly it made Alex's teeth rattle. Her legs stung as if cut, and the monster's tail swished against her leg. At the end of the tail was a ridiculous-looking, fluffy tuft of fur.

*Why? It's almost as if it's there for fun. No, it can't be!*

Alex stepped back to avoid the tail slapping her again and realized who was standing before her. She tripped over the body of the wolf she'd killed and fell backward onto her rear. Lynx had finished off the other wolf and transformed back into her human form. Despite being completely naked, she rushed to Alex's side and put pressure on her shoulder to stop the bleeding. Alex struggled to her feet and grabbed Lynx.

"Is that ... ?" Alex asked.

Lynx nodded.

Gryphon roared at his mother, and she howled back as though they could understand each other. Imelda smirked, and a moment later, she howled in Alex's direction.

"Makes a magnificent beast, doesn't he?" Imelda chuckled. "Careful, though—the longer he stays that way, the more his animal instincts kick in. Wait long enough and you'll never get him back."

Alex heard a crack behind her. *Lygari.* She spun, dodging the first ball of fire he threw at her. She stopped the second with a shield of water.

Her cousin's face went red with rage. But being so close to Gryphon, she felt his Ares powers entwining with her own and strengthening them both. When she felt full of their combined power, she attacked Lygari. He moved to dodge her, but she spun and punched him in the face. His head snapped to the side, sending blood flying from his nose.

"That was for trying to hurt Megesti," Alex spat. She punched him in the gut. "That is for ruining Emmerich's burial celebration. And this, this is for Arthur." Alex kneed him in the balls, and Lygari dropped to the ground like a stone.

There was a snarl behind her. Alex turned around, and everything went dark.

# CHAPTER 26
# GRYPHON

His blood burned with excruciating pain. Never in his life had he felt such pain from his own powers. It took everything in him to harness the Ares and Tiere powers rushing through him and lock them away in his well. Now, another ache he knew too well radiated down his back and legs. Every time he shifted back from his animal form, it hurt. Lynx told him it would lessen if he did it more often, but it took all of his power to control his gryphon's animalistic nature. He feared losing control. It was usually bloody.

Lynx knelt beside Alex, trying to wake her. When it had become clear his mother would lose, she'd unleashed her well and exploded a good portion of the field, sending rocks and wood everywhere and leaving a gaping crater on the training field. Alex had been struck by the debris and knocked out cold. *I let her get hurt. I wasn't watching her.*

"Her heartbeat's strong," Lynx said, standing up, "and the bleeding stopped."

Gryphon crossed his arms and tried to calm his rage.

Lynx rubbed his shoulder. "It wasn't your fault."

"Tell that to Aaron. He's going to blame me."

"I will. He likes me." Lynx examined the cut on Gryphon's shoulder. "Though I do suggest you put on some pants before you bring her back. Being nude would send the wrong message."

"Says the sorceress strutting around a field naked."

"I'm not naked," Lynx protested. "I'm clearly covered in blood." She grinned before she summoned extra clothes from her room and held out an outfit to Gryphon.

"Do I even want to know who these belong to?" he asked, accepting the clothes and putting them on.

"Just the mortal I've been pursuing."

"*The* mortal? Only one? I'm surprised at you, Lynx."

"They don't seem to enjoy sharing the way that we do." She walked over to the bloody corpse on the opposite side of the crater.

Finally dressed, Gryphon joined Lynx, who was standing over his mother's lifeless body. "Thank you, Lynx."

She rubbed his good shoulder. "I know you would have done it to protect your Heart, but I couldn't let you. Besides, I did it out of mercy. No one should have to suffer through red steel."

Gryphon felt conflicted looking at his mother. Imelda's cold blue eyes stared up at him, and her skin was covered in blood. Her entire throat was gone. Lynx had finished her off in animal form, and the blood now coating her body was Imelda's. *A mercy killing befitting a Titan of Tiere.*

"Goodbye, Mother," Gryphon whispered. He held his hand over her heart and cracked her deep into the woods of the Tiere territory in the Forbidden Lands. Exhaling, he turned back to Alex, who had passed out from the blast.

His mother's last words to him echoed through his head. *She'll choose him. She always will, unless you get rid of him. You're exactly like me, Gryphon. You'd do anything to get the sorceress you want, just as I did everything I had to in order to get your father.* He shook his head to silence her words, but they wormed into his heart. He kneeled down and picked up Alex, then sniffed.

"What's wrong?" Lynx asked.

"I frightened her."

Lynx glared at him. "You've never seen yourself in your animal form. You aren't exactly cuddly."

Gryphon chuckled and cracked him and Alex into Alex's bedroom. The room was chilly, so he laid her on the bed and waved his hand to light the fireplace. He paced the room and waited until the door flew open and Lynx arrived with Aaron.

"Alex!" Aaron rushed to her side and stopped, staring at her face.

"Only the blood on her cheek and shoulder is hers," Gryphon said before Aaron could ask. "The rest of it is from when she beat Lygari to a pulp."

Aaron turned to Gryphon, his eyes wide with fear. "Lygari was here?"

Gryphon barely nodded. "They know everything. My mother confirmed it."

"What happened?" Aaron sat on the bed and took Alex's hand.

"She fought bravely," Lynx said. "But she was hit in the head by a rock when Imelda realized she'd lose. Ares sorcerers are known for their violent tempers." She glared at Gryphon.

"And I scared her when I arrived in my other form."

"She usually tries to hide it when she's scared. How could you tell?" Aaron asked. He moved her head to examine the bump behind her ear along the hairline.

"The urine." Gryphon smirked as Lynx elbowed him. "Ow."

"I'm pretty sure she doesn't need the entire world knowing that," said Lynx.

"How is her princeling the entire world?" Gryphon snarled at Lynx.

Aaron groaned and pinched the bridge of his nose. "You two

are as bad as Alex and Stefan." He turned toward Lynx. "Will she be all right?"

"Considering how fast she heals, I suspect she'll recover by the morning," Lynx said.

"You'll want to get her out of that dirty dress," Gryphon added. "And probably burn it."

"Was anyone killed?" Aaron asked. The tone in his voice made Lynx swallow hard enough that Gryphon heard.

"My mother," Gryphon replied.

Aaron's face went white. "Did Alex—?"

"No!" Lynx spoke up and moved toward Aaron and Alex. "I did it. Your father wounded her with red steel. It's one of the most painful ways we can die, especially if you delay the effects until the end. She deserved to die for what she'd done, but she was my mentor. I couldn't let her go through that."

"The others got away, but at least we know why they're coming after Alex," Gryphon said.

"Is it her power?" Aaron asked.

"Because of me. My parents believe if they bring her to the Forbidden Lands, I'll return. Then they can turn her to their side and use her as leverage to control me."

Aaron stood and marched to Gryphon with his fist clenched, then shoved his shoulder. "You were supposed to stay with her."

"Me?" Gryphon growled. "Where were her guards? I had to turn into a gryphon to break the spell my mother put on your ferflucsing castle."

"I don't care if you turned into a pumpkin!"

"She ordered me to leave. To bring Megesti to safety."

"You don't get to make that choice," Aaron shouted at Gryphon.

"Your Royal Highness?" Michael appeared at the door.

"GET OUT!" Gryphon and Aaron both shouted. Gryphon threw

his hand toward the door. It slammed shut, barely missing Michael's face.

"I *didn't* make that choice. Alex did!" Gryphon said. "She told me I had to get Megesti to safety because he's the only link to her mother she has left. That's why they went after him."

"What is the point of having you around if you abandon her and she gets hurt because of it?" Aaron's words shot out like daggers at Gryphon.

"I didn't abandon her," Gryphon growled back at him. "I listened to her. She is *my* Heart. You have no idea how much power is in me and how hard it is to use only enough so I don't destroy your entire kingdom. It will be the same for her soon, if it isn't already! So don't shout at me about things you know nothing about."

Lynx frowned and cracked away in a huff.

Aaron pushed Gryphon. "Get out."

"I'm not going anywhere," Gryphon retorted. Aaron's hand went to his blade, and Gryphon laughed. "And what exactly do you think you're going to do with that?" Gryphon mocked. "You know she'd never forgive you if you hurt me. Especially after you promised to change and be a better man." Gryphon leaned down until their faces were inches apart. "I get her for centuries. You have a few decades. Do you really want to risk that for some petty, jealous revenge? Besides, I promised her I'd teach her how to manage her powers. If I'm dead, I can't do that."

There was another soft knock on the door.

"What, Michael?" Aaron shouted.

The door opened, and Stefan stormed in, followed by Michael and Lynx.

"Is she all right?" Michael's voice was soft.

Stefan went to examine the bump on her head. "She's had worse. This isn't even as bad as the time she pushed you out of the tree and then fell after you."

Michael nodded. "Not as bad as my injuries after that incident? Or hers?"

"Hers. You always got hurt worse," Stefan said. He moved Alex's hair out of her face and then exchanged a look with Lynx before turning back to Gryphon. "Thank you, Gryphon. I spotted her across the field but couldn't get to her. I feel like this is my fault."

"She'll be fine," Gryphon said. "Assuming you get her out of that dress." He turned to Michael and Stefan before they could ask. "It's not her blood. But the urine ... let's just say my beast is scary."

Michael snorted. "She is going to freeze you for telling us that."

"Gryphon?" Stefan asked.

"Yes, Stefan?"

"Why are you wearing my clothes?"

# CHAPTER 27
# AARON

The air was always stale in the royal crypt deep beneath the castle. As in Warren, before each crypt stood a carved stone statue of the royal entombed within. Emmerich's had been carved shortly after Aaron was born. Aaron placed his father's sword in its stone sheath. Harold and Edward moved beside him, while Jerome, Stefan, Michael, and several senior knights of Datten carried his father's casket to the large stone crypt that had been built for him.

Aaron gazed at the statue of his mother, already in place beside his father's. Guinevere had gone to bed and left him and Edward to inter his father. She was exhausted after everything they'd been through in only a few days. Across from them was his brother's crypt, and next to Daniel would be his. *Where will Alex be buried? Will she go back to Warren, be buried here with me, or stay in the Forbidden Lands?*

Edward put his hand on Aaron's shoulder. "I think we should have an ale in Emmerich's honor," he said.

"Agreed," Harold said.

Aaron looked at Gryphon, but the sorcerer spoke before Aaron could. "I'll see how Lynx and Alex are doing."

"See if you can get Lynx to read to her. She'd like that," Michael said.

"Where did you get that idea?" Stefan asked. Michael and Aaron chuckled, remembering how Alex read to Stefan for hours each day when he was unconscious and healing from her attack at Verlassen Castle.

"Anyone who wishes to have an ale in my father's honor is welcome," Aaron said to the knights. They quietly headed to the dining hall.

❧ ❧

DRINKS WENT LATER than Aaron expected. What was going to be a drink or maybe two turned into an hours-long celebration where the men shared their favorite tales of the late king. Aaron refused to be the first to leave, despite his own exhaustion. Early in the morning, after far too much ale, he crept back into his room. Birch and Lynx were standing at Alex's side of the bed, watching her sleep.

"How is she?" Aaron whispered. He could feel the ale clouding his thoughts.

"She'll be fine in the morning." Birch picked a book off the bed and set it on the side table.

Lynx shrugged. "Ares explosions aren't as painful as you'd think. We've all gotten hit by a few of Gryphon's and lived to tell the tale."

"The bump on her head concerned me," Birch said. "But her healing powers took care of it. Come see."

Aaron squeezed between the sorceresses and saw that the large bump on her head was nearly gone. "You'd think I'd be used to her getting into trouble, but I'm not," he whispered. "Every time she puts herself in danger and I don't save her, I feel a piece of me die."

"Love weakens us all by giving us something to lose," Birch said. "I'll check on her in the morning. For now, sleep well, Your Royal Highness."

Birch and Lynx both bowed and left the room. Aaron looked over Alex, checking for any missed wounds, but there didn't seem to be any. He adjusted her blanket and dressed for bed, tossing his dirty clothes on the chest. He paused and tapped at the book on the table. *Torian Legends* was a favorite of Alex's, and Lynx had promised to write out the sorcerer versions for her. Aaron crawled across their enormous bed and lay beside Alex. When he wrapped his arms around her, she turned toward him, moving into the curve of his body and snuggling closer.

He kissed her head and whispered, "You need to be more careful, Your Royal Highness. You're stronger than any woman I've ever met, and my generals, but you aren't invincible. And I need you by my side. I can't be king without you as my queen." He felt her nuzzle into him. He pulled her as close as possible and fell asleep with her in his arms.

❧❧❧ ❧❧❧

A FIRM HAND shook Aaron's shoulder. He groaned and pulled his pillow over his face. His head was throbbing. *Why did I drink so much? Did I lose my tolerance to Datten ale?*

The visitor cleared his throat. "Sorry to disturb you, Your Royal Highness, but there is much to do before the coronation tonight, and Her Majesty is insisting you help since Her Royal Highness has left."

"What?" Aaron pushed himself up so fast his head swam. He had to close his eyes for a moment to let the nausea pass, but when he opened them, Alex's side of the bed was empty. He rubbed the silky fabric with his palm. It was cold.

"Where is she?"

"I'm not sure, King Aaron." Aaron's childhood friend looked clammy and was fidgeting.

"You can relax, Caleb," Aaron said. "I won't scream at you because you don't know where Alex went."

"Good, because then I'd have to scream at *you*," came a voice from the stairs. Jessica crossed her arms and shot Aaron one of the Wafners' stern looks.

Aaron forced himself to stand, and he slapped his cheeks to wake himself up. "How is it that *your* glare is more terrifying than your father's?"

"I've had a lot of practice. Get dressed. Your mother is looking for you, and she will not be happy when she learns you're hungover."

"Do you know where Alex is?" Aaron ran his hand through his hair and went over to his wardrobe.

Jessica hummed as she moved to the bed. "Our queen is in Warren with her father, General Nial, Stefan, Michael, and Gryphon. His Royal Highness wanted to make sure Warren was represented at Alex's coronation today." Jessica paused. "At least, that's what he told everyone. Between us, I think he's trying to give her a break from the gossiping nobles of Datten."

"Can't blame him for that," Caleb said. "It's been a rough few days."

"Edith didn't go with her?" Aaron grinned at Jessica and wiggled his eyebrows.

Jessica smiled. "No. Her father insisted she stay here to entertain King Harold."

"Good. Another royal wedding would take some of the attention off Alex and me. We wouldn't be the newlyweds anymore."

There was a knock at the door. "Enter," Aaron ordered.

It was Lynx. "Good morning, Your Royal Highness." She tried to smile at Aaron but stopped when she spotted Jessica. "Alex wanted you to know that she'll be back in time for the coronation. She had something to attend to in Warren."

"So I heard," Aaron said.

"She felt well after she woke, and after the attack yesterday, she was determined to put the protection spell on Warren. Gryphon refused to let her do it by herself, and Stefan refused to let her go with Gryphon alone."

Aaron chuckled. "And Michael?"

"Michael didn't want to be left out," Jessica replied.

Lynx chuckled. "I'm heading over to help Megesti, Birch, and Kharon try another protection spell on Datten, if you'd care to join us."

"What does that entail?" Jessica asked suspiciously.

"Come and find out."

"Sounds like fun." Aaron threw on a formal shirt over his tunic and beckoned Jessica over. Grabbing their hands, Lynx cracked them out to the courtyard.

# CHAPTER 28
# ALEX

Alex yanked Stefan down the small side hallway, where no one would see or hear them.

"You have a plan, right?"

"Of course I have a plan!" Alex said. "My father and Randal want to bring Michael to the duchess in Datten. But I want to confirm his lineage before we get his hopes up."

"Then lead the way, Your Highness." Stefan motioned for her to leave, but Alex didn't move. "What?"

"I need you to come to the crypt with me. When Ember attacked me, I left something down there."

"What in Torian did you forget there?"

Alex gulped and clenched her fists at her side. "My grandfather's sword." She muttered it so fast while turning to leave that Stefan grabbed her arm and pulled her back.

"If you're going to tell me, then say it."

Stefan could always make her feel like a little sister in trouble. Alex's voice was soft as she said, "I broke into my grandfather's tomb and stole his sword."

Stefan's mouth dropped open, and he stared at her for so long she looked away. Finally recovering, he leaned close. "You mean the one he used to …"

"Yes, that one. But don't tell my father. I need to be the one to tell him, but we haven't had time to talk. The sword is red steel. I have to learn where he got it. Plus, having an extra red steel blade will help."

"Have you given Aaron his sword?"

"Not yet. I wanted to, many times, but it's never the right time," Alex said. Stefan chuckled, and Alex smiled. "I missed big brother Stefan. Head guard Stefan is bossy."

"Well, if you're right about Michael, you'll have to give both of them their new blades to celebrate." They meandered down the large main hallway toward Alex's room to fetch Michael. He'd needed to change after making a mess of himself at breakfast.

"Does it bother Lynx that you carry red steel around?" Alex asked.

"Why would she care?" Stefan asked.

"For the same reason she gave *your* clothes to Gryphon yesterday."

Stefan's face went ashen as he glanced down the hallway before turning to her. "It makes her nervous, so I don't wear my sword around her. What gave us away?"

"Nothing you did," Alex said. She tried and failed to hide the smirk that was spreading across her face.

"I know that look. I don't like that look."

Alex snickered and bolted toward the door to her room, with Stefan hot on her heels. She burst into the room and slammed the door in his face. Michael leaped off the couch where he'd been sitting and hurried to her side.

"Are you all right?" he asked.

"Of course. Why wouldn't I be?" Alex asked, leaning against the door. A second later, a pounding sound started.

"Alex, open this door right now!"

"No!"

Michael crossed his arms and raised his eyebrows at her. "Who started it?"

Alex smirked at Michael. "I called him out on Lynx."

"You didn't! If he admits anything to us before he tells Jessica, she'll be furious," Michael said.

Alex slammed her body into the door and raised her voice. "Admits what? That he already has feelings for her?"

"Don't push him."

"Why not? I distinctly remember being judged for being alone with Aaron when we tried to keep our relationship a secret. At least I never lost my clothes in Aaron's room!"

Stefan stopped banging, and Alex spun around and threw open her door.

"How did you—?"

Alex cocked her head to the side. "I know who she is, Stefan. I was eleven the first time I saw your future wife."

"Did you know I would end up with Jessica?" Michael asked.

"No. Parts of your future were always muddy to me, but Stefan's is as clear as the Oreean Sea." Alex glanced around her room. "Where's Gryphon? I thought he was with you."

"I thought he went with you," Michael said.

"We don't need him for this task," Stefan said. "You brought him for the protection spell, right?"

"I did." Alex swallowed.

"What is it?" Michael asked, rubbing Alex's shoulder and watching her closely.

*Stop that. You can see through too much when you look at me like that.*

"Aw. Did you miss me already?" came a voice from the stairs. The grin that covered Gryphon's face vanished in an instant. "What's wrong?"

"Nothing."

"What were you doing in her bedroom?" Stefan asked, glaring at Gryphon.

"Snooping, and something is clearly wrong if you're making that face."

Alex growled in frustration at the three men and threw her hands in the air. "I need to get my grandfather's sword from the crypt, but I'm scared to go back after Ember attacked me there. Happy?"

"Yes," Stefan said.

"Being honest with us isn't a weakness, Alex," Michael said. "Your father's honest with Randal, Harold is with Macht, and Aaron is with Jerome. It's time you learned what your obligation is to us."

Alex's mouth dropped open. "I don't like it when you get philosophical."

"Of course not." Michael winked. "It only happens when I'm right. Your father has the keys to the crypt, so go get them, please, since we're not supposed to know where his copies are."

Alex scrunched her nose at Gryphon.

"I won't defend you. They're right," he said.

She huffed and stomped up the stairs to fetch the keys.

❧❧❧ ❧❧❧

ALEX HAD DROPPED the sword next to Arthur's crypt. Gryphon refused to even go near it, so Stefan tucked it in his belt beside his own. With the first mission accomplished, Alex took out the keys and led them into the oldest crypt.

The torches sprang to life, and Gryphon asked, "Why is the older one less creepy?"

"Because these ghosts are at peace and don't have malicious intent," Alex replied.

"Wait, how many ghosts do you see when you come down here?" Michael asked.

"Most of them. I've only seen my grandmother twice. My grandfather, however, I see far too often. He stalks the castle."

"Is it because you desecrated his grave?" Stefan asked.

"No. Though he is bitter about being buried so close to my mother."

"I could fix that." Gryphon smirked.

Alex snorted despite herself. Stefan raised his eyebrow at her, but she noticed the slight curl at the edge of his lips.

"No one would notice if his body vanished." Gryphon strolled ahead of them and walked to the end of the path, running his fingers along the wall.

With Michael ahead of them and out of earshot, Alex grabbed Stefan's arm.

"What?" he whispered.

"Tell Michael the trick for the door. If I open it, we won't know."

"As far as your plans go, this is great."

"Edith suggested it," Alex reminded him and scurried after the others.

"Where's the door?" Michael asked.

"You have to make it appear," Alex said, handing him the keys. "It's enchanted."

Gryphon leaned against the icy wall. "For a kingdom that supposedly hated sorcerers in the past, you have an awful lot of enchanted things."

Alex stuck out her tongue at him.

*Careful, Princess. One of these times, I might do something with that tongue you keep pointing at me.*

A wave of heat surged within her, and she shot Gryphon an angry look. He winked at her.

*Oh, good. I was worried I couldn't embarrass you anymore.*

*Catch your tongue, Sunset.*

*You're welcome to make me.*

"It's actually simple," Stefan said to Michael. He hadn't noticed the interaction between Alex and Gryphon. Alex breathed slowly, trying to banish the red from her cheeks. A burst of heat hit her back, and a tingle ran up her spine.

"Stop it," she muttered through clenched teeth.

"Spoilsport," Gryphon said.

Michael was looking at the patch of wall. "So I prick my finger and say the spell? But how will the spell know that I'm friend and not foe?"

"Because I'm here," Alex said from behind them.

Michael shrugged. He pulled his sword far enough out of the hilt to cut himself on the blade. Then he pressed his finger against the wall. "Nial the brave. Veremund the wise. Warren the true."

Alex held her breath, waiting for what felt like an eternity, but nothing happened. Finally, Michael pulled his finger off the wall, and the wall moved. Alex sucked in a breath. The door appeared with a click.

Michael turned to Alex and Stefan, but his smile faded when he saw their expressions. "Alex?"

She ran up to him, threw her arms around his neck, and burst into tears. He caught her. "Clearly I've missed something. Would someone enlighten me?"

"She was right, as usual," Stefan said.

"About what?" Gryphon asked.

"Alex figured out who Michael's family was," Stefan continued. "Only a blood descendant from one of the three founding families of Warren can summon that door."

Michael gulped so hard Alex felt it as he held her tighter. He trembled slightly. "Is that true?" he asked Alex.

"Yes."

"So, you don't need to get into the treasure room?"

"I couldn't get your hopes up and be wrong. But now we know and can get you your title."

"Title?"

Stefan held out his hands to calm Michael's panic. "It's okay, Michael."

"Your name is Percival Veremund," Alex said. "Matthias Veremund was an earl on my father's council, which means that as his son, you're now an earl."

Alex felt Michael stumble, but Stefan rushed over and caught him as he released Alex. "Weren't the Veremunds killed?"

"They were," Alex whispered. "They sent you away to keep you safe. My grandfather found out and sent Kruft to get rid of you, but he obviously failed. That's what brought you to me."

Michael put his hands on his forehead and exhaled. "I wasn't abandoned?"

Alex shook her head. "No, Michael. You were loved so much that your parents disguised you as a poor boy and tried to send you to Datten."

"And you have *family*, Michael. A grandmother in Datten, and a pair of distant cousins," Stefan said. His voice was reassuring.

"Oh, no. What if they're worse than the Rassgats?"

Alex snickered.

"What?" Gryphon asked.

Michael looked to be on the verge of hyperventilating. Alex took his hands and squeezed them.

"I'm named after my grandmother—Elizabeth Veremund. My father and I are your distant cousins, Michael."

"So I wasn't abandoned, and now I'm a blood relation to one best friend and brother-in-law to the other."

"Yes," Alex said.

"And you're an earl!" Stefan said.

"That's not important," Michael said.

"It is in Warren," Alex said. "You belong to one of the three founding families. You'll have duties, an estate, money—"

"Duties? They'd better involve being your guard because I'm not leaving you." Michael backed away from Alex.

"Do you need to sit down?" Gryphon asked.

"Who else knows?" Michael asked.

"Edith, Randal, and my father. I haven't even told Aaron. I didn't want to until we knew for sure."

Michael exhaled a few times and composed himself. He smiled at Alex and kissed the top of her head. "I need to process this, but I couldn't be more excited to have you and your father be part of my family."

"You're stuck with both of them now," Gryphon said.

"It explains the connection you and Alex had from the start. Can't your line sense kin?" Stefan asked.

Alex nodded and hugged Michael tighter. "We won't say anything to anyone until you've told Jessica and Jerome."

"Thank you. Now if you didn't actually need to go into the treasure room, can we go? It's creepy in here."

Alex tried to look innocent, but Michael laughed and shook his head. "My father has your inheritance in there, but it would be too much for us to carry."

Gryphon piped up. "In that case, shall we head to the beach to try the protection spell, Princess?"

# CHAPTER 29
# AARON

Harold, Edith, and Jessica joined Aaron in the courtyard of the Datten castle. Megesti and Birch stood near the center of the courtyard, crowding around a book of spells. Lynx and Kharon were close by, talking among themselves, but they were too far for Aaron to hear, so he moved closer.

Birch finally closed the book. "Are you all ready?" she asked, loudly enough for Aaron and the other mortals to hear. "We'll need to concentrate and really help Megesti. The last spell didn't take hold properly, which is why Imelda was able to trap us all in here. This time, Megesti and I will try a spell from Merlock's family. The Cassandra line created it, so he will have to perform it, but he should be able to draw strength from me since I'm his mother, and from you two as the Usurper."

Lynx and Kharon nodded and moved into position. The four sorcerers held hands and stood in a circle. Megesti chanted the words, and after a few repetitions, the others joined in. A violet light flowed from Megesti into the grass and raced toward the mortals. Edith let out a startled squeak, and Harold put his arm around her. Soon the others glowed, and their light flowed into

Megesti before surging across the ground and flying along the castle wall to the roof. It penetrated the stones until every brick glowed.

"It's so bright it's almost blinding," Harold said.

"I think it's beautiful," Edith said.

Aaron grinned watching Megesti, his lifelong friend who'd lived in his father's shadow, now leading the group of sorcerers with his mother at his side. Aaron felt a sense of calm come over him as his castle glowed.

"Do you feel calmer?" he asked the others.

"Yes," Jessica said.

A minute later, the light rushed back past them to the sorcerers. The group released their hands, and Megesti stumbled the same way Alex did when she drained herself. Aaron rushed to his side and steadied him.

"Thank you, my king," Megesti said.

"Friend first. King second." Aaron patted his back.

"Thank you for being there for him, Aaron, for all those years. I know you weren't there the whole time, but you were a great comfort to him," Birch said, making Aaron feel warm.

"How does this protection spell work?" Aaron asked.

"The magic is from the Cassandra and Merlin lines, so it will be strengthened by a Merlin and Cassandra. Only they, and those they welcome, may enter," Kharon explained.

Lynx smiled. "As we weren't sent flying out of here, we're clearly welco—"

Thunder cracked through the courtyard, along with an enormous wave of water. Aaron drew his sword and turned toward the sound. Harold did the same, with Edith and Jessica behind him.

Gryphon stood in the middle of the courtyard ankle-deep in water, glowing dark orange and growling. He whipped back his head and shouted, "Common courtesy dictates you warn someone before you soak them, *Princess*."

Aaron spotted Alex, Stefan, and Michael further behind Gryphon. They were as wet as Gryphon but didn't seem bothered.

"I didn't know that would happen," Alex snapped back, stomping through the water toward Gryphon with an equally vicious look on her face.

"I told you it would!" Gryphon shouted, storming toward her. Before Aaron could react, Michael was between them, holding Gryphon back, but the sorcerer continued shouting at Alex as if Michael wasn't even there. "When you borrow strength from another sorcerer, you risk taking on their powers. I warned you, I'm as drained as you and not fully in control of my powers."

"Stop being so dramatic." Stefan pushed Gryphon away from Alex and Michael and glared at him. "It's only water. You don't hear us complaining, and we've spent years getting soaked by Alex."

"I'm a fire sorcerer! We detest being wet." Gryphon flicked his hands and burst into flames. Stefan had to throw his arms in front of his face to block the flames from burning him. Gryphon shook his arms, and the fire vanished. Completely dry, he sneered and fixed his tunic.

Slinking out from behind Michael, Alex looked Gryphon up and down. "You missed a spot." She flicked her fingers and splashed dirty water from the ground on him, soaking him again, and hurried away, cackling. When she saw Aaron, she gulped. Fear crossed her face for a moment before she threw her shoulders back and smiled.

Aaron put an extra-large smile on his face and strutted to his wife. *I hate this. I don't want you being scared of me. We need to talk about this. I just want you free to be your beautiful, confident self.* "Good morning, my love. I see you've already been up to mischief this morning." He held out his hands to her, letting her come to him. She flinched when she took them. Aaron pulled her close and gazed lovingly at her in his arms. Soon all the nervousness melted from her face.

"Protecting Warren from evil sorcerers is hardly mischief," she said.

"Taking someone's powers without permission is," Gryphon grumbled, storming past them into the castle, still dripping.

As soon as Gryphon was out of earshot, Aaron broke out into laughter. "I do not know what he's talking about, but if you made him that angry, I'm fine with it."

Alex turned to the others, staying in his arms. "Did you cast the spell on Datten?"

"We did," Megesti said. "But what happened to Warren?"

Alex hesitated for a moment. "I wasn't strong enough to do the spell alone. Gryphon offered to help me, but when I took his hand, I took on his explosive nature and couldn't control it. First, I exploded water through half the castle. Father and Randal are dealing with that. Then it worked, but we weren't sure if I had gotten it all the way through the castle. The last time, this flood came with us."

Birch came over with a reassuring smile. "Be thankful you're skilled in the line of Poseidon. When a Salem sorceress loses control over explosive powers, it's terrifying."

"Or one from the line of Tiere." Lynx laughed.

Alex laughed. "How does that happen?"

"Ever wonder where plagues of locusts come from?" Kharon asked.

Michael and Stefan started laughing.

"We should change," Alex said.

They nodded in agreement. Aaron turned to their friends. "You two can go change. I'll escort Alex."

Stefan narrowed his eyes for a moment, then nodded.

Aaron held Alex's hand, and they walked back to their suite in silence. Once inside, Aaron dismissed their maids, leaving them alone.

"Are you angry?" Alex asked. "I didn't think you'd be upset if I went to Warren with my father, and my guards and Gryphon—"

Aaron cut her off with a kiss. "None of that. Let me put your mind at ease. I'm not going to be angry with you for living your life. You went to finish a job we all knew needed doing, *and* you brought help with you—something you aren't always the best at." Aaron ran his hands along her biceps.

"I'm going to hold you to that."

He gently ran a hand along her neck and cupped her face. "I expect nothing less." He moved up his fingers to where she'd hit her head the day before. "The lump is gone."

"I didn't even have a headache when I woke."

Aaron raked his eyes across her body. "Perhaps we should get you out of those wet clothes before you catch a cold."

Alex blushed.

"Still?" he asked, affectionately pressing his forehead to hers. "After a year and a half, I can still make you blush?"

"Only when you catch me off guard," Alex said. She pulled her wet tunic over her head and hung it near the fire to dry. Once she'd slipped off her pants and hung them too, she searched for her robe. It lay at the end of their bed, but as she hurried across the room, Aaron intercepted her. Alex giggled when his stubble tickled her neck. Then she spotted a red dress hanging on her wardrobe. "That looks like the dress I wore at the tournament."

"It's the same style. I had another made for you. Call me sentimental, but you saved my life that day and showed you loved me. I wanted that reminder."

"Should I try it on?"

"Afterward." Aaron smiled mischievously, pulling Alex toward their bed. She yanked his tunic over his head and threw it on the floor. Aaron pushed them back onto the bed and cupped Alex's face to kiss her. Just as Alex kissed him back, there was a knock on the door, and Aaron groaned.

Alex kissed his cheek. "Later," she said.

He stood and held up her dress for her. She slipped into it before calling out, "Enter."

Michael and Jessica came in, and Jessica immediately went to Alex to do up her corset.

"Is everyone all dry now?" Michael eyed Aaron's wet clothes by the fire.

"Yes. Does Alex need to retrieve Edward?"

"No," Jessica said. "Lynx and Gryphon went. You need to run through the coronation."

Alex turned around, her nose scrunched.

*I love you and your funny faces.*

"You need the practice in front of people," Jessica said.

Alex groaned and adjusted her belt. She pulled away, but Jessica stopped her.

"I'm not finished," Jessica said, holding her crown.

"I know. But I keep forgetting." Alex threw her wardrobe open, squatted, and started throwing things out of it.

"Are you all right?" Aaron asked.

"Found them!" Alex leaped up and spun around. The grin went across her entire face, and her eyes sparkled. In her arms was a big gray bundle.

"What is that?" Michael asked.

"Presents." Alex placed the bundle on the bed. She peeked inside, then took out a smaller bundle from it and handed it to Michael. She whispered to him, and his face went serious for a moment before he shook his head to the side. Alex rubbed his shoulder before she gave another bundle to Aaron. "These are your coronation gifts. Harold helped me with them."

Aaron looked at Michael and then looked back to Alex. Somehow her smile had become larger.

"Stefan already has his. Open it," she said.

Aaron unwrapped the bundle. "A sword?" A large ruby adorned the end of the gilded handle. But the blade was different. Aaron held it up to the sunlight coming through their balcony, and a shaft of red light reflected onto the walls.

"Are these made with red steel?" Michael asked. Michael's sword was the same as Aaron's but was decorated with a sapphire.

Alex grinned. "They are. Harold melted the chains they had and turned them into swords for you." Alex reached into the bundle and handed a hideously embroidered bag to Jessica. "And cloak pins for my ladies. Sorry the bag isn't neater. I tried. Harold already gave Edith hers."

Jessica laughed and hugged Alex. When Jessica let her go, Aaron handed Jessica the sword and kissed Alex. "Thank you."

Alex hugged him back tightly. "We thought you'd feel better having a sword that can actually hurt a sorcerer for when I get into trouble, as I inevitably will."

"Very much so," Aaron said.

"Sorry to break up this party, but Her Majesty is waiting for you both," Jessica said, picking up Alex's crown from the bed and holding out Aaron's sword to him.

Aaron took his new sword and sheathed it on his hip, placing Daniel's on the side table. Jessica handed him Alex's crown. Once he placed it on her head, he tucked her loose hair behind her ear. Alex put his crown on him, and they headed to the throne room, with Jessica and Michael a step behind them.

❧❧❧ ❦❦❦

"I THINK we should take it one more time from the top," Guinevere said.

"Mother, I think we're prepared." Aaron used a gentle voice, trying to be polite.

"We've done this seven times," Alex whispered from her throne beside Aaron's. "I don't know what she thinks is missing."

"Aaron." Guinevere sighed. "I just want everything to be perfect."

Aaron stood and held out his hand to Alex. She allowed him to pull her up from her throne. "We appreciate that, Mother, but we're finished for now. We cannot go through it again. Seven times is enough."

"Seven?" Guinevere asked Michael and Stefan. "Has it really been seven times?"

"Seven, Your Majesty," Sir Bishop replied, taking the pressure off the young knights.

"That certainly is enough. I'm sorry, dear, I hadn't realized."

Aaron grinned and gave his mother a kiss on the cheek. "It's fine, Mother. Tonight after supper, we'll have the ceremony, and I'll formally accept the crown of Datten before our people."

Guinevere had tears in her eyes. "It feels like only yesterday you were chasing after Daniel on every adventure he went on. Now you're a grown man, hoping to start a family of your own, taking your father's place on the throne." Guinevere gave Aaron a soft kiss on the cheek and moved toward the door. "You're right. You'll do wonderfully tonight."

Alex gave Aaron a confused look. "She left so suddenly. Did we offend her?"

"No. She thinks we're right." Aaron grabbed Alex's hand and gently kissed it.

Alex stood on the balls of her feet and kissed Aaron. Immediately, they heard the loud clink of all the knights turning away. She groaned.

Aaron pressed his forehead to hers. "I keep forgetting to talk to Jerome about that."

"Forget it. Might as well give them a reason to look away." Alex grabbed Aaron's shirt, pulled him close, and kissed him passionately.

Aaron was startled but happily complied with Alex's request. "We have some time before the ceremony. What would you like to do?" Aaron asked, grinning.

"We have to practice our first dance. You may be an exceptional dancer, but we all know I need practice, especially with Datten dances."

Aaron led her to the open area of the throne room. He took his position, held up his arms, and waited for Alex to take her spot, just as he'd done the first time they danced.

Alex sighed contentedly and walked over to him, inspecting his positioning. "Much better than the first time we danced." She contorted her body into his grip and gasped in delight as she fit perfectly.

*I know your body, my queen.*

Aaron closed his hand over Alex's and led her across the floor in a traditional Datten dance. Michael and Stefan were in the corner, chuckling and whispering to each other. When the dance ended, they applauded.

"Stop it," she ordered her guards, blushing more deeply than Aaron had seen her do in ages.

"You dance beautifully," Lynx said from the doorway.

"Is there anyone who wasn't watching?" Alex asked.

"It's all because of my partner." Aaron caressed Alex's rear and pinched her playfully.

Alex hiccupped and nuzzled him. "He lies. I'm a truly terrible dancer. The only times I dance without hurting people are when I dance with Aaron."

"Your Royal Highness?" Jerome called from the main door.

"Jerome?" Aaron asked.

"I'm sorry to interrupt, but your presence is needed."

Alex looked sad for a moment before she hid it away again. "Go." She pushed him toward Jerome, more firmly this time.

Michael was already adjusting his sword belt and heading toward Jerome. Aaron turned to Stefan.

"I won't leave her side," Stefan said.

Alex wrinkled her nose and groaned loudly.

Lynx winked at Alex and held out her hand to her. Alex grabbed it and they cracked away.

"Get back here," Stefan shouted.

Michael laughed. "Stefan, I think you're going to have to learn to get along with Gryphon if you ever hope to find Alex when she vanishes on you," he teased.

Aaron chuckled. He and Michael followed Jerome out of the room. They walked to the library, where three of the kings from the southern kingdoms were waiting for him. The families had been at war with one another for decades. Aaron knew his father had always refused to interfere, and while he knew he'd stay out of things, he wanted to give them the respect they deserved and hear them out. He took his father's seat at the table, with Michael and Jerome on either side of him.

# CHAPTER 30
# ALEX

Alex tilted the barrel of wooden swords. "How long before Stefan and Gryphon find us?" She and Lynx had changed and arrived at the vast training grounds only a few minutes before.

"Any minute now. Gryphon can't read your mind, but he can read mine."

"Cheaters," Alex grumbled. She spotted Jessica and Edith ahead of them.

"Excited to learn to fight like a mortal?" Alex asked Lynx.

"If it'll impress Stefan," Lynx said.

"Ready, ladies?" Alex braided her hair and threw it over her shoulder before handing each of her ladies a wooden sword.

"I'm ready," Edith said, leaning against the hilt of her sword. "We'll see how your ways compare with Daddy's." Out of all of them, Edith looked the most comfortable with a sword in her hand, even if it was wooden. Jessica didn't struggle with the sword either, but she kept adjusting her tunic.

"Jessica, your tunic isn't magically going to become a dress, no matter how much you tug at it," Alex teased.

Jessica huffed, making Edith and Lynx giggle. "Some of us enjoy dressing like ladies."

"How did your father teach you to fight when you were younger?" Lynx asked.

"In sparring clothes, naturally. But that doesn't mean I liked them."

Alex began her lesson on how to stand and hold the sword properly. Jessica and Edith easily mimicked her movements, but Lynx struggled.

"They feel unnatural," Lynx protested. Alex adjusted Lynx's position and reiterated the difference between a fighting stance and a sorcerer's stance, stressing that the leg and hip position were more defensive and how the arms needed to be lower to start, close to the hip where the sword would be.

A familiar voice resounded through the courtyard. "It took Alex forever to master the stance. You're doing fine. Keep trying."

Alex spun. It annoyed her to see Stefan with Gryphon already, but she quickly recovered and stuck out her tongue at them.

"Nice to see you two getting along for a change," Edith said.

"What are you doing?" Stefan marched toward them.

Gryphon abandoned the wall he'd been leaning against and sauntered after Stefan. His eyes were wide and his mouth was agape. "What are you *wearing*?" he asked in horror.

"We're training," Alex answered. "Lynx is wearing training clothes, the same as the rest of us."

Edith was clad in Warren blue and Lynx in Warren green. Alex and Jessica were dressed in Datten fighting outfits. Aaron had several gold ones made for Alex, while Jessica's were dark red, the color reserved for the highest noble families such as the Wafners.

"Clearly, but I'm talking about your clothes, not theirs," Gryphon said.

Alex could feel Stefan's eyes on her, clearly trying to figure out what Gryphon meant.

"Nothing's wrong with her clothes," Edith said defensively.

"They're even her line color," Lynx said.

Gryphon groaned and pinched the bridge of his nose before looking back at Alex. "Why didn't you tell them?"

Alex flushed, and her pulse raced. She remembered the smile on Aaron's face when he'd gifted her the Datten clothes. He'd been so excited that his kingdom's color matched her line color. Alex squeezed the necklace around her neck, feeling her friends' eyes on her.

"Alex, what's he talking about?" Stefan asked, crossing his arms.

"You don't have to tell us if you don't want to," Edith said, putting her hand on Alex's shoulder.

Alex swallowed hard. "Every tunic Moorloc forced me to wear was gold. Everything I wore there was gold … because it was my line color."

Edith's gasp was audible, while Stefan went pale. Jessica visibly winced. "I'm so sorry. Aaron wanted to make them red. I was the one who suggested we get you gold instead."

"That explains why they keep getting ruined or magically disappearing," Edith said, rubbing Alex's arm. Alex grabbed Edith's hand and squeezed.

"I'll see that you have red ones tomorrow," Jessica said. "And again, I'm sorry."

"You didn't know," Alex whispered.

"Feels better to tell them, doesn't it?" Gryphon asked, nudging her with his shoulder once Edith stepped away. Alex shot Gryphon a dirty look, but Lynx snapped her fingers and switched their tunics. Looking down at the green, Alex sighed with relief. Now that she was back in her mother's color, she felt the wave of nausea leave her.

Stefan slid his arm around her shoulders. "Don't get angry at him because he's right." He pulled her close. "You should have told us. The colors you wear don't matter to us."

"I just didn't want to seem ungrateful for the effort that was made to make me feel at home in Datten."

"Clothes can easily be replaced," Jessica said. "You need to feel comfortable in your clothes so you can be yourself. That's what will win over the Dattenites, not the color of your tunic."

"Enough chitchat," Lynx said. "You're done interrupting my lesson." She pointed at the wall they'd come from. Stefan and Gryphon shrugged and moved back a little.

Edith held up the wooden sword, and Lynx stood across from her with her own sword up. The sword trembled in her hand while Edith smiled sweetly.

"You're going to be great, Lynx," Alex said. She adjusted Lynx's stance and as soon as she was perfect, Alex hit Lynx with the wooden sword she'd been hiding.

"Ow!" Lynx cried out and turned to Alex.

"That wasn't as bad as you thought, was it? The biggest fear people have when they train is how badly a hit will hurt."

Lynx rubbed her thigh. "I get your point, but you could have warned me."

"That wouldn't be realistic. Right, Stefan?" She smiled at him.

Stefan laughed at them all. "She's right. You never know when a hit will come, and you can't always be prepared for them."

Gryphon eyed Stefan. "So, how many bruises have you given Alex?"

"Too many to count," Stefan replied, crossing his arms and grinning. "But that's why she is as strong and quick as she is."

"Edith, you're up," Alex said.

Edith moved toward Lynx, who screamed and started waving around her sword like a wild animal. Alex grabbed it with her hand to stop her.

"I think you need a visual demonstration. Stefan!" Alex beckoned him over.

"Do you have your actual sword with you, or just the toy?" Stefan asked. Alex went over to another barrel, pulled out two metal swords, and gave him one.

"Let the experts show you how it is done." Stefan walked to the training circle Lynx and Edith had vacated. Alex motioned for the others to join Gryphon, then marched after Stefan. They nodded to each other.

"You better not go easy on me," she said.

"I'd never dream of it, Your Royal Highness. Watch our feet and arms, ladies."

Alex aimed for Stefan's thigh, but he was too quick and blocked her. Lynx gasped as Stefan lunged at Alex, and she mostly dodged him, but he hit her back with his sword's hilt. A breeze hit her, and the ground beneath her feet felt different. Glancing around, she realized Gryphon or Lynx had cracked them from the training grounds to the inner courtyard. Alex focused on Stefan, blocking everything else out.

The cracking had thrown Stefan off balance. Alex lunged at him. It was a move Stefan knew well. He jumped back, but Alex saw the tip of her blade scratch his thigh.

"You'll notice," Stefan announced, "once Alex draws blood, her stance tightens and her movements become swifter ... and more vicious."

A rush of adrenaline flowed through her, and she called a wind to remove the stray hairs from her face. Stefan's stance shifted too. He switched his legs to protect his injured thigh. He was getting more defensive. *Good.* Alex made her own movements faster and more economical. She charged him and struck his sword with hers, sending him back a few steps. He dodged her next move and struck her hard in the back again.

Someone gasped, but Alex ignored it. She caught herself before she went down and turned back toward Stefan. He tried to readjust his stance, but she struck him hard in the shoulder, slid under his legs, and leaped up behind him. Alex kicked him hard in the back of the kneecap, sending him to his knees. She slammed the hilt of her blade into his shoulder, knocking him face-first on the ground.

"I surrender!" Stefan laughed, rolling onto his back, hands in the air. Alex placed her foot on his chest.

"Good." Alex smirked down at him, and applause erupted around them. The Datten courtyard was full of knights clapping for her. She bowed to them, and Stefan reached for her ankle.

"Don't even think about it," Alex replied, pointing her sword at Stefan again.

"I want to be as good as you," Lynx said excitedly to Alex, despite her wide eyes fixing on Stefan on the ground.

"With some time and training, you could be," Alex said. "You have the advantage of magic on your side."

"Show off," Stefan muttered.

"Are you going to let your man up?" Aaron came over to them with a big smile on his face, clapping his hands. "Stefan's going to need to get cleaned up for the coronation after that loss."

"How's your back?" Michael asked Alex upon arriving at her side. He held out his hand to Stefan and hauled him up.

"Her back is in better shape than my shoulder and thigh," Stefan groaned.

Alex felt a hand graze her back. Gryphon held out his hand to her and when she took it, he summoned her healing powers to the surface. A gold light flowed out of her into Gryphon. Aaron watched intently as Gryphon moved his hand over her back in a counterclockwise circle where Stefan had hit her. The instant the ache was gone, Alex pulled away from Gryphon and went to Stefan to heal him where she had struck him.

"What did you do?" Aaron asked Gryphon, crossing his arms.

"I sped up her healing powers. It's an ability fostered by our Head and Heart connection," Gryphon said and walked away.

After Alex healed Stefan, Jessica looked her over. "I think it's about time you all got dressed for tonight."

"Especially those of you with blood on your clothes," Edith added grinning.

Aaron chuckled. Alex and Stefan both sheepishly headed toward the doors.

# CHAPTER 31
# AARON

Aaron entered their room to find Alex drying her hair with a towel. Without taking his eyes off her, he dropped his crown on the bed and leaned against it, taking in the sight of her naked body.

She narrowed her eyes at him. "Don't even think about it." As she strutted across the room, Aaron caught her and playfully pulled her toward him.

"I can think about it and not act on it. I'm not a beast." He pressed his forehead against hers and ran his hand down her back.

Alex grinned. "True. You only get wild late at night."

Aaron slid his hands around Alex's waist. Resting his chin on her shoulder, he nuzzled against her neck. "When did Gryphon learn your magic?"

"He helped me bring out my healing powers when I was at Moorloc's," she said. "Like today, he summoned my power to help heal an injury. I didn't realize he was that good with it already."

"Or that sneaky?"

"That too," Alex replied. "What do we wear tonight? Neither Jessica nor your mother told me which dress to wear."

Aaron opened his wardrobe and pulled out a king's shirt embroidered with real gold. He tossed it on the bed next to his crown. Next, he went to her wardrobe and pulled out a gorgeous red and gold dress. Alex gasped at the dress, making Aaron smile.

"I had it made for you. It's a more regal version of your green one. I had another one made, but it will have to wait for another day." Alex caressed the sleeve gently with her fingers. It was simple in design but incredibly elegant by Datten standards. The entire dress was red, with gold detailing that ran along the bottom of the skirt, around the neckline, and on the edges of the long, graceful sleeves. The belt was fabric woven from gold, matching Aaron's golden crest, and at the front, a long piece of the gold fabric flowed down to the floor.

Aaron held out the dress for her and let her use his shoulder for balance as she stepped into it. When he pulled it up her back, he gently ran his finger over her birthmark before tightening her corset.

"Aaron?" Alex's voice wavered, and his attention shifted to her face. She was biting her lip, and her hands were pressed to her neck. The neckline rested low on her shoulders and showed off her entire collarbone and more of her cleavage than anything he'd seen her wear before. "Are you sure it's tight enough? And is it supposed to be this low?" Alex's hands struggled to cover the area she clearly didn't want exposed.

Aaron couldn't help but chuckle at her reddening cheeks. "You have nothing to be nervous about. The dress won't show any more than it does right now. Queens of Datten have been wearing this style for centuries. It displays the feminine beauty of our queen before she sneaks up and kicks you in the kneecaps. That's why it's snug in the bust and core but loose in the legs."

Alex laughed and pushed him playfully. He fetched her necklace from the table on her side of the bed, and when he turned around, he caught her spinning in her dress. "I thought you didn't like dresses." Aaron held up her necklace.

*You look like the little girl in the Warren garden.*

"I don't like blue dresses or the overdone Warren ones. But the Datten ones are simpler and ..." Aaron fastened her necklace, and she turned to face him with fire in her eyes.

"And?"

"And I like how I feel when you look at me in them."

"How does it make you feel?"

"Loved," Alex whispered.

Aaron could only grin. "I can't help looking at you. You're enchanting. Now, I have another surprise for you—a new crown."

"What?" Alex froze. "But I have a crown."

"You have several, but you're Datten's queen after tonight, not just mine. And our queen needs a different crown."

Aaron stepped toward his table and picked up a crown from the back. This one looked like a larger version of her normal Datten crown, but rather than having only four large sections, every other prong was large with a small one between it. They were equally spaced apart, and each large prong held a ruby to honor Datten's crest. At the front was one large obsidian stone. Lining the inside of the crown was a piece of luxurious velvet that helped hold it up on her head. Alex eyed Aaron suspiciously.

"Was the large stone always an obsidian?"

"No," Aaron said. "I had the ruby replaced in honor of Warren, our queen's homeland."

"So, should I put it on now?" Alex asked.

"Not yet. Your father will place it on your head during the coronation."

"I thought your mother was doing our crowns." Alex was fiddling with her shoulders again.

Aaron realized she was trying to hide the scar from his sword. "You haven't healed it?"

"Gryphon had to touch me to heal my scars. He wouldn't move his hand off my back to heal anything on the front. And then I didn't know if I should."

"Why wouldn't you?" Aaron slid the fabric to the side and examined the scar he'd given her. The guilt was nearly unbearable.

"You won't let me heal your arrow scars," Alex retorted.

Aaron sighed. "So if I let you heal mine, you'll heal yours?"

"Yes. The guilt you feel seeing my scar is the same as the one I feel seeing yours."

"Not quite the same. You hurt me because I was an idiot. I threatened you and you needed to protect Michael. I hurt you because I was jealous. My lack of faith in you is why I hurt you."

"Aaron." Alex grabbed his arm and gently squeezed it. "You were cursed, and that version wasn't the real you."

"But it was a part of me. The violent part of my Datten side."

"I wish you didn't hurt so much when I've already forgiven you."

"You may have, but others haven't. I need to figure out how to make things right with your father. Maybe then I can try to forgive myself." Aaron kissed her forehead and moved to put his shirt on.

"We both need to figure things out with my father. He looks exhausted, but there's never enough time to really talk with him. Now please explain why your mother isn't crowning us."

"She expects to be too emotional to properly do it, so Harold and Edward agreed to."

"I assume my father crowns me, and Harold you?"

"How'd you know?"

"He's your Edward." Alex laughed. They heard a knock on the door. "Come in," she called.

Edith and Jessica entered the room in their best Datten dresses. "We came to help you finish getting ready, Alex," Edith said. She and Jessica looked Alex over, assessing the work they had cut out for them. Edith grabbed a brush and began fixing Alex's hair.

Jessica adjusted Alex's corset. "You did a good job, Aaron."

"Datten dresses are easier." There was another knock at the door. "Enter," Aaron called, and their guards walked in.

"We're here for the crowns," Stefan said. "We've been tasked with delivering them to Her Majesty."

"She runs a tight ship," Michael said. "It's intimidating."

"Now you know where Jessica learned it." Aaron laughed and handed the crowns to Michael.

"We have larger necklaces, if you don't want so much skin showing," Edith said. Aaron looked over and saw Alex covering her neck with her hand again.

"The queen's collection in Datten is extensive. I'd be happy to get you one," Jessica offered.

"No," Alex said, shaking her head. She swallowed hard enough for Aaron to hear as she stepped back from her ladies.

*Oh no. You're breaking.*

"Everyone out," Aaron ordered.

Her ladies looked at him, shocked. Aaron cocked his head toward Alex, who had fled to their balcony. Edith and Jessica nodded and left the room.

Aaron padded out onto the balcony and déjà vu hit him. He recognized this scene: Alex hyperventilating before a big event, and him desperate to take her pain from her. *Only this time, I probably won't make it worse. Last time, I was nervous you'd set me on fire or worse, throw me out, but today ... you're my wife, and I just want to make this whole mess easier for you.* He stepped up behind her and gently caressed her arms. She turned around and wrapped her arms around his chest. Aaron kissed the top of her head and tightened his grip on her as she cried.

"I know tonight's hard. It is for me too," he said. "Every day we celebrate something meaningful is hard without them." She sniffled and buried her face in Aaron's shirt. "The difference now is we have each other. You'll never have to face times like this alone again."

"Thank you," Alex whispered, and Aaron gently stroked her back. "There is so much I need to tell you, but we haven't had the time between curses, attacks, and ceremonies."

"We have time now."

Alex exhaled hard enough that Aaron felt her chest move. "Your mother will be upset if we're late."

Aaron cupped Alex's cheeks in his hands. "She can wait a few more minutes. It isn't as if she can start without us."

The corners of Alex's lips curled up. *I love it when you smile. I have so much to make up for with you, and moments like this … they make me believe I'll actually be worthy of you one day.*

His fingers went to Alex's necklace. The three teardrop-shaped gems rested flush on her slender neck and collarbone. "A sapphire for Datten, an obsidian for Warren, and an emerald for your mother, and to match your eyes," Aaron said, kissing her cheek softly.

Alex sighed. "Promise me we'll make time to talk tomorrow."

"I promise," Aaron said and released her. "Tomorrow you will have as long you need to tell me everything weighing on your heart."

Alex held out her hand to Aaron. "Then I'm ready."

"Princess." Aaron bowed to her, grabbing her hand to kiss it.

Alex placed her free hand on her bust. "Your Highness," she gasped. "I'm spoken for. Haven't you heard? I've caught the eye of the king."

Aaron laughed and proffered his arm. Alex accepted, and they headed out into the hallway. Aaron took them the long way around so they could greet as many of the servants and knights on guard as possible on their way to the throne room. When they neared the hall, Aaron shuddered, and Alex squeezed his hand.

"You have nothing to be nervous about. You're going to be the greatest king Datten has ever had," she whispered.

Aaron grinned. "How do you know that?"

"I've seen it," Alex said, as they arrived at the doors to the throne room. When they were ready, Aaron nodded and Sirs Reinhart and Wafner opened the doors for them.

They both exhaled, held their chins up, and marched up the aisle to the thrones. Standing at the front of the room before the dais that held their thrones were King Harold and King Edward. Beside Harold was Michael, holding Aaron's crown, and Stefan stood beside Edward with Alex's crown. Aaron and Alex strutted up to the thrones of Datten and stood before Edward and Harold.

Harold stepped forward first, and Alex dropped Aaron's hand and stepped back.

"I, King Harold of Betruger, Datten's oldest enemy and newest ally, have been honored with crowning the new king. So for the last time, Crown Prince Aaron Edward Johnathon Arthur, do you accept the crown of Datten and the responsibilities that come with it? Will you put the lives of your people over your own, and their needs above those of your own family? Will you put aside petty differences and uphold the motto founded by your family centuries ago: honor, above all?"

Aaron kneeled on one knee before Harold and bowed his head. "I pledge to give my people my sword, my honor, and my life, until the last breath leaves my body."

Harold nodded and lowered the crown of Datten onto Aaron's head. "Then for the first time, and from this moment on, I present to you King Aaron of Datten."

Aaron stood and turned to face his knights, lords, subjects, and family, and the room erupted in applause. He beamed at Alex and stepped away from the dais as Edward moved toward her.

"I, King Edward of Warren, Datten's oldest ally, have been given the honor of crowning the new queen, my daughter. So for the last time in *this* kingdom, Princess Elizabeth Katrina Alexandria, will you accept the title of Queen of Datten, and the burden of it? Will you put your husband and king first? Will you put the lives of your people over your own, and their needs above those of your own family? Will you put aside petty differences and uphold the motto founded by your husband and king's family centuries ago: honor, above all?"

Alex was kneeling and now looked up at him. "I agreed to all of that and more when I agreed to marry a crown prince."

Edward nodded and placed the crown on her head. "Then arise, my daughter, as the new Queen of Datten."

Edward held out his hands and helped Alex up. Aaron swooped in and took her hand as the room erupted in applause.

"My first act as King of Datten is to invite you all to the coronation banquet being held in the dining hall next door." The people erupted in applause again. Alex lifted her dress skirt with her free hand and allowed Aaron to lead her down the aisle.

He noticed she was walking a step behind him. "What are you doing?" he whispered.

"I'm trying to stay a step behind you, as a Datten queen does."

"Not us," Aaron said, pulling her forward to him. "We're equals."

Aaron squeezed her hand, and they arrived at the dining hall for the banquet on equal footing. Michael and Stefan moved ahead and threw open the doors for them. The instant they entered the hall, Aaron learned how different things would now be. Lords of Datten and kings of the southern kingdoms rushed toward him. They pulled him away from Alex to talk about the open positions on the king's counsel and gain favor from the king.

When he glanced back, noble ladies, queens, and princesses of the southern kingdoms surrounded Alex. They were fussing over her, whispering to her and laughing. Alex was clearly uncomfortable, but Aaron couldn't find Edith, Jessica, or his mother to save her. Stefan and Michael took their places next to Alex's and Aaron's chairs. Mischievous grins formed on their faces as they watched Alex's predicament.

Crown Prince Jesse of Darren was talking to him. "It seems your wife has trouble socializing with other royal ladies. No doubt a result of her years running wild in the woods. Such a shame, really. She had potential."

Aaron glared at the prince. "It sounds as though you're still upset that Her Royal Highness pushed you into the sea when you put your hands on her? Or is it because she found you unworthy of her time?"

"I meant no disrespect, Your Royal—"

"I suggest you keep in mind what I did to Wesley when he spoke ill of a princess I had hoped to court. As she is now my wife and queen, I'd use the entire army of Datten to defend her."

Jesse gulped and straightened his tunic. "I shall remember that, Your Royal Highness." The prince nearly tripped in his hurry to get away from Aaron.

"Who's that?" King Coilen of Bearen asked, nodding to the ladies on the other side of the room. Aaron looked where Gryphon leaned and whispered into Alex's ear. She furrowed her brow and turned back to the surrounding women. They curtsied, and Alex followed Gryphon across the hall to Caleb.

"That would be Gryphon of the Forbidden Lands," Aaron responded. "He's tutoring the queen in the use of her magical abilities."

"I'm impressed you could find her a tutor for her powers. Your father and Merlock always feared them so much."

"Alexandria's *gifts* are already stronger than her uncle's ever were. It would have been dangerous to allow them to grow without proper instruction."

King Coilen chuckled. "You sound like your grandfather."

"I do?"

"Oh, yes. My father told many tales of King Johnathon. He was fearless but intelligent. He always said if you are not the best at something, then you must employ the best to help you."

Alex squatted to be face-to-face with a young girl who was clutching Caleb. She was Ruby, Caleb's little sister, and she had tears on her face. Alex's hands lit up and glowed gold. She smiled and held them out to the youngest Reinhart. Ruby placed her tiny hands into Alex's, and the queen covered them and pulled them to her mouth. Aaron couldn't see what Alex did, but when she released Ruby's hand, the little girl's eyes widened and her mouth dropped open. Before Caleb could stop her, she threw her arms around Alex. Aaron beamed when Alex returned the hug, obviously not caring about how improper it was.

*If that's how you treat the most vulnerable in my kingdom, you'll be loved in no time.* Caleb bowed to her, and Alex patted his shoulder. She held out her hand to Ruby and led the girl to the dessert table, with Gryphon and Caleb a step behind.

Aaron looked over at Stefan and then back at Gryphon and chuckled. *You'll be furious with me tomorrow, Stefan, but it's for the best.* After excusing himself from the royals, he went over to Alex. The Reinharts had moved on, and now she was talking to Edith's mother with Gryphon at her side.

"Good evening, Your Royal Highness." Lady Judith Nial curtsied to Aaron.

"Lady Judith. Where is Edith?" Aaron slid his hand along Alex's back and stole a piece of chocolate off her plate.

"She attended the coronation as King Harold's guest." Lady Judith gracefully motioned with her head. Aaron and Alex turned to see Harold handing Edith a plate of chocolate. "I'd never presume to know a king's intentions, but her father is keeping a close eye on them."

"Them?" Gryphon asked.

"King Harold and my daughter." Lady Judith gave a sly little smile.

"Gryphon means to ask not who, but why," Alex said. "Harold's intentions are nothing but virtuous. Both Aaron—uh, His Royal Highness and I know distinctly that Harold intends to ask Randal for Edith's hand."

"That would explain why she's abandoned all my attempts to find her a husband these last few months. I suspected she'd found herself a candidate, but I never expected a royal, let alone a king."

"Is Harold still a king if he doesn't have a kingdom?" Gryphon asked.

Aaron almost choked on his chocolate, but the look Alex shot Gryphon made Aaron snort back a laugh.

"It is not land or location that make a king, but how he leads his people," Alex snapped. "Besides, Harold still has the entire Betruger territory. He just doesn't have a castle, something I've been meaning to discuss with you."

"Why does that sound like you're giving me work?" Gryphon asked.

Alex turned back to Lady Judith. "The thing the Betruger people value the most is family. I'm not surprised Edith and Harold were drawn to each other."

"It was her archery skills," Aaron said. "The look on Harold's face when she beat Caleb on Randal's birthday told me all I needed to know. He was smitten." He popped another chocolate into his mouth.

"Perhaps Randal wasn't mistaken, letting her grow up a little wild," Alex said.

"It would seem kings of Torian are drawn to wild Warren women." Aaron smirked, and Alex's cheeks turned a darker shade of pink at his comment.

Lady Judith bowed and excused herself. Aaron was about to ask Alex to dance when several Datten nobles surrounded them and pulled him away. He listened to their requests, but when he looked around the room, Alex had vanished. He shook his head and realized a baron had asked him a question.

"Apologies, Baron Oakes. I was preoccupied."

"I know it's a busy night for you, Your Royal Highness. I'm hoping to know whether there will be a place at court for my sons, Lucas and Elijah. Lucas is ready to settle down now, but Elijah has a wild spirit. It seems to be a common trait among secondborn sons of Datten."

Aaron laughed at the baron's jest and put his hand on his shoulder. "Hubert, I'll be frank. Not only did both your sons fight bravely when my father called, but they also volunteered to go with me to Betruger Castle. They're exactly the type of men I need around me." Aaron raised his hand to Michael, who immediately came over. "What were our plans for Lucas and Elijah Oakes?"

"We will promote Lucas to manage the royal coop and train all our messenger birds. He'll remain in Datten. Elijah is in the next group to go to the Stronghold to train with the best knights. I recall his tactical knowledge was exceptional for his age."

"Would that do?" Aaron asked the baron.

"You're too kind, Your Royal Highness. You have truly blessed my house."

"Your sons earned their places. You should be very proud of them," Aaron said.

The baron nodded and headed off into the crowd. Aaron pulled Michael aside. "Where's my queen? I lost her a minute ago."

"It was closer to thirty. It became too hot for her, so she took Stefan and her ladies to get some fresh air."

"Welcome to being a king, Aaron," Edward said, coming up behind him. "You're very busy now. The oath you took about putting your people before your family was quite real. This is the hardest thing you'll have to do as king."

Aaron felt the weight of his commitment, knowing it would be difficult to choose between Alex and anything else, but that he *would* do it.

"We're here to save you for a bit," Harold said.

"How so?" Aaron said.

"When other kings such as Warren's and Betruger's appear beside you, everyone else vanishes," Harold said.

"We are rather intimidating," Edward added.

Aaron turned to Harold. "Have you talked to Sir Nial yet?"

"Not yet."

"About what?" Edward asked curiously.

"I intend to ask Sir Nial for Lady Edith's hand," Harold said.

"We'll see to this right now," Edward said. "After the past week, I think we've all learned there is no point in waiting for things like this. Aaron will be fine now. My daughter has returned."

Edward practically dragged Harold over to Sir Nial, and soon after, Harold and Randal left the hall. As they left, Alex came over to Aaron and he grabbed her.

"Save me from all the knights and lords!" he joked.

"Only if you save me from the noble ladies. They're terrible. They only want to talk about how beautiful I am and ask who made my dress and why I'm not pregnant yet. A few of them tried to give me advice on how to get you to visit my room. Apparently they don't know we actually share a room."

Aaron snorted and grinned at her. "Sorry. I find it funny, considering it's you who can't keep your hands off me."

"It's frustrating. I don't feel ready to try again, but they keep asking. I thought Jessica told them."

"When I was ... *occupied* after you left, everyone assumed I left with you and that we went to get your things from Warren and Verlassen Castle. Our parents kept it private, so no one knows what happened."

"That explains why everyone keeps asking me about dresses

and babies. Apparently to the Datten people, all I'm here for is making your heirs."

Aaron pulled her close. "Not for long. Your sword fight with Stefan this afternoon is all the knights are talking about. And after things have settled and we begin the second council, they'll be too busy yelling at me to ask you about dresses and babies." Aaron put his hands on her cheeks and kissed her passionately, making the knights turn their heads. "I think it's time for our first dance."

Aaron led Alex to the dance floor, and they performed beautifully for the nobles of Datten. Once they'd finished, they invited the guests to dance. Aaron was going to suggest they try to eat while they could, but Alex was already maneuvering him toward the food.

"I'm starving," she said. "You're coming with me to get food, or those horrible noblewomen will never leave me alone long enough to eat anything."

"I'm happy to be of service to my queen," Aaron said. After almost a year home, Alex nearly had her strength back. Training with Stefan, Michael, and Jerome was bringing back the muscle she had spent so many years building, and her hair was thicker. Starving at Morlock's castle had changed so many of her habits. Aaron wouldn't admit it to her, but he'd been terrified she'd never recover. Despite his concerns, her healing powers seemed to have finally worked their way through all of her.

Alex gasped at the sight of the banquet table bursting with food. Aaron reached across the table and placed a piece of swordfish on her plate. "I insisted your father bring some."

The smile that filled her face warmed his soul. *This will fix us. I'll fix us with one small, loving gesture at a time.*

Alex filled her plate with her favorite Datten delicacies and caught Aaron staring at her. "What?"

"Nothing," he said. When she gave him her wife-stare, he laughed and admitted, "I'm happy to see you so healthy again."

"Training is much easier when I'm well-fed and stronger."

Aaron tried to steal a piece of cheese from Alex, but she was too quick and stuffed it in her mouth. "Mine." She raised her eyebrows at him.

"I thought you agreed to put me first." He laughed as they headed to their seats.

"In everything except food," she said.

As they were eating, Harold arrived back in the hall and came to join them.

"Did your talk with Randal go well?" Aaron asked.

Harold nodded. "Very. I must find an appropriate time to ask her."

"The moon's out by now. It's full tonight, and the forest will be romantic. But take Jessica as a chaperone. Warren and Datten are rather strict about that sort of thing," Alex said.

"Do you have the ring I gave you?" Aaron asked.

Harold nodded. He took Alex's hand and kissed it. "Thank you, Your Royal Highness." Harold hurried off to Jessica. She nodded to him and they headed off into the crowd.

"May I have the next dance?" Edward bowed to Alex, and she glanced at Aaron.

"The Queen of Datten doesn't need my permission to dance with anyone, least of all your father."

Alex accepted her father's hand. "If you're not worried about getting hurt," she said to him.

"For you, dear, I'll risk it."

Alex nervously let her father lead her along the dance floor. The dance wasn't nearly as smooth as when Aaron danced with her, but they looked happy. After they'd finished, Edward kissed Alex's cheek. He nodded at Aaron and then headed toward the hallway. Alex turned to walk away and bumped into Gryphon.

Gryphon smiled and held out his hand to her. Aaron noticed the redness that covered her cheeks as she shook her head, but

Gryphon's hand remained out. Alex relented and Gryphon took her hand and pulled her onto the dance floor. The music began slowly and he spun her, pulling her close.

Several Datten lords approached Aaron as he watched Alex dance with Gryphon.

"You're a much stronger man than I am, Your Royal Highness."

"Why's that, Duke Nimbly?" Aaron asked.

"I wouldn't let another man dance with my wife like that."

Aaron bit his lip to keep himself calm. Michael and Stefan arrived at his side, and the lords left.

"Aaron?" Michael asked nervously.

"It's a dance," Aaron said, but his eyes never left Gryphon's hand on her side.

"Then why do you look like that?" Stefan asked.

"Dancing was the first time she let me through her walls."

"Then cut in," Stefan said.

"I just told her she didn't need my permission to dance with someone. Won't it seem as if I'm marking my territory? Something we all know Alex hates."

"Gryphon's different," Stefan said. "Risk it."

"You get to draw a line with him somewhere," Michael said. "This can be it."

Aaron strolled out to the dance floor. Alex shot Gryphon a dirty look, and the sorcerer smirked in response. Aaron gently tapped Alex's shoulder and smiled when she turned to him. "I'm cutting in. Thank you for dancing with her while I was detained, Gryphon. But I'm no longer occupied. You can go."

Aaron slipped his arm around Alex's waist, pulled her against him, and danced her away from Gryphon.

"Your Royal Highnesses." Gryphon bowed and vanished into the crowd.

"Aaron?" Alex whispered.

"I'm drawing my line. Spend all the time you want training,

working on your powers, reading, riding, teaching him about humans, but no dancing ... please. Dancing is special for us."

"All right," Alex replied, without dropping the smile from her face. Aaron, however, couldn't hide his shock.

"No argument?"

"Why would I argue? You're being completely reasonable. I don't know if I could be so reasonable if our places were reversed."

"Thank you."

"I'm ready to retire to bed," Alex said. "It's wonderful that nothing attacked us tonight, but it's been a long few days and I'm exhausted."

"I'll join you."

"You don't have to." Alex placed her hands on Aaron's chest and looked up at him. "You promised to put your people first."

"I promised to give you time to talk about things. Besides, it'll quell some of those wagging tongues if you leave with me."

Alex giggled and nodded. Aaron twirled her one last time and turned to his guests. "Thank you, my wonderful guests, and thank you to the people of Datten. The queen and I are retiring for the night, but we do not expect you to end your festivities. Please continue to celebrate in our absence." Then he bowed to the people. It was an act a King of Datten rarely did, but he knew who had put him here. He slid his hand around Alex's hip and nuzzled against her. Out of the corner of his eye, he saw the noble ladies of Datten whisper to each other as he left the hall with Alex.

# CHAPTER 32
# AARON

Aaron wandered the halls, his arms crossed. The celebration had gone on long into the night, but he was thankful he'd left with Alex. Despite being tired, they had stayed up late and talked about many of the things on Alex's mind. *I'm sure she isn't telling me everything, but at least I can help her introduce Michael to his grandmother, work through the memories that still haunt her from her time at Moorloc's, and cope with the guilt she feels for losing the baby, all while managing her fear of me from my curse. Hopefully Warren and Datten are safe for her now with the spells put on them.*

Aaron headed to the library to distract himself with a book, but he found it was already occupied. Gryphon sat at the massive table with at least fifteen books open in front of him. He was holding up his head with his hand and feverishly writing on a piece of parchment, flipping pages at random without touching them by flicking his fingers in the air. Aaron thought he recognized the line books from the Poseidon and Salem lines. *I think Salem is the fire line? Some of them seem to be Merlin and Celtics books, too. What are you up to?*

The sorcerer hadn't heard him enter, so Aaron cleared his throat.

Gryphon's head slipped from his hand, and he caught himself before his face hit the table. His eyes snapped up to see who'd interrupted him, and Aaron could see the gold shine in them. The annoyance on his face held on a moment longer than it should have.

"Good evening, *Princeling*," he said.

"That's Kingling now, *Fire Pumpkin*."

Gryphon scowled. "I had hoped you'd forget that name."

"As long as my wife calls you Sunset, I'll go with Fire Pumpkin. It suits you much better."

Gryphon opened his mouth to say something but stood instead. "If you want the library, I'll leave."

"Stay. I didn't come here to fight. I didn't even know you were here."

"I'm trying to figure out how to safely push Alex out of her magic comfort zone. It's the powers she's afraid of that put everyone at the most risk."

"That makes sense," Aaron said. "A small push to face her fears is necessary right now. I actually want to speak with you."

"I won't ask her to dance again."

"What?"

"I saw you watching."

"Thank you, but that's not why I wanted to talk to you. I intended to find you tomorrow, but this is easier. Fewer witnesses."

"What exactly is this request?" Gryphon sat back down.

"I'm asking you to train Alex."

"I already offered to train her, and she accepted."

"I know," Aaron said, sitting down opposite Gryphon. "But you said it before—she wouldn't follow through with it without my approval. I give it now, wholeheartedly. She needs help, and you're the best person to give it."

"You wanted to gut me a few days ago. Why the change of heart?"

"I'll still gut you if you try anything inappropriate. But I was informed of something my grandfather said, about finding your own weaknesses and surrounding yourself with the strongest people with those skills."

Gryphon sat up and eyed Aaron suspiciously.

"I can't teach her magic; only you can. So I'll trust you with her."

"That's big of you."

"There's more. Beyond being her tutor—"

Gryphon snorted.

"Don't interrupt a king." Aaron looked him in the eye until he blinked. "I also have a job for you. One that I won't force you to accept, but I really hope you will."

"You've allowed my friends and me to remain here and have asked for nothing in return. I'll do what you ask."

"The queen's guard."

"What about her guards?" Gryphon asked.

"I want you to co-captain her guard with Stefan. The curse and attacks have made it clear we cannot protect her from sorcerers, but you can. I might as well make the role official. She has a habit of leaving her guards behind, but you can hunt her down."

Gryphon's mouth dropped open. "Even I struggle to find her sometimes."

"But you can at least follow her. We cannot."

Gryphon's palm burst into flames, and he extinguished it. This happened several more times before he finally spoke. "I accept the job so long as Alex approves. She'll need to understand that I will invade her privacy if needed to protect her, and she probably won't like that. But I'll do whatever's necessary to keep her safe."

"That's the other reason I want you."

"I'm sorry for what I said to you, Aaron, after her memories came back."

"Don't be. If I could go back, I would never let her get those memories back. The things she has to live with are burned on her soul. But at least she had a reason to act that way. I was jealous of you, and the curse made me take it out on her instead of you. A proper Datten king would have taken it out on you."

"She'd have loved that."

"We both know she'll work through this, and I will too."

Gryphon smiled at Aaron. "Only Alex would forgive us both for our indiscretions so easily."

# CHAPTER 33
# ALEX

Alex felt Aaron's fingers running down her back, giving her goose bumps all over. Outside their balcony, a sliver of red and orange flared over the castle walls, the telltale sign morning was coming. She rolled over into Aaron's arms and curled up against his chest.

"You're tickling me," she said, cuddling into him. She wanted to meld their bodies into one and stay there forever.

"I'm sorry I woke you. I can't help touching you. It's simply amazing that the scars have all disappeared."

"Now you should let me heal your shoulder and stomach scars." Alex nuzzled against Aaron's chest.

"So ... shall we discuss boundaries?"

"What are you comfortable with? When it comes to Gryphon, I promise I'll respect whatever you decide."

"I want him to help you with your powers. He threw it in my face that you won't take him up on it because I'm jealous."

"That isn't true," Alex said. "I only said I needed to discuss it with you, and that we'd decide together. He sees that as a weakness, but I think it's our strength. It keeps your temper in check and lets me feel useful."

"You are useful." Aaron laughed, then gave her a look. "And not just for babies and dresses."

"Then why are you giving me your scolding look?"

"Okay," Aaron said and kissed her. "I'd prefer you not to be alone every lesson. I'm still dealing with finding the truth in the memories I have from the curse."

"Gryphon won't try anything if I'm not in control. But I'll bring Stefan whenever possible. It is his responsibility to watch me. Or perhaps Birch, Lynx, Kharon, or Megesti, depending on what we are doing. You know ... it wouldn't hurt Megesti to learn from Gryphon as well."

"I like that idea," Aaron said. "Him teaching you and Megesti. It simplifies things."

"I'm teaching Lynx how to fight. She's very keen to learn."

"Is that why you were fighting Stefan yesterday?"

"I want to offer it to any of the sorcerers who want to learn."

"I like it. Gryphon teaches you magic, and you teach them to fight." Aaron kissed her forehead and pulled back to look at her. "Now your turn."

"My turn?" Alex asked. *Surely he couldn't mean—*

"I gave you my boundaries for you. Now, what are yours for me?"

Alex froze. She hadn't been expecting this. Finally, he nudged her. "Alex?"

"I'm sorry ... I don't understand."

"You don't understand what boundaries are? You accepted mine without complaint."

"Why are you even offering? I'm a princess." Alex exhaled nervously. "I've been controlled my entire life. My father, then Stefan, then my father again, and guards ... and now I'm a Datten queen. Doesn't that mean you are *supposed* to control me?"

Aaron furrowed his brow. "First, when have any of those people actually had control over you? Second, they were only trying to *protect* you, not control you."

"I'm a woman. It's the same thing."

"Well, no more. You are our queen. If you can't set rules and receive respect from your husband, how can we expect our people to follow suit?"

Alex paused. "I don't know ... I'd like for you to listen more ... really listen." She huffed and covered her head with the quilt. "I know you're right about setting an example, but I've never had the opportunity to give it any thought."

"There's no rush. Take your time, and let me know when you decide. You've already given me a few items to start with."

"I have?" She peeked out from the quilt.

"You don't want the guards looking away when we kiss, and you want only your ladies and brothers to enter the room first thing in the morning."

Alex realized Michael and Jessica would normally be in the room by now. "Wait. Where are they?" she asked.

"They aren't coming this morning."

"What do you mean?"

"I told Michael that the morning after our coronation was off-limits, and that we were not to be disturbed until we summoned them. That I needed alone time with my wife."

Alex grinned at Aaron and kissed him softly. "What's keeping them away?"

"I ordered Jerome and Caleb to guard the doors." Aaron rolled on top of Alex and kissed her. "And then I told them the first person to interrupt us would be beheaded."

Alex laughed. "You're terrible."

Aaron smirked at her. "How are we expected to produce heirs if we're never alone together?" He softly kissed her as she ran her hands through his hair.

When Aaron and Alex were finally ready to start the day, Alex put on her favorite green sparring tunic and Aaron threw on one of his crested shirts. Alex felt him wrap his arms around her.

"I love you, and I trust you," he whispered. "Now go to your sorcerer. You have lessons to start."

Alex spun around in Aaron's arms, wrapping her own around his neck. "We could call him my governess if it would help you."

"I'd like that very much. I'll let Stefan know." Aaron smirked, then turned to the door. "You can come in now!"

At once the door opened, and Michael came in, beaming. "Morning, Your Royal Highnesses."

"Good morning, Michael." Alex pulled away from Aaron to give him a hug. "Where is Jessica this morning?"

"Still in bed. She wasn't feeling well."

Alex noticed he wouldn't meet her eyes. "It's all right, Michael," she said. "I'm happy to talk about Jessica's pregnancy. Our loss shouldn't diminish the joy you two should have right now. I know I'll have children with Aaron when the time is right."

Michael relaxed.

"What did she say about being a countess?" Alex asked.

Michael laughed. "Still can't believe it, but I'm ready for you to reach out to Duchess Veremund. Jessica and I would like to meet her."

"Of course," Alex said.

"I'll ask Mother to set up a tea with her today," Aaron said.

Alex looked at him in surprise. "Are you sure? I don't want to trouble Guinevere."

"Her life has changed as much as ours has. I think she'd like to help."

Alex smiled. Lately, she never knew whether Aaron was trying to make up for being cursed, or whether he would have done it anyway. Either way, it would take some getting used to. "If you're sure, then give her my thanks."

"I will."

"And mine as well," Michael said. "Aaron, they sent me to ask as tactfully as possible when you might be ready."

Aaron groaned and reached for his crown, but Alex snatched it from the bed and hid it behind her back. "Oh no. You are not putting on your own crown," she said, laughing.

Aaron walked to her and lowered his head. As she placed it on his head, he grabbed her waist. She wanted to protest, but he kissed her before she could make a sound. When he finally pulled away, Michael handed him Alex's crown from the other table and Aaron presented it to her with a flourish.

Alex shook her head. "Not for training. I'd hate to damage it." She turned back to Michael. "Where exactly are you taking him?"

"We're starting trade negotiations with all the southern kingdoms," Michael said. "Edward will be there for that, too."

"Shouldn't I be as well?" Alex interrupted.

"You're welcome to come if you'd like," Aaron said, and Michael nodded in agreement.

"But it will be tedious," Michael warned. "Each of the kingdoms insists on its own deal, and they will all try to get a better one than the last. I'm told it takes ages."

*Poor Michael. He already looks bored.* "No, you go on. Enjoy yourselves." She grinned. "At least you'll have the tea to break it up."

Stefan appeared at the doorway. Like Michael, he wore the shirt of a Datten guard.

Alex glanced at his uniform and laughed. "Getting comfortable in Datten, I see."

"I ran out of Warren shirts," Stefan said. "This is my father's."

"I see," Alex said, looking at Aaron. When he didn't speak up, she glared at him.

"Michael, add a note to make sure we provide all our knights and guards with extra crested uniforms. A gift from their new queen," Aaron said. "And see that you and Sir Stefan get triple the allotment. Guarding my queen results in a lot of ruined shirts."

Alex gave Aaron a playful shove, scowling at him, while Michael laughed.

"I'll ask Jessica to handle it," Michael said.

Stefan finally stepped out of the doorway. As soon as he saw Aaron's crown, he groaned. "I thought you'd take the day off." He winced as the light from the window hit him, and he rubbed his face.

"Someone had too much Datten ale." Alex giggled. "You're welcome to stay back here, Stefan. I'm only going to figure out training my magic with Gryphon and, if there is time before the tea, teach the sorcerers more swordplay."

Alex noticed Stefan giving Aaron a questioning look. "You do not report to him," she said. "You're the head guard to the Crown Princess of Warren. That takes priority."

Aaron gave Alex a kiss on the cheek. "Unless you're in Datten. Then you're the queen and he's a Wafner, and all Wafners answer to me."

Alex shot Aaron a dirty look.

"Stefan, obey your queen." Aaron grinned and headed to the door with Michael.

"You should start with Harold and my father," Alex called after them. "See what trade requirements they have for both Datten and the southern kingdoms before you make any agreements with the other kingdoms."

Michael's and Aaron's mouths dropped open, and she smirked in satisfaction. "Stefan, shall we go? The boys have enough work to do without us."

Stefan and Alex burst out laughing as Aaron and Michael huffed and closed the bedroom door behind them.

"Where's Gryphon now?" Stefan asked.

"We have to go get breakfast first."

"Breakfast ended hours ago," Stefan said. "You and the king slept so long you missed it."

"Yes, *sleeping*. That's what we were doing." Alex winked at Stefan, making him pretend to gag. "Lucky for us, the kitchen maids love me."

Alex grabbed Stefan's hand and took him down the small back stairwell Aaron had shown her years ago. The kitchen maids were happy to provide their queen with a snack when she showed up hungry at their door. With a loaf of fresh bread and some smoked boar sausage in her hands, Alex and Stefan set off to find Gryphon.

They walked down the main hallway, away from the kitchen. They saw Harold and Michael head into the library, so they knew he wasn't in there.

"Wait!" Alex exclaimed. "I have to find Edith! I never found out what happened!" She began to jog down the hall.

"What are you talking about?" Stefan asked, chasing after her.

"Harold asked Randal for Edith's hand! He left the celebrations with her, but then Aaron and I left before they came back! I have to find Edith!" Alex charged up the stairs, taking them two and three at a time. At the top of the third floor, she slammed into Gryphon so hard she fell backward.

"Whoa!" Gryphon quickly grabbed Alex's arm, saving her from falling down the spiral stairs. "You have to learn to watch where you are going."

"Actually, we were looking for you. But I need a minute. I have to find Edith. Can you wait here with Stefan?" Alex asked, bouncing anxiously.

"Lynx brought her to Warren this morning," Gryphon said. "With her parents."

"What?" Alex asked. Disappointment flooded her. *I spend one morning alone with Aaron and I miss everything?*

Gryphon eyed her suspiciously. "I'm sure she didn't mean to neglect to share her good news."

"They'll be back for dinner," Stefan added.

"Hopefully," Alex said.

"Where are we going for training?" Stefan asked, turning toward Gryphon.

"If you're open to it, I'd like to go to the Stronghold. We trained there before, so it'll be easier to see changes."

Alex gulped. Stefan put his hand on her shoulder and gently squeezed it.

"I'm all right with it. Race you there." Alex grabbed Stefan's hand and cracked them to the beach.

As Stefan looked around the beach, his forehead wrinkled and his lips became a hard frown. "This is where you first met Gryphon?"

"Yes."

"And where he saved you from Kruft?"

"One time, yes."

"And where he saved you when you ... broke?" He chose his words carefully.

"Yes." With the sounds of the lapping waves, she wasn't sure if Stefan heard her.

"I'm sorry I wasn't there for you."

"Stefan—"

"I know. There wasn't anything I could do, but I still feel as though I abandoned you."

Gryphon appeared beside Alex. "That's ridiculous. You did everything you could. You even let me beat you up to try to break the oath."

Stefan snorted. "*I* beat *you* in that fight."

"Did you? That isn't how I remember it." Gryphon's focus

shifted to Alex. "All right, Princess, show me what you've learned. I know you're stronger from our battles, but I want to see what you're capable of when you're not under pressure."

Alex turned toward the water and inhaled deeply before shifting her stance. The moment she raised her arms, Gryphon cleared his throat. Alex shot him a scowl.

"Form," he said.

Stefan crossed his arms. "Her form is perfect."

"Not for magic."

Alex let out a frustrated groan and dropped her arms to her sides. "Remind me?"

Gryphon squatted in front of her. He moved her left foot forward, then considered her side for some time. When he stood behind her and grabbed her hips, he twisted her body more toward the sea. Alex heard Stefan growl.

"Stefan," she warned.

Gryphon merely chuckled as he pulled her shoulders back. *Elbows up, Princess.*

Alex closed her eyes and felt for the lid on her well. Gently, she pushed it off and focused. A year earlier, she had used her Poseidon powers to split the sea, but now she could do more. She kept the left side of the sea calm while making a storm on the other side. After that, Alex demonstrated her control over her Salem and Celtics gifts by growing a grove of small trees on the sandy beach and creating a wall of fire around them that stayed exactly where she put it. Gryphon made minimal sounds, but Stefan chuckled any time Alex concentrated hard enough to stick out her tongue.

"How do you feel? Drained at all?" Gryphon asked.

"Not really," Alex said.

"We've been working on combining her magic with her fighting skills since she returned from here," Stefan said.

"Why?"

Alex said, "My magic still doesn't come the way I need it to when the circumstances are less than ideal, and so combining it with my knight training gives me the best of both."

"Have you managed two powers at once?"

Alex's mouth dropped open. "That's possible?"

"Only for the strongest of sorcerers. Observe." Gryphon walked onto the dry seabed between the cliffs of water Alex had opened. His eyes flashed orange, and without blinking, he twisted his wrists. As he thrust his palms upward, the ground beneath them trembled, and a mountain rose from the sea.

Alex stepped forward in complete awe, but Stefan pulled her back in fear.

"I won't hurt her, Little Wafner. Let her go." Gryphon's fingers closed to a point. Stefan let go, and she went to stand beside Gryphon.

Fire exploded from the top of the mountain, which was still rising from the sea. Alex gasped and leaped back. Gryphon slammed his palms together and threw his hands down, sending the volcano crashing back into the earth. The sea rushed in to fill the void, crashing into the molten rocks. A heavy wave of steam blew at them, nearly searing their skin until Alex threw her ice wind at it. Her lungs burned from her forceful breaths.

Gryphon smirked at her. "That is what we're going to work on next, Princess."

Alex gulped, and the sea churned around them.

# CHAPTER 34
# ALEX

Alex waited in the royal carriage for the others. She'd changed her gown three times before deciding on a gold one to match Aaron's royal tunic. She fiddled with the hem, working a loose thread. The fear of having chosen wrong made her anxious.

Jerome was with her, and he watched her with the intensity that only a Wafner could. "How are you holding up?" he finally asked.

Alex scoffed. "About which part?"

"Any of it. All of it."

Alex looked out the window. "Not as well as everyone thinks. I'm having new nightmares that leave me scared and anxious all day. I'm worried Aaron will turn back into a monster, or that someone we love will be killed by the sorcerers hunting me and it'll all be my fault."

"I'm not surprised your nightmares are worse. You were still struggling to process your memories before the curse and everything that came after. You've also gotten married, become a queen, fended off sorcerers, and invited other sorcerers to live in the castle. Be kind to yourself. It's a lot for anyone to adjust to."

Alex started twisting her skirt again.

"They're here." Jerome stood and opened the carriage door, holding out his hand. Jessica stepped in, followed by Michael, Stefan, and Aaron.

Aaron and Stefan sat on either side of Alex, while Michael sat across from her. He was pale and sweating.

"It'll be fine, Michael. I promise," Aaron said. He squeezed Alex's hand as if he could feel her nervousness.

"I don't understand why any of you are nervous," Stefan said. "He opened the treasure room in Warren. Only a blood descendant of the three founding families can do that."

Michael took Jessica's hand. "I'm not nervous about being rejected as a Veremund. I'm scared that my blood family won't be as good as the one I've found in this carriage."

Jessica kissed Michael's cheek as the carriage lurched forward. Despite Stefan's confidence, Alex's stomach jumped with the carriage.

Aaron took her hand. "What can I do?" he asked.

"Nothing," Michael said. He grinned at Alex and hummed. It was their song, and Alex couldn't help but hum back. Before long, Alex's nerves had settled. She looked out the window of the carriage, bouncing along the road that headed past the town. Datten homes were sturdier but less colorful than those of Warren. The stone walls were strong enough to withstand storms and attacks, and the roofs looked easy enough to replace. After a few twisting turns on different roads, the houses became larger. Here they were all two stories, with substantial land around the properties.

They turned down an obsidian cobblestone road, and Alex's heart pounded in her chest. Her hands were slick, and she turned away from the window to calm her breathing, but everyone in the carriage knew her too well.

"Why are you panicking?" Michael asked.

Alex choked back a sob.

"You remember," Jessica said.

Alex nodded and buried her face in her hands.

"Remember what?" Michael asked.

"This is the road to the old Wafner estate. The house we hid her in before it burned down," Jerome said.

"On the way home, I insist we take a different route." Aaron rubbed Alex's back.

Alex held her breath as they passed it. The field was over-grown, but she could see the burned-out house in the distance. She could still remember the warm sun on her face before Stefan threw her over his shoulder because she didn't want to leave the Wafners.

"We'll be there in a few minutes," Jerome said.

Alex could breathe again. Soon the carriage turned down a narrow road, toward an old estate. The house was not as grand as the estates in Warren, but Alex found beauty in all things, and this house was perfect. An immaculately kept garden that made her father's pale in comparison surrounded the duchess's manor.

"I didn't know homes in Datten were made from logs," Alex said.

"Only the oldest ones are. Those made in the last century are stone," Jerome explained.

The logs made her think of Kirsh, and she smiled. Iron shutters were decorated with flowers, and the grandiose front door was made from planks of dark wood. As they pulled nearer, Alex spotted a small stable to the side, and another beautiful garden that would rival any in Warren.

The driver stopped the carriage in front of the door, where Jerome and Stefan climbed out and held out their hands to her.

Worried her legs wouldn't hold her, Alex grabbed both their hands, and Aaron gave her a concerned look.

The main door swung open, and a handsome man with auburn skin and hair greeted them. His eyes were moss green, making Alex smile. His uniform consisted of simple black pants with a deep red tunic, which sported a crest Alex didn't recognize.

"The Veremund crest," Aaron whispered in her ear.

"Your Royal Highness." The man bowed lower than Alex thought was possible. "The duchess is expecting you."

"Thank you, Aldo." Aaron nodded.

The butler smiled at Alex. "Queen Alexandria, your beauty has not been exaggerated, and your father's crown suits you, King Aaron. General Wafner, Sir Wafner, Lady Wafner." He paused, and his eyes went wide when they hit Michael, but he recovered. "Apologies, Sir ..."

"Wafner. My son-in-law," Jerome replied.

Aldo nodded with an awkward smile but didn't stop staring at Michael. "If you'll allow me to bring you to the sitting room, I'll retrieve the tea."

The group followed Aldo down a simple hall. Michael motioned for Aaron and Alex to go ahead of him and Jessica. Everything smelled rich and woodsy, like the Dark Forest. The scent of pine engulfed Alex, and she relaxed. Aaron walked beside her, gazing at the paintings of Datten and Warren that spanned the length of the hallway. Aldo opened the doors and bowed as they entered.

Alex brought her hands to her face. Before them was a giant painting of a young couple on their wedding day. The woman stared lovingly at her new husband, who looked exactly like Michael except for the eyes. A side door opened, and a beautiful old woman made her way into the room. She leaned on a cane but still appeared as if she were gliding. Like her manservant, her skin was a radiant auburn, and her blue eyes sparkled almost as much as her silver hair. Her dress was in the same style as the ones Guinevere wore, but it was deep red, like Warren's wine.

"Pleasure to see you both so soon, Your Royal Highnesses. I know it's customary for you to visit the higher nobility after taking the throne, but surely there were more pressing families for you to visit."

She moved as if she were bowing, but Alex rushed to her. "Please don't bow on our account."

Veronica turned to Jerome and Aaron, a smile spreading across her lips. "She's clearly Edward's daughter."

"Let me help you." Michael hurried to Victoria's side.

"Thank you, dear boy. You're—" She gasped and almost stumbled back, but Alex and Michael kept her upright. "Bruno? But it can't be." Cautiously, she moved her hand toward Michael's face. He took a knee before her so he could be face-to-face with her.

Silence filled the room as the duchess and Michael stared at each other. Finally, she inspected his hair, looked behind his left ear, and then tilted her head to the side. "Take off your shirt."

"I'm sorry?" Jessica asked.

The duchess turned toward Jessica. "My grandson Percival fell into the Datten castle fireplace when he was three years old, leaving a long scar across his back. Victoria healed it so it wouldn't hurt, but Matthias insisted the scar remain as a reminder. If you are my grandson, you'll have that scar."

Michael looked from Jessica to Alex. Alex pursed her lips and held out her hands for Michael's shirt.

"I owe you an apology, Alex," Michael said, pulling off his crested shirt.

"For what?" Aaron asked.

"Michael said the scar came from Alex pushing him out of a tree when she was six and he was seven," Stefan said.

"I'm disappointed," Alex said. "I really wanted it to be from pirates."

Michael laughed at Alex and turned around, showing a faded scar that ran across his entire back above his hips.

The duchess motioned for everyone to take a seat. Only then did Alex notice the beautiful couches and table in the middle of the room. The duchess sat and patted the spot beside her. Alex obeyed and sat next to her great-aunt.

"Now dears," she said, looking from Alex to Michael and back again. "Tell me how exactly you came to find my grandson, young lady."

"How'd you know she found me?" Michael asked.

"Victoria told me that one day her daughter would return something I lost, and that I shouldn't question it."

Heat crept up Alex's cheeks as she told the tale of all those years ago, when she was five and found Michael alone and injured in the Dark Forest, near Kirsh. Aldo brought them tea, and Aaron prepared Alex's cup while she finished the story.

The tea lasted for hours. Veronica told story after story about Michael's parents, and about the trouble Matthias had gotten into with Randal and Edward as boys. Stefan, Alex, and Michael told of their adventures growing up in the camp. They even shared some stories that Aaron and Jessica hadn't heard. Through it all, Michael couldn't stop smiling.

"Now the hard part," Veronica said, turning to Alex. "Is your father aware of who Percival is, dear?"

Alex tried desperately hard not to snicker every time the duchess called him Percival, but even Jessica and Aaron were struggling not to laugh.

"Yes. He asked me to assure you he's handling the transfer of title to make Michael the new Earl Veremund."

"Perfect. Thank you, Jerome, for allowing my grandson to borrow the Wafner name, but now that he's discovered his heritage, he'll need to use Veremund. Just as Wafner is revered in

Datten, a lot of history and responsibility comes with the Veremund name."

"What do you mean?" Michael asked.

"Your father was not only an Earl of Warren, but also one of the king's closest and most trusted advisors. In every generation since the kingdom's founding, the ruling Warren has had a Nial *and* a Veremund at their side. As one of the oldest families, one of those large estates in Warren now belongs to you. It must be fixed up before you return home."

Michael turned pale. "Home? But I serve the Queen of Datten. I won't leave Alex."

"You'll need to show your face in Warren for certain duties, but outside of those, you may, of course, stay with Alexandria. And when she takes the throne of Warren, she'll need you."

Michael nodded, swallowing hard.

"You have time, Michael," Alex said. "My father is healthy, and I have no intention of becoming queen of two kingdoms anytime soon."

"I suggest you take a few days to figure out what this means for you," Aaron added.

"But what about our responsibilities?" Michael's eyes widened.

"I hate to say it," Stefan grunted. "But Gryphon and I can manage Alex for a few days."

Aaron smiled. "Edith will need help planning her engagement party, and I'm sure Alex would enjoy helping."

"I would. I can get revenge on her sisters for that tea."

"Thank you," Michael said. "I'd like some more time to get to know my grandmother."

"Then it's settled," Jerome said, rising. "I'll escort them here in the morning, Duchess Veremund."

"What tea?" Stefan asked.

# CHAPTER 35
# AARON

*I'm exhausted. All I want to do is go to my bed with my wife and sleep for a week.* Aaron rubbed his throbbing head. Before today, he'd never realized how much trade occurred between the three kingdoms. Even more would be needed now to rebuild Betruger Castle and the town after the sorcerers had sunk everything. He'd spent the morning talking about the trade negotiations with Edward and Harold, and he was already drained when he left the meetings to go to the tea with Alex and the Wafners. The trip was important for Michael, and Alex wanted everything to go well, so he'd put on his best king's face for them.

For once, everything went perfectly. Over the next few days, Michael and Jessica visited the duchess to help Michael learn about his past, and the way Alex's face lit up when Michael met his grandmother made it all worth it. Somehow Alex had convinced their parents that a quiet dinner with their closest friends was called for after the attacks of late. The idea of a simple meal was a relief. Aaron pulled his royal tunic over his head and tossed it aside, along with his gold shirt. Putting on his favorite red training shirt made him feel more normal than he had in forever.

"How did you do this, Father? Being a different version of your-self to everyone all day is exhausting."

"He says you get used to it." Alex closed the door.

"Does he follow me a lot?" Aaron rubbed his neck and glanced at Alex.

"Only sometimes. He mostly comes when you're struggling with something, then leaves when you figure it out."

"Thank you, Father."

"Are you ready for dinner? I'm starving."

"In a minute. I have a surprise for you." Aaron took her hand and led her to sit at the foot of their bed. He noticed she had to keep shifting to fix her long, heavy skirt. *Perfect timing.* He felt her eyes follow him to his wardrobe. He came back with a large red box wrapped with a gold bow.

"That looks suspiciously familiar."

"It should," Aaron said. He pressed his forehead to Alex's and kissed her. "Consider it an apology. A second chance, after messing up your training clothes."

"I didn't mind that they were gold. I just … I can't always be in gold training clothes. I wore nothing else at Moorloc's."

Aaron tapped the box. "Hence the present."

Alex's smile took up her entire face as she pulled the bow and opened the box. She dug through the tissue paper, and her smile flickered, but she recovered. "A dress? How thoughtful."

"You must be exhausted too, because that lie was horrible." Aaron took the box from her. "Take the gift."

Alex pulled out the dress and gasped. She stood and held it against herself in the mirror. The skirt was short.

"What do you think?"

"Where's the rest of it?"

Aaron laughed.

"What is *everyone* going to think?" Alex asked, swinging her leg out.

Aaron grinned. The top of the dress resembled her usual gowns but had a higher neckline and more room in the shoulders. The corset was in the front, and the remaining chest material was made of sturdy, brown leather with a soft lining. The skirt ended at the knee, allowing her full use of her legs. "You'll wear your training pants under it. Now you can wear a skirt, the way Jessica and my mother want you to, but you also have the freedom to move that Stefan and Jerome need."

"Who thought of this?"

Aaron laughed. "I did. My mother said the Datten people will see and treat you as I tell them to. I want them to see you as the powerful and brave queen who knocked a Wafner to the ground, but also recognize you for the beautiful woman I see."

Alex clutched the dress, and a genuine smile spread across her face. "Thank you."

"You're welcome. Now let's head to dinner. I recall that you're starving."

In the dining hall, the servants had pushed together three knight's tables to form a large square so they could see each other while they ate. In the center of the table were all Aaron's favorites: roasted boar, potatoes, green beans, ale, and two fresh breads.

"I asked the kitchen to make your favorites," Alex whispered. "Not a carrot in sight."

"It's perfect."

They took their seats, and their friends soon joined them. Stefan, Michael, and Jessica updated the others on their visit to the duchess. Megesti told them of his and Birch's plans to redo his lab and make it larger for all the sorcerers who now used it. Edith had returned in time for dinner, allowing her and Harold to proclaim their engagement. Once they had, the conversation turned toward wedding plans.

Edith's mother wanted the engagement celebration in Warren. Alex loved the idea and said she'd ask her father to let them use the castle for the wedding, since they would not complete the construction of Betruger's new castle in time. Aaron admired that despite everything, she was still herself.

When Alex excused herself to go to the restroom, Aaron stood to let her get up from the bench, and Megesti slid next to him. But before Aaron could speak, Megesti closed his eyes and held his forehead.

"Megesti? Are you all right?" Aaron was holding his friend's shoulder, trying to look at his face to see what was going on, when a crash echoed in the hall.

"Alex!" Aaron shouted.

Alex had fallen to her knees in the middle of the hall, and Michael and Stefan rushed to her. She knocked over an iron candelabra, and Stefan put out the flames.

"Alex?" Michael said, standing in front of her. "I think she's having a premonition, but it seems different."

"Different how?" Stefan moved to Michael's side and looked at Alex with surprise. "Her eyes are black!"

Megesti's head jerked toward Aaron. His eyes were solid white, as they usually were when he got a vision, but the way he spoke was eerie. Then, Alex and Megesti spoke in unison, with a single deep voice that rattled and didn't sound like either of them.


*"He will betray her. With that single act, he'll release the beast and Datten will pay the cost.*

*The pain will destroy her, releasing it into the world so she may watch it burn.*

*He left her once, but never again. From the broken ruins shall rise the protector they need.*

*Ties that bind are snapped, and the choices made are etched in stone, never to be undone.*

*She will earn her name and make her line proud. To be the greatest of her people, she will give up all she knows.*

*He will break the laws to protect her and make one into two. His love is strong enough to push him to the end.*

*He shall protect the cub as he always has, and was always meant to do.*

*The unexpected gift will save them all.*

*If they survive the trial, then all will be right, but if they perish, Torian will burn to ash."*

Megesti slumped forward into Aaron's waiting arms, but Alex continued to stare. Her fully black eyes bore into Aaron's as if she could see through him. Michael wrapped his arm around her chest to hold her up. Edith moved slowly toward Alex, and her head spun to face her. Edith's hands flew to her mouth and neck, and she shook her head. Aaron had never seen her so terrified. A shrill cackle burst from Alex and she smirked wickedly. *That's not my wife.*

"Gryphon!" Stefan's voice tore through the heaviness. A moment later, he appeared, and Aaron knew something was very wrong.

The cocky sorcerer's mouth dropped open. "I didn't imagine it. Your eyes really do turn black." He crept toward her and placed his hand on her forehead, and Alex's head finally dropped forward.

"What's causing it?" Michael asked, letting Stefan take Alex from his grip. Stefan hoisted her up the same way he'd done hundreds of times.

Megesti groaned and blinked his eyes. Aaron passed him to Harold and rushed to Alex.

Edith was there, trembling.

"What did she say?" Aaron asked.

Edith swallowed. "She said, 'You know who I am' and then laughed."

Gryphon came beside Aaron. "*Do* you know—?"

Edith nodded. "It's a fury."

# CHAPTER 36
# AARON

Aaron worked with Stefan, struggling to remember and write down every word of the disturbing premonition, but Kharon pacing the library and muttering to themself wasn't helping. The others watched from their seats. Randal and Edward had joined them, while Jessica had gone to rest. Gryphon and Lynx looked bored.

Finally, Kharon stopped and turned to Edith and Michael. "She said 'fury'?"

"No—not Alex. Edith," Michael said, pressing his lips into a tight line.

Aaron tightened his grip on Alex's waist, and her father grasped her hand. His face was pale, and he looked as exhausted as Aaron felt.

"What's a fury?" Alex asked.

"A legend," Gryphon said, glancing at Kharon to get their approval before going on. "They stem from the line of Hades and were originally called the Erinyes. They were goddesses who sought revenge on Hades's behalf."

"There's more to it than that," Kharon said, rubbing their eyes with both hands. "I can't remember all the details, since it's been almost a century since I read that titan book. They went after specific types of crimes as defined by Hades but then mysteriously vanished. We never figured out where they went."

Edith looked at her father, who was leaning against the wall, and Randal glanced at Edward. "They went into the line of Cassandra," Edith said.

"Went *in*?" Birch said.

Edward tensed and narrowed his eyes at Randal. "How does she know that?"

"The legend's been passed from generation to generation in the Nial and Veremund lines," Randal said. "One day, a Cassandra sorceress would bring down the curse of Warren from within. But if the wrong Cassandra took power, she'd destroy the kingdom and leave it in ruins."

Alex trembled in Aaron's arms, while Edward went eerily silent.

"How?" Stefan asked.

"They're born that way," Edith said.

"Are you saying that Cassandras are born possessed by a fury?" Birch asked.

"Not possessed, and only the titans," Randal answered.

Kharon paced again. "That explains why there have never been more than three daughters of Cassandra alive at once. There were three furies. How did I not realize this sooner?"

Gryphon stared at Alex in disbelief, and she avoided his gaze. Aaron hated the silent moments that passed between them, hated knowing he could hear her thoughts and she, his. But hatred wasn't what Alex needed from him, so he swallowed it down.

"Is that why we treasure Cassandras?" Lynx asked.

Kharon paused and scratched their head. "I don't know. I wish I had my books."

Edith whispered, "The fury cannot take control of a sorceress until she undergoes trauma connected to all the crimes avenged by that fury."

Silence filled the room. Everyone stared at Edith and her father.

Edward broke the silence when he slammed his hands on the table. "Exactly how long have you known this?"

"Since I was young. Long before you met Victoria."

Edward rose and marched to Randal. "And you never said a word?"

Randal exhaled and glanced at Michael before replying. "Matthias and I agreed. You were in love with her, and we didn't know if Victoria was the one who would save us or ruin us."

"So you kept me in the dark about my wife and daughter?" Edward's voice rose with each word.

*This is getting dangerous. I've never seen Edward this angry. Not even when Alex was in danger.*

"The warning passed through our lines claims a Cassandra would break the curse. After Alexandria was born, Matthias and I believed that the curse had ended, that we didn't have to worry anymore. Since our founding, there had never been a girl born to the throne until ... you."

"Do not address my daughter," Edward growled, moving closer to Randal.

"Edward, we were young and arrogant. We never should have let down our guard."

"When exactly did you let down your guard?" Alex asked. She eyed Randal, but then her eyes flashed gold and she whipped her head toward Gryphon. Her mouth fell open, and her voice came out as a whisper. "*You knew.*"

"Knew what?" Aaron asked.

"You left us, knowing what my grandfather had planned!"

The torches tripled in size. Startled, Aaron released Alex, whose breath became ragged. He turned to Edward. His usually calm demeanor was gone, replaced with a level of rage he would have expected to see on his own father.

"No! That's not true," Edith shouted. "It can't be. Right, Daddy?"

The air in the room became heavy. The king's face was stoic, but his shoulders were drawn back and his body full of tension. No one spoke a word until Randal's head dropped. "We thought she'd kill Arthur. That if he went after Alexandria, she'd retaliate, and we'd be free of him. We were wrong."

Edward lunged at Randal. "You were her guard. Your duty was to protect us—all of us, and you left my wife and daughter alone, knowing my father planned to kill them!"

"Edward, we thought—"

But Edward didn't let him finish. He punched Randal in the face and grabbed him by the collar, slamming him into the bookshelves. The general made no move against his king. Harold, Stefan, and Michael all leaped to their feet, knocking over a bench, but Alex and Edith were faster and rushed toward their fathers.

"Father, stop." But Edward hit Randal again.

Chaos broke out in the room. Harold pulled Edith back so she wouldn't get hurt. Michael and Stefan didn't know what to do and watched in shock, while the sorcerers stood back, trying to stay out of the way.

Randal's blood covered Edward's fist, and he struck his friend again. Randal wouldn't even defend himself as Edward whaled on him.

"Alex, don't!" Aaron pleaded.

But Alex was already pushing herself between them. She grabbed her father's arm to stop him, and Edward reacted with rage and adrenaline. He twisted his arm to force Alex off him, and when she wouldn't let go, he shoved her and slammed her into the ground. The moment Alex hit the ground, rage burst through Aaron, and he banged his fist on the table.

"Enough!" Aaron's voice echoed off the walls, and Edward finally stopped. Aaron rushed to his godfather and ripped him off Randal, leaving Gryphon and Stefan to help Alex up. It only took a glance for Aaron to see she was cradling a glowing wrist.

"Aaron," Edward growled. "This isn't your concern."

Straightening to look Edward in the eye, Aaron summoned every ounce of courage and his own father's strength. "The moment you laid your hands on my wife, it became my concern."

That snapped Edward out of his rage. "Alexandria," he said, moving toward her, but Alex leaped back, bumping into Stefan. Seamlessly, Gryphon stepped before them and burst into his orange glow, growling at Edward.

*And that's why you're her guard. To take the pressure off Stefan.*

"Daddy?" Edith rushed to Randal, ignoring the blood covering his face and chest, and wrapped her arms around him.

"I'm all right, sweetheart."

Running his hands through his hair, Aaron turned around. "Birch, please send Edward home."

"Excuse me?" Edward snarled.

"We won't get anywhere with you here, and we need to sort this out."

"Young man, if you think—"

"Do not 'young man' me!" Aaron shouted at Edward. "My father would do exactly the same thing. You're enraged, and I of all people understand that, but taking it out on your best friend or your daughter is not okay."

Clearly surprised by the tone Aaron used, Edward cleared his throat. "Wait until you've been king for more than five minutes before judging another."

"Now, either Birch can take you back to Warren with the dignity befitting a king, or Gryphon can."

Edward stayed silent.

The sorceress nodded to Alex and cracked away with Edward.

Alex moved around Gryphon to get to Randal. "Stefan, I need water." When Birch returned, Alex had healed Randal's face, and Edith had washed away most of the blood.

"I'll start from the beginning," Randal said.

# CHAPTER 37

# GRYPHON

The fire in Gryphon's room crackled as he lit and extinguished his palm. They'd talked for over an hour after Edward left, but all they knew was that every Cassandra titan had a fury inside her. Not how, or why; only that it was there. Kharon knew they originally came from Hades. Randal and Edith knew the prophecy that one of these Cassandras would break the curse of Warren, but one could also cause Warren's downfall.

*I shouldn't have read Randal's mind when he was arguing with Edward. I hope Alex isn't angry with me for exposing him. Randal mentioned that two Cassandras would matter to Warren. Was Victoria the savior, or is it Alex? Alex is the daughter, so either she broke the curse or Victoria did by bearing her. No wonder I was so drawn to her. She has not only the power of a Heart, but also this vengeful beast. There has to be a way to free her of it, but where do we even begin?*

Gryphon breathed in sync with the flicker of the fireplace, touching the Head and Heart marking on his neck.

*What if the Hades books could help? Would it be worth the risk of getting them?*

His room in Datten was simple, but he'd added a few touches: books he'd pilfered from various castles, a few tins of potions he'd brought with him, a pillow from Alex's couch in Warren, and the letter she'd written to him at Moorloc's castle—not a happy letter, but it reminded him of how close he'd come to losing her. He'd sworn never to let it happen again. He swung open the doors to his wardrobe, grabbed his loosest clothes and his only non-titan cloak, and threw them on the bed. It was the thick black wool one that he used to sneak around his parents' castle.

Running his fingers along the shelf, he paused at the smallest tin. "Ares protect me."

"If you're asking *him* for help, you're obviously planning something stupid."

Gryphon clasped the tin in his hand and turned to face Alex. "What makes you so sure?"

Alex frowned and pointed at the cloak and satchel on the bed.

"I could say that same thing to you." Gryphon grinned, looking her up and down. She wore sparring clothes, carried her satchel, and had on a solid black cloak that smelled of Michael and their horses. "Are you wearing Michael's things now?"

"Aaron owns nothing without red or gold on it," Alex said. She stepped toward him. "Where are we going?"

"*We* are not going anywhere. You are going back to bed." He grabbed his satchel and cloak.

"You're not going alone."

"Where do you believe I'm going?" Gryphon stepped into her space and looked smug.

"To your father's library to collect the Hades titan books."

Gryphon's smirk vanished. "How—?"

"I had a nightmare." She swallowed.

"What did you see?"

She turned away. "You can't go alone."

"Tell me, or I'm not bringing you."

"Blood. Screams. Your father … burning you. I thought fire couldn't hurt Salem sorcerers."

Gryphon tugged on the collar of his tunic. "It can if it's from a powerful Salem sorcerer."

"So you lied to me." Alex crossed her arms.

"'Lied' is harsh. I believe what I said was that *your* powers couldn't hurt me, which is true."

"Did your father burn that handprint on your shoulder?"

"Yes."

"Then I'm coming."

"Alex—"

"Stop arguing. You're wasting your breath." She held out her hand to him. "I'm waiting, Sunset."

"You know Aaron's going to gut me if he finds out about this."

"Let me deal with Aaron."

"Bringing you is going to set off a hundred alarms. You're an unknown power, and if the Head and Heart appear together, they'll know."

"I don't care. That nightmare can't come true."

Gryphon rolled his eyes. Opening the small tin, he rubbed the ointment in his hands to soften the wax. When he held out his hands to Alex, she stepped toward him.

*Why do you always smell so good? It's torture.*

Gryphon placed his fingers on the middle of her forehead and rubbed the wax into her skin. He drifted down her cheeks and under her chin. He paused at her ears. "Can you lift your braid?" he asked. When she did, he rubbed her ears and finished putting the wax down the back of her neck.

When he removed his hands, Alex trembled. "That's cold. What did it do?"

"The peppermint makes it feel cool." He held up the tin. "This is all I have left of the wax I made to hide myself from other Mystics, specifically my father."

Alex's mouth dropped open. "Is that how you hid your location when you trained me?"

"Yes. It stops Mystics from looking through your eyes." He put the tin back on the shelf and turned back to Alex. "Avoid using your magic while we're there. We all give off a unique aura of power."

"I assume your father knows everyone's."

"He does. And I'd like to keep yours from him for now."

"But he's met me."

"Fighting you in the open would not be enough to learn it, but if he caught us in tight quarters, it would be."

Gryphon grabbed her hand and his cloak and cracked them away from Datten.

THE ROOM WAS spotless and sparse, like the one they had just left. There were a few books and the odd trinket. Alex spun to take in the space.

"Is this your bedroom?"

When Gryphon nodded, her face fell. "What is it?" he asked.

"Lygari's room didn't have personal things either. Is that normal?"

Gryphon snorted. "No. If you saw my bedroom at Birch's house, you'd see the room I considered my true home. We're not here to analyze my belongings."

Gryphon got to work gathering everything he wanted. He draped his cloak across the bed. With inhuman speed, he grabbed the items he wanted out of the wardrobe and tossed them onto the blanket. Alex slipped past Gryphon to the corner bookshelf. Gryphon had so many books that the shelf extended onto the ceiling.

Gryphon followed her and scanned the shelves to grab a

few. When he snapped his fingers to retrieve a book on the ceiling, Alex's mouth dropped open.

"Now what?" Alex whispered.

He braced himself against the shelf and closed his eyes. Focusing on his father, a wave of nausea hit him. "My father's in the throne room. We'll hurry to the library and get out." He tied his cloak, bundling the items inside it, and handed it to Alex. "Send it home. But do it quickly so no one senses your powers."


"I THINK I sent it to your room. There or the kitchen." She shrugged, and he couldn't help the smile that spread across his face.

"Come on," he said.

Gryphon grabbed Alex's hand and led her to the fireplace. Ducking his head, he pushed against the back wall, and it opened. He slipped through the door and took Alex with him. The tunnel was smaller than those in Warren and as dark as night. Gryphon heard Alex's breath speed up and pulled her closer to him.

"I know the way, and I won't leave you."

It was slow going, but he didn't dare summon light. He held Alex's hand and used his free one to feel along the wall until he found the turn that would take them to the library. He went faster until he felt the carving in the stone. With a sigh of relief, he released Alex and put both his hands on the stone to check for heat. It was cool to the touch, so he pushed the stone, but nothing happened.

"What's wrong?"

"I'd usually use magic."

Alex placed her hand on his arm. "Where do I push?"

"It's a specific spot, so come here." Alex slipped under his arm and stood caged between him and the door. Gryphon found her hands and covered her hand with his. "Count to three?"

She whispered, "One ... two ... three!"

Together they pushed, and the stone door opened, barely wide enough for one person to fit. Gryphon slipped out first, and Alex after. Distracted, she bumped into Gryphon. "It's beautiful," she whispered.

Of all the labs and libraries he'd seen in the mortal world, this dwarfed them all. She gawked at the ceilings, which were as tall as those of Warren's great halls. The ladders along the outer bookcases almost disappeared at the top, and Alex smirked.

Her thoughts reached him. *Michael would be terrified up there.*

*Troublemaker.* Gryphon chuckled. Before them was Garrick's lab table. It ran half the length of the room and could seat fifty men comfortably. Alex ran her fingers over the wood, taking in the shelves of pots, powders, and plants before her, and the wall of ancient weapons owned by the Head.

Gryphon moved to her side and waited while she took everything in. When she turned the other direction, her gasp was audible. The Head's library held all the titan and founding books for each of the lines except Merlin and the missing portion of Cassandra that Alex had. Bookshelves along the outside went up to the ceiling and crossed it to the other side. The central shelves were lower, with crates stacked on top in places. She walked toward the front shelf as if entranced. She reached out to touch a book but stopped herself and turned back to Gryphon. When he nodded, she moved for the book's spine, and a tiny static charge hit her finger. Alex snorted and grabbed the book anyway.

He came up behind her and peeked over her shoulder. "Figures it would be Poseidon."

Alex ran her finger along the book. "As in *Poseidon* and not 'line of'?"

"Yes. This bookcase is full of the journals and books from the line founders. Only the Heads and Hearts can remove them."

Alex bit her lip and slid the book back. "Do you see the Hades books?" she asked.

Gryphon scanned, but there were no books with gray spines. But it wasn't only Hades's books that were missing. The Ares ones were gone, too.

Alex walked to the end of the row, searching in vain. "Where are the rest?"

"We have thousands of books here, but there's one other place we keep the most valuable things." Gryphon grabbed her hand and tugged. "I'm sorry you can't explore the shelves, but know that one day ... as the future Head and Heart, these will be ours."

Alex looked back at the shelves longingly, so Gryphon tugged her again, and they hurried past the rows of bookcases to the last one at the very back of the room.

"Why is this one different?" Alex asked.

"What do you sense?"

Alex walked along the shelves and paused at a large obsidian stone slab covering the middle of the shelf. "Power," she whispered.

Gryphon placed his hand on the stone and muttered a spell under his breath. Alex jumped back, and the large stone broke in two and slid aside. At the front were two pearls, one black and the other white, sitting on their stands, with a third empty stand beside them. Next to the empty stand were two identical black crowns. The gems jutting up from them had always reminded Gryphon of dragon teeth. Behind them was a row of unusually shaped bottles and vials, and on the shelf beneath were journals of gray and orange coloring. Gryphon grabbed the oldest-looking gray book and handed it to Alex. She tucked it into her satchel, and Gryphon grabbed a few more before a low, guttural growl emanated from behind them. Quickly, Gryphon grabbed Alex's hand to crack them back to Datten, but nothing happened. *Ferflucs!*

"What?" Alex's voice trembled.

"I can't crack." His heart nearly leaped into his throat when he heard another growl.

Alex went pale, her eyes wide with terror. "It's the dog I saw in my nightmare," she whispered.

Gryphon nodded. *Don't be scared. I'll protect you.* He gripped her waist, pulling her close as the giant shadow of a dog's head appeared down the aisle. He slammed his hand over Alex's mouth before she could scream and pulled her down the aisle. At the end, he listened for Cerberus's breathing and steps. Hearing nothing, he took Alex out of the aisle.

He peeked down the next one and sighed with relief. Nothing but books. *Stay between me and the bookshelf.* He released Alex, and they were slinking toward the front of the library when Alex squeezed Gryphon's arm.

Her arm was trembling. *What is that?* Even her thoughts sounded terrified.

Gryphon followed her gaze to the top of the bookcase before them. Squatting on it was Cerberus.

"Gryphon ..." she wheezed, squeezing him tighter.

Gryphon clenched his jaw at the sight of his mother's dog. The beast leaped down and stalked toward Gryphon. He shoved Alex behind him to protect her from all three of the mutt's heads. Just as he thought it couldn't get any worse, the door groaned open.

"Cerberus? Did you find them, boy?" The beast growled and yipped in reply. "Don't bother trying to crack out, Gryphon. Your hexa cast a spell on the castle that only lets you crack in. We wanted to make sure you'd stay put the next time you came home, though I'm delighted that you convinced Victoria's daughter to join you. I assumed her husband would want you two far apart."

Gryphon could feel every tremble that went through Alex. Her fear was so strong he could smell it in the surrounding air, making his Ares powers froth to protect her. *Don't lose control.* He focused on Cerberus. The beast in front of him snarled, showing razor-sharp teeth. Each of the three heads was the size of a horse's head, and the entire beast was large enough to take on a bear. Cerberus watched every movement with three sets of black eyes. Gryphon inched them toward the front of the room and realized the dog was tracking Alex, not him.

"Stay away from her, you useless mutt. You may have used me as a chew toy before I got my powers, but I'll set your heads on fire if you so much as sniff her."

Alex and Gryphon crept away from the beast as one. It stalked them with each step. After what felt like an hour, they'd made their way up the long aisle and out of the bookcases. Gryphon kept Alex between him and the wall.

"I can protect myself, Gryphon."

"I know you can, Princess, but I won't bring you home with holes in you."

"Gryphon," Garrick admonished, looking them up and down. "I'd never let our first sorceress Heart in millennia come to harm. What do you take me for? A monster?" His smirk made Gryphon's blood run cold.

Cerberus trotted across the open space toward Garrick, taking a seat beside him. Two heads snarled while the central head enjoyed a quick pet from Garrick. Together they blocked the only door that led out of the room.

"You *are* a monster," Alex said, and Gryphon squeezed her tighter.

Garrick chuckled and fixed his collar. He wore his simplest black Head robe, which stopped at his ankles to allow more movement. A crown, the symbol of the Head, was stitched on it, and his sleeves were rolled up. On his right hand, he wore the ring he'd inherited from his father, which would one day go to Gryphon. It supposedly contained the magic of their line's founder. It had been forged from a metal no one could identify, and it held a large blue moonstone.

*Don't worry. I'll get us out of this.*

*How?* Alex thought back.

*I haven't figured that out yet.*

Garrick stepped closer. "Regardless of why you're here, I'm thrilled to have you, daughter of Cassandra. I'm feeling so generous that if you surrender yourselves, then all your little friends—Lynx, Kharon, Birch, and her son with Merlock—can spend the rest of their lives in the mortal world. I won't seek revenge as long as they never set foot in the Forbidden Lands again."

Gryphon felt Alex's hand stroke his back, and heat and strength filled his body. *Are you sharing your powers with me?*

"I'm trying to," Alex whispered.

Gryphon eyed his father and smiled. He took one large step back and then another, until he heard a soft thump when Alex hit the stone wall. Cerberus sensed something was amiss and stood.

"It's rude to keep people waiting, Princess," Garrick growled.

Alex gulped and stepped beside Gryphon. "I'm not giving you anything. Gryphon belongs with me now."

Gryphon's throat went dry as he twisted his neck to look at Alex. Her eyes were fixed on his father, and glowing gold.

"How sweet," Garrick mocked. "You certainly warmed up quickly to my son. What does your husband think about that?"

"Aaron trusts me."

"What made you take to my son? Was it him helping you? I assure you, it wasn't the first time he visited your world. How would you feel if you knew we sent him?"

Alex's shoulders drew back and her eyes flipped back to green. "You're lying."

"Are you certain about that?" Garrick patted Cerberus and stepped toward them. "Mystics can read minds and dreams, dear. In that regard, is anything ever safe?"

"Gryphon?" Alex's voice trembled.

*Lies. Don't let him in your head.*

*But ...*

*Alex, get angry. Remember what he did to your family ... threatened your uncles, drove your mother away, and tried to kill your father.*

Gryphon couldn't read the expression on Alex's face, and her thoughts were silent.

*Please don't believe him. I admit I hate seeing you with Aaron, but I would never do anything to hurt you.*

"Since you're here now, I should gift you your marks. You're old enough, and it's fairly obvious what lines you belong to." Garrick snapped his fingers.

Alex's hand flew to the base of her neck on the left side, and tears welled in her eyes as she bit her lip, clearly trying to hide her cry of pain.

With his father distracted by Alex, Gryphon moved his arm behind him and thrust his palm against the wall. He summoned his powers and, using his free arm, yanked Alex to his chest before sending his explosive fire at the wall behind them. With a deafening bang, his Salem and Ares powers combined to blow a gaping hole in the wall. Ears ringing and lungs burning from the ash and dust, he shoved Alex through.

"Run!"

# CHAPTER 38
# ALEX

Alex nearly fell when Gryphon shoved her through the jagged opening he'd ripped in the wall. Sucking in dust and debris, she coughed and blinked to focus. They stood in a hallway, and there were only two directions. She couldn't see Gryphon through the mess, but she heard Cerberus's growl clear as day. Not knowing which way to go, Alex picked a direction and ran.

*Left!*

Gryphon was steps behind her, and Stefan's words echoed through her head. *Don't look back. You have to push yourself endlessly. One day, your life might depend on it.*

The snarling behind them grew louder, and she was forced to speed up.

"Left!" Gryphon shouted.

Alex turned, narrowly avoiding hitting a wall. This long hallway was busier, and they barreled past several surprised sorcerers. Alex could see the spiral stairs at the end of the hallway and pushed herself hard to get to it. Her lungs ached as if they'd explode.

A sorceress cracked in front of them.

Ember cackled and dropped her arms, causing her entire body to erupt in flames so intense they set the stone floor ablaze.

It was too late to avoid the inferno, and Alex's fear took hold, making her send out icy bursts that extinguished the flames.

*Ares, that's cold!*

Alex glanced behind her to see Gryphon covered in frost. *Sorry.*

"Welcome home, Gryphon," Ember said, stalking toward them. Her eyes and body glowed red. "I see you brought your little witch."

Alex leaped back and collided with Gryphon. He grabbed her waist and pulled her closer.

Ember smirked, but before she could speak, claws clattered against stone, and a growl echoed in the hallway behind them.

Cerberus had caught them, and then Garrick and an older sorceress cracked beside Ember. The old one was wearing an orange robe like the one Alex had laughed at Gryphon over.

"Who's that?" Alex asked.

"My hexa," Gryphon said.

Before Alex could ask anything else, Gryphon was ripped from her so hard the force sent her crashing to the ground. She half turned, terrified to turn her back on the sorcerers. Two of the dog's heads had knocked Gryphon down. The third head leaned down and sniffed Alex before growling. Massive front paws held down Gryphon's chest while he struggled to free himself. The claws stretched and shredded Gryphon's shirt, ripping at his flesh. Alex scrambled to her feet, but she could only stare while the hound began biting Gryphon's arms as he tried to fight it off.

Alex struggled for her satchel. It had shifted when she fell, and the strap was tangled around her braid. She twisted it around her wrist and yanked it over her head, wincing when it ripped out some of her hair. She lunged toward the beast, swinging the bag of ancient books as hard as she could at the closest head. It made contact, and another head turned and clamped its jaws around her shoulder. Alex screamed, and the walls shook, startling the beast enough to release her and back away. All three pairs of ears tucked back.

Power surged through Alex. She stared down the beast, and it ran back down the hallway, whimpering. The pain in her shoulder was excruciating. Gryphon writhed in agony on the ground. Ember and Garrick watched as she mustered all her strength, preparing to fight, when Gryphon shouted in her head.

*You cracked the bundle from my room! His spell only works on me. Take us to Birch's cottage. I'll show you where.*

Garrick was saying something, but Alex dove and grabbed Gryphon's hand. Her well exploded, and she cracked them away from the castle.

It was pitch-black outside when they arrived. Alex couldn't see anything, but the smell of charred wood was all around them. She felt around and found Gryphon groaning on the ground. He struggled to his feet. Alex bit back a cry when he gripped her injured shoulder.

"I can't crack far enough," she said.

"Focus on Datten. Together, we might make it." Gryphon's grip shifted to her elbow and tightened as a warmth filled her.

Alex closed her eyes and pictured the throne room. "Aaron. Datten. Home."

With a crack, they arrived not in the throne room, but in the Datten courtyard. She struggled to hold up Gryphon and looked around for someone to help.

A small group of guards approached with swords drawn. "Who goes there?" one said.

"Caleb, help!" Alex cried.

"Your Royal Highness!" Caleb sheathed his sword and hurried toward them.

"Are Lucas and Hunter with you?" Caleb took Gryphon's weight from her.

"We are," Lucas replied.

"What happened? Should we sound the alarm?" Hunter asked.

"No alarm," Gryphon groaned.

"They shouldn't be able to follow us," Alex said. "Hunter, help Caleb get Gryphon to the lab. Lucas, fetch Aaron and my guards. Try not to worry them. I'll find Megesti and Birch."

"I'll help," Gryphon said.

"Ignore Gryphon's protests and get him to the lab as fast as you can."

"At once," Lucas said.

Alex stopped listening and cracked herself to the east tower. She ran up the steps to Megesti's room, rushed to his bed, and shook him awake. "Get up! I need your help."

Megesti shot up and lit the room with a wave of his hand. He rubbed his eyes and looked at Alex. "Why are you always covered in blood?"

Alex ripped the quilt from his bed. "Get to the lab, now. Bring your mother."

Alex had reached the stairs when Megesti shouted after her, "Her name is Birch."

The moment Alex hit the third floor, she heard Gryphon scream in pain. She rushed forward and threw open the lab door. Stefan and Caleb struggled to keep him from getting up. Lynx was shaking while grabbing frantically at several herbs and piling them on the table.

Michael was standing in the corner with Aaron. He took one look at her blood-soaked tunic and asked, "What happened to—wait, that's his blood, isn't it?"

"Most of it."

"Do something before he bleeds to death!" Lynx cried.

"He's not allowed to bleed to death," Aaron said. "Because I want to kill him."

When Birch, Kharon, and Megesti cracked into the room, Gryphon's pain became so intense that he lost control of his powers and burst into flames. Clearly terrified, Caleb and Stefan dropped him hard on the floor, and the rug caught fire.

Alex groaned. She summoned water and threw it on Gryphon, extinguishing both him and the rug. Lynx dropped to his side and moved the hair from his face as he moaned.

"He burst into flames!" Caleb said.

"He cauterized his wounds, so I can heal him easier."

"Caleb, go," Aaron said. "Gryphon's level of chaos is reserved for head guards only."

Caleb nodded and ran from the room, letting the door slam behind him.

"Who's going to tell us what happened?" Kharon asked.

"And what's on your neck?" Aaron asked.

Everyone turned toward Alex. Birch gasped. A moment later, Lynx smacked Gryphon, making him cry out.

"Ferflucs, Lynx!"

"You took her to the castle? How could you risk that?" Lynx slapped him again for good measure before Stefan pulled her away from him.

Alex kneeled beside Gryphon and closed her eyes, thinking of warm summers in the Warren garden, picking flowers with Aaron and seeing her mother smile. Heat pooled in her palms, and when she opened her eyes, both arms were gold. She placed her hands on Gryphon's back, and his seared flesh softened and reverted to smooth bronze.

When she'd finished, Aaron helped her to her feet. He moved her messy hair to examine her neck.

Megesti stood next to him and squinted. "Now I'm the only sorcerer without line marks. Lovely."

"What were you two thinking?" Birch asked, shaking her head at them. "If they'd captured you, Cerberus would've been the least of your concerns."

"We needed the books," Gryphon said, slowly getting up. Kharon offered their hand, and Gryphon let them pull him up. Once he was on his feet, Gryphon grimaced, pulled his shredded shirt over his head, and threw it in the fireplace.

Alex reached inside her satchel and offered the volumes to Kharon.

They rushed forward to take them, eyes wide. "You got the Hades journals?"

Gryphon took a deep breath and looked at Aaron and Stefan. "Our only lead about the furies was something Kharon remembered reading in a Hades book from a hundred years ago. We went to the library to find the books so we can figure out what's going on with Alex."

"But I had a nightmare and made Gryphon take me," Alex said.

"How?" Aaron asked.

"It doesn't matter," Gryphon said, crossing his arms. "I let her come, so I'm at fault."

"No, you aren't," Alex snapped. "The only people who actually ever listen to me are Michael and Gryphon. So all of you can stop blaming Gryphon for *my* choices." She turned to Gryphon. "And that includes you." *Men.*

Everyone went silent and avoided looking at Alex until Stefan pointed at her. "You're bleeding."

Gryphon examined her shoulder. "Someone hold her." Before Alex could ask why, Stefan and Aaron locked her in their vice grips, and Gryphon ripped something out of her shoulder. Alex shrieked in pain, but once the thing was out, the pain vanished, and her skin glowed gold. Gryphon held up the giant fang that had been embedded in her shoulder.

"I think it would be best if everyone got some rest. We can discuss this further in the morning," Birch suggested.

"Fine." Kharon was already seated at the table, examining the Hades books.

"I'll stay and help," Megesti said, and Kharon smiled and handed him a book.

"Tomorrow, you're both explaining yourselves," Stefan said. He shot a glare at Gryphon and left with Michael.

Alex looked at Aaron. He was looking at her, rubbing his neck with one hand. She cracked the two of them to their bedroom. "Thank you for not scolding me in front of our friends," she said.

"We agreed to be more honest. Do you really think I don't listen to you?"

"Listening and honesty between us only work if you don't try to control me. Would you have let me go if I had told you the truth before I left?"

Aaron pursed his lips and looked away.

"Exactly." Alex wrapped her arms around his back and pressed closer to him. "I woke up panic-stricken from a nightmare and knew in my heart he was going to do something stupid."

Aaron ran his fingers over her collarbone, shook his head, and smiled. "So you had to do something stupid too. Does your neck hurt?"

"Not anymore." Alex moved her fingers to her neck, grazing her line marks. "Are they ugly?"

Aaron smiled and kissed her sweetly. "Nothing about you could be ugly. Let's get some sleep. We can discuss everything in the morning."

# CHAPTER 39
# ALEX

Someone was nuzzling her neck. Alex gradually awakened and let out a contented sigh. Aaron wrapped his arms around her and pulled her tightly against him. "Morning," he mumbled between kisses.

"Morning." Alex wriggled out from his grasp and rolled over to face him. "I'm sorry," she said.

Aaron opened one eye and stretched.

"I need to apologize for last night."

"No, you don't. We've had more chaos and insanity recently than I would expect in a year. You don't owe anyone an apology, least of all me."

"If you're sure ..."

"More than sure. I'm King of Datten, and I command it. No more apologies, just cuddles with my enchantingly beautiful wife. If you insist on discussing it, we can do so in a few days, when everything has settled and you have figured out your boundaries."

Alex rolled over and let Aaron pull her against his chest again. His light kisses down her neck and shoulder stirred something within her.

They were going to be late for breakfast.

ALEX AND AARON strode to the dining hall, talking quietly.

"Are you meeting with the lords again today?"

"Yes. Edward was supposed to help, but I'll ask Jerome and Harold instead. I'm sorry I sent away your father without asking you."

"I understand. I can't believe he fired Randal. Can you imagine Warren without him?"

"Hopefully Edward will come to his senses. What are you up to today: training or being trained?"

"I have a plan and you'll love it." Alex laughed and rushed ahead into the hall. She was dressed in her red Datten sparring clothes for the morning's magic lesson.

Most of their friends were already eating breakfast. Megesti and Gryphon were missing. Aaron pulled her toward breakfast, and Alex scrunched her nose. For the first time in days, Alex was properly hungry. She ate a massive plate of hard-boiled eggs, herbed cheese, and fresh, warm bread. She didn't miss the smiles that spread across Aaron's and Michael's faces when she took another small loaf of bread after finishing her plate.

"Using magic makes me hungry," Alex said and took a big bite of bread.

"If that's the case, you should train more," Stefan joked from across the table.

Gryphon and Megesti arrived and found seats at the large table. Though it was unusual for Datten royalty, Aaron and Alex still ate with their friends at least once a day. Alex was desperate for normalcy after everything they'd both endured, and Aaron wanted her happy. They tried for breakfast as often as possible since dinners often included nobility and other guests.

"What training are you doing today?" Jessica asked Alex.

"That depends on what my head guards have decided," Alex said.

"Head *guards*?" Stefan asked.

"Oh, did I forget to tell you with all the fistfights and curses?" Aaron asked. He took a bite from his smoked venison. "I made Gryphon co-captain of Alex's guard."

Stefan spit his bread across the table. Alex quickly flicked her fingers, and a wind deflected the food away.

"You're letting him guard your wife after what he did last night?" Stefan shouted.

"We can't protect her from sorcerers, but he can. I'm not saying you aren't talented, Stefan, but—"

Alex put her hand on Aaron's arm. "Aaron wanted someone who can track me no matter where I go. So you'll continue to train me in physical fighting, and you'll be my head guard inside our castles. Gryphon will train me in magic, and he'll be my head guard outside the castle, where I'm more likely to be attacked by sorcerers."

"How long have you known about this?" Stefan asked Gryphon.

"A few days."

"You know I'm not leaving you alone with her when you train," Stefan growled.

"We won't be alone," Alex said, glancing down the table toward Lynx and Birch. "Since Gryphon has so kindly offered to train Megesti along with me."

Gryphon's mouth dropped open. *What did you say, Princess?*

Alex stuffed a hunk of cheese into her mouth to stop herself from smirking.

"Gryphon, that's wonderful news!" Birch's smile lit up her entire face. "I can't thank you enough. If Megesti learns along with Alex, then he'll be able to handle the powers of all the lines, and I won't have to worry about another accident." Tears filled her eyes.

Gryphon smiled weakly. "Of course. With all this titan magic floating around, I'll ensure that he can handle himself."

Alex looked down the table at the other sorcerers. "Gryphon told me you could help me too, Birch and Kharon, since I have Celtics and Hades powers. Sorry, Lynx. I don't seem to have any Tiere."

Lynx chuckled. "Yes, you do. There's a reason you connect so deeply with horses, and why they move so well for you. But that appears to be the extent of it."

"That, I believe," Michael said. "We've never met a horse that didn't like you, Alex."

Stefan crossed his arms. "I suppose if your magical lessons are now a group event, I'll allow it."

"You'll *allow* it?" Aaron smirked and looked at Alex. "Would you like to reply to that or should I?"

"We are in Datten."

"Enough mortal chatter," Gryphon groaned. "We'll need a large, open area to begin with their Celtics powers. Someplace where they can grow plants."

"Could we use the old stable area?" Alex asked.

"Of course. It isn't doing anyone any good now," Aaron replied.

Gryphon and Stefan glared at each other, standing. Aaron leaned over and whispered, "I'm glad he's not growling at *me* for a change."

"Stefan, today you should stay back," Birch said. Everyone turned toward her. "I intend to push Alexandria to the limits of her Celtics abilities, and I know she worries when those she loves are nearby."

Aaron nodded and kissed Alex's cheek. "Have fun."

Alex and Megesti led the others to an overgrown field that had served as the royal stables when Aaron and Daniel were young. The sprawling paddocks where royal horses had once trained were now returning to the shadowy forest that had originally stood there. Bushes and trees had taken root, and the main area was a sea of green and brown leaves and stems swaying in the morning breeze.

Birch and Gryphon strode silently while Lynx chatted away about whatever animals she sensed nearby. Kharon remained with their books; they would test Alex's Hades powers another day.

*This is where Aaron's carefree childhood ended and we thrust the expectations of a future king upon him.*

Megesti grabbed Alex's hand and squeezed.

"Why didn't they rebuild?" Lynx asked. "I can see there was a fire, but the design is lovely. I can sense how happy the animals were here before."

"This is where Aaron's older brother, Daniel, died," Megesti replied quietly. "Lygari attacked them, and only Aaron survived. After that, Emmerich moved the stables to the other side of the castle. No one wanted to come here."

Alex surveyed the field. The fall flowers and grass came to their thighs, but the stable was completely bare. Nothing she'd sent to seed when she had visited with Aaron had grown back yet.

"This'll do nicely," Birch said. "Who would like to go first?"

Megesti spoke before Alex could. "I will."

"Remember our training," Alex said.

Birch scanned the tree line, then closed her eyes and curled her fingers into a fist. A moment later, a large, freshly fallen log came flying out of the woods and gently fell in front of the stables. It was long enough to easily fit them all, and everyone but Megesti took a seat.

Megesti wiped his hands on his black pants and cracked his neck. He fidgeted awkwardly. Alex had done her best to teach him the correct magical stance, but she knew it wasn't perfect. Gryphon had just gotten up to help when Birch touched his arm.

"I need to see what he and Alexandria can do without your interference," she whispered.

Gryphon huffed and settled onto the log, and Lynx giggled. Megesti was positioning his hands and trying to focus.

*He drops his elbows too, Princess. And his hands are all wrong.*

*If you have nothing nice to say, Gryphon, then shush.*

*I'm not saying anything. I'm thinking it.*

*Give him a chance. He's more powerful than he realizes.*

*He absolutely is, so I'm worried what'll happen with you and Birch nearby. Usurpers can take from any sorcerer, but from family they can …*

Megesti's eyes flashed violet. The surrounding grass came to life, slithering toward the group like thousands of tiny snakes. Alex pulled her legs up onto the log to avoid them. Sweat covered Megesti's forehead, and another burst of magic left his upturned hand, causing the ground to rumble. A towering pine tree erupted from the ground, growing wider and taller as it shot skyward. Alex lost her grip and slid off the back of the log. Megesti's tree ascended farther into the sky than the towers of the Datten castle.

Birch's voice cut through the loud rumbling. "Megesti, enough!" She was glowing green with both her hands on his shoulders, sending her pale green light into him. Megesti closed his eyes. The violet glow left him, and his arms dropped to his side.

Alex took Gryphon's outstretched hand to get up. "Is that what Michael does to me?" she asked him.

"Strangely enough, yes."

Megesti shook his head, and his eyes went back to emerald green. He gazed up at the tree, astonished. "I didn't do that, did I?"

"You don't remember?" Alex asked.

"It's common for Usurpers not to remember taking someone's

power," Birch said. "He's merely the conduit. My magic went through him on its way to create the tree. You'll have to work on controlling the magic you take, Megesti. Once you can control the powers you use, you'll remember everything."

"You should sit, Megesti," Lynx said. "You look a little pale."

He nodded and stumbled to the log. Alex and Gryphon moved aside to let him sit. Once he'd caught his breath, Birch nodded to Alex.

Alex approached Megesti's tree. With her hand on the rough bark, she shifted her feet, then searched deep inside herself. Her well was open and ready, but she only needed a little of its power. She reached for the grass that was still slithering around them, and it stilled. The blades sank back into the ground until they were at ankle height. Then she raised her arm toward the field behind her. Her face scrunched in concentration. Soon, a lone stalk thrust out of the ground. As she focused on it, a branch grew, then more branches, leaves, and flowers. Lynx and Birch oohed when the flowers burst into plump, green apples.

*Let yourself go, Princess. Show Birch everything you're capable of.*

Alex let her well burst out. She raised another fifteen apple trees and released the bark, sending Megesti's tree back into the ground. With subtle flicks of her fingers, spring flowers rose from the soil like smoke from a fire, and their lovely smell filled the air. Finally, she lowered her arms.

Birch was grinning, and Lynx was staring in surprise.

"You better close your mouth, Lynx, or you might swallow a bug," Alex said.

Gryphon laughed, and Lynx shoved him backward off the log.

"Lynx doesn't eat animals, so I think the bugs will leave her alone," Birch said.

"That," Gryphon said, standing and slowly clapping his hands, "was the utterly worst stance I have seen in many years. Your form is terrible, Megesti, and Princess, you're rusty. We'll have to begin with the basics. Take your stances and I'll correct you."

Alex and Megesti looked at each other but did as Gryphon asked. Celtics powers required subtle movements, which both Megesti and Alex needed to work on. Gryphon's training was grueling. When Alex held out her arms for him, they trembled and ached. She glanced at Megesti, but if he was feeling it, he didn't show it. She made a note to ask Stefan and Michael to help her work on her arm strength.

# CHAPTER 40

# AARON

Aaron settled into the library's reading couch as the fire crackled in front of him. Meeting with all the lords and noble families continued to wear on him. They all wanted something, and Aaron just wanted peace and quiet. He opened his father's journal, hoping there'd be some advice to help him with the Edward and Randal issue. He and Emmerich had never seen eye to eye, but now he had a new perspective on things, and he soon became absorbed in reading the stories behind the decisions his father had made. After a while, he sipped his ale and gazed into the fire, lost in thought. The door creaked open behind him. *What now?* He slammed the drink on the table a little too roughly, and some ale splashed out.

But the smell of sea air surrounded him, and Alex's arms wrapped around his neck as she kissed his cheek. "I thought you'd be happy to see me," she said. "I'm way more fun than the lords you've been meeting with all day."

Aaron smiled, and Alex dropped onto the couch next to him. He tossed the journal aside, pulled her onto his lap, and greeted her with a passionate kiss. Alex had declared that she wouldn't kiss him in front of the knights, because of the rule requiring that they look away, so Aaron made up for it whenever the two of them were alone. "You, my love, are much more entertaining than all the lords in Torian. How was your magic lesson?"

"Exhausting. I made the mistake of telling Stefan and Michael that my arms were sore from my magic lesson, so they forced me to work them my entire time training. We didn't even run."

"I suspect you made *them* do it to build the stamina you need for your magic."

Alex stuck out her tongue at Aaron and picked up the journal. "What are you researching in your father's journals?"

"I'm looking for advice on how to handle your father," Aaron said with exasperation in his voice.

Alex's lips pursed. "Are you still angry?"

"Not about Randal. I understand. But for hurting you when you tried to interfere ..."

"Aaron."

"I'm allowed to be upset. Edward lectures me about putting you at risk with my behavior, so I think I can return the favor."

"I'm going to Warren tomorrow."

"No." Aaron squeezed her tightly.

Alex laughed. "I wasn't asking for permission. I need to see my father."

Aaron groaned.

"I know you don't want me around him right now, but remember what we talked about last night ... about honesty and listening."

"You have duties here."

"What duties? Your mother is still handling my job as queen while I train, so what could be so important that it cannot wait a day?"

Aaron grinned at her. "I intend to throw Harold and Edith their engagement party here."

"Considering Edith is Warren nobility, we agreed to host it in Warren." Alex teasingly pinched his arm.

Aaron scoffed. "I highly doubt your father will allow it now."

"He's angry with Randal, not Edith. He wouldn't punish her for her father's sins."

"Fine, ask him, but when he refuses, we'll hold it here, and you'll have to plan it."

Alex kissed his cheek. "Deal. I do have other reasons for going to Warren. Michael wants to see how the repairs to the Veremund estate are coming, and I need to speak with your uncle Bernhard about transferring the estate to Michael. He and Reilly were handling it for my father."

"Take both your captains."

"You enjoy torturing Stefan with Gryphon too much," Alex giggled. "You're welcome to come too."

"Thank you, but I don't want to leave my duties to Jerome yet."

"I know. You're a new king and want everyone to see you working hard to make things better. Now come to bed. My father's feud with Randal won't change with you here reading yourself into exhaustion."

Aaron woke to Alex's screams. Their bedroom door banged open, and Stefan and Jerome charged into the room. Alex was gasping and pointing at the balcony. Aaron glanced at Stefan for a moment before the two of them threw open the balcony doors and leaped outside. It was early dawn, and they could hardly see.

"Alex, nothing's here," Stefan said. He turned to Aaron and whispered, "Is she all right?"

The morning dew chilled Aaron's feet. He nodded.

Alex sat on the edge of the bed. The straps on her red night-gown were askew and gave the illusion of blood running down her pale shoulders and chest. Jerome stood beside her protectively as she clutched a pillow, shaking.

"What is it?" Aaron asked.

He was about to come inside when Jerome threw up his arm to stop him. "Aaron, don't move."

Aaron paused. Alex was staring at something on the ground with a look of horror. Jerome squatted down to take a look.

*Shoe prints. Muddy shoe prints.* Aaron was barefoot, having dashed out right from bed.

Jerome tapped Stefan's foot, and Stefan lifted his leg to present his clean sole to his father.

Jerome rubbed his chin. "It's too small to be Stefan's and doesn't match the soles of the guard uniform."

Aaron exchanged a look with Stefan. *Someone was on the balcony and fled.* Aaron dashed to the stone railing and glanced down. "How would they have gotten up or down from here without a ladder?"

"Maybe they took it with them," Stefan said. "If there were several of them, they could have fled while we were looking around. Or they cracked."

Aaron strode back to Alex. "Are you all right?"

Alex nodded.

"What did you see?" Jerome asked.

"I woke from a nightmare. When I rolled over, I saw a dark shadow through the glass on the doors. I screamed, and it ... ran."

"I need to point out that you both made a serious error," Jerome said.

"Because someone dared to break into my bedroom?" Aaron asked.

"No, because you abandoned the queen."

Aaron and Stefan looked at each other nervously.

"I know you have issues with each other, but that cannot interfere with your duty to protect Alexandria," Jerome said. "In Datten, it's you, Aaron, who protects her, and in Warren, it's Stefan. That confusion led to you both leaving her unprotected. I'm aware you can defend yourself, Alexandria, but there are protocols to follow. Especially considering how you and Aaron are working to start a family. I recall that your mother struggled with her powers while pregnant with you."

Alex's mouth dropped open, and she looked up at Jerome. Stefan looked as guilty as Aaron felt.

"I don't like when you two fight," Alex said.

"I know," Aaron said. He took the pillow from her. "Who do you want to guard you when something like this happens?"

Alex glanced back and forth between the two for what felt like forever. "Stefan," she finally whispered.

Stefan sighed happily, but Alex grabbed Aaron's hands. "Because he—"

"No explanation needed. This is why he's your guard."

Alex avoided Aaron's gaze.

"What's wrong?" Aaron asked.

She didn't move. Aaron counted her breaths, waiting for her to answer him. Just as he was about to ask again, she answered. "I'm scared to go to Warren without you or Randal there."

Aaron sucked in a breath. He hated that Alex was scared, especially given all that had happened. Before he could reassure her, Stefan intervened.

"You'll have Michael, Gryphon, me, and Julius. I sent word to Matthew yesterday to let him know we'd be coming and asked him to summon Julius from Verlassen Castle."

Jerome beamed at Stefan, who stood tall and straight, looking down at Alex. "You can bring any Datten knights you'd like," Jerome added. "Jessica will be occupied trying to convince Edith to hold the celebration here, but Caleb or Lucas could join you."

"Or Lynx," Stefan said.

Aaron groaned.

"I'd like for Lynx and my ladies to come." Alex stood and turned to Aaron. "Did you really ask Jessica to interfere?"

"I want to celebrate Harold's engagement here as much as you want Edith's in Warren. We'll see who wins," Aaron said.

"I'm going to win," Alex said, straightening her nightgown.

"I'll wait in the hallway for you to get dressed," Stefan said, and the Wafner men departed. Alex pulled out a set of training clothes.

"I don't want you afraid in Warren," Aaron said.

She threw her damp nightgown at him. "I know, but I can't help my feelings. So much has happened that I find I'm always a little anxious and waiting for something to happen."

"You know, whoever was on the balcony could have been looking for me."

Alex pulled on her tunic and scoffed at Aaron. He couldn't help laughing at her scrunched up nose. "If that was supposed to make me feel better, you failed."

Aaron chuckled and walked to Alex to pull her close. "You'll have Michael and Stefan. Don't leave their sides for once, and if you're in trouble, any sort, call Gryphon and he'll get you away."

Alex inhaled so deeply Aaron felt her stomach move. "And if you can't sleep, come home," he added.

Alex peeked up at him and smiled. "I might do that. I don't enjoy sleeping alone anymore."

"Neither do I. Now go. You have a busy day ahead of you."

"I hope Michael is happy with what they've done."

"Michael won't care what his estate looks like," Aaron said. "All he cares about is his family. Now you're his distant cousin, and Stefan is his brother-in-law. He's got you both forever, and he adores Jessica."

Alex kissed Aaron on the cheek and headed into the hallway to leave for Warren. Aaron dressed and went to the library for his meeting with Harold and the builders. They discussed the supplies needed to rebuild Betruger, as well as the location for the new town. Harold insisted on building the houses for his people first. He'd stay in a knight's estate until everyone else had their homes back, and only then would they begin work on the castle. Aaron suggested they ask the sorcerers to help the building go faster. Harold thanked him but admitted that Betruger hands built the homes in Betruger. It was a sense of pride for them, and it wouldn't be the same if magic did it.

After the meeting, Aaron checked in with Megesti and Kharon. Both were so engrossed in their Hades books that they barely acknowledged Aaron. He had food brought to them and found Harold again. They collected Caleb, Lucas, Hunter, and Macht, and headed out for a brief hunting trip. Aaron realized he hadn't done anything fun in ages. With Alex and Edith busy in Warren, he wanted to do something with Harold to take their minds off everything that had happened.

# CHAPTER 41
# ALEX

When Alex stepped out of her suite, Stefan was waiting. "Should we gather everyone and head to Warren?" he asked.

"Already done." Michael's cheery voice came from the long main hallway. "I asked Lynx to go ahead with Jessica and Edith. My wife was desperate to start the planning for the engagement celebration. She barely slept a wink last night."

"Do you think your father will host Edith's celebration, after his falling-out with Randal?" Stefan asked.

"I hope so. It isn't Edith's fault that her father made a poor choice," Alex replied.

"A poor choice?" Gryphon came down the tower stairs to join them. "He left you and your mother defenseless against your grandfather. It was reckless, irresponsible, and treasonous. His decision cost your mother her life."

"I'm well aware of what it cost," Alex snapped. "I don't need reminding of that."

The men stood silently, evidently afraid to risk drawing Alex's wrath. She took a slow breath and straightened her tunic. "If everyone's ready, I'll take us to Warren," she said. When the men nodded, she cracked them into the throne room in the usual spot.

Julius was waiting for them despite the early hour. "Welcome back to Warren, Your Highness."

"How did you know we'd be here so early?"

Julius smiled. "I've been in your guard long enough to expect the unexpected with you."

Michael chuckled, and Alex shot him a warning look.

"Don't be mad that we know you so well," Michael said.

"Where are her ladies?" Stefan asked.

"I escorted Edith, Jessica, and the sorceress to the Nial estate before settling in to wait for you here," Julius replied. "They suggested you head to the Veremund estate first, and they'll meet you back here for dinner."

"They don't want Alex's help?" Gryphon asked.

"To plan a celebration?" Michael smirked at Gryphon, making Alex bite her lip to avoid laughing. "They adore Alex, but party planning isn't in her skill set."

"It's fine. I still have a very important duty for the party," Alex said.

"Oh?" Stefan asked.

"Aaron and I are paying for it." Alex laughed and started her walk to the royal stables.

Gryphon complained endlessly about having to ride to the estate, but Alex refused to crack everywhere. Her horse, Snow, had not yet been brought to Datten, and she wanted to continue bonding with him. Julius provided updates from Bernhard, confirming that they had transferred the estate to Michael. He'd be able to swear his oath to Edward at any time.

Michael gulped hard, and Julius trotted ahead with Gryphon, seemingly to give Michael a moment with his friends.

"There's no rush, Michael," Stefan said.

"Stefan's right. You're in my guard, so your loyalty isn't in question."

"I know, but I want Jessica and our baby to have their titles."

"My father won't expect you to be a perfect earl overnight, Michael," Alex said. "I've only been home a year and a half, and he doesn't expect perfection from me."

"He'd be waiting centuries if he wanted perfection," Stefan added.

Michael laughed, and Alex stuck out her tongue at Stefan. They passed the Bishop estate and hurried onto the Veremund property. The midday sun cast a warm glow over the estates. Alex marveled at the changes since their last visit. The worn path had filled in with new stones, the garden had been tended to, and the broken shutters and windows had been replaced.

"His Royal Highness has half the builders in Warren working on it. With how much he's paying, no one wants to be left out," Julius said.

Michael's eyes were wide, and he seemed to take in every detail. Alex pushed Snow beside him and slipped her hand into Michael's, the same way he'd do to her when she needed strength. "Ready?"

Michael nodded, and the group clopped down the cobblestone path to the doors of his childhood home.

Alex dismounted from Snow, and Julius took the reins. The smell of cedar hit her, and she turned to see a beautiful, newly built stable. It wasn't as ornate as most of the stables in Warren, but Alex suspected that would come later. The touches of life would come after Michael and Jessica moved in.

"This door is certainly an improvement," Stefan said. "And not just because you can open it."

Michael and Stefan continued to whisper to each other, standing outside the wooden door, but Alex couldn't hear what they were discussing. The door was less ornate, but no less beautiful than other estate doors. Curious, Alex got closer. "Is that black pine?" she asked.

"It is," Michael said.

"I thought black pine only grew along the edge of the Dark Forest and the Ogre Mountains. How on earth did it get here?" Alex asked.

"Birch," Gryphon replied. "When you discovered who Michael was, your father asked her to supply the builders with black pine so that you'd have the wood you all grew up with. She enjoyed being part of this secret."

Alex saw Michael touching the wood with a smile on his face. In their camp, nearly everything had been fashioned from black pine. The huts and the beds inside, the stable, their wagon; even the inn in Kirsch was made from black pine. Julius handed Michael the large brass key, and once he'd unlocked the door, it swung open easily on its hinges. Michael paused on the threshold, looking into the house, so Alex playfully pushed him through. The refreshing scent of freshly cut wood had replaced the lingering, musty smell. The decorative tables and couches were all uncovered and polished to a shine, and a beautiful harp stood in the corner. They'd repaired the loose stones in the wall and replaced the windows. The bearskin rug on the floor brought back the memory of parents when they had visited before. Alex took a step back and bumped into Gryphon. He had a strange look on his face, as if he were concentrating on something.

"Are you all right?" she asked, touching his arm.

"There's powerful magic here," Gryphon said.

"Are you sure? It's a mortal home."

Gryphon pursed his lips in annoyance. Alex grinned at him. "Sorry. How dare I forget the Ares' ability to sense power?"

"This harp is beautiful." Michael's voice brought Alex's attention back to him.

"You're lucky Jessica plays," Alex said.

"I'm lucky for more than that," Michael said. He had a big smile on his face. "Do you think Jessica will approve?"

"She'll love most of it. She won't like the sky blue couches. You'll need to get those reupholstered, but besides that, it's perfect."

"Excellent. On to the next room!" Michael clapped his hands and brushed past Alex and Gryphon. Julius remained at the entrance to keep watch. Michael headed into the hallway lined with paintings and stalled. Alex followed him to the painting she'd discovered in the treasure room, now on the wall. The younger Michael couldn't have been older than five, and he stood between his parents. Both his parents had their hands resting on his shoulders, and the love they had for Michael was clear even in the painting.

Michael stood transfixed. Alex rubbed his back, and he sighed. "Do you think they're proud of me?" he whispered so only Alex could hear.

An icy breeze blew past them, and the ghost of Matthias appeared further down the hall. He nodded to Alex and looked at Michael with the same expression of love that was in the painting before them.

"He's very proud of you, Michael."

"The breeze. Was that—?"

"Yes."

Michael exhaled and tried to peer past Alex down the hallway. Alex stayed with him, letting him compose himself. Stefan and Gryphon were nowhere to be seen.

Finally, he smiled at her. "Should we keep going? I know you're not as style-oriented as Jessica, but I think together we can decide if she'll like the decor."

Alex couldn't help but laugh. "Are you saying I'm not stylish, Michael?"

"Of course not, my queen." Michael winked. "But my wife is the one who dresses you."

Alex playfully shoved Michael, and the two of them turned toward a small door that creaked open on its own. When they entered, Alex froze.

Michael laughed. "Is this an office or a library?" he asked, pointing toward the oversized, elaborately carved desk in front of the window. The remaining walls were covered in bookshelves, save for the fireplace and door they'd entered through. Michael walked over to the desk. The front of it held a carving of a book with a quill. He slowly traced the image with his fingers.

"I remember this desk, and this carving. I used to sit here and trace it while my father worked." He crossed the room to the fireplace, turned, and surveyed the room. "There was a wolf pelt on the floor. I would lie on it and read by the firelight. My parents' reading chairs are missing. They were navy blue." He held out his hands, waving them in circles and trying to decide where the chairs had once been. Alex pictured her own green reading chairs from her suite. She could almost see them in this space.

"We'd read in the evening, before dinner. I loved to read in here with them. And my mother ... she'd tell me tales of the other kingdoms. Of their riches and battles."

"Maybe we should get Jessica so she can be here for you."

"We discussed it. She's lost family too, so she understands I need to do this with you and Stefan. You're the family I have left, the ones who got me through the dreadful nights when I was little ... who saved me."

"Does that mean I get to borrow your books?" Alex asked, and Michael burst out laughing.

"You can borrow any books you want." He looked at the fireplace and cocked his head.

Alex followed his gaze to the old, worn hearth. "Why is one stone different?" she asked.

"I don't know ... but I remember it. When the fire is going, you can see it from the floor."

Alex leaned into the fireplace, and Michael squatted to get a better look. "Do you think it comes out?" he asked.

Alex grinned at him. "Only one way to find out."

Michael reached for the stone and ran his finger around it. Impatient, Alex bumped him with her hip, and his palm slipped and hit the stone. A rumble echoed throughout the room, and Michael leaped to his feet and pushed Alex behind him. The bookshelf beside the fireplace slid back, and Michael stared in shock at the secret entrance to another room.

"Stefan! Gryphon! We found something!" Alex shouted.

Michael finally woke from his stupor. "Do we wait or go in?"

Alex smirked at Michael, and he shook his head. "After you."

They stepped through the threshold. Alex produced a glowing orb, lighting up the narrow room hidden behind the shelves and walls of the office. There was another bookshelf here, identical to the ones in the office, but the books on it were yellowed with age. Some shelves held other items, such as maps of the Ogre Mountains and the Dark Forest, jewelry, a compass, something under a velvet cloth, and a small chest covered in gold and gems. Alex had picked up the chest and opened it. Inside were letters addressed to Percival.

"Michael, there are letters to you in this chest."

She handed it to him, and as he flipped through the letters, Alex moved down the shelf. She picked up the old compass. The arrow spun strangely. *It's pretty. Too bad it's broken.* She replaced it, and the velvet cloth caught her eye. "It can't be."

"What can't be?" Michael asked.

"Alex? Michael? Where are you?" Stefan's voice sounded far away.

"In the study," Michael shouted back. "There was a secret room behind the fireplace."

Alex pulled the velvet cloth away, exposing a cobalt pearl. Flecks of other colors ran through it. "I've seen this pearl. There's an identical one in my grandfather's study hidden by the treasure room in the castle."

Michael folded up the letter and set it on the shelf with the chest.

"No, don't stop reading your letters on my account," Alex said.

"They aren't going anywhere," Michael said. "Besides, I'd rather read them with Jessica. The first one is from my mother, telling me where to find her engagement ring. I'm supposed to give it to my future wife."

Alex was afraid to touch the pearl after what had happened with the white one, but Michael had no such fear. He grabbed it with both hands. "Let's bring it into the study, where there's more light."

Sunlight was shining into the study, so Michael held up the pearl to the window. Unlike the other pearl, this one was opaque. Its gold and silver flecks sparkled as Michael turned it around to examine it.

"What's that?" Stefan asked, arriving in the doorway.

"We don't know," Alex said. "But there's one in my grandfather's office too."

Stefan crossed the room and took the pearl from Michael. He looked at it, shrugged, and handed it back.

"Where's Gryphon?" Michael asked.

"Tell me you didn't lock him somewhere in the house," Alex said.

# CHAPTER 42

# GRYPHON

*Mortal houses are so strange. How are you supposed to fit more than two people in these tiny beds? Ridiculous.*

Gryphon had gone upstairs while Stefan searched the main floor. As head guards, they'd gone ahead to check for any threats to Alex. It was possible the builders had overlooked something, and according to Stefan, anything off might be a sign of someone trying to get to her. But all Gryphon found upstairs were bedrooms. Most appeared as though they had never been used, not even years ago.

Only two of them had any life or character. One looked similar to the suite he stayed in at the castles. The other, at the end of the hall, was filled with children's clothes of the same style as in the paintings. The boy's room was full of life. Artwork was strewn about. It seemed ships and stars had fascinated young Michael. *Makes sense for a kingdom full of merchants and ships. Does he still like the stars? It would actually give us something meaningful to talk about.*

"Stefan! Gryphon! We found something!"

Alex's voice reached him even upstairs. He closed the door to Michael's childhood bedroom and took the stairs at the back of the house that led to the kitchen. Crossing through an overly formal dining room, he saw a small door and heard Alex speaking to Michael and Stefan.

*Never fear, Princess, I'm right here.* "It wouldn't be possible for a mere mortal to trap me," Gryphon announced. He strode into the room but stopped in his tracks as soon as he entered. "It can't be."

"What are you babbling about, Gryphon?" Stefan asked, but Gryphon ignored him, his eyes fixed on the orb in Michael's hands, and how dangerously close Alex was to it.

Without thinking, Gryphon leaped toward them. "Alex, get away from Michael—now!" But his actions had the opposite of the intended effect. His warning startled Michael, and he almost dropped the pearl. Alex lunged to help, but the moment she touched the blue orb and Michael's hand, a *pop* sounded through the room.

Alex, Michael, and the pearl were gone.

"What did you do?" Stefan spun around. His face was a combination of rage and terror, but his eyes made Gryphon step back.

"Nothing," Gryphon snarled. "It was the blue pearl Michael was holding. It's a magical orb used by non-Mystic sorcerers. It is connected to a location and takes the sorcerer there, even if the location is too far away for the sorcerer to crack there on their own."

"So follow them and bring them back!"

"I can't. I don't know where they went."

"I thought you could read Alex's mind!"

"I can't hear her or Michael," Gryphon snapped.

"If we had another pearl, could you use it to find them?"

"We'd need another pearl that goes to the same spot. But the blue pearls only work for non-Mystic sorcerers." For Stefan's benefit, Gryphon added, "I'm the Titan of Mystic."

"But other sorcerers could? Lynx? Birch?"

"Clearly."

"Good, because we have another one."

"Blue pearls are rare. How do you have two? Only the most *powerful* sorcerers could manufacture such objects." *But if they actually had another, it was likely from the same batch.*

"I don't have any, but I know King Edward has one," Stefan said. "We should get the ladies."

They rushed to grab Julius and rode the short distance down the road to the Nial estate, where they waited outside for Edith.

"Are you sure it was a blue pearl?" Lynx asked.

Gryphon glared. "I sensed magic in that house the instant we arrived. Alex didn't believe me, but clearly I was right."

"Have you told Aaron or her father?" Jessica asked.

"Once we're at the castle," Stefan said, rubbing his sister's shoulder. "I promise we'll get Michael back."

"I could retrieve Aaron from Datten," Lynx said.

Gryphon exchanged a look with Stefan. The younger Wafner looked as nervous as Gryphon felt. A knot the size of a brick weighed in Gryphon's gut. He nodded to Lynx. She vanished in an instant, and Edith appeared in the doorway.

"Sorry for the delay. My father asked our stable boys to take the horses back to the castle, so we can crack there," Edith said.

"Isn't your father coming?" Stefan asked.

"Edward doesn't want him anywhere on the grounds."

"The crown princess has vanished. I think he'll make an exception," Jessica said.

"He won't," Julius said. "He has my father with him."

"Mortals," Gryphon grumbled and cracked them into the Warren castle courtyard. Julius left to find his father while they went to get the key to the treasure room. The group was heading down the hallway when Lynx and Aaron came around the corner from the throne room.

"What happened?" Aaron demanded, looking back and forth from Gryphon to Stefan.

Stefan briefed Aaron as they raced to the bowels of the castle, where Matthew and Julius were waiting for them.

"Where's His Royal Highness?" Jessica asked.

"I chose not to tell him," Matthew said. "He doesn't need anything else to set him off at the moment."

"Who'll open the door?" Lynx asked.

"Edith," Julius said. "She's a blood-born Nial."

Matthew unlocked the door and Gryphon let the others head in first. He closed his eyes, searching for Alex's thoughts.

"Gryphon?" Lynx touched his arm.

"I can't hear them, Lynx. What if the pearl was a trap?"

Lynx squeezed his arm.

Gryphon closed his eyes, focusing on his father, but all he could sense were rage and confusion. *So you don't have her. At least, not yet.*

"Gryphon. Lynx. Let's go," Aaron shouted.

Edith opened the door to the treasure room. Stefan, Edith, and Jessica went inside, but when Gryphon went to follow, Aaron grabbed his arm.

"Is she all right?" Aaron asked.

"I can't hear her, which could be a good thing. If she was terrified or hurt, I think I would, even from this distance."

Aaron rubbed his neck. "She promised she wouldn't keep running off."

"She didn't. Nothing happened when Michael held the pearl. The other pearls all react to anyone, but blue pearls only react to a sorcerer without Mystic powers. Michael's mortal," Gryphon explained.

Aaron's hands shifted to the sides of his head, and he groaned. "Why can't one day be calm?"

Gryphon chuckled. "You're married to the most powerful sorceress ever born. I don't think any day is going to be easy."

"What's keeping you two?" Jessica asked, peeking out of the

treasure room. She beckoned them to come, and they followed her into the immense room piled high with gold and treasure. They passed rows of bookshelves until they got to the end, where the hidden door was open.

"Another secret tunnel. I wonder how I never found that one," Aaron said.

"Are there many tunnels in this castle?" Gryphon asked.

"Yes. There are a few in Datten, but nothing compared to what you find in Warren."

Gryphon sent floating orbs of fire to light the way and followed Aaron down the tunnel, where the others waited.

"It's true! Another blue pearl." Lynx's voice was soft and full of wonder.

As soon as Gryphon took it in, he could see why. Another precious object from the Forbidden Lands had found its way into the hands of the Warren mortals.

"There could be three," Aaron said. "The two we know of were held in the Warren and Veremund homes. I wouldn't be surprised if the Nial estate housed one as well. They are the three founding families."

"Why wouldn't my father have told us when you arrived?" Edith asked. "It seems like a lot of trouble to make us come here when we have one too."

"Unless he needed us to take time," Aaron replied.

Edith exhaled and crossed her arms. "Just because my father made a mistake all those years ago does not put every action and decision he has ever made into question."

"Unfortunately, it does," Matthew said.

Edith's eyes widened, and she turned away from Matthew and wiped her eyes. Julius went to comfort her.

"How do we get Michael and Alex back?" Aaron asked.

Lynx spoke up. "As a Tiere sorceress, when I touch the pearl, it will send me wherever it's enchanted to take me. Considering how two were hidden in the homes of the founders of Warren, I can't see them going to completely different places."

"And Gryphon can't do it?" Aaron asked.

Stefan picked up the pearl and tossed it to Gryphon. He caught it and looked at the craftsmanship of the sphere in his hands. Cobalt blue with flecks of gold running through it, providing the magic needed to transport a non-Mystic further than they could ever go on their own. He tossed the pearl back to Stefan.

"Since Mystics make them, they have no effect on us. It would be the same if you gave Alexandria the black pearl. It shows the future, so it doesn't work on her."

"If they're in the Forbidden Lands, how do I get them back?" Lynx asked Gryphon.

"As soon as you leave, I'll head for the beach at Moorloc's castle. Once you have them, you and Alex call for me. Together, I should hear you anywhere."

Lynx held out her hands to Stefan, waiting for the pearl.

"We'll wait for you in the library," Matthew said.

"What if it doesn't work?" Jessica asked, her voice shaking.

"Only one way to find out," Stefan said, and he shoved the pearl into Lynx's hands.

# CHAPTER 43
# ALEX

Alex and Michael stumbled and found themselves on a stone path. The woods surrounding them were so thick that it was dark despite it being morning. Michael dropped the pearl and kicked it as far away as he could.

"What happened?"

"I don't know," Alex whispered.

"Was it you or the orb?"

"I don't know," Alex snapped. She could barely see, so she rubbed her palms together until a large orb of fire appeared, filling the space with a soft glow. Gnarled bushes and vines surrounded them, so she opened her hands and sent the plants back to seeds.

Michael's elbow brushed hers.

Alex heard something. "What's that?" The deserted path revealed a decrepit old house. Something called to her, and she stepped toward it. Michael pulled her back and insisted on going first.

"I hear someone calling me," Michael said.

"You hear it too?" Alex listened and gulped.

"It's not frightening." Michael grabbed her hand and led her down the path. The house's door was barely hanging on to the doorframe. He gave it a gentle tug, and the rotted wood ripped from its hinges and fell to the ground with a loud thud. They startled at the sound but calmed when silence filled the air again.

Alex swished a finger, sending her orb into the house before stepping over the threshold. Inside, she was glad to see candles still attached to sconces on the walls and in holders on the table. Alex focused, and they burst to life.

"Where are we?" Michael asked. They'd entered a large, open room with a round table in the center. On it stood an empty vase surrounded by gray powder. Alex leaned down and ran her finger through it. She could sense the flowers that had been. To the left seemed to be an ancient kitchen, and the other side had shelves filled with jars and bottles. Many of them were cracked and broken, but in those still intact, Alex spotted several plants and animal parts she had never seen before.

An unintelligible voice made the hair on Alex's neck stand up.

Michael pushed Alex behind him and rested his hand on his sword. "You heard that, right?"

Alex merely grunted. Her eyes adjusted, and she noticed a shadow in the far corner. She slipped past Michael, and he followed her through an arch into a long, narrow hallway. Rot replaced the musty smell. Alex covered her nose and mouth as they crept down the hallway past several doors. Without thinking, she dropped her hand on one, but she gasped and ripped it away.

"Are you all right?" Michael asked.

Memories flooded her. "This is where our story began," she whispered and pushed the door open with her hip. A lone bed was pressed against the far wall. Michael squeezed Alex's shoulder.

"Your relatives?" he asked.

On the wall was a portrait of a sorcerer who looked like an older version of Moorloc and a woman who was clearly another daughter of Cassandra. Alex was drawn to the painting. "I think they're my grandparents. Alexandria is the one I'm named for, and Hermes was my grandfather."

Suddenly, a voice behind them whispered, "Keep going."

They dashed into the hall but found they were alone. Then Alex's orb began moving further down the hall on its own. She glanced at Michael, but he shrugged.

"Something brought us here," said Michael. "I say we follow it."

Alex nodded, and they walked by a few more doors. The hall ended at a locked stone door. Michael frowned at it, but the voice whispered to Alex. *Only the noblest may enter.*

"Blood, but whose?" she asked.

"We'll both offer." Michael pulled out his dagger and handed it to Alex. She pricked herself and then Michael. When they pressed their thumbs into the door, it swung open, revealing a dark dirt tunnel that spiraled downward.

"Why are all your secrets underground?" Michael teased.

Despite everything, Alex smiled and held out her hand to Michael. Together they entered the dark tunnel, with only Alex's orb to guide their way.

As they descended, the tunnel narrowed, and Alex smelled dank earth. Soon they arrived at a small room. It reminded Alex of the alcove in Moorloc's castle where he'd hidden the people he enslaved. Sure enough, when she approached the wall, it shimmered, and a larger space appeared. A fireplace roared to life, illuminating the room. Michael walked to one side, and that wall revealed more shelves covered in jars filled with strange ingredients.

"Welcome," said a strange voice.

Alex yelped and jumped back. Michael dashed before her and drew his sword.

A petite ghost stood at the end of the room. "That won't be necessary, young Veremund," she said. She was glowing with a faint white light, similar to Alex's gold sorcerer glow. Long blonde curls flowed down her shoulders onto her back and chest. Her skin was as pale and smooth as Jessica's, but her eyes were the same sparkling emerald green as Alex's. She wore a simple white robe. *I've never met her, but she feels so familiar.*

"You're correct, Alexandria. You do know me. My name is Cassandra."

Alex touched Michael's arm, and he sheathed his sword while she stepped around him. Alex examined the sorceress before her with suspicion. "Besides the eyes, I don't look like you."

Cassandra smiled at Alex. "That, my dear, is because only the true *daughters* of Cassandra look alike. So you resemble my daughter, not me, and she was very much a combination of her father and myself."

Alex felt a sudden rush. "I have so many questions. Who is the original father? Did my mother really have visions of my future? Am I going to be more powerful? Will Aaron and I be able to have children? Will they be sorcerers?"

Cassandra raised her hand. "I wish I could address all your concerns, my dear, but your arrival was sensed. The blue pearl did not hide you as I hoped it would, and they are coming. I only have time to provide you with the information you require. The rest will have to wait."

"How?" Michael asked.

"The pearls in your possession were gifted to the founders of Warren to provide help if needed, as they were punished for helping me."

"Who punished them?"

Cassandra smiled and told her tale. How she'd arrived at the Forbidden Lands with Ares, Hades, and Poseidon, and been gifted a lifespan beyond a mortal's and the ability to see the future. She fell in love and had a daughter, but her partner became abusive and controlling, so she fled in the night, leaving everything behind. Her lover could sense their daughter because of their blood connection, but couldn't sense Cassandra, so although it broke her heart, she left her daughter behind and ended up washing ashore in Warren. The founding families of Warren gave her sanctuary and let her live in their kingdom. Soon she fell in love with a mortal man and married him. When her former lover found out, he and his friends combined their powers and cursed everyone involved.

"Cursed you how?" Alex asked.

"Warren's nobility would only bear sons. The curse lived in the royal family to punish their mercy, and when their younger prince married into Datten, the curse followed."

"But why?" Alex asked.

"I had two sons with my mortal husband. I'm a sorceress, so my powers could only be inherited by my daughters. Sons carried the powers in their blood but could only pass them to the next generation, until a daughter was born to claim the built-up power. By forcing the royalty to have only sons, they prevented my powers from being claimed."

Cassandra walked over to a portrait and touched the frame. "They also took back my long life, but since my husband was mortal, it was a blessing."

Alex gulped and looked down. A cold hand touched her cheek.

"Your future holds two great loves, my dear. You will not be left mourning your remaining centuries."

"What about the daughter you left?" Michael asked.

"Her father protected her and punished me. He went to Hades and convinced him to bind a fury to each true daughter of Cassandra."

"That's why we're here," Alex said.

Cassandra nodded. "To ensure no daughter of Cassandra would be hurt the way my daughter was when I abandoned her, they tied a fury to you, and should you suffer, that fury will awaken, take control of you, and seek revenge on everyone who ever wronged you."

Alex gulped.

"Suffer how?" Michael asked.

"The crimes the furies avenged: murder, betrayal, and blood guilt within a family. These things have to be done *to* you, and you have to enact them."

Alex trembled. *Murder is done. Blood guilt within the family. Does kissing Gryphon count as betrayal? No wonder it's waking.*

"How do we stop it?" Michael's voice was desperate.

"You must seek the scepter of the first King of Warren. The sons of the three founding families hid it after the king died, to ensure it wouldn't be lost to time. The secrets of its location and how to wield it were passed down the Nial and Veremund lines for generations."

Michael's face went ashen. "My father died before he could pass on anything to me."

Cassandra smiled at him. "You have already found everything you need. They kept it with the pearl that brought you here. We tied it to my favorite place, my first home, and allowed you to receive help in the event this occurred. So ask quickly."

"How is it that I can calm Alex when she's upset?"

"A gift from me to the Veremund line. A Veremund can calm the volatile emotions of their Warren. So your gift for calming is exclusive to Alexandria."

"Sorcerers bond for life. How can I have children with both Aaron and Gryphon?" Alex asked.

"Gryphon and you share a nature bond and will bring about the next evolution of sorcerers. It was predetermined, and fate cannot be undone, except in a case such as yours."

"What does that mean?" Alex asked.

"In rare cases, a sorcerer bonds to someone before their powers come in. This allows them to bond again once they have come into their full powers. The birthmark on your shoulder is not as it appears. You bonded yourself to Aaron as a child. As your bond to Gryphon grows stronger, the one with Aaron will too. You will always be connected to them both."

"So the burn scar on Aaron's shoulder …"

"Masks his bond mark to you."

Alex swallowed hard and tried to slow her racing heart. *I took away his choice. That's why he never wanted anyone else.*

"None of that," Cassandra said sternly. "Destiny put you with Aaron as much as it did Gryphon."

Michael rubbed Alex's shoulder as if he'd sensed what she thought too. Alex exhaled and turned back to Cassandra. "What do we do about the fury?"

"Find the journals that do not match."

"What?" Michael asked.

Cassandra quickly explained what they had to do. Alex had so many questions she could barely keep up. Suddenly, Cassandra looked up with a worried expression and broke off.

"They're nearing. We must finish—"

"What will break the curse in Warren and Datten?" Alex blurted out.

"The curse of birthing only sons?" Cassandra asked. "Your mother broke it the day she birthed a daughter. The idea of a sorceress marrying a mortal was inconceivable to the sorcerers of old, so the moment your mother fell in love with your father and had you, that curse ended."

All the hairs on Alex's arms rose at once.

"They're almost here. I must go. Trust yourself, your Nial, and your Veremund. Find the scepter. It will help keep the beast controlled. But beware, once the crimes have been committed, it'll take the combined power of a Head and Heart to stop the fury."

There was a loud *pop*. Alex and Michael glanced behind them, and when they looked back, Cassandra was gone.

"We have to leave," Michael said.

They raced down the narrow hallway and ran up the spiraling dirt path to the main floor of the house. Alex was running hard when she slammed into someone and screamed. Arms gripped her tightly before she could fall backward.

"It's all right, Alex."

"Stefan? How'd you get here?" Michael asked.

"He hitched a ride with me," Lynx said, standing behind them. "We need to leave now. I can smell other sorcerers. They can't crack here, but they can feel your and Cassandra's magical essences and are hunting you."

"How are we going to get home?" Alex asked.

"I'll crack us to the furthest point possible. Then you and I are going to summon Gryphon. I only hope we'll be strong enough."

Lynx gripped Stefan's hand and held out her other hand to Alex. Alex grabbed Michael's and Lynx's hands and they landed on a beach. A wild storm raged. Wet wind whipped against their faces, and the Oreean Sea was rough.

"There wasn't a storm when we arrived," Michael said.

"It's the Titan of Poseidon," Lynx said. "Pearl's trying to make it hard for us to leave. If her magic engulfs the area, it will be harder for Gryphon to focus on us."

"Then we'll have to get closer." Alex shifted her stance toward the sea, facing the direction she hoped was Warren, and threw open her well. She slapped her palms together and thrust them toward the sea as she had done in her first lesson with Gryphon. *Elbows up, back straight, and hips forward.* She slowly exhaled and pulled her palms apart. Despite the raging storm, the sea split open to reveal a path between the waves.

"Go!" Alex shouted, dropping her arms and running onto the dry seabed. Lynx ran after her, with Stefan and Michael trailing behind.

"How long will it stay?" Stefan asked.

"Until someone puts it back, so keep running," Alex shouted over the roaring winds.

"Gryphon!" Lynx screamed, but nothing happened, and they kept running further out into the sea.

The ground behind them trembled. A brown light flickered up the beach from them. Dread filled her. "Ridge is here. Run harder!"

Terror and adrenaline propelled them forward, and they ran harder than Alex thought was possible, until Michael and Lynx skidded to a stop. Alex glanced back in confusion and nearly tumbled into a gaping canyon. Stefan grabbed her arm and yanked before she could go over the edge. Pain shot through her shoulder and collarbone, but she ignored it, knowing that without it, she'd be dead now.

*Gryphon! Please! We're trapped.*

Others joined the brown light, and red, orange, and blue lights moved toward them. Alex's chest heaved from her terrified breaths, and the smell of campfire surrounded her.

Gryphon stepped out of nowhere and stalked toward them. Lynx had Stefan and Michael, and the moment they touched Gryphon's shoulder, the sea vanished.

# CHAPTER 44

# AARON

Aaron paced in the library, avoiding Edward's gaze. He'd caught them on the stairs and berated Matthew for not telling him about Alex. Jessica couldn't stop fidgeting on the couch as the clock ticked on.

Edith was sitting beside her, doing her best to calm her friend.

"They'll be fine," Edward said to the ladies. "No thanks to Aaron."

Aaron glared at him. "If you hadn't started a fistfight with your general, he could have accompanied her. Randal knows more about the furies than he was able to tell us."

Edward stood to face him. "You may be a king, but you have a lot to learn. Insulting another king's choices is not wise, young man."

"I'm speaking not as a king but as your godson and your daughter's husband."

"You're a child, and you know nothing of losing someone you love," Edward snapped.

"You're right. I don't know the pain of losing the love of my life, but I know Randal. I intend to hear things from his side, even if you're not interested in it."

Before Edward could answer, a damp wind tore through the library.

"Aaron!" Alex appeared across the library. She ran and threw herself into Aaron's arms. He squeezed her tightly, feeling her tremble in his grip.

"Michael!" Jessica rushed past Aaron and Alex, crying when she reached Michael.

"Is everyone all right?" Edward asked.

"They are," Stefan replied. He remained beside Lynx at the other end of the room.

"I'm so sorry. I didn't mean to go to the Forbidden Lands. Please don't be angry." Alex spoke so quickly she didn't even breathe. "It wasn't my fault—it was the pearl, and it took Michael and me to her house, and I'm sorry I locked you into this relationship by tricking you into falling in love with me when you were a boy. I didn't know and I'm so sorry and please forgive me!" Alex whimpered as soon as she finished.

*What?* Aaron cupped her face and pressed his forehead to hers. "You have nothing to apologize for. Gryphon told us about the pearl. I don't need an apology for anything ... I'm just glad you're safe."

Alex kissed him, and Aaron felt her heaving chest slow.

"As am I," Edward said. Begrudgingly, Aaron released Alex, and she turned to embrace her father. "Now what was that nonsense about tricking Aaron into marrying you? Aaron's been in love with you since he was a boy. You didn't trick him into anything."

Alex stayed silent and hugged her father.

"Where'd you go?" Edith asked.

Michael glanced at Alex before replying. "An old house," he said.

"An ancient house in my family," Alex added.

"We saw the ghost of the original Cassandra," Michael said. "Apparently Alex looks like her daughter—not her."

"I'm confused," Lynx said. "Why were there blue pearls in the Veremund house and the castle that took you there?"

Alex and Michael exchanged another look and stayed silent.

Stefan crossed his arms. "No more secrets, you two."

Michael rolled his eyes and spoke. "She told us they cursed Warren long ago because the kingdom's founders helped her when she fled the Forbidden Lands. Those sorcerers cursed Warren to only have royal sons and cursed her line to carry a fury."

"Why would they do that?" Jessica asked.

"To protect them," Edward said.

"Father?" Alex asked.

Edward was standing stiffly with his lips pulled to one side. It was the same face Alex made when trying to memorize something in a book. "Your mother once said protecting you would be important not only for us, but for all of Torian. Could this be what she meant?"

Alex went over what they'd learned about the three furies. "I don't know which fury I carry." She looked at Gryphon for a moment too long, and his eyes went wide. *Telling him something again? I thought we talked about this.*

"She told us about a scepter," Michael said. "Our priority should be to find it, but how to do so was passed down the Veremund and Nial lines. If we want any chance of figuring out the clues, we need Randal."

"We don't need Randal," Edward growled. "The scepter is a legend."

"Let him back into the castle," Alex said. "Even if you think it's a legend, *I* need to know if he knows anything. And I can't throw an engagement ball for Edith and Harold without the bride's father. Randal needs to be there."

"Absolutely not." Edward's kingly voice echoed through the room, making the Wafners stand straighter.

Alex pulled the hem of her shirt and looked at Aaron. He winked, and she smiled. His wink had become their secret sign around Datten nobility that he'd support whatever she was about to do. She crossed her arms and thrust her chin up. "If you won't let Randal back into this castle, I'll bring him to mine."

Tension filled the room. Edward slowly turned toward Alex and stared at her a long while before addressing Aaron. "This rebelliousness is your doing."

"Your Royal Highness, I can assure you it isn't," Michael said. He smiled at Alex. "Alex has always been like this."

Alex took her father's hands into hers. "If you want me to be Warren's crown princess, then I have to act like it, even when I disagree with you. The best chance we have at keeping the fury at bay is to find the king's scepter, which you told me has been lost for centuries. Now you claim it's a legend. If the founders know of its location, then we need Randal and Michael to figure it out."

Edward pinched the bridge of his nose. When he turned to Edith, she flinched. "Lady Edith, would you do us the honor of allowing my daughter to host your engagement banquet with King Harold?"

Edith's smile took up her entire face. "Yes, of course!" Jessica abandoned Michael and hurried over to her.

"But." Edward pointed a shaking finger at Alex and Aaron. "You meet Randal beforehand, and not in my castle. And at the celebration, I do not want him on the same side of the hall as me. Understood?"

"Yes," Aaron and Alex replied in unison. Alex glanced at Gryphon again, and Aaron tightened his lips. *Enough of the secrets. Can you just tell me the whole truth for once? And not share a part of it with him.* Aaron reached for Alex's hand, but a wind hit him and he found himself back in Datten, standing alone in their suite. He heard footsteps from their bedroom, followed by a door slamming.

"What is going on now?" Aaron growled. The door opened, revealing Michael and Stefan.

"You're losing your temper as usual," Stefan said.

Michael sighed loudly and crossed his arms. "You can't keep getting upset at her."

Aaron was about to reply but stopped. *There's nothing I can say to that. They're right.* Before he could figure out what to say, Gryphon cracked into the room with Lynx. Gryphon held a gold pitcher of ale and a stack of wooden cups. Lynx held a platter covered with cheese, smoked venison, and boar.

"Edith went to her father's estate," Lynx said. "She'll see what she can find out and report back later. Now we're missing one."

"Who?" Aaron asked.

"Me." Alex's voice beat her into the room. She was carrying a large basket overflowing with rolls. "I figured we'd eat while Michael and I fill you in on everything else that happened on our brief trip."

"So there *is* more to the story." Aaron caught the frown that crossed her face at his tone. She set down the basket and grabbed his hand, and with a soft crack, they were upstairs in their bedroom.

"We'll be down in a minute," Alex shouted. "I need to change out of my sandy clothes."

"Just change. None of that other stuff you two do. We have plans to discuss," Michael shouted back, and Stefan made a loud groaning noise mixed with a gag.

Alex snorted. When she turned back to Aaron, she gently cupped his face and kissed him. "Yes, there is much more that happened that we need to discuss, but I never planned to keep any of it from you."

"Then why not—?"

"Because I do intend to keep it from my father." Alex pulled off her green tunic and handed it to him. Sand cascaded from it onto the floor.

"How did you get your clothes full of sand?" he asked.

"It happened when the sea was put back by Pearl. She's the Poseidon titan, the one who helped Garrick go after my father." Alex put on a red training shirt and turned back to him. "I promised you honesty, and I'm really trying to keep that promise."

Aaron moved her braid off her shoulder, shaking out more sand. "Thank you."

"Come downstairs, and I'll tell you everything."

Aaron took Alex's hand and kissed it before leading her down the stairs. When they got there, Lynx's palms were flat on the table, and the table was bleeding.

"What are you doing?" Alex asked. Blood was welling up from the wood, well away from the food, and dripping off the edge into a bucket on the floor.

"I heard Aaron doesn't like this table because of the bloodstain, so I'm asking the wood to release it. You're very lucky. Usually dead wood doesn't listen to me."

Relief swelled in Aaron when the last of Alex's blood was drained away and his father's table had lightened, reverting to the colors he remembered from his youth. When Lynx had finished, Gryphon cracked the bucket away. Aaron ran his fingers across the smooth wood. "Thank you," he said, taking his place at the newly restored war table.

Michael threw a roll at Alex, but she caught it easily and took a bite.

"All right, let's hear the rest," Aaron said.

It took Alex and Michael over an hour to fill them in on the details Cassandra had shared with them. Alex repeated the crimes that needed to be done by and to her to weaken her control over the fury. Everyone agreed that murder and blood guilt within the family had been completed, which only left betrayal. Michael explained how the scepter of the first King of Warren had disappeared and how they needed to find their way through a maze built into the Ogre Mountains to find it. The worry came out in his voice when he spoke of how his father never got to pass on the Veremund's knowledge to him. Alex spoke about the journals that could help them come up with a plan.

"What do you mean by 'journals that don't match'?" Gryphon asked.

Alex twirled her braid in her fingers. Aaron recognized her tell. She was getting overwhelmed and needed time to process. If she continued to fidget, he'd step in, but he trusted her to know her own limits.

"There's a pair of Hades and Cassandra journals that don't match the rest. If we put them together, they'll tell the full story of how to handle the fury and vanquish it," Alex said.

"That's great," Stefan said. "Let's get the Cassandra one from your books and worry about Hades later."

"It's not that simple," Alex said. "The books are coded. Nothing makes sense unless you have both, and even then, it might not work."

"You don't always have to be so optimistic," Gryphon teased.

"I am realistic," Alex snapped. "The only way to stop the fury once it's released is with the combined power of a Head and Heart. But if I'm no longer in control, you can't use me, and I'm fairly sure your father won't help. So if we don't stop this, the fury inside of me will destroy Warren and Datten. And ... I'll be gone."

The room fell silent, and Alex looked at her lap.

"Is that what you didn't want your father to know?" Aaron asked.

Alex nodded, her eyes full of tears. Aaron leaned over and kissed her cheek.

"We will not lose you, Alex," Stefan said. "I didn't spend most of my life protecting you so some vengeful ghost could take control of you."

"Stefan's right," Lynx said. "Birch and Kharon will have ideas on how to help too. Gryphon and I will speak to them. Maybe you grabbed the Hades book when you went to the Head's library. Kharon will know."

"And we don't know what Randal knows," Michael said. "Maybe the Nials and Veremunds talked about the secrets they guarded."

Alex leaned into Aaron. "We've already survived so much," Aaron said. "If betrayal is what sets off this whole mess, you have nothing to worry about, because I love you."

# CHAPTER 45
## ALEX

Alex shivered as she lay awake in bed watching the moon outside her balcony. They'd spent hours coming up with a plan and backup plans for how to control the fury growing inside Alex. So far, its influence was limited to eye color changes, the odd voice in her head, and a feeling of being watched when she was alone, but Alex knew it would only get worse. In the morning, Aaron would accompany her to Warren to visit Randal, along with Edith and Michael. Gryphon, Lynx, Kharon, and Megesti were to search through their magic books for the supposed pair that didn't match. Afterward, they'd regroup to see what they should do next.

Despite everything that needed to be handled in Datten, Aaron promised her he'd come to Warren in the morning. His work would wait for him, and he'd proclaimed that nothing he had scheduled was as important as protecting her. Alex shivered again. Though she was wrapped in Aaron's arms, a chill crept up her spine. Every time he exhaled, his soft breaths warmed her neck. A chill washed over her each time it cooled and night air replaced his warmth.

*Who was on our balcony? Were they looking for me or for Aaron?*

*Will they come back? What if the book we need is one of the missing journals? We never figured out my premonition. What if this is just a part of it? Did Matthew find out if the Vinur on my father's council was related to Reinhilde? Does her family know about what I did? Are they angry? What if I forced Aaron into bonding with me? Would he have picked me if he'd had the choice? What if we fail and my fury hurts Aaron?*

Alex picked up Aaron's arm and slipped out of bed. She flicked her wrist so the fire would grow larger to warm the room, then crossed to the balcony doors. It was still dark outside, and frost was collecting on the door. Alex closed her eyes and tried to calm the panic that was raging through her.

*Who do I go to now that Emmerich is gone? Jerome is the closest, but Randal has more experience with daughters, and Matthew is the oldest.*

*You talk to whomever you want, Princess.*

Alex stopped and felt for Gryphon. She hurried down the stairs and threw open the door to the suite's main floor. Gryphon turned around slowly and looked her up and down.

"Nice nightgown. Rarely see a sorceress in white."

"Get out of my head."

He leaned against the doorframe and crossed his arms. "I don't go there on purpose. That whole bond thing we have makes my powers look for yours."

"We don't have a bond," Alex snapped. "One day we will, but not now."

"Sorry, Princess, but you're wrong. Look at the bond mark on your shoulder."

Alex tried but couldn't see it. Gryphon snickered and cracked two mirrors into his hands. He stepped into her room, lit the fireplace, handed Alex one mirror, and held up the other. Alex gasped. On her left shoulder was their crown on a heart, signifying the Head and Heart, but hers had a sword through the back of it.

"How is that possible?"

"Cassandra was correct. You're bonded to both of us. As one bond grows stronger, so does the other."

"No," Alex stammered. "I don't want a bond with you—not until I've lived my life with Aaron."

"Seems you don't have a choice."

"Wait, does that mean … ?" Alex grabbed Gryphon's collar and yanked on it.

"Ow."

"What is your mark? Do you have two or all three? Can you feel Aaron too?"

"Unfortunately, yes," Gryphon snapped and pulled away. With a crack, the mirrors were gone. "It would seem your bonds to both of us are strong enough that I can feel Aaron through yours. Not always, but more often than I'd ever want to."

"I'm sorry." Alex dropped her hands and spun the wedding ring on her finger.

"It is what it is."

"Why isn't any of this easy?" Alex asked in exasperation.

"Because you're the Heart. If you look back in our history, nothing about the life of the Head was easy. Most of them started their time in power by killing their Heart and the living Head. They deserved what they got."

Alex sighed and rubbed her bare arms.

"Talk to Aaron," Gryphon said. "You have other options if he doesn't help you through this, but you should at least give him a chance."

Before she could say anything else, Gryphon walked out of the room and closed the door. She sighed and went back upstairs. Aaron was sound asleep, so she crawled across their bed and gently shook his shoulder. He moaned and nuzzled his pillow. When she shook him harder, he jerked up, startled.

"Are you all right?" he asked.

"I can't sleep," Alex whispered. "I've got too much on my

mind."

Aaron grabbed her hand. "Do you want to talk about it?"

Alex nodded, and Aaron's eyes lit up. He moved closer to her until their knees touched. "Then I'm ready to listen."

Alex woke up in confusion. She was facing a wall, not the balcony. The events of the night slowly came back to her. Aaron had given her his side of the bed to put himself between her and the balcony. He'd promised to have a stronger latch affixed on the door while they were in Warren and repeatedly assured her she hadn't forced him to bond with her. He'd had many opportunities to choose a Datten maiden but had never wanted to. Alex wasn't fully convinced.

There was a click, and Alex sat up. Aaron was at her wardrobe. He wore his training clothes, which, despite being designed for comfort and ease of movement, were ridiculously embellished in gold. He faced her with her green tunic draped across his arm.

"I thought you'd want to dress like yourself, without representing either kingdom," he said.

Alex smiled. "Thank you."

Aaron placed her clothes on the edge of the bed. "That fury isn't getting you, because I love you too much to ever betray you. I'll see if Matthew has tracked down the Vinurs." He kissed her sweetly. "Get dressed, Your Royal Highness. We'll summon your Veremund and Nial and find out what Randal knows."

When they got to the Nial estate, Edith escorted Alex, Michael, Stefan, and Aaron down the long hallway that led from the front door to Randal's office. Alex gazed at the paintings that lined the hallway. To the left were the family portraits of generations of

Nials, and on the right were the Nials with their Warrens and Veremunds. Alex spotted a painting of her grandfather with Bruno Veremund and Randal's father, and she paused. The figures were in the Warren throne room, frowning in serious poses. In contrast, the portrait of Randal, Matthias, and her father had them seated in casual clothes in the library with enormous smiles. They'd never be so close again. Aaron gently squeezed her hand.

*I hope our generation doesn't follow in our fathers' footsteps.*

When she entered the room, she stood there and blinked. Randal's office wasn't merely similar to Matthias's—it was *identical*, with the same large, ornately carved desk in the corner, two large blue velvet chairs, and a couch facing the roaring fire. There was even a brown bear hide on the floor.

Randal glanced up from his paperwork and smiled at Alex. "You look surprised. All the estate offices look the same. Warren builders don't change things that work."

Before Alex could reply, two servants entered, carrying a pair of extra chairs. When they had left, there was enough seating for everyone.

Randal finished his document, then walked over to sit with them before the fireplace. He crossed his ankle over his knee. "Where do we begin?"

"You can tell us what else you know about the fury," Alex said.

"Since the founding of Warren, our families have passed down the secrets through the lines. That includes the Warrens."

"Then why doesn't Edward know anything?" Aaron asked.

"You've met Arthur. He was neither a helpful nor a loyal man. He received the knowledge his father shared with him but refused to pass it to Edward."

"Why?" Edith asked.

"Because of me," Alex whispered. "If the stories foretold that a girl would bring about Warren's downfall, he wouldn't have told my father that."

"He never would've trusted Edward to handle it," Aaron added. "He'd have taken matters into his own hands. I remember that much about him. Even when Edward was acting king, Arthur meddled with everything until he lost his mind completely."

"Precisely," said Randal. "Three brilliant men founded Warren: Arthur Warren, Patrick Nial, and George Veremund. They each had gifts the others lacked, and together, they created the Warren we love today. But when they gave refuge to a young sorceress who'd fled from violence, they were punished. When the first king died, the sorceress named Cassandra met with the firstborn sons of each of the three families. She blessed them with gifts that they would use when the daughter who would finally break the curse was born."

"How did you know Alex would break the curse?" Stefan asked.

"Because no daughters were born until her, and also because of Edith. My Nial ancestors were told that the curse would break when 'the name of Nial stopped.' At least one son has been born each generation to pass on the name until my three girls. After Edith was born, we couldn't have more children, and that told me this was the generation that would end the curse."

"How would the daughter break the curse?" Alex asked.

Edith glanced from her father to Alex. "The only way a daughter could be born into the royal family was for a sorceress to marry into the line. It reasons that a curse placed by magic would need magic to end it."

"Once you were born, all the royalty could have daughters again," Randal said.

"That's all well," Aaron said. "But I need to know why you left Alex and Victoria that day if you knew Arthur was going after them."

Randal sucked in a breath. He dropped his food and reached out for Alex's hands. "Matthias and I suspected he was planning to do away with Victoria so that Edward would need to remarry to have a more acceptable heir—a son."

Alex squeezed Randal's hand.

"But we never thought … Alex, your mother was a powerful sorceress. She saved Warren from a storm that would have flooded the entire town!"

"She did?" Alex asked.

Randal nodded. "It was shortly after you were born. Matthias and I wondered if it was a warning about the curse being broken, but your mother handled it even though she had given birth only days before. She brought you to Catherine and Matthias and strode down to the beach and out into the sea until the black sky vanished and the sea was smooth as glass. Then she disappeared, and a week later, she retrieved you from the Veremunds and returned home."

"Where would she have gone?" Stefan asked.

"Verlassen Castle, most likely. To recover," Alex said.

Randal pursed his lips and nodded. "I thought so, too. After that show of power, I never thought Arthur or anybody else could hurt her. If I'd had any doubt, I never would have left you. Please believe me."

"I do," Alex whispered. "My grandfather had Kruft working with him, and somehow he got red steel. You couldn't have known."

"We don't blame you, regardless of Edward's opinion," Aaron told him. "Now, what else do you know about the fury?"

"My father told me the fury was both a punishment and a protection. The punishment was for the sorceress who abandoned her own sorceress daughter in favor of her mortal sons. She would live knowing that her line, a line that should heal others, would eventually harbor a monster who would cause nothing but pain and death."

All the sorcerers feared the furies, so for generations, they had done everything in their power to protect and treasure the Cassandra daughters—that was where the protection came from. But, Randal said, all the attacks on Alex seemed to show that the sorcerers had forgotten about that over the centuries. Or they didn't care anymore.

"Is the scepter real?" Alex asked.

"It's very real," Randal said, making Alex sit up straighter. Her heart pounded in her chest. "However, the location of the scepter was entrusted to the Veremunds, as they were known for their wisdom."

Stefan snorted so loud that everyone faced him. Michael smiled so smugly Alex choked back a laugh.

Aaron gave Stefan a warning look. "Michael is more clever than you give him credit for. He never gets to show it with you bossing him around."

"The bossy one is your lovely wife," Stefan replied.

Alex smiled sheepishly and tried to avoid Aaron's gaze, but Michael's laugh made it hard to deny.

"So, we have to search my house to figure out how to get the scepter back?" Michael asked.

"It seems that way," Stefan said. "Looks like we'll be reorganizing your father's office sooner than you expected."

"What is the Veremund item?" Edith asked.

"Item?" Aaron asked.

"A scepter, sword, and compass," Randal answered. "The first king's scepter is enchanted to help control the fury. The sword of the first Nial glows green around foes and gold around friends. I don't know about the compass, but it must have some power."

Aaron's eyes grew wide. "I've always admired how well you can read people. Is it because of your sword?"

Randal nodded, then stood. "We need to find that scepter and the map hidden in the Veremund estate."

Aaron's arms reached across Alex's belly, sending a warmth through her. His chin rested on her shoulder as he stared at the opening in the Veremund bookcase. With all the secret doors and passages in their lives, Alex had expected him to be bored with them, but he was delighted by the secret room, and now he wanted one in Datten.

After the incident with the pearl, Alex refused to touch anything besides books, so Aaron stayed with her while the others investigated the secrets the room held. Edith had gone into town with her mother and sisters to plan the engagement celebration. Stefan, Michael, and Randal were inside the secret room, digging through the items. Suddenly, there was a loud crash.

"We're fine!" Michael called. Aaron chuckled, making Alex's shoulder tremble.

It wasn't long before the desk in front of them was covered with historical treasures of the Veremunds from generations gone. There were crumbling journals written by the men of Michael's family, the chest of letters from his mother, some older books on medicinal plants of the Dark Forest, a few books about the Ogre Mountains, and other odds and ends. A small wooden horse that was painted black especially pleased Alex. It reminded her of Flash, and Michael insisted she keep it.

She rested her elbows on the desk and flipped through the antique plant book. *It's a first edition of the book I gave to Aaron when he came to Kirsh for his honor rite.* Alex ran her fingers along the painted flower on one page.

Michael came out of the room with another armful of papers and dropped them on the desk. He looked up and saw what Alex was reading. "If I give you that family copy, will you finally stop making me feel bad about ruining yours?" he asked.

"Maybe." Alex smiled at him.

"Or you could give hers back, Aaron." Michael said.

Aaron had been trying in vain to make the compass work and now looked at him, dumbfounded. "Give what back?"

"He never figured it out," Stefan said. He came out of the secret room, carrying a large ceramic pot.

"What's in that?" Alex asked. Stefan shook his head and carried it to the far corner.

"What are you all talking about?" Aaron asked, but they all ignored him. "Excuse me—"

"Excuse what? Did you fart, or are you sorry for being a spoiled king's son who can't tell the difference between poisonous and non-poisonous bush mushrooms?" Alex turned to face him and smiled innocently, having quoted their childhood exchange.

Aaron's mouth dropped open, and his eyes bugged out. "It was you! You gave me the plant book all those years ago?"

Alex and Michael burst into laughter. "She couldn't very well let your idiot friends get you killed," Stefan said, wiping his hands on his pants.

"Stefan won the bet," Michael said, holding his side from laughing so hard. "Stefan guessed you'd never figure it out. I thought you already knew, and Alex guessed you'd figure it out after you saw her plant powers."

"You recognized me?" Aaron asked.

"I started seeing Daniel's ghost when my powers arrived, and he was always dressed in a Datten tunic. So when you arrived, the resemblance was obvious. That, and my grandfather wouldn't have taken part unless Emmerich had forced his hand."

Aaron's hands cupped Alex's cheeks. "And you think I ever would have picked anyone else." He caressed her face with his thumbs before he leaned down to kiss her.

Stefan groaned and fled to the other room. Michael's laughter grew softer as he followed Stefan.

"You'd think finding his own sorceress would have made him less grumpy," Aaron said.

"Shhhh," Alex whispered. "He doesn't know I told you."

"I'll keep your secret." Aaron kissed her quickly and then turned back to the desk. "So, you'll take the parchments on the left and I shall take the right?"

"Deal."

After a few hours, they had emptied the entire room and gone through all the items, papers, and books they'd found in the hidden room. There was no sign of a map. Frustration and fear churned through Alex. She tried to hide it from Aaron and her brothers by clutching her gifted plant book and her horse statue. Aaron took them from her and squeezed her hand. *He knows I'm upset.*

"What do you want to do now?" Aaron asked as they walked out of the Veremund estate. Michael stood in the doorway with Stefan, answering some questions from the builders. Stefan crossed his arms and observed Alex.

"I don't know," Alex said. "Part of me wants to stay here to talk to my father ... but I'm tired, and I want to know if the others found anything in the books."

"Then let's go home. You can come back tomorrow to help the ladies with their plans and talk to your father," Aaron replied.

Alex shook her head. "You know they don't need my input. I'd be in the way, but that's okay. I know they love me."

Michael and Stefan approached them. "Ready to go home?" Stefan asked.

"Since when do you call Datten home?" Aaron asked.

"Datten isn't home," Michael said. "Alex is. Wherever she is, that's home."

Aaron kissed the top of Alex's head. "That, I understand. Ready?"

Alex nodded and cracked them away.

## CHAPTER 46
# GRYPHON

Gryphon stood and stretched. He and the other sorcerers had spent all day going through the journals. Kharon had read every page of the Hades books, but they all seemed normal. The only hope they had was finding the Cassandra half in Alex's books and possibly being able to decipher some of it. The others had given up for the night, but Gryphon couldn't stand the idea of disappointing Alex, so he'd stayed. Despite the roaring fire, the fall air chilled the library, and Gryphon shivered. He was concentrating so hard on the books that he didn't hear the footsteps coming toward him. It wasn't until the smell of wildflowers and sea air surrounded him that he realized he wasn't alone.

Alex stood behind him, gripping a mug in her hands. "I didn't mean to disturb you." She placed the mug before him. "I ran into Lynx when we got back, and she told me you were staying, so I thought I'd keep you company ... if you'd be all right with that."

Gryphon's gaze lingered on her. Alex had worked tirelessly to regain her strength, and it was paying off. For the first time since he'd met her, Alex's clothes fit properly, and she appeared confident in her skin until she fidgeted with the belt around her waist.

320

"Why are you nervous?" he asked.

"I'm not nervous." Alex's voice was defensive, and she dropped her hands from her belt.

"You're acting it."

Alex sighed and took a seat at the table. "What if we can't figure this out?"

He tapped his book. It closed itself, and he faced her. "I take it your trip to Warren didn't provide answers."

Alex shook her head. "Randal told us about the magical items owned by the founding families, but my grandfather kept my father in the dark about them, and Matthias died before he could pass on his knowledge to Michael. We're working with only part of the story."

"I can help you look through the mortal estates to see if we can find anything."

Alex laid her arms on the table. "We went. There's nothing. No map. No book of details or instructions. Even the Veremund compass seems useless." She dropped her face into her arms and groaned.

"So you came here hoping for good news?"

Alex's emerald eyes peeked over her arm at him, and she nodded once.

"Sorry. Nothing yet."

*How am I supposed to handle all this? Even with Aaron sharing the burden, no one knows what it's like to know that this thing is inside of me. I wish I had my mother.*

Gryphon raised an eyebrow at Alex. "Would you like me to fetch Kharon? Perhaps they can get your mother to speak with you."

Alex frowned, then dropped her face back down.

*She won't come. She only shows up when she wants to, and now even Daniel is staying away.*

Gryphon reached out and squeezed her hand. "He's probably

with Emmerich. I'm sorry you feel alone, but you aren't. Aaron, Michael, Megesti, your father, Lynx, Birch, Lynx's plaything—"

"Lynx's plaything?"

Gryphon smiled. "They will not rest until they solve this. You mean more to them than anything, and you have the future Head on your side. I shall not stop until that fury is banished from you."

"Why?"

"Our kind did this to you, and I'm going to make it right."

Alex tilted her head at him. "That's not all of it."

Gryphon felt his face heat. No one could see through him the way Alex did—not even Birch or Lynx. As she examined his face, a tingle radiated from his shoulder, where his bond mark itched. Alex's face twisted, and she scratched her shoulder.

"It's normal."

"What is?"

"The itching. Nature bonds burn into your skin as you grow closer to the person you're bonded with. So they itch when we're getting along."

Alex's face went pale.

"You aren't betraying him. You have many friends whom you trust with your life, so the more I become that for you, the more our bond grows." *I hope one day it will be more than that.*

"Don't change the subject."

"The furies ... if you and I are supposed to bring a new evolution of sorcerers to life, I suspect our future daughter will be better off without a fury holding her back." He spoke softly but clearly, hoping to convey his sincere concern.

"I never considered that my daughters might have them."

"Only the daughter of Cassandra. Your youngest daughter, as Cassandra passes power to the youngest."

"Then we'd better get to work." Alex gestured toward the piles of books. Gryphon chuckled and shoved the Merlin books he wanted to review between them. She grabbed one off the top.

Gryphon tapped his book, then took a large swig of ale as it fluttered open to his page.

# CHAPTER 47

# ALEX

Alex read until the words blurred. The dark circles under Gryphon's eyes told her he was as tired as she was. The book they needed wasn't anywhere in this pile, but they'd discovered some fascinating spells. Alex had snuck one particularly useful book onto her lap. Gryphon would be furious if he knew what she was planning.

His head shot up.

Alex closed her eyes and yawned extra loudly while cracking her neck.

"Looks like you need rest," Gryphon said, stretching his arms. His back and neck cracked so loudly that Alex had to cover her mouth with her hand to hold back a laugh.

"It seems we both do."

Gryphon shrugged, dropping his arms. "Grab your books. I'll walk you back to your room."

Alex picked up her small stack of books, deftly tucking the one in her lap into the pile. "That's all right. I can crack."

Gryphon barely had time to nod before Alex vanished. She arrived in her suite's meeting room and set her books on the table, next to the stack from Michael's home. With a flick of her wrist, the torches and fireplace burst to life, filling the room with dancing lights.

She picked up the antique plant book Michael had gifted her and smiled as she traced the letters of the title. She closed her eyes and remembered that day in Kirsh so many years ago when she had come face-to-face with Arthur and a young, precocious Aaron. Alex pushed away the memory of the terror that had overtaken her upon recognizing her grandfather. It was seeing Aaron that gave her hope. It had been almost seven years since she'd fled. All the other noble children she'd played with vanished from her memory, but Aaron remained. His kind and curious nature made him Alex's favorite playmate, and his sweet smile was impossible to forget. She'd yearned to tell him everything the moment he stood before her, but she'd stayed silent, afraid to risk her grandfather's wrath. Alex exhaled and set aside the plant book and her memories of Kirsh.

She grabbed the book she'd snuck by Gryphon and flipped through it until she found the spell.

*3 foxtail leaves, large*
*1 lily-of-the-mountains flower*
*3 bleeding heart flowers*
*1 gryphon feather*
*5 drops of bat blood*
*White pine sap for thickening*

*Most of those ingredients are at Verlassen Castle. I could go there to try it. I'm sure I can find a feather in the training area or the courtyard and white pine sap in the forest.*

She was so focused that she didn't hear the footsteps that crept up behind her.

"What are you reading?"

Alex startled so badly she knocked all the books off the table onto the floor.

"You're awfully jumpy." Aaron winked at her before setting her books back onto the table.

"Sorry. My book distracted me."

"I can think of something else that would distract you." Aaron stepped up to Alex and gently pressed her into the table behind her.

Alex bit her lip to stop herself from giggling. She slid her arms around his neck. "And precisely what would that be, Your Royal Highness?"

Aaron smiled and pressed his forehead to hers. "If you'll follow me upstairs, I'll be happy to show you."

Alex scrunched her nose and stared into Aaron's soft blue eyes. Slowly she moved her hands to his solid chest and stalled there. "You'll have to catch me first." She shoved Aaron away from her and raced to the stairs at the far end of the room, which led to their bedroom. Aaron's feet pounded behind her. She laughed as she ran from him. In their room, she leaped across the bed, but Aaron was too fast. He grabbed her waist, and they both fell onto the soft covers.

A girlish squeal erupted from her when Aaron's palms landed on either side of her head, trapping her beneath him. Her hands shot to her mouth, and they both glanced toward the door. There were three quick knocks.

*Sorry*, she mouthed. "I'm fine, Jerome. Thank you."

Aaron caressed her cheek.

"Does it bother you?" she asked.

"What?"

"That our guards insist on checking whenever any sound comes from our room?"

"Not after what happened. They guard you from everything, including me, and it won't last forever."

Alex leaned up and kissed him, bringing his attention back to her. A wicked grin spread across his lips. He sat up only long enough to rip his shirt from his chest before plunging back down to kiss her.

The door to the balcony hadn't been secured yet, so Aaron gave her his side of the bed again to help her sleep. She rolled over groggily. *Where'd he go?* Instinctively Alex felt sad at Aaron's absence, but she remembered the spell and jumped out of bed.

At her wardrobe, she pulled out the new, shorter dress Aaron had designed for her and her training pants. She ran a brush through her thick hair and braided it while hurrying down the stairs to find her book. Caleb was on guard duty outside her door, and she asked him to summon Michael.

While she waited, she glanced over the books and noticed that her plant book from Michael was missing. She quickly counted the books on the table. More were missing. She stepped up and looked frantically around the room. *Maybe they slid under the chairs.*

There was a quick knock, and the door opened. "Um, Alex, why are you on the floor?"

"Michael! I can't find your book."

"How did you lose it already?" Michael squatted down beside her.

"I didn't lose it. I knocked the pile onto the floor, so it has to be here somewhere."

"I'll help you look for it. Is that why you needed me when it's supposed to be my morning off?"

Alex sat up on her knees and stuck out her tongue at Michael.

"Jessica stayed with Edith to help plan the engagement party. What else do you have to do?"

"Sleep in?"

Alex waved her hand at him and crawled further under the table. She grasped a book, but it turned out to be another spell book.

"Alex!" Michael's voice was husky and wavered. Alex spun so fast she almost hit her head on the table. Michael was in front of the fireplace, holding an open book. His face was as pale as the ash in the fire pit behind him. She crawled across the floor to him and noticed that the book he was holding had a map drawn inside.

"Michael," Alex whispered. "What book is that?"

Michael turned to her and held up the book, showing the cover. Even upside down, Alex could recognize the Plants of the Dark Forest book. Michael held the antique Veremund copy. "Come see." He pointed to the compass in the top left corner. It looked identical to the one in the Veremund room. His finger was pointing to the spot on the map at the base of the Ogre Mountains, where the mountains met the Dark Forest.

"Kirsh?"

Michael nodded. "Our journey to find the scepter starts in Kirsh."

"Stefan and I ended up there."

"And your grandfather tried to have me killed there," Michael added.

"We have the map, Michael!"

He nodded back. "We do."

"Do we tell them?" Alex whispered.

"No." Michael turned the page and handed Alex the book. On the back of the map was a set of instructions. Written neatly as the first instruction was, "Tell no one."

*One descendant from each of the three founding families must travel together. They cannot bring any extra and cannot leave anyone behind. Together they will achieve their end.* Alex's legs trembled when she tried to stand.

Michael grabbed her. "It'll be okay, Alex. You can't do this alone. The instructions say it must be you, me, and Edith. No one else can come. I guess Randal or your father could, but—"

"No. We need to be from the same generation. Each Warren has a Nial and Veremund. I need mine."

Alex and Michael stared at each other as Alex's heart pounded in her chest. *We can do it. We can find the scepter!*

"But if you didn't call me to help with the book, why did you summon me?" he asked.

"I need to try a spell, and it involves you." Alex grabbed her satchel from near the door and dropped the plant and spell books into it. Before she could throw it over her shoulder, Michael grabbed it from her and slung it over his.

"Send Edith a message and then you can explain the rest to me while we walk," he said.

Alex nodded and led Michael outside. They nodded to the other guards and knights as they headed to the extensive training fields where the funeral had been held.

"A gryphon feather? Couldn't you ask Gryphon to give you one?"

Alex rolled her eyes. "He can't know."

"He's your guard too, Alex. You're supposed to trust us."

Alex stopped. She bit the inside of her cheek and exhaled forcefully, then dug through her bag and pulled out the spell book. Glancing around, she opened it to the spell and turned it toward Michael.

His eyes widened and his mouth dropped open. "You can make this?"

"I'm going to try," Alex said. She closed the book and returned it to the satchel. "I sent Edith a message already, so she'll be ready, but first we have to find that feather."

Michael joined Alex as they tried to inconspicuously stroll around the field. "We should find a few to give you extra chances," he said.

Alex laughed. "That's my Veremund. When we're finished, we'll get Edith and go to the Verlassen Castle lab."

"What if Aaron and Stefan ask questions?"

Alex kept her eyes on the ground. "We'll tell them we're going to Warren. It's true, since we need to get Edith, but we'll say the new Earl Veremund had things to do."

"You lie too easily."

"The trick is that you don't lie. We'll ask Randal what the next steps are for your title, because I don't actually know. Matthew's handling the process, but he has so many extra responsibilities now that I don't want to bother him with simple questions."

Michael's eyes narrowed. Alex smirked and resumed searching the tall grass. Despite the recent funeral attack, most of the field had been restored to a proper training ground. The holes Imelda created had been filled in by the knights, and then Lynx and Birch had grown grass to hold the earth in place. The grass had turned brown quickly in the cool fall air, but at least they could use the fields without worrying about falling into a pit. More knights headed into the fields. It was late morning, so she headed to the tree line with Michael at her side.

Closer to the trees, there were a dozen feathers of various colors and sizes. Alex scooped them up and turned back to Michael. "How do we know which are Gryphon's?" she wondered.

"By the magic." Lynx's voice made Alex spin so quickly she bumped into Michael. Stefan was standing beside her, his arms crossed and his steely Wafner glare fixed on her. Michael gulped and pushed her forward.

"And what are you two up to?" Stefan asked. His eyes narrowed at Alex before they shifted to Michael.

"Why do you always assume we're up to something?" Alex replied.

"Because it's too early for Michael to be awake on his day off," Stefan said.

"It's your day off too," Michael replied.

"Yes, but I'm not the one snooping around the woods at dawn."

"We aren't snooping," Alex snapped. Finding her courage, she stepped into Stefan's space and stared him down, even though she had to tilt her face up to look at him. "I need gryphon feathers for a spell I want to try when we go to Warren today. We're up early to find them before we're due at the Nial estate to discuss Michael's title and duties."

"What sort of spell are you trying?" Stefan asked.

"It's a surprise," Michael said.

"We typically use gryphon feathers in more advanced spells. If you need one, you'll likely need assistance," Lynx said.

Alex pushed back her shoulders and exhaled. "I'm never going to become confident with my magic if I'm not allowed to fail. I learn best from my mistakes."

"It's true," Stefan said. "The worse she fails, the harder she works to keep from repeating the mistake. Who's on guard duty today?"

"Technically Caleb, but I let him go with his father, since we're going to Warren," Michael replied. "No need to have unnecessary guards, since Randal and I can watch Alex."

"And Gryphon?" Lynx asked.

"He watched me last night," Alex replied. "We read through the spell books when I couldn't sleep. That's when I found the spell I want to try."

"All right, give me the feathers," Lynx said and held out her hands. "I'll teach you how to detect his magic on them."

Lynx walked Alex through the steps, and soon Alex could feel a warmth coming from the gryphon feathers that wasn't present in normal bird feathers. Stefan and Lynx escorted them back to the castle. Alex glanced back at her brothers and grabbed Lynx's arm to pull her close.

"How are things going with Stefan? I presume you weren't out looking for me when you found us."

Lynx's sandy cheeks flushed and she grinned at Alex. "Stefan took me for a walk in the woods to see what animals we could find. Many only come out when it's dark."

Jessica and Guinevere would have frowned at the lack of romance in such a walk, but Alex found it sweet. "He knows you well," Alex replied.

"I have a lot of experience with wild sorceresses," Stefan announced behind them, making Alex and Lynx giggle.

When they reached the castle, Alex hugged Lynx and Stefan, but Stefan grabbed her arm and pulled her back. "Whatever you're up to, stay with Michael?"

"Stefan," Alex huffed, pulling away. "I gave Aaron my word, and I intend to keep it. I'm escorted everywhere. You should be happy."

"I know you, and I know that's not the entire story."

Alex groaned. "I'm going to Verlassen Castle after Warren. Happy now?"

"Very." Stefan grabbed Alex's cheeks and kissed the top of her head. He shivered, stepped back, and then smiled. "Daniel, if she gets into anything she's not supposed to, tell Kharon."

Alex crossed her arms and was about to respond when Michael interrupted. "How'd you know we weren't staying in Warren?"

"Because the only lab she likes is her mother's," Stefan replied.

"Sorcerers are quite particular about our labs. Celtics and Mystics are the worst," Lynx said.

After leaving Stefan and Lynx, Alex dragged Michael to the room he shared with Jessica. She dug through his uniform pieces until she found his archery arm guard. She examined it, running her fingers over the leather fasteners crisscrossing the length of the guard. They held it on his arm when he used his bow. Without a word, she threaded them through her fingers and ripped them off the guard.

"Alex, what are you—? Stop!"

The eyelets that held the leather tore and spilled onto the ground. Alex held up the leather strap. "I'll buy you a better one. Promise."

"That's not the point, Alex. What are you doing?" Michael snapped at her. Alex dropped the sleeve and looked up at him. *Michael's never snapped at me.* He was pinching his forehead with his hands and staring at the ground.

"What did Stefan say? You're clearly upset."

"He felt it necessary to remind me how much is at stake now when you leave Datten. As if I'd ever forget how important you are to people." He rubbed his forehead with his hand.

"Stefan's overprotective. He always has been."

"I know." Michael crouched down and started picking up the pieces of leather.

"You can tell Jessica," Alex said.

"What?" Michael tossed the leather onto a table. Alex tied the thread and put it into her satchel before holding out her hand to him.

"I know it's hard not to tell her things, and this is big, and she's expecting."

"Thank you. Let's see what Edith says first, though."

Alex took Michael's hand and cracked them to the Veremund

estate. They were hurrying down the hall to the office when they heard laughter. They found Edith sitting on the desk, dressed in her sparring clothes and kicking her legs. Jessica was standing beside her with her arms crossed, dressed in one of her prettiest Datten gowns.

Jessica eyed Alex's knee-length skirt. "I knew he designed it, but I didn't think he'd actually find someone to make it."

"Being king helps," Alex replied.

"Sorry. I had to tell her," Edith said. "She was there when I got your letter, and it's harder to lie to her than my father!"

Alex chuckled and hugged them. "We wanted to tell her everything too."

"It'll help keep everyone calm if one person knows everything after we're gone," Michael said.

"Are you sure you can't tell everyone?" Jessica asked. "I know my father and brother are controlling, but I'm sure Edward and Aaron can talk some sense into them."

"No," Alex replied, and she nodded her head toward the secret room. Michael went in and came out with a key ring. Handing it to Edith, he bowed playfully.

"And this will get me into my father's room?" Edith asked. She slipped the keys into the small pouch hanging off her belt.

"The little key matches the one that got me into my grandfather's room. What else could the third key be? Now, to Verlassen Castle. I have a spell I need to try."

"What does it do?" Edith asked, hopping off the desk and joining the group.

"If I get it right, it'll keep Gryphon out of our minds," Alex said.

"What if you need to call for help?" Jessica asked, her hand moving over her stomach as if she wanted to shield her child from Alex's reply.

"We can't risk someone following us," Michael replied. "The

instructions with the map state that only one of each line can go. Anyone else, and we would find nothing."

"Where'd you find the map?" Jessica asked.

Alex and Michael looked at each other and laughed. "It's a long story, but Michael can tell you while I work on the spell. Edith, I'll need your help with the garden, if you don't mind."

"So what do we do?" Jessica asked.

"Keep Julius from asking questions," Michael replied. "He's almost as bad as Stefan."

Edith and Alex spent the first hour collecting sap from the nearby white pine trees around Verlassen Castle. The recipe didn't specify how much she'd need, and Alex wanted to have extra. They talked about the engagement party and how Randal was holding up. He was hurt, so any chance at a reconciliation was still far-off. Alex was worried Edward would remain stubborn as well. Losing her mother had nearly destroyed him, and if Randal had had any inkling of what would eventually happen—it was understandable that he was furious.

"Do *you* forgive him?" Edith asked as they walked into the lab.

"Yes. I don't believe he suspected my grandfather would succeed in killing my mother. But it's different for me. I don't have the memories my father does. If it happened to Aaron ... love complicates things."

Alex flicked her wrist, sending the fireplace and torches to life in the lab, and dropped her satchel on the table. Edith added the jar of sap to the table and swung the cauldron over the flames.

"We have to bring back some of the potion," Alex said.

"What for?" Edith asked.

"To help Aaron and Gryphon." Alex told Edith what Gryphon had said about being able to feel and sense Aaron.

Edith picked up the leather strap and examined it. "This is good quality. How did you get it so quickly?"

"I'll need your help to find Michael a new arm guard when this is over."

Edith burst out laughing. "How mad was he? I'd throw a fit if someone damaged my archery gear."

"Your brother-in-law handcrafts yours. I can take Michael into any archery store and most of their supplies will fit him."

Scanning the recipe, Alex grabbed the jars and dropped the bleeding heart flowers and foxtail leaves into the boiling water. "So what did Harold give you when he proposed? Aaron told me they don't give jewelry in Betruger and that Harold only gave you a ring because it's our tradition."

Edith glanced down at her finger and rubbed the gold band emblazoned with a beautiful pearl. "Well, I got a Betruger horse, a new bow, clothes suited for the mountains, and my choice of as many hunting dogs as I want."

Alex smiled. "Do you like your ring?"

"I do. Harold told me you and Aaron helped, which leads me to believe it was all you."

Alex shrugged. "I used the royal wedding portraits for inspiration. Aaron gave Michael Jessica's ring, so I gave Harold yours."

They kept working on the potion, adding the flowers, bat blood, gryphon feathers, and finally the sap. Alex expected the sap to make it thick and stinky, but at once, the smell vanished. It was completely clear and smelled only faintly of pine.

It was the strangest potion Alex had ever made. She bottled a small amount for Aaron's ring and then dropped the long leather band into the liquid. She pulled it out with long tongs and examined it. The leather, once stained, was now clean and shiny. Edith grabbed a knife and measured the strap, both for Michael's wrists and for her own. Alex grabbed the last strip and slipped it inside her satchel.

"You need one too?" Michael asked, arriving at the lab door with Jessica.

"Sometimes. I struggle to keep Gryphon out of my head. It would be nice not to have to try so hard. Besides, I can test them without suspicion." Alex held up the plant book Michael had given her and motioned for them to sit at the lab table.

# CHAPTER 48
# AARON

Aaron shifted in his throne. Despite the beautiful cushions, the obsidian stone was cold—a flaw the Warren king had not considered when he'd gifted it to Datten. *I'll have to ask Randal what Edward does to keep warm when he sits on it for hours.* Surrounding him were ceiling-high paintings of former kings, family portraits of Aaron with his parents, and his wedding portrait with Alex. Their coronation portrait would take a while to finish, since Alex could never sit still for paintings.

Jerome cleared his throat, and Aaron reluctantly focused on the nobles before him. Nearly every noble family had visited, all wanting to tell their new king what they were entitled to under his rule. It was exhausting, especially considering how those whose requests he'd happily grant were the ones who didn't ask for anything. Today it was the Rassgats, and they were particularly long-winded.

Aaron stepped off the dais to shake his cousin Nathaniel's hand. There had been no mention of Aaron's threats to the Rassgats after they'd insulted Alex and Aaron's plans to save her from Moorloc. Emmerich had begged Aaron not to cast them out after his death, all because of Simone Rassgat, Aaron's great-grandmother. She'd lived to hold Daniel but died before Aaron's time. Emmerich had loved her dearly, so Aaron reluctantly agreed to spare the Rassgats. Today, standing before Wesley, he regretted that decision immensely. Wesley kept listing off the demands he had for his family's estate. *More land, a larger stable, more animals, better servants, and a title change. Do you actually do anything for the kingdom?*

Jerome stood stoically behind them, but Aaron saw the small pull of his lips as he tried to hold back his scowl.

Aaron impatiently cut off Wesley. "I'll take your requests under advisement and will let you know my decision in a few weeks."

"A few weeks?" Wesley crossed his arms and scoffed.

"His Royal Highness is very busy," Jerome interjected. "He has to meet with all the noble families before he makes any choices about duties or land."

"I don't want a job, I want my land that other people can work and pay me for. We're blood. We shouldn't have to wait like commoners."

Aaron stared at Wesley. Under all his formal, pretentious clothing, he was still the boy Aaron had been forced to play with, and who'd made his life terrible after Daniel's death. "I am well aware of what you *want*, Wesley, but my obligation is to *all* my people. I'll consider all requests and make my decisions then. You're excused."

Aaron nodded to Wesley's father and stepped between them, but a hand grabbed his arm.

"We aren't finished."

Aaron gave Jerome a look to tell him to remain where he was and turned toward his cousin. A wind ripped through the room.

"If you wish to keep your hand, you'll remove it from your king immediately," Alex said.

Wesley dropped Aaron's arm and stepped back several paces from him. The color drained from his face.

*I love when she gets protective.*

Her eyes narrowed and glowed gold, and her lips wore a thin scowl. In training pants and the new short dress, she appeared ferocious. "Seems you haven't learned your lesson from last time," Alex growled at Wesley. She snapped her fingers, sending him and his father away.

"Where'd you send them?" Jerome asked.

"I sent Nathaniel to the cow field and Wesley into their duck pond." She smirked wickedly. "I assume he can swim."

Jerome chuckled and shook his head.

"What about *your* requests, general?" Alex asked.

"My requests?"

"Almost every noble family fought to be the first to make its demands before the new king and queen, but the Wafners, Averys, and those we actually like have stayed away."

Jerome smiled. "Those who have served the kings for generations would never be so presumptuous. We accept what we're given."

"You must want *something*," Aaron said. Alex smoothed his sleeve where Wesley had grabbed him. "You have a grandchild on the way. Perhaps a larger estate, so you'll have room for your children to stay when they visit?"

"Yes," Alex said. She bit her lip, and her eyes glazed over for a moment. "Something with at least fourteen bedrooms."

"Fourteen!" Jerome looked as if he might collapse.

"Wafners have a lot of children." Alex laughed. "Jessica and Stefan will be no different. If my visions are accurate, they'll have ten between them."

A smile spread across Jerome's face. "Ten grandchildren? Gwendalin would have loved that." He wiped his hands on his pants, then crossed his arms and returned to his usual position as general. "I accept this gift from my new king. Thank you."

"You'll keep the existing house as well," Aaron ordered.

"Should any of your children or grandchildren wish to live in Datten, you'll have another home for them." Alex slid her hand down his arm and locked her fingers into his. He moved his free hand to her cheek and kissed her. Alex stiffened, but with only Jerome in the room, there was no sound, and she soon leaned into it.

"If you'll excuse me, Your Royal Highnesses." Jerome bowed and turned to leave.

"Jerome, wait." Alex pulled away from Aaron. "If Wafners have a tradition for when the firstborn son chooses a wife, I suggest you remind Stefan of it."

Jerome's face softened again. "He's found someone? How? He never leaves your side."

"Neither does Lynx," Aaron added, chuckling. "After chasing a princess sorceress for years, it seems Stefan has found himself a sorceress as dedicated to keeping Alex safe as he is."

"Thank you for telling me," Jerome said, letting slip a quick smile. "If you'll excuse me, I should check on the young guards."

"Find Stefan first, then the young guards," Aaron said, and Jerome left, grinning.

"What did the Rassgats want?" Alex asked.

"My annoying cousin thinks that he shouldn't have to work and that he deserves to continue to live off the kindness of the royal family."

Alex scrunched her nose and stared at Aaron. "It's a hard choice. On the one hand, it makes sense to let him work for what he has, but on the other, do you really want to subject any of your people to the torment of working alongside him?"

Aaron snorted. "I hadn't considered that. How was your day?"

"I have a spell I want to try." Alex led him through the back door of the throne room. They crossed the hall to their suite. Inside, there was a jar of clear liquid sitting on the table, with a few books. Aaron picked up the jar.

"I know it looks odd, but I need your ring," Alex said. She held out her hand, and Aaron passed her the jar and removed his wedding band. Alex grabbed a string off the table and slipped it through his ring. Once the jar was opened, she lowered the ring into the liquid and watched intently. Aaron watched Alex's face, but she was fixated on the ring. Shaking the string to make it shift, she moved the ring up and down a little before removing it from the jar and dropping it into her open palm.

"May I?"

Aaron nodded and held up his hand, and Alex returned the ring to his hand. When Aaron examined it, his ring looked the same.

"What did it do?"

"If it works, this spell should keep Gryphon from reading your mind."

Aaron spun the ring. "Gryphon reads my mind? I know he can read all of ours, but he actually reads mine?"

"Not like that." Alex's cheek moved and Aaron recognized her nervous tic of biting it.

He grabbed her hands. "Tell me." Alex looked up at him but shrank back. Aaron's heart fell. "I won't be angry. I promise."

"It's our bond. You and I are linked, but so are Gryphon and I. Through our bond, he connects to you, even when he doesn't want to."

Aaron grabbed Alex's hands, pulling her to him. "Thank you. I appreciate you finding a spell to keep him out of my head." As he held her hands, he noticed a thin leather strip tied around her wrist and turned her hand to look at it.

Alex smiled at him. "A test. He'll eventually notice he can't hear you, but if he stops hearing me, we'll know sooner."

"If it works, you'll have to make a lot more of the potion. But why did Gryphon never mention this spell?"

"I don't think he knows about it." Alex moved the jar to the bookshelf beside the fireplace. "I found it in one of Merlin's journals. He was incredibly talented and came up with a lot of ideas that no other sorcerers had."

"That explains your inquisitive nature."

"I like to think so." Alex crossed her arms and leaned against the fireplace. They discussed Edith and Harold's party in Warren. Edith's mother had told Alex that Edward insisted on paying for it. Alex suspected he was trying to get her forgiveness for what had happened when he fought Randal. Alex assured Aaron she wasn't ready to forgive him yet, and she had told Edith's mother to send her the bill for the new dresses for the Nial women. Aaron rubbed Alex's back, knowing how hard it was for her to stay angry with her father. Alex leaned her head against his chest and sighed.

"How about we lock ourselves in the library and have dinner brought to us?"

"But don't you have work to do?"

"I've had enough of people's demands for today. My night is yours."

There was a knock at the door. "Come in," Alex said.

Guinevere came in, dressed in a simple Datten mourning gown that went down to the floor and flowed around her legs. "Good evening, dears. I hope I'm not interrupting anything."

"Of course not," Alex said.

"I was hoping you'd be free for dinner. I'm eating in my room, and I know you have been trying to adjust to everything, but—"

"We'd love to," Alex replied.

Alex squeezed Aaron's hand before moving to his mother. "I met with Jessica and Edith today, and I have so much to tell you about what they're planning."

When she slipped her arm into Guinevere's the same way Aaron would, the smile that spread across his mother's face warmed his heart. He knew she was struggling to adjust to life without his father, but he didn't want to push her to join them.

Alex was forgoing their alone time to comfort his mother, and it touched him more deeply than he could ever tell her.

"Are they going to do the Warren waltz?" Guinevere asked.

"They are, but *someone* has to teach it to Harold."

In a breath, his mother and wife turned toward him, grinning. Aaron burst into laughter and followed them. "If Edith helps, I'm sure I can teach Harold the man's part," he said. "After all, I taught Alex, and Harold is a much better dancer."

Guinevere coughed to hide her laugh. Alex stuck out her tongue at Aaron and led his mother to her room.

# AARON

The day of the celebration was a complete blur. Aaron barely remembered waking up or eating before Jessica, Edith, and Alex took over his room to get ready and banished him to Harold's royal guest suite.

"Were you told to get out of the way, too?" Michael asked when Aaron arrived. Harold chuckled.

Aaron took a seat on the overly formal couch beside Michael. Harold's room was a much more elaborate version of Aaron's childhood room in the castle. Along with the oversized bed with sea dragons carved along the beams, there was an extensive wardrobe on one side and a couch facing the fireplace. Aaron leaned back, locking his hands behind his head.

"I'm glad this is your show and not mine," Aaron said.

"How noble of you," Harold replied. "Macht already abandoned me. He ran off to hide with your generals to avoid having to wear anything too formal."

"Smart man," Michael whispered to Aaron, and he snorted.

"Well, if it makes you feel better, as King of Datten, I'll be dressed completely ridiculously."

"What about Alex?" Michael asked. "Is she dressing as Queen of Datten or Princess of Warren?"

Aaron groaned. "*She's* going to dress as Princess of Warren so she can get away with a simpler dress. Nope, it'll be all up to me to wear the stupid official garb."

"In that case, they'll probably make it extra ridiculous to make up for it," Michael said.

Harold started laughing. "I do feel better."

"She's not dressing down to make you look bad," Stefan said from the doorway. He was holding a pair of large bundles across his arms. "Alex is dressing simply to let Edith shine. A queen's dress catches the eye, and since Harold asked Edith to dress in Betruger fashion, Alex wants to vanish into the Warren nobility. She might even wear blue." He handed a bundle to Michael and tossed the other to Aaron.

Michael looked down at his clothes and back at Stefan. They matched in their formal Warren queen's guard shirts, but Stefan shook his head. "You're an earl, Michael. That's your formal tunic as the Earl Veremund. Alex had it made and insisted you wear it today. She also had a new gown made for Jessica. You'll love it. My sister looks like a princess."

Michael unpacked the new clothes, and Harold nodded to Aaron's bundle.

"I know what's in mine. You saw what my father wore to my wedding."

The others all laughed. Aaron couldn't help but grin and roll his eyes. The official Datten king ensemble was ridiculously ornate. There were extra layers, all trimmed with gold, and perfectly polished boots with gold snaps. Even the belt was large and made of solid gold. The shirt and crest on the tunic were woven from gold thread. The cape was lined with actual gold, and the fur around it was ostentatious. To top it all off were gold shoulder plates and arm guards. *Why I even need shoulder plates and guards for formal attire is beyond me, but so long as my mother and Jerome are alive, I'll wear them.*

Stefan stared at Michael until he reluctantly put on the new tunic. Only those related to the king had the privilege of wearing the black tunic. The elegantly embroidered *V* in the top left corner told everyone he was the Earl Veremund.

Aaron smiled at him. "You remind me of Cameron and his father."

"Is that a good thing?" Michael asked.

"A marvelous thing," Aaron said, patting Michael's shoulder.

Both sets of doors were open, joining Warren's dining hall, throne room, and spare hall, and making the largest possible space to celebrate Harold and Edith's engagement. Per tradition, Aaron waited with the guests in the halls, whereas Alex would arrive with her father. Aaron stood with his mother and the Strobel side of the family. Cameron was standing between their mothers. His tunic was a rich blue, almost as dark as the deep sea. It was the color given to the highest-ranking noble families. The Bishops had it too, and the Nials, though Aaron wasn't sure if the Nials still would after what had happened with Randal.

His mother kept adjusting his cape. While it irritated him, he said nothing. His mother had always fixed his father's cape, and she probably wasn't even aware she was doing it. Two of the halls were decorated in blue and silver, while the central one was decked in Betruger green, gold, and brown. The feast was already laid out in the dining hall, and the wafting smell of roasted boar with garlic and onion was making Aaron's mouth water. He counted three different roasted meats besides the boar, and more fish than he could recognize. As always, there were barrels of bread on either end of each table, and many of the guests had already helped themselves to the Warren wine.

Suddenly, the throne room doors opened, revealing Edward, Alex, and General Bishop. Matthew's outfit was identical to Cameron's. Edward's was as glittery as Aaron's but with silver in place of gold, and blue in place of red. His fur was spotted rather than a solid color like Aaron's.

Alex was enchanting. Her dress hugged her figure and was the same dark blue as Cameron's tunic, with a silver belt and trim all around. Her sleeves hung long and almost touched the floor, and her bodice was covered in intricate waves of silver lace. From the way it sparkled in the candlelight, Aaron suspected it had been crafted from fine silver thread and sewn in place by the royal seamstress. Alex wore her mother's silver crown with the pearls, and her wild, unruly chestnut tresses had been brought to heel and cascaded down her left shoulder, covering the spot where her burn mark had been. Gryphon and Megesti may have taken the scar from her, but the memory of it, and the habits she'd developed to hide it, remained.

The room fell silent when Edward held out his arm to Alex, and she looked at it for a breath too long before she took it and faced the room. Instantly her cheeks became bright red. She forced an awkward smile and glanced around the room nervously. It wasn't until her eyes found Aaron that her smile became genuine, and the tension left her. Edward led them to the center of the hall and released her next to Aaron. He stepped forward to offer his arm, and she took it, her whole body softening.

Edward praised Harold's decisiveness in joining Aaron to save Alex from Moorloc. Through gritted teeth, he spoke of Patrick Nial, who had helped found Warren, and of how important the family was to the kingdom. Then he praised the living Nials and commended Harold on his choice of an exceptional Warren lady, who not only represented the best Warren had but also carried a family legacy that was hard to compete with in all the kingdoms, outside of royalty.

Betruger's royal musicians played the kingdom's song, and Harold appeared in the doorway. Like Edward and Aaron, he was dressed in a fancy crested shirt of forest green. His tunic was sunflower yellow, and his cape and boots were lined with fur. But his belt was made of simple leather and wasn't covered in jewels or gold like Aaron's. Still in the doorway, he looked to the side and held out his hand, and Edith stepped into view. She was dressed in a floor-length Betruger gown made of forest green fabric, with yellow mountains decorating the bottom of the skirt and the bodice. Along the neckline and sleeve edges was the same solid fur that lined Harold's boots and cape. They matched perfectly. Alex let out a soft, happy sigh and leaned closer to Aaron. He wrapped his arm around her shoulders.

Edith and Harold paraded to the center of the room to accept congratulations from Edward, then from Aaron and Alex. Once they'd finished, it was time for Harold and Edith to have their first dance. Alex smiled at Aaron, and he kissed her forehead before they watched their friends complete the traditional Warren Waltz. Edith was confident in the moves, and though Harold made a misstep once or twice, he recovered quickly. As soon as they finished, the celebration was officially underway, and guests swarmed the couple to offer congratulations.

"She looks stunning," Alex said.

"She does, but nowhere near as enchanting as you," Aaron said.

Alex stood on her toes to get closer to him. "I'm starved. It took hours to get us ready, so we didn't have time to eat."

"Well, I can't fix things between Randal and your father, but I can get you food." Aaron grabbed her hand and led her through the crowd. Some nobles tried to stop him, but the instant they saw Alex, they bowed to her and moved away. It took some careful navigating, but Aaron got them to the tables that had venison and fish, both their favorites. Alex searched for and then found bread, grabbing three small loaves for her plate. Aaron grinned at her and added two more to his own plate for her.

"It's strange, being on the outside of one of these celebrations," Alex said before taking an oversized bite of her bread.

"Good or bad?" Aaron whispered to her.

Alex finished chewing before answering. "Good. It's nice not to be the center of attention tonight. Edith deserves her moment, and they look so happy."

After they'd finished their food, Aaron convinced Alex to dance with him. She was nervous, as always, but they ended up dancing perfectly. He didn't want to let her go. Her presence kept away not only the annoying royals from the other kingdoms but also all the Datten nobles in attendance. It seemed no one would risk offending Alex in her kingdom by trying to take Aaron.

Jerome listed off the royals and nobles he was supposed to schmooze with, and Aaron noticed Alex scanning the hall. Michael was moving through the crowd toward them.

"Apologies, Your Royal Highnesses, but could I borrow Alex? Edith is having some trouble, and we can't find her sisters or Jessica."

"Of course." Alex turned to Aaron. "You don't mind if I leave with Michael and Edith to take care of this?"

"Are you escorting them?" Aaron asked Michael, and he nodded. "Then by all means, you may take her as long as neces-sary, so long as you bring her back."

Alex pushed Aaron playfully. "I love you, Aaron. You know that, right?"

Aaron narrowed his eyes. "That sounds like a goodbye."

"Hardly. I just like to say it." Alex kissed him and turned to go.

Aaron stopped her. "I love you more than anything in Torian, and I will spend the rest of my days reminding you of that fact." He cupped her face and kissed her passionately, not caring who was watching. "But if you doubt my words, I can prove it later tonight when we're alone."

Alex's cheeks darkened for a moment before she composed herself. She winked at him, then left with Michael. Aaron turned back to Jerome. "Who's first?" he asked.

# CHAPTER 50
# AARON

It took hours for Aaron to finish greeting and conversing with the Torian royalty. A mix of interesting and downright terrible royals had journeyed from the southern kingdoms, and it was always a guessing game as to how a chat with one of them would go. He'd been lucky—most of the ones in attendance were of the younger generation, which he had more in common with, though he had a little too much fun teasing Prince Jesse and Prince Rudolph.

At last, he'd finished his royal obligations. His mother and Jerome had already left when Stefan hurried over.

"When did you last see Alex?"

Aaron tried to remember. "Before I had to complete the royal tour, she left to help Edith with something."

"I haven't seen her in hours. I assumed she was with you, but then I saw you alone with the royals, so I started searching. She isn't with her father, your mother, Jessica, or any of her guards."

"Just ask Michael. He'll know," Aaron said. He was trying not to worry.

"I can't find him either."

Aaron's stomach dropped. "Edith?"

Stefan shook his head. "Should I summon Jerome and Matthew?"

"Not yet," Aaron said. "I want to talk to Randal first. With everything going on with the fury and the founding families—I think more's going on."

"What about Gryphon?"

"I'd like to avoid his help if possible." Aaron searched the room for Alex but couldn't find her or Randal. He rushed toward the next room and almost tumbled over as his cape snagged on a table. *Enough of this useless thing.* He ripped it off, bunched it up, and shoved it at Stefan before hurrying to the next room. Alex wasn't in either of the other two rooms, but Randal was in the spare hall. They hurried toward Randal, who'd kept his promise and stayed away from Edward for the evening. Randal nodded goodbye to the knight he was talking to and turned to Aaron and Stefan. "Everything all right?"

"We can't find Alex, Michael, or Edith. They left together a few hours ago, and no one has seen them since," Aaron said. "Should we be concerned that those three are gone?"

All the color drained from Randal's face. "I need to go home and check my office to be sure, but I suspect they have gone looking for the labyrinth." His voice was flat and devoid of life.

The three of them headed for the closest door. The hallway was quiet, and they kept their voices low.

"Michael wouldn't have let Alex run off again," Stefan said.

"If they went to find the scepter, he would have had to," Randal said. "Edward may believe it's a myth, but it isn't, and the scepter is magically protected. To get to it, they'll pass through a labyrinth filled with trials to prove their worth."

Aaron grabbed his arm and spun him around to face Aaron and Stefan. "Why didn't you tell us this before?"

"Edward wouldn't have believed it. He'd have made things

difficult for them, and you ... you would have increased her guard and never left her side."

"You're right. We would have!" Stefan said. His body was rigid with rage.

"That's the problem," Randal said. "The journey to retrieve the scepter can only be completed by those from the Warren, Nial, and Veremund bloodlines. Anyone else, and they'd end up wandering the mountains endlessly."

"So why do you need to go to your office?" Aaron asked.

"To confirm it's where they went. Edith told me Michael found the Veremund compass in his house—"

"The compass didn't work," Stefan said.

"Not here. It will when they get to the starting point of the journey."

"Where exactly is that?" Aaron asked.

"The Veremund family has the map."

"What good are you, then?" Stefan asked.

Aaron tried to fight the pressure building in his chest. *Why didn't she tell me?*

"Any help would have kept them from completing their mission," Randal said.

"Go," Aaron said, rubbing his neck and looking around to make sure no one had been listening. The narrow hallway was still deserted. "I'll summon Megesti, and we can try to get the others here. Maybe Gryphon can see where they are."

Randal nodded and headed down the hallway.

"So ... who's going to tell Edward?" Stefan asked.

"Let's start with Harold and Jessica. They're less likely to blame me." Aaron scratched his head and looked around the hallway.

"Try not to panic," Stefan said. "Michael loves Alex as much as we do. He'll keep her safe."

Aaron nodded. "Bring them to the library. I'm going to put on some reasonable clothes; I expect tonight is going to be a long one."

Aaron tried to still his nerves, but he couldn't stop his legs from bouncing on the floor. Harold paced the room, grumbling to himself. On the couch between Aaron and Stefan, Jessica rubbed her pregnant belly.

"Welcome to real life with Alex," Stefan mumbled, making Harold's head snap in his direction.

"Stefan, don't start," Jessica said.

The door flew open, and Randal rushed in. "The sword of Nial is gone, and Michael's office is empty, too. Alex's, Edith's, and Harold's horses are all gone. Apparently, Alex asked to move them and a few others to the Veremund estate to make room for the guests' horses, but now those three are nowhere to be found."

Aaron gulped and bounced his knee.

"How can we believe you don't know what's on this map?" Harold demanded. "You kept all this from Alex and Edward for years."

"I don't know what the map says, but even if I did, I couldn't tell you."

Harold threw his arms up and grumbled louder in Betruger, stomping around.

"Do you know what he said?" Aaron asked Stefan.

"You don't want to know."

A breeze hit the group, and Megesti and Gryphon appeared in the back of the room.

"Apparently, I was summoned. Did you miss me already, Princeling?" Gryphon asked, holding out his hands to the group before him, but his smile dropped immediately. "Where's Alex?"

Stefan and Jessica brought them up to speed while Aaron tried to calm Harold. When Alex had been taken by Moorloc, Harold had been his rock. Now that their places were reversed, Harold was struggling as badly as Aaron had.

"I promise you, Michael and Alex will take care of Edith," Aaron said before whispering, "Just remember, love makes fools of us all."

Harold groaned. Aaron smiled, remembering that morning on the Ogre Mountains when Harold had said it to him, back when he was scared he'd never get Alex back from Moorloc.

"How long since anyone's seen them?" Megesti asked.

Stefan rubbed his forehead. "Four hours."

"How did you all lose track of them for *four hours?*" Gryphon threw up his hands, looking from Jessica to Aaron and back. "You're married to two of them."

"I was speaking with my father," Jessica said.

"And I had responsibilities to see to," said Aaron.

Stefan scoffed. "Playing the friendly king with the other Torian royalty isn't a responsibility."

"Your father says otherwise," Aaron snapped. "It was he and my mother who made me leave Alex to talk to them. Besides, I left her with Michael, and she gave no indication—"

*I love you, Aaron. You know that, right?*

"What is it?" Jessica asked.

Aaron groaned loudly enough to make Harold stop pacing. "She's diabolical. She asked if I minded if she left with Michael and Edith to take care of *some issue*. I told her it was fine because it was Edith and Michael."

"You gave her permission to do this?" Harold asked.

"I watched Edith go to Michael. He said he couldn't find her sisters or Jessica, and Edith needed help. I assumed it was a dress issue, not that they were secretly asking permission to run off on an adventure together!"

"Not an adventure," Randal corrected. "Getting there could be one, but the labyrinth is also a test to ensure that the descendants embody the virtues of their founders."

"How does that work?" Megesti asked.

"I can't say for sure, as it wasn't written anywhere. All I know is that Edith will need to prove that she is as brave as Patrick Nial, Michael that he is as wise as George Veremund, and Alex that she is as true and honorable as Arthur Warren the First."

"And if they fail?" Jessica's voice was barely a whisper.

Randal frowned. "Then they'll die in there."

# CHAPTER 51

# ALEX

The Veremund estate was freezing cold. Alex hurried down the hallway to Michael's office. Michael and Jessica had not moved in yet, and with the restoration completed, the place was empty. Alex had enchanted it earlier to keep the future occupants safe, but now, with nobody here, it was the perfect place for them to hide their supplies. When she arrived at the office, Michael was already in the secret room, grabbing the bag of things they'd collected from the estate.

"I put the bags behind the desk. The tent and sleeping mats are already in the stable," Michael called. A crash and a clatter came from the room.

"Try not to break the compass."

Michael stumbled out, holding an old bow and a quiver of arrows. "The compass and the book are in my satchel, beside you. I wanted to get my father's hunting bow. It wouldn't hurt to have an extra one, and no one will notice if this one is gone, but they would if we took any of ours."

"Are you okay riding Harold's horse?" Alex asked.

"Edith said she'd switch with me if I ran into trouble. This time of year, we need three Betruger horses to make it across those mountains. Winter in Warren is mild compared to the camp, but those mountains, they're something else."

"At least we don't have to carry much water with us."

"One of the many advantages of traveling with a powerful sorceress." Michael threw his satchel around his neck and offered Alex the bow. She took it and examined the carvings along the limb. Despite its age, it was beautiful. The secret door rumbled shut, and Michael slid his arm around her shoulders. "You know I won't let anything happen to you or Edith, right?"

Alex nodded, and they made their way through the hall. They locked every door they could and headed out the back door to the stable. "Do you really think locked doors will slow them down?" Michael asked.

"If they don't bring sorcerers with them, then yes."

Snow, Alex's white colt, was happy to see her and kept stamping the ground, making it hard for Alex to grab his bridle. Harold's horse, Hestur, was looking around, clearly searching for Harold. Alex rubbed Hestur's snout and neck to soothe him. Michael arrived beside her and gently led the horse out of the stall and checked that the packs were secured and not pinching. Hestur was carrying Michael's things and the tent.

Alex left Snow and took Quiver from her stall. The mare Harold had given Edith was dark brown, like wet sand, and matched Edith's eyes. As with Alex's horse, they loaded Quiver with everything Edith needed. Edith's bow was secured above her sleeping mat, and Michael had both a bow and a sword strapped to his.

He caught her staring. "I promised Jessica I wouldn't let anything happen to you two."

Alex pulled out her red steel dagger, adding it to Snow's mat along with the bow Michael had given her. They were all overprepared. Alex and Michael settled in their saddles and headed to the Nial estate with Quiver on a lead line. Alex had never been happier to see a deserted road. They arrived at the Nial estate and silently headed down the large, ornate cobblestone path to the back of the main house. Alex climbed down and knocked quickly. Edith threw open the door, grinning like a madwoman. She had a sword, and it was glowing faintly.

"The sword of Nial." Edith held it up and looked at the blade. "It glows gold with friends and green with foes."

"It's beautiful," Alex said.

"It's also enchanted to be the perfect weight and balance for whoever wields it," Edith said. She twisted the blade toward the ground and held it out to Alex. "The Nials got the sword, the Veremunds a broken compass, and you a scepter. I think our items were supposed to be used to retrieve yours."

"Are you ready?" Michael asked. Edith nodded, then attached the sword's sheath to her bags, took the sword back from Alex, and climbed onto Quiver. Once Alex and Edith were settled on their horses, Michael and Alex exchanged a look she knew too well, and she cracked them away.

They arrived on a deserted trail in the middle of the Dark Forest. Edith's and Michael's horses reared up from being cracked suddenly, but Snow didn't even flinch. Once they had gotten the horses under control, Michael and Alex looked around until Alex got her bearings, and they headed east along the trail. Alex slipped the reins up her arm and rubbed her hands together, producing orbs of light that floated above them to light their way. Their breath fogged as they clopped down the dirt path toward Kirsh. Michael was searching his satchel for something, so Alex leaned over and grabbed Hestur's reins.

Edith asked questions about where they were. She hid her fear well, but Alex heard the slight pitch in her voice.

"It's okay to be scared, Edith," Michael said.

"What? Nials are brave. I'm fine."

Michael pulled the ancient plant book from his bag and turned to Alex, giving her another look she knew too well. She gently kicked Snow and overtook Michael to ride beside Edith.

"It's understandable to be nervous. You've never left home like this. Michael and I grew up in these woods, so we're used to cold nights and empty bellies."

Edith gulped and twisted Quiver's reins.

Alex leaned toward her and squeezed her hand. "You have nothing to worry about. Michael and I know exactly where we are, and for the first bit, we know exactly where we're going. Hopefully by then the map becomes useful, and I can summon all the apples and water you could want."

Edith smiled weakly and turned back to the road ahead of them.

"Are you sure we're going the right way, Alex?" Michael called from behind them.

"Yes."

"But the river sounds are coming from the north."

Alex glanced back at him. "Trust the weather and water sorceress, Michael. We're in that strange part of the woods where the sounds reflect off the nearby mountains and old-growth trees. I brought us here. I know where we are."

"All right, Your Royal Highness. Lead the way."

Michael grinned wickedly and held out his hand for her to lead the way. Rolling her eyes, Alex flicked her wrist, bringing Michael's light orbs back to her. She cackled as he grunted and tried to catch up to her and Edith.

They rode on, with only the pounding of the horses' hooves and their ragged breaths breaking the nightmarish silence. Despite the chill in the air, the fur-lined Betruger cloak kept Alex warm, and she was thankful to Edith for sharing her clothes. After half an hour of riding, they spotted lights ahead. Michael and Edith perked up almost immediately, but Alex swallowed hard. She'd ended up at the back of their group and was thankful Michael couldn't see how nervous she was. *How are the people in Kirsh going to react to me? They knew me as a poor boy, and now I'm their queen. Will they even recognize me?*

"You're going to love Kirsh, Edith. The people are wonderful," Michael said. He turned back to Alex and winked.

The forest gave way to a rickety old bridge. The horses clattered across it without reservation, and Alex noticed Edith's reaction to the little village. *It must seem so insignificant.*

Alex glanced nervously toward the mill, but Michael grabbed her hand and shook his head. They took the single road toward the inn that was run by Ian and Irma.

The camp for orphaned boys was hidden in the forest on the outskirts of Kirsh, and Ian had been second-in-command when Alex and Stefan had stumbled upon it so many years ago. Alex hadn't yet reached five years, and Stefan was twelve. The boys saw how capable Stefan was and wanted him to join them. They tried to get him to bring Alex to town to find a family who would take her in. Girls were easy to find homes for in the small towns where housework was plentiful, but he refused. It took some convincing by Ian, but in the end, the boys agreed to allow Stefan and Alex to stay. She'd lived as a boy for twelve years until Aaron, Megesti, and Jerome had arrived to bring her home.

Alex had considered this place to be her home for so long. *How has it only been two years?* The inn had expanded into a second building. While not as fancy as Warren homes, or as sturdy as those in Datten, the building had a homey charm. The logs that formed the walls were abundant in the Dark Forest and provided shelter from the cold mountain storms. There would be a garden in the back, even if it wasn't growing anything this time of year. The former boys now lived here and thrived under the loving care of Ian and Irma. Michael, Stefan, and Alex had sent back enough gold to get them all proper homes or apprenticeships and allow the rest to stay with Ian to be cared for.

The shops and homes were as dark as the surrounding woods, but the inn windows were illuminated and welcoming. Alex nudged Snow to encourage him toward the stable beside the inn, and Edith followed suit. The stable looked exactly as it had when Alex had left.

She took Quiver's and Hestur's reins and asked Michael to see about some rooms for the night so they could leave early in the morning. With luck, no one would notice them. Warm light spread across the dirt road, and her friends disappeared into the inn. Alex turned back to their horses to unload them for the night.

"You're supposed to go inside," said a young voice from behind her.

A small boy with bushy dark brown hair looked up at her. Alex wrinkled her nose at him. "My friends have gone inside. I'm unloading the horses while they arrange our rooms."

"My father won't like it. *He* always handles the horses."

Alex leaned against Snow, who stood still as a stone for her. "I'm confident Ian won't mind."

The boy's eyes widened. "You know my father?"

"You don't remember me, Felix, but I know you, your mother, your father, and your grandfather too. I was one of the boys in the woods for many years."

"But you're a girl."

"I am."

The boy's mouth dropped open. "That means you're ..."

"Alex!" Ian strode up behind his son, the same bushy dark brown hair covering his head. He held out his arms to her.

She threw herself into Ian's arms, and he gave her a big bear hug.

"Go back inside with your grandfather," he called to Felix. "Michael asked a few of the older boys to come help Alex with their bags."

"Michael's here too?" The boy darted to the inn's kitchen door.

Alex rubbed her hands, sending out light orbs to illuminate the stable. "I have magic, but Michael's the favorite? That doesn't seem fair."

"Michael's funny. Kids like funny," Ian said. He petted Snow on the head, looking over the three horses. "You have fewer things than I expected."

"We have clothes, shelter, and some food. With my magic, we'll be fine. And we'll be purchasing a few things from you as well."

Ian cleared his throat and looked away from Alex as he unloaded Snow. "Michael didn't mention Stefan."

"He's in Warren."

"So what do I tell him when he figures out everything and shows up in a few days?"

"The truth," Alex said. "I won't ask you to lie. By then, we'll be too far for him to find us."

"Is there a reason you left him behind?"

Alex explained why it had to be she, Michael, and Edith alone who made this journey, while they unloaded and groomed the horses. When the horses had been fed and put into their stalls for the night, Ian wrapped his arm around Alex's shoulders and led her through the kitchen door.

Irma almost knocked over Ian in her rush to get to Alex. She marveled at how much Alex looked the same and updated her on all the happenings in town. A pair of boys who looked to be only twelve took their things to the three rooms Irma had provided. Some patrons had been waiting awhile. Michael went behind the bar with Ian to retrieve drinks, and Alex helped Irma in the kitchen, scooping rabbit stew into bowls and adding fresh bread loaves to the side. Edith took a seat in the kitchen, right in the middle of all the activity.

Alex tossed her a loaf. "Try one. Irma makes the best sunflower bread you'll ever taste." Irma shook her head but smiled at the compliment.

Once the patrons had eaten and left, Irma brought out food and drink for the visitors, and they settled into the chairs around a large table. They enjoyed some stew and talked about life in Kirsh. Ian filled them in on how things had changed at the camp. Since the boys lived in Kirsh, the huts in the forest were mostly empty now. Oliver and Graham worked as hunters and trappers and would stay in the huts while they were out there.

Irma mentioned the miller had moved to a different town after passing the mill to his son- and daughter-in-law. Alex sighed with relief knowing he wasn't around anymore. Michael asked about each of the boys they'd grown up with. Many of them had found apprenticeships and were now thriving in other towns. It lifted Alex's heart to hear this. They talked well into the evening, until Alex noticed Edith yawn and they finally excused themselves to go to bed. They all knew that in the morning, things would get a lot harder.

# CHAPTER 52

# ALEX

Alex tossed and turned for most of the night. She already missed Aaron. She wanted to crack back to him, explain everything, and return before anyone realized she had gone. But what if he and Gryphon followed her? *No, I can't risk it.*

She got up and headed outside. Last night, she'd been so tired she'd slept in her clothes. Now, in the icy morning air, she was thankful for them. She tightened her cloak and, with only the moon for illumination, strolled down the small dirt road toward the wooden bridge. A familiar silhouette leaned on the railing.

"You couldn't sleep either?" she asked.

Michael shook his head.

"I'm sorry, Michael. I know lying to Aaron and Stefan was hard for you."

"I'll survive. I'm thankful we told Jessica the truth."

Alex leaned on the railing next to him. "I wouldn't risk your baby for my secrets." Looking into the black water of the Darren River, she shivered and pulled her cloak tighter.

Michael put his arm around her shoulders. "How are you

holding up? I mean, you're lying to your husband, brother, father, friends, future partner, cousin—"

Alex shoved him away playfully. "Sadly, with twelve years of my life spent in hiding, I'm quite accustomed to lying."

"That's fair. Old habits are hard to break."

Alex twisted her shirt hem.

"You want to go to the camp, don't you?" Michael asked.

She nodded.

"Then we shall. For now, let's see if we can't get some sleep before Edith wakes up. We'll stop by the camp after breakfast."

Edith was up earlier than either Michael or Alex had expected. Irma served them a hearty breakfast of fresh bread and hot oat porridge with sweetened applesauce. After they'd eaten their fill, Alex and Michael hugged their friends goodbye. Alex slipped Irma a letter and some extra gold before she and her travel companions went to the stables to prepare their horses. After they were loaded, Michael checked the horses to be sure none were overburdened. Edith and Alex snickered and compared him to Cameron, making Michael throw hay at them. The ladies laughed, mounted their horses, and rode out of the stable, soon followed by Michael.

It was early in the morning, and the only sounds they heard were the clopping of hooves as they crossed the wooden bridge into the woods. The rising sun sparkled like gemstones on the frosted, grassy trail. Edith was breathing hard enough that her breath fogged up a good distance before her face. When Alex brought it up, Edith laughed it off and admitted she wasn't used to being out of touch with her family for even a day.

"I can still crack messages to your father or Harold for you," Alex said.

"I know, but they can't reply."

"Oh." Alex had forgotten that without knowing where they were or being able to sense them, Megesti and even Gryphon couldn't send back anything. "I'm sorry, Edith."

Edith smiled weakly. "You have nothing to apologize for, Alex. You're my Warren, and I'm your Nial. It's my job to support you."

"And mine," Michael chimed in.

"Now let's go to this camp you grew up in. After listening to all three of you talk about it for years, I'm excited to see it in real life."

Alex nudged Snow to the front of the group. She glanced at Michael for a second before tugging the reins. Snow obeyed and shot forward, cantering down the path. Edith laughed and chased after Alex. Michael cursed and spurred on Hestur to catch up.

The ride was chilly, and Alex was grateful when the sun rose and warmed the air. Though she had spent decades in these woods, she missed the milder weather of Warren and Datten.

"Is it me, or is it colder here than we're used to?" Michael asked.

"How did you two live in these woods? I'm freezing," Edith said, pulling her gloves out of her satchel.

"This isn't even bad," Alex said. "In the winter, we'd get some nasty storms from the Ogre Mountains that would settle here in the valley. It would snow for days."

"Days?" Edith's jaw hung open. "Warren is challenging enough when we get a few fingers of snow. How did you manage?"

Alex laughed. "Well, the camp was full of young, strapping men. So they got the snow out of the way for us, and after my powers came in, I helped."

"She'd melt it," Michael said, moving his horse into the lead.

"That would have been amazing to see," Edith said.

"I'm sure you'll get the chance to see it," Michael said. "If

Betruger is as cold as it is here, she'll have to come thaw you out regularly."

"Well, at least I have some time before we have to move so far away. I'm excited to marry Harold, but I never saw myself leaving my home."

"I understand," Alex said. "I didn't want to leave Warren, and Aaron promised me it would be years before we had to, but then ..." She shrugged.

"I will go wherever Alex needs me to, and Jessica will come with me," Michael said.

Alex and Edith turned to Michael and made faces at him. They laughed and chatted about life in Datten versus in Warren. Michael told them what he'd seen in Betruger when he'd stayed with Aaron and his men. It wasn't long before they forgot the cold from all the laughter echoing between the trees.

Michael and Alex both spotted a familiar pair of trees and veered their horses to the right on instinct. The small clearing had scattered wooden huts. The stable was over a river running through the clearing. Michael leaped from his horse. Alex grabbed Snow's bridle and climbed down. She did a full circle to take everything in. *It's all still here. I thought for sure it would have vanished into the woods it came from.*

"If Oliver did anything to my bed, I'm going to be so mad." Michael laughed and rushed to his old hut. Alex smiled and turned to Edith. She'd gotten off her horse, but she looked as if she might retch at any moment.

"Edith?" Alex took her arm. "Are you all right?"

Edith gulped and trembled. "You grew up *here*?"

"Yes. From a week or two after I vanished until Aaron found me."

"Here? This is where you lived?"

A hut door slammed, and Michael called across the yard. "I know it's silly, but my favorite blanket was still in there, so I'm taking it." He strode over to them and held up his prize. "The musty smell will be gone with a few days of fresh air, don't you think?" He stopped short when he noticed Edith. "What's the matter?"

Edith shook her head. She stepped away from them and walked toward the first small hut. She tilted her head, examining the building.

"That was Alex and Stefan's," Michael said. Edith walked up the two steps to the door and slowly opened it. She stepped in, letting the door close.

"Do you know what that's about?"

"I don't," Alex said. "But she seemed really upset the moment we arrived. I thought she'd be excited to see the camp."

Michael pursed his lips. "I know it was a home when we were here with the boys, but looking at it now ... well, it's not the same. Your sitting room at the castle is larger than all these buildings combined."

"With the damage from being abandoned, it looks small and depressing."

Michael slid his arm around Alex's shoulders and pulled her close. "Especially after the warm and loving home Irma and Ian have made for the boys in Kirsh."

It was hard to believe Alex had shared this tiny cabin with Stefan for years. "I'm going to check on Edith. Then we can water the horses at the river and go. I've seen enough." Alex forced her feet to move, and her boots softly crunched beneath her as she drew closer to the hut, while Michael tended to the horses behind her.

Once Alex was in front of the cabin, she could hear soft crying. She hurried up the stairs.

"Edith?" Alex let the door close behind her and walked toward her friend.

Edith was sitting on what had once been Alex's bed, holding

her face in her hands. She sniffled. Alex sat beside her and held out her hands. Edith gave them a squeeze but wouldn't meet her eyes. Not knowing what to say, Alex sat with her until Edith had stopped crying.

"This is where you lived? In here?"

"Yes. We're on my bed. Stefan slept on that one." Alex nodded to the rickety old bed. "When I got mad at him, I'd stuff his pillow under it so he'd have to hunt for it. And when he made me really mad, I put a snake in his bed."

Edith chuckled and released Alex's hands. "I wish I'd have thought of that with my sisters." She pulled out a handkerchief and wiped her tears. "I'm sorry that I'm being silly."

"Not at all."

"You grew up here." Edith motioned to the small room. "Crown Princess of Warren, the future Queen of Datten, and the most powerful sorceress to grace Torian, and you grew up in a room that my father wouldn't have let our dogs live in."

"I know it may not look like much, but we had what we needed. I had food, shelter, protection, and love. Some winters were harder than others, and yes, it was a struggle some days, but it made me what I am today. I think growing up here was good for me as a queen. I won't ever look down on any of our people because they live without."

Edith sniffled again. "I know, but the idea of my princess living like this ... breaks my heart for you and makes me furious at my father. He's the reason you ended up here. He could have done more ... *should* have done more. Instead, he tarnished the Nial name, and I don't know if we'll ever get it back."

"My father may not see it this way, but I'm a believer in fate. It comes with seeing the future so much. I believe he did what he was supposed to do, and that we have to move on from this. Edith, you are not responsible for your father's sins, and neither my father nor I hold Randal's actions against you."

Edith threw her arms around Alex and hugged her neck.

Alex squeezed her back. "You're my Nial, just as Michael is my Veremund. I wouldn't take anyone else, ever."

Edith sniffled, and Alex felt her chest shudder. "Thank you. I'm honored to have you as my Warren. Who'd have thought that there would be two women in our lines in one generation?"

"And that we'd both be queens, no less." Alex stood and held out her hand to help Edith up.

They headed outside to find their horses back in the clearing. Michael was beside them, holding the plant book and the compass and wearing a worried expression.

"What's wrong?" Edith asked.

"Did you drop the compass in the river and now it's water-logged and broken?" Alex teased.

"No, it's working." Michael held it out to her.

The moment Alex took the compass, the needle spun wildly, then slowed down and pointed toward the mountain range. She looked at Edith and Michael, who both looked as confused as she felt.

"But it didn't work in Warren," Edith said.

Alex handed the compass to her and grabbed the book from Michael. She flipped it to the back to get another look at the map and gasped. Beside Kirsh was now a small green dot. And far into the mountain range was a second small dot, near the top of one of the largest mountains.

"We found the starting point of the map, and that fixed the compass," Michael whispered.

Alex slammed the book shut. "Well, we'd better follow it."

# NEED MORE OF TORIAN?

If you enjoyed the book be sure to leave a review since they are a huge help to indie authors like me! They can even just be a few words that you enjoyed the book!

Join the Facebook Fan group to engage with other fans and get fun updates from Alice!

https://www.facebook.com/groups/theheadheartandheir/

Sign up for the monthly newsletter via my website!

alicehanov.com

Support Alice on Patreon and get early or exclusive access to things.

patreon.com/AliceHanov

# TORIAN TIMELINE

| | |
|---|---|
| Sorcerers arrive | No one knows |
| Founding of Datten | year 0 |
| Founding of Warren | 50 |
| Founding of six Southern kingdoms | 50-100 |
| Merlock arrives in Datten | 1469 |
| Megesti is born | 1483 |
| King Arthur of Warren is born | 1484 |
| King Emmerich of Datten is born | 1503 |
| Prince Edward of Warren is born | 1510 |
| King Emmerich is crowned king of Datten | 1516 |
| Prince Daniel of Datten is born | 1522 |
| Prince Aaron of Datten is born | 1530 |
| Princess Elizabeth of Warren (Alex) is born | 1533 |
| Princess Elizabeth vanishes and Prince Daniel dies | 1538 |
| Princess Alex returns home to Warren | 1550 |
| Princess Alex is taken by Moorloc | 1550 |
| Datten brings Princess Alex home | 1550 |
| Present day story | 1551 |

# KINGDOMS

## DATTEN

HONOR ABODE ACC

Motto: Honor above All

***Royal Family***
King Emmerich (1503–)
Queen Guinevere (1504–)
Dead Prince Daniel (1521–1538)
Prince Aaron (1530–)

***House of Wafner***
Jerome (General of Datten) and dead Lady Gwendalin
Seven children: Patrick (Stefan), Jessica, dead Ryan, Arthur,
Samuel, Olivia, and David

***House of Merlock***
Merlock: royal sorcerer and king's advisor
Megesti: sorcerer apprentice and Merlock's son

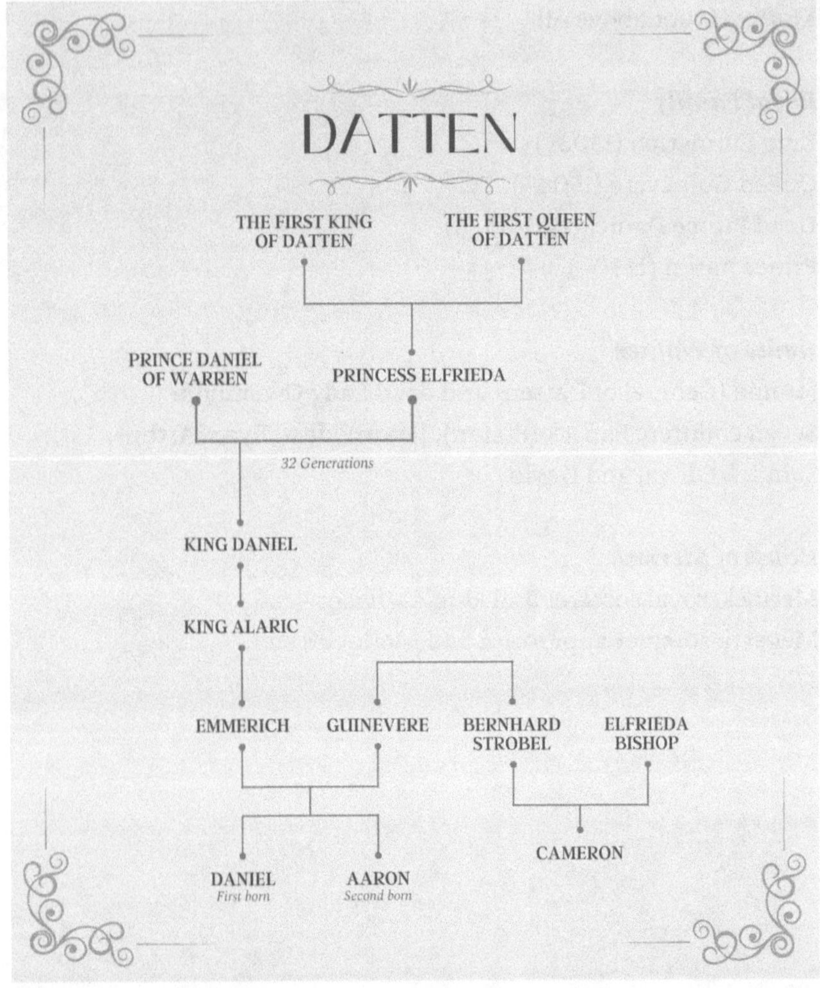


DATTEN

THE FIRST KING
OF DATTEN

THE FIRST QUEEN
OF DATTEN

PRINCE DANIEL
OF WARREN

PRINCESS ELFRIEDA

32 Generations

KING DANIEL

KING ALARIC

EMMERICH

GUINEVERE

BERNHARD
STROBEL

ELFRIEDA
BISHOP

CAMERON

DANIEL
First born

AARON
Second born

# KINGDOMS
## WARREN

Motto: Prosperity through Courage

***Royal Family***
King Edward (1509–)
Dead Princess Victoria (1451–1538)
Princess Elizabeth aka Alex (1533–)

***House of Nial***
Randal (General of Warren) and Lady Judith
Three daughters: Abigail, Diana, and Edith

***House of Bishop***
Matthew (retired general) and Lady Lillian
Three sons: Marco, Aiden, and Julius

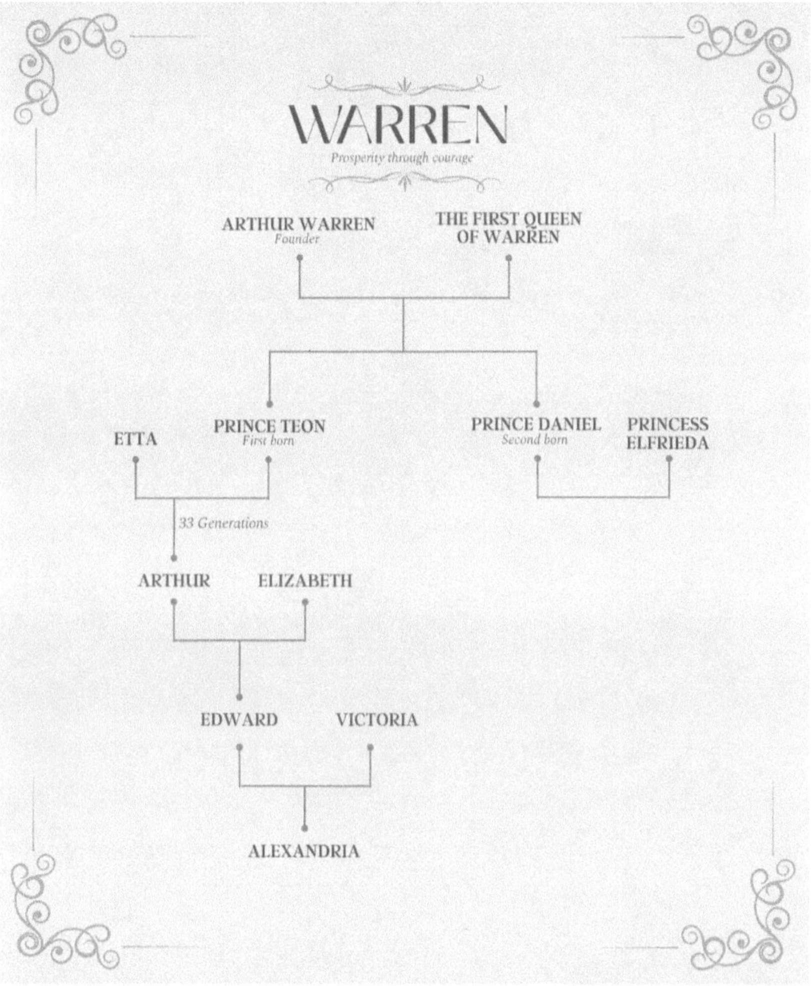

WARREN
Prosperity through courage
ARTHUR WARREN
Founder
THE FIRST QUEEN
OF WARREN
PRINCE TEON
First born
PRINCE DANIEL
Second born
PRINCESS
ELFRIEDA
ETTA
33 Generations
ARTHUR
ELIZABETH
EDWARD
VICTORIA
ALEXANDRIA

# KINGDOMS

BETRUGER

LEGACY NEVER DIES

Motto: Legacy Never Dies

**Royal Family**
King Harold (1525–)

**House of Macht**
Bruno (Head Guard of Betruger)

# SORCERERS OF TORIAN

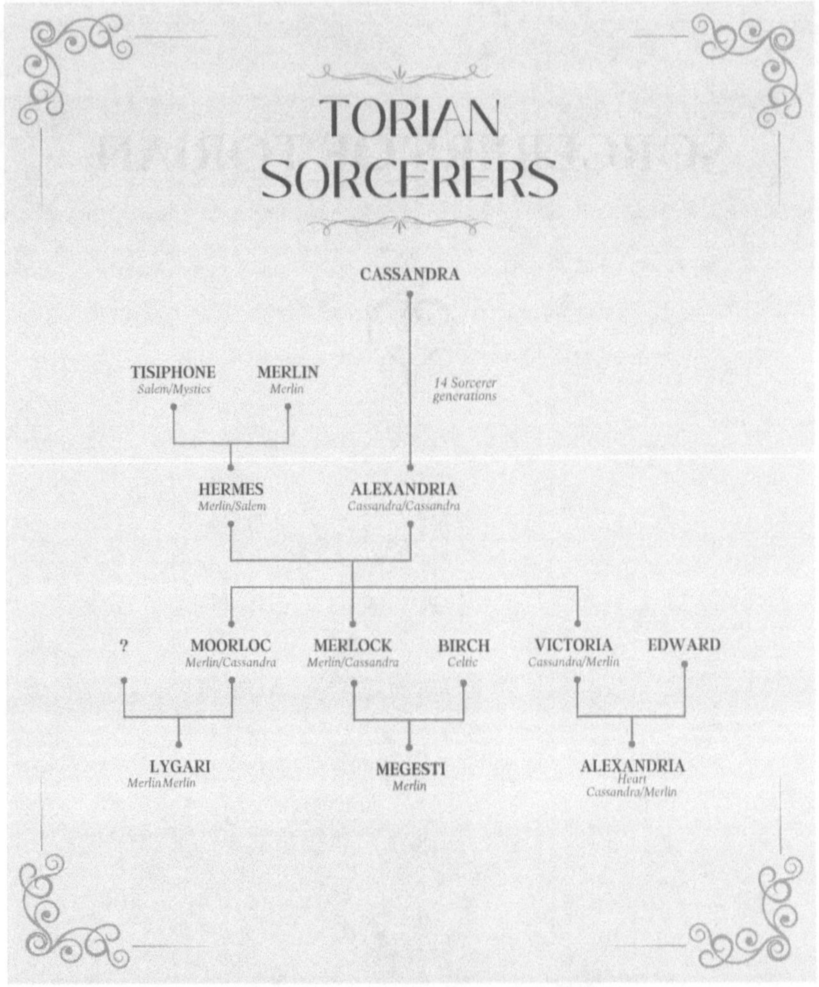
TORIAN
SORCERERS

CASSANDRA

TISIPHONE
Salem/Mystics

MERLIN
Merlin

14 Sorcerer
generations

HERMES
Merlin/Salem

ALEXANDRIA
Cassandra/Cassandra

?

MOORLOC
Merlin/Cassandra

MERLOCK
Merlin/Cassandra

BIRCH
Celtic

VICTORIA
Cassandra/Merlin

EDWARD

LYGARI
Merlin Merlin

MEGESTI
Merlin

ALEXANDRIA
Heart
Cassandra/Merlin

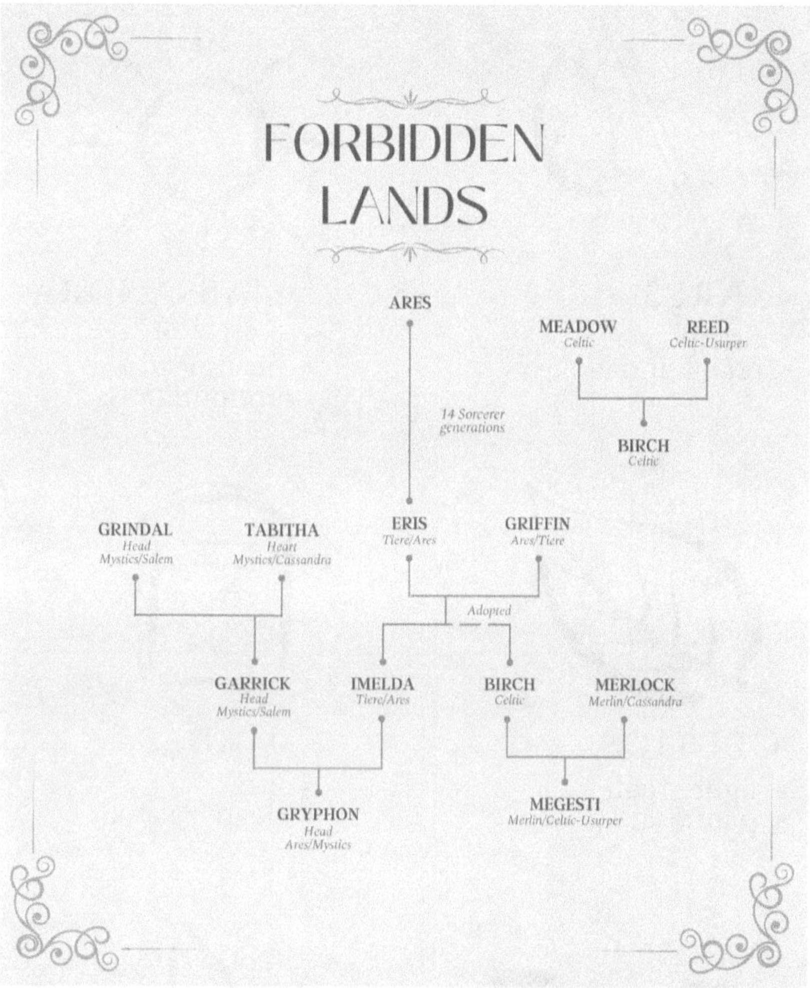
FORBIDDEN LANDS

ARES

MEADOW
Celtic

REED
Celtic-Usurper

BIRCH
Celtic

14 Sorcerer
generations

GRINDAL
Head
Mystics/Salem

TABITHA
Heart
Mystics/Cassandra

ERIS
Tiere/Ares

GRIFFIN
Ares/Tiere

Adopted

GARRICK
Head
Mystics/Salem

IMELDA
Tiere/Ares

BIRCH
Celtic

MERLOCK
Merlin/Cassandra

GRYPHON
Head
Ares/Mystics

MEGESTI
Merlin/Celtic-Usurper

# ARES

- orange
- chaos and violence

# CASSANDRA

- gold
- healing and premonitions

# CELTICS

- light green
- plants and peace

# HADES

- grey
- death related

# MERLIN

- violet
- varies

# MIRE

- brown
- earth powers

# Mystics

- royal blue
- mind control

# Poseidon

- dark blue
- water and weather

# Salem

- maroon
- fire and explosions

# Tiere

- dark green
- animal powers

# Head

- one of two strongest born in a generation
- logic ruled

# Heart

- other strongest born in a generation
- emotional ruled

# PRONUNCIATION GUIDE

Ares: Air-ease

Bernhard: Burn-hart

Betruger: Beh-True-Grrrr

Cassandra: Cas-an-draw

Celtic: Kel-tick

Datten: Day-ten

Ferflucs: Fair-f-looks

Hades: Hay-dees

Lygari: Le-garh-ee

Kirsh: K-ear-sh

Kruft: K-ruff-t

Merlin: Mer-lin

Merlock: Mer-lock

Mire: Mirr-ah

Moorloc: More-lock

Mystics: Myst-ics

Nial: N-aisle

Ogre: O-grah

Oreean: Or-ian

Poseidon: Poe-sigh-done

Rassgat: Ras-gat

Salem: Say-lem

Tiere: Teer-rah

Torian: Tore-Ian

Warren: War-en

# GLOSSARY

**Betrayer:** term used for a sorcerer who tries to kill or severely wound their own family. Appears as three *x*'s stacked on top of each other on the left inner forearm.

**Bond marks:** a mark that a mated pair of sorcerers share. Each is unique, made up of their line marks, and can appear on the back of either shoulder or neck.

**Hexa:** sorcerer grandmother.

**Hexen:** sorcerer grandfather.

**Line marks:** images used to show the ten sorcerer lines.

**Magician:** insult that implies a person has no power as all human "magicians" were frauds.

**Pearls:** magical spheres that show the past (clear), present (white), and future (black).

**Returned one:** a sorcerer who dies but is brought back.

**Sorcerer line:** also known as a line, this is the legacy of sorcerers born from a founding sorcerer. For example, the line of Merlin includes all Merlin sorcerers born from him with Merlin powers.

**Sorcerer awakening:** a time in a sorcerer's life when they go through puberty and subsequently receive their powers and learn which line they are.

**Sorcerer:** sorcerer who identifies as male.

**Sorceress:** sorcerer who identifies as female.

**Sorcerous:** sorcerer who identifies as neither male nor female, nonbinary.

**Titan:** strongest sorcerer of a particular line.

**Usurper:** a special sorcerer born every two or three generations who can borrow or siphon the power of sorcerers around them. Only one can ever be alive at a time.

**Witch:** insult that implies a person has no power as all human "witches" were frauds.

# SERIES LIST

The Spare Who Became the Heir and Other Stories

The Head, the Heart, and the Heir

Broken Sons

The Heir Rises

The Last True Heirs

Book 5 - coming late 2024

Book 6 - coming 2025

Book 7 - coming 2025

Extended Omnibus Kickstarter

Volume 1 - May 2024

Volume 2 - February 2025

Volume 3 - November 2025

# ACKNOWLEDGMENTS

ALWAYS first. Thank you to my husband, Steve, and my children, Lillian, Katrina, and Zack. They believe in me, love my characters, and give up time with me to write my books.

To my mom, Elke, and stepdad, Al, thank you for supporting all my crazy dreams.

My amazing friend **Andrea** who is always there for me and gives me the best ideas and lets me ramble at her until I figure things out. I love you more than you know! And her cat is a lovely purrball.

To my amazeball friend **Brittany** you are AMAZING and I can't thank you enough for taking on my crazy.

To my amazing online BookTok and Bookstagram friends, thank you for bringing a smile to my face and giving me a safe place to vent and talk books and cry when I needed. To my fantastic author friends I found online—you are shining lights in my dark days. Killian, Nikki, Sonja, Rosalyn, Laura, Bekah, and countless more—you all make writing so much more enjoyable!

To my ferflucsing photographer, and FRIEND **Brittany Nosal** —I hate the way I look in photos, but you made the entire process painless and, more importantly, made me feel beautiful and gave me photos I love and can use knowing they captured the real me in all my happy, loving craziness! You are the best.

My editors are the bomb! **Sam,** my amazing developmental editor! You love my characters a much as I do and I know they are always safe in your hands! **S. E.,** I can't thank you enough for keeping me on track and keeping things rolling. You are so easy to talk to you and I value you so much. **Supriya** my amazing copy editor! Thank you for helping me keep things consistent and making sure people can read my words.

To my cover designers, **Alan and Ian**—I cannot thank you enough for making magic again! I love my covers.

# ABOUT THE AUTHOR

Photo by Brittany Jean Photography

Alice Hanov was born in Germany and then raised on Pelee Island in the middle of one of the Great Lakes, spending her days imagining grand adventures in the woods around the island. She has never stopped writing and has a degree in rhetoric and professional writing from the University of Waterloo. Alice lives in Ontario with her hubby and three kids, various pets, and many, many books.

You can visit her online at alicehanov.com.

www.ingramcontent.com/pod-product-compliance
Lightning Source LLC
Chambersburg PA
CBHW031828310726
48972CB00005B/1203